T0322853

SHOT WITH CRIMSON

SHOT WITH CRIMSON

NICOLA UPSON

faber

First published in 2023
by Faber & Faber Ltd
The Bindery, 51 Hatton Garden
London EC1N 8HN

Typeset by Faber & Faber
Printed and bound by CPI Group (UK) Ltd, Croydon CR0 4YY

Extract from *Rebecca* by Daphne du Maurier reproduced with permission
of Curtis Brown Ltd, London, on behalf of The Chichester Partnership.
Copyright Notice 1938 © The Chichester Partnership

The right of Nicola Upson to be identified as author of this work
has been asserted in accordance with Section 77 of the Copyright,
Designs and Patents Act 1988

*This book is a work of fiction. Any references to historical events,
real people, or real places are used fictitiously. Other names, characters,
places, and events are products of the author's imagination, and any
resemblance to actual events or places or persons, living or dead,
is entirely coincidental*

A CIP record for this book
is available from the British Library

ISBN 978-0-571-37367-3

2 4 6 8 10 9 7 5 3 1

For Walter Donohue, with love

The sky above our heads was inky black. But the sky on the horizon was not dark at all. It was shot with crimson, like a splash of blood. And the ashes blew towards us with the salt wind from the sea.

Rebecca, Daphne du Maurier

SUMMER, 1917

The road was long and dreary, at least to my ten-year-old eyes. I was used to a life of colour, and I found its absence puzzling: vast grey skies that weighed heavily on the day; the dark fenland soil, stretching for miles on either side; a ribbon of tarmac, scarcely wide enough to hold the car. Every now and then, the monotony was broken by a house with a brightly painted fence or a thicket of green, but those moments were rare, and, when they came, only emphasised the blandness of the world around them. It depressed me, that landscape, for reasons I would have found hard to explain; the house itself was a happy place, but the journey never failed to make me sad.

'Daphne?' My father's voice was sharp, as it always was when he found me quiet or withdrawn, too lost in a world that didn't involve him. He caught my eye in the rear-view mirror and smiled, still happy and affectionate in those early years. I sat in the back of the car, sandwiched contentedly between my sisters, listening as he and my mother talked about the friends they were going to visit, the children we would get along so well with, the adventures we would have in a house so much bigger than our own. He was right about the house. Dear old Milton, the essence of Manderley – a fine country mansion, set in sprawling parkland and loved by one family for generations. Milton was as open as Manderley would be secretive, her life lived robustly in the present moment, but the spirit of those rooms found its way so easily to the pages of Rebecca, as vivid to me then as at our first meeting, on that summer's day when the war was grinding slowly to a close.

The journey seemed interminable, but at last we entered the grounds by a single-storey lodge, its windows wide open and a family's washing hung on the line in a neat, enclosed garden. The driveway didn't twist and turn like Manderley's; its bushes weren't hostile or menacing; instead, the lane cut politely through ground that rose and fell, flanked by heavily wooded plantations kept firmly within their boundaries. By the time the trees cleared, the sun had burned through and we emerged into a different, cloudless day. In keeping with the fairy tale, another building appeared up ahead, a sort of miniature chapel made from honeyed stone, with little turrets and a circular window above the door – Gothic, I would say now, but back then it seemed too strange and too magical to be so easily classified. The building fascinated me, but it held no novelty for my parents and we drove quickly past, stopping only at a crossways where several drives met. I heard my father mutter something about Piccadilly Circus; to this day, I don't know if it was a joke or if that's what the junction is really called.

The car swung with a flourish onto the gravel at the front of the house, and there it was before me for the first time – elegant rather than imposing, with handsome Elizabethan stonework and a host of mullioned windows, embattlements and attic rooms that seemed to promise adventure. I'm not sure I can say why it made such an instant and lasting impression on me. Perhaps it was simply the exhilarating freedom of childhood and the first big house I had known, or the feeling – so tangible during the war – that our world was hovering on the brink of change. Lately, I've begun to think that it was more than that, even then; a premonition of some kind, a certainty that what happened while we were there – innocent, illusory, never fully understood – would eventually touch us all.

There were glasshouses and a walled garden nearby, and a stable block adjoined the house. As we got out of the car, hot and sticky from the drive, I could hear the sound of horses' hooves, and – in the distance, somewhere over to my left – a fountain. The tranquillity barely had time to register before it gave way to other noises growing louder through the trees, the choke of an engine and the crunch of heavy tyres over stones. Behind us, the door of the house flew open and five or six people emerged, but they were not the family that my parents had described; they were women in nurses' uniforms and men dressed in khaki, and they looked at us with annoyance, as if we were in the way. My father drew me protectively towards him, and I felt the heat of his hand on my shoulder. 'It's all right, Daphne,' he said. 'The house is a hospital for the war, but there's nothing to be frightened of. They're taking care of our boys, making them strong again.'

In spite of his reassurance, I remember thinking at the time that the war was coming straight towards me, that the invasion we'd been conditioned to fear had finally arrived. There were five vehicles in all, three ambulances and two open-topped buses, and, from where I was standing, the convoy looked as if it were forcing its way through the line of lush, green laurel bushes. As it drew closer, the atmosphere amongst the men on board seemed to sap every bit of hope from the day. Some of the soldiers hung their heads, and all I could see was the top of a helmet; others leant quietly against their neighbour for support. A foreign sun had tanned their skin as it had bleached the colour from their clothes, and rusted blood stains stood out against white rags, incongruous in the English countryside. What struck me most, I recall, was how dirty they were, like animals rolling in a field. I could never have known at that age how apt a comparison it was.

The walking wounded disembarked in a muddle of boots and elbows and breath, and the exhaust fumes that had been so overpowering were replaced by the pungent smell of sweat and leather. They stood bewildered in a group, waiting for someone to tell them what to do while their less fortunate colleagues were unloaded gently but efficiently from the ambulances and taken into the Hall first. I remember wondering why my father had called them boys when they seemed so old and defeated. As I stared, unable to help myself, I locked eyes with the man on the nearest stretcher, his sunburnt face stark against the pillow, the mud of the trenches still thickly encrusted on his boots. I felt myself flush, but the soldier simply looked back, doggedly blank, as if the world I belonged to was something he had long ago lost touch with.

We were rescued by my mother's friend – kind and gracious and ethereal, like something from a Barrie play. She swept us through the house to the family's wartime quarters, a modest set of rooms between the kitchen and what was now an operating theatre, and I could see by the look on my parents' faces how much had been lost in the relinquishing of privacy and comfort. To my sisters and me, though, the hustle and bustle seemed noble and exciting, an adventure in which we could share without any noticeable hardship to our own lives. My earliest memories from inside the house are jumbled now, and some seem more dreamlike than others:

6

men in loose-fitting convalescent uniforms, huddled round one end of a dining table while a butler looked on; a group of soldiers playing billiards under a Rembrandt; rows of empty deckchairs stretched out along the south terrace; dishes piled high with mashed potato. I remember very clearly the banter and the coughing, the clatter of knives and forks and the scraping of chairs across polished floors. When we got to the family's private dining room, which had pink and white walls and an enormous clock built into the fireplace, we ate delicate food off plates that were painted with birds.

After lunch, we were told to run along and play while the grown-ups talked. The hospital areas were strictly out of bounds, but the gardens and family rooms would be ours to explore for the duration of our stay. If we'd done as we were told, the afternoon would have passed innocently enough, I suppose, but our guide was a pale-faced little boy who seemed unfazed by the invasion of his home, and he was as eager to break the rules as we were to lead him astray. Within minutes, we found ourselves in a long gallery which had been transformed into a ward. I waited to be shooed away, but the nurses smiled at the boy of the house, obviously used to seeing him there, and nobody asked us to leave. The room was naturally light and airy, decorated in a restful green with white stucco leaves and ribbons; generations of the family looked down at us from the walls, but their disapproving stares were obscured now by bed railings and medical equipment, and the essential femininity of the room jarred with those who occupied it. There was an air of calm about it, and I wondered how it must feel to these men to come from the world of blood and dirt that I had glimpsed outside to this haven of peace, where the only disturbance was the shaking and folding of a sheet, the scrubbing of a floor. Every now and then, a cry of pain rose above the ordinary sounds of the afternoon, and a nurse moved silently to one of the beds, a red cross emblazoned on her chest. Another sat by a soldier's side, her face close to his as he struggled to dictate a letter home, and I found myself imagining what he might be saying and who was waiting anxiously for those words. I was so caught up in my own invented world that I didn't notice the others leave.

Less brave on my own, I went back to the hallway to look for my sisters, but they were nowhere in sight. There was a breeze coming from the end of the passage, so I went towards it, hoping to find a way out to the garden and drawn, in any case, to the sound of a gramophone. This room was smaller than the converted ward, but just as light and pleasant, with pillars at intervals all the way down and a sarcophagus filled with ferns in the centre. It led out to the terrace, and the French doors were all wide open, their curtains billowing gently. Some of the soldiers were resting under awnings in the open air. Beyond them, on the lawn in front of the house, others played croquet, the blue of their uniforms patriotically offset by red ties and white lapels. Those inside painted a less cheerful picture, their injuries more obvious, their manner more subdued – brave, vital young men, reduced to knitting or playing chess. One in particular caught my attention, seated in a wheelchair next to the window with a blanket across his lap. Another man was at the table with him – not a soldier, because his uniform was brown and drab, and not a doctor, although he was obviously caring for the patient, intent on helping him to construct a model house from matchsticks – and it was this that captivated me rather

8

than the men themselves. As I watched, the soldier's hand slipped, knocking down the roof section that he had been working on, and he swept the matches onto the floor in frustration. Undeterred, his friend picked them up and managed to coax a smile, then the process began again. He glanced up and caught sight of me watching from the doorway, and I didn't hesitate when he beckoned me over and invited me to take a closer look. His voice was beautiful – soft and lyrical, with a lightness to it that made me think of the sun dancing over water.

The model was exquisite, a miniature replica of Milton that somehow seemed more real than the building we were standing in. He smiled when he saw my delight in it, and turned it this way and that to show me the detail – the bays and the central porch that we had entered by, the softer south side that I had yet to see, the chimneys and parapets. Everything was perfectly proportioned, so vivid and lifelike that I half expected to see a figure at one of the windows, and I watched as he showed the soldier how to cut the matches to form joints for the angled rooftops, waiting patiently while he got the hang of it. There was a sheaf of papers on the table, designs for all sorts of models drawn carefully to scale, and he pushed them towards me to look through, then gave me his name and asked for mine.

'Are you a clever girl, Daphne?' he asked, when we had chatted about my family and what we were doing there. I'd often been told that I was, so I answered truthfully, without hesitation, and he smiled. 'Then would you do something for me?'

He reached into his trouser pocket and took out another model, this time of the Gothic folly that had intrigued me so much on the way in. It was even smaller in scale than the miniature of the Hall, but its features were perfectly formed, and my face must have lit up as I studied the spires and arches that had disappeared too quickly through the window of the car, hardly able to believe that something so delicate could exist. 'I made this for someone who's not very well, but I'll get in trouble if I leave the ward. Would you deliver it for me if I tell you where to go?' I hesitated, unsure of the vast house and labyrinthine corridors that were still so strange to me, but he had the measure of a curious ten-year-old. 'I'll make you one just like it if you'll do this for me – but keep it to yourself, do you understand?'

Who doesn't love being part of a secret? The challenge was almost as irresistible as the bribe, and anyway, I wanted to please this clever, gentle young man who could apparently do magic; there could be nothing wrong, I told myself, in such an act of kindness. I took the present and listened carefully as he told me where to go, then he squeezed my shoulder and wished me luck. 'Come and tell me when you've done it,' he said, 'and thank you, Daphne.' I turned to look back from the doorway, wanting, I suppose, a last scrap of encouragement, but he was already engaged with the soldier again, talking to him as if he were the only other person in the world, and I wondered briefly what it must be like to have that sort of attention. Disappointed, I hurried to the main hallway before I could forget the directions he had given me. That huge staircase, with its gilded, wrought-iron banisters, still seems grand to me, even now, but it was a thousand times more daunting to a child, and I felt very small as I climbed timidly up to the first landing, where a lead-paned window looked out over parkland and grazing sheep. The stairs split to left and right and I hesitated for a while, waiting for a nurse to pass me and hoping that I wouldn't be challenged, then glancing in both directions and taking the right-hand side as instructed. The window leads threw crisscross patterns onto the walls and carpet as I climbed another short flight of steps and found myself at the head of a long, narrow corridor with closed doors on either side – never had I seen so many closed doors. A welcome shaft of light came from the window at the end and I moved forward slowly, conscious of the alternating patches of sun and shade on my face, counting the doors carefully to make sure I chose the right one. When I was certain, I reached up towards the handle, startled for a moment by the silhouette of my own hand against the wood, enlarged and distorted in the shadows.

It should have occurred to me that someone else might be in the room, but I was too intent on my mission to stop and think. The door was opened from the inside before I had a chance to touch it, and I was confronted by a woman dressed entirely in black, a crucifix hanging at her neck. I had no idea who she was, of course, and I never knew her name, but she stood looking down at me, an expression of pure hatred on her face, and instinctively I put my hands behind my back, hoping to hide the model. I wanted to run, but she seemed to hold me with that stare. Forced to articulate her now, I find myself automatically falling back on the words that were always in my mind when I wrote Danvers – the hollow eyes, the white skull's face, a child's view of the witch from a fairy tale. Was she really like that? Those memories may or may not be real and I have no way, now, of knowing, but – accurate or not – they refuse to be shaken. How foolish of me to imagine that I had ever made her up.

She asked me who I was and what I was doing there, her voice taut with anger, and I backed away down the corridor. My silence only infuriated her more, and, as she stretched out her hand to shake the answers from me, I found my feet and ran. Everything is a blur after that, although I know that she followed me as far as the stairs, shouting as she went, and I know I heard a noise like the crack of a whip soon afterwards – but I was too desperate to get outside to consider what that might have been, and, in any case, as soon as the sun hit my face and I saw my sisters playing on the lawn, the whole thing seemed like a terrible dream. I never told anyone what had happened, not even Angela or Jeanne. For a while, I dreaded bumping into my magician and having to admit that I had failed him, but I needn't have worried: I never spoke to him again, and eventually he faded from my thoughts. Until today, I had no idea what became of him, no notion that – in a very different way – he had worked his magic for me a second time. I wonder if he made the connection, or if he even remembered the clever little girl who let him down.

When I saw the model of the Hall again, a few days into our stay at Milton, it had been smashed to pieces, although I don't know by whom. I still have the miniature he gave me, a gift made for another, and it was wrong of me to keep it. It's there on the bookshelf, next to the jay's feather from the woods at Menabilly and the photograph of my father in his dressing room, and every time I look at it now I can't help but wonder if I could have changed things. If I'd got there earlier, if I hadn't hesitated on the stairs, if I'd been braver in facing her, would the years have turned out differently? But that was in the past, I tell myself. The trick, as most of us know, is to keep it there.

SEPTEMBER 1939

I

The boat train pulled slowly into its designated platform by the side of the ocean dock, and Josephine breathed a sigh of relief, taking more pleasure than she would ever have believed possible from the prospect of leaving the country. The sense of anticipation amongst the passengers had built steadily during the short journey from Waterloo to Southampton, and now that they were within walking distance of the ship that would take them across the Atlantic, some could barely contain their excitement. She wished her own emotions were that simple, but this impatience to get underway had very little to do with the romance of travel or the thrill of America. Whichever way she looked at it, the ticket that she clutched in her hand smacked of running away, but she didn't care. For the moment, all she longed for was to see Marta again, and to put as much distance as she could between herself and the memories of the last few days.

Her conversations with Archie were sporadic and subdued on the way down, neither of them wanting or needing to make small talk. A sombre mood had fallen across the whole country as months of fear and speculation suddenly became a reality, but not even the outbreak of a new war could eclipse a more personal horror. Her friendship with a police detective meant that she was never far away from the sadness of his job: even when Archie couldn't talk about a case explicitly, the tragedy of one murder enquiry or another invariably governed his moods and shaped his outlook on the world; this time, for Josephine, the anguish had been closer to home – the abduction of a child in a place she had come to love. Perhaps not surprisingly, she was struggling to come to terms with a gnawing sense of loss and betrayal. 'I'm glad you came to see me off,' she said, as Archie lifted her bag down from the luggage rack.

'So am I.'

They had a shorthand, she and Archie, and she didn't need to explain that it helped to be with someone who had lived through those events, even if they didn't discuss them, who understood how tainted and responsible she felt, no matter how irrational that might be. He smiled at her, but whatever he was about to add was lost in a flurry of activity on the train. People began to push towards the doors, eager to get a first glimpse of the ship that had rarely been out of the news since she was launched into the Clyde, five years ago almost to the day, and Josephine and Archie joined them. By now, the *Queen Mary*'s statistics were legendary – taller than the Eiffel Tower, faster than any ship in her class, bigger than the *Titanic* – and they allowed themselves to be swept along with the other passengers, caught up in the swell of chatter and expectation. There was a dramatic hush when the liner suddenly came into view, towering above the transit sheds and dwarfing dockside cranes until they looked like something from *Gulliver's Travels*. The huge, black bulk of the hull, stretching off into the distance, seemed menacing rather than romantic, and Josephine found it hard to believe that something so colossal could float at all. Once the initial impact had passed, though, she saw beyond the boat's sheer size to the beauty of her lines and the majesty of her presence, and understood exactly why the nation took such pride in her. Although she was built for an English company, it was Scotland who had given her life, but not without a struggle. Josephine remembered seeing the photographs of the half-built shell in the newspapers, slowly rusting to death in its shipyard, such a striking symbol of the hardship and poverty of those Depression-ridden years. Many feared that she would never be completed, but they had been proved wrong, and – when the prosperity of the country improved and work on the ship began again – she became just as potent an emblem of hope and a better future. It seemed to Josephine that the *Queen Mary* had been asked to stand for a lot in her short life, designed in peacetime to link the old world with the new; she might epitomise the style and elegance of the decade that was drawing to a close, but now it was her strength and unconquerable spirit that wartime Britain needed.

'Extraordinary, isn't she?' Archie said admiringly. 'Perhaps there's hope after all if we're capable of something like this. Let's get you on board.'

That was obviously going to be more easily said than done. In spite of the size of the boat and the length of the quay, the crowds seemed too big for both and it was difficult to do anything more than inch slowly forward. 'There won't be many more crossings now,' Archie said, shielding Josephine from the worst of the crush. 'People are obviously getting out while they can.'

He was right, and Josephine felt naïve for failing to notice a change of mood between the train and the pier. She looked more carefully at the other passengers, listening to the voices around her, and saw instantly that a good proportion of the tickets were likely to be one way – Jewish families fleeing the

Nazis or Americans returning home while there was still a commercial ship that would take them. The outward appearance of luxury and pleasure was as robust as ever – smiling stewards in pristine uniforms, trolleys of expensive-looking luggage – but there were pockets in the crowd where a sense of urgency had replaced the carefree. For a moment, it felt unreal to her, and the idea of sailing into the unknown took on a completely different connotation, something rather less like a blessing. 'Are you all right?' Archie asked, touching her arm.

She nodded, and they pressed on towards a series of covered gangways that sloped gently up from the quayside, the words 'RMS Queen Mary' emblazoned proudly on the canvas. A purser stood in the gangway, checking tickets, and he welcomed Josephine aboard as if she were the most important person ever to travel with Cunard, then directed her to the lifts that would take her to the state rooms. Her cabin was on B Deck, which – apart from a variety of hairdressing and beauty salons – seemed to be made up entirely of passenger accommodation. As she walked along brightly lit corridors, looking for the number that matched her ticket, she glanced through the open doors of cabins that had yet to be occupied, noticing that – although united by a feeling of luxury and sophistication – each one was designed differently and had its own distinct character.

'Do you think anyone would notice if I came with you?' Archie asked, as they passed a particularly enticing suite with gleaming chrome surfaces and art deco sculpture.

'Virginia might have something to say about it. Marta, too, if I'm honest.'

'I'm not sure I've ever seen anything quite so opulent. I

hope you don't get used to it, or I won't be able to take you anywhere once you're back.'

Josephine laughed. 'There's no need to worry about that. I've blown far too many of my savings on this ticket. It was a bit reckless, I suppose, with everything so uncertain, but a once in a lifetime trip suddenly felt like now or never.'

Her own cabin, when they eventually found it, was lavish in a more traditional way, with rich, warm woods and gentle lamplight. A marquetry panel above the bed pictured ducks flying over a lake, and a flower-patterned rug competed for attention with three vases of the real thing, fresh chrysanthemums in autumnal shades that complemented the colours of the room. Every convenience had been thought of – plenty of storage space and a thermos jug and telephone recessed into their own alcoves – but there was also a light system above the outer door if she needed to summon a steward. She put her bag down on one of the four polka dot chairs that had been arranged around the room, and gestured to Archie to sit down. 'I don't know how many people they think I'm going to be entertaining, but you might as well make yourself at home when they've gone to all this trouble.' The room was more spacious than she had feared, and a large mirror opposite the bed made it feel bigger still; even so, she felt a little claustrophobic, and walked over to the outer wall to lift the blinds that covered the portholes.

'I had no idea they had their own newspaper,' Archie said, picking up *The Ocean Times* from the coffee table. The paper carried the day's date and a front-page story about the ship being 'home to the world', and he flicked through it. 'This is a refreshing change. What I wouldn't give to pick up one of our papers and read only good news. Nothing about murder, not even much about the war.'

There was an edge to his voice that Josephine understood only too well: the headlines that most people mulled over in horror at their breakfast tables were something that Archie lived through personally – finding a child's body, breaking the news to grief-stricken parents, coming face to face with the killer and knowing that justice would never really be enough. He had been through all that and more in the last few days, and – not for the first time – she wondered how he did it. 'You'll talk to Virginia when you need to, won't you?' she said. 'I know what you're like, Archie. You shut people out and deal with everything on your own, and that never works in the long run.'

'And you won't be here to help?' He smiled, acknowledging how well they knew each other. 'I don't want to take all this home to Virginia and the children. It's still early days for us, and I don't want her to think that's all she's going to get if we have a life together – just one sadness after another.'

'I'm sure that's not what she thinks. I know I've only met her once, but she didn't strike me as the sort of woman who has to be shielded from reality. On the contrary. Look what she's been through herself.' Virginia's first marriage had been an unhappy one, and she had met Archie because of it; the strength she had shown since in protecting her children and moving on was something that Josephine admired tremendously. 'You wouldn't want her to be anything other than honest about her feelings, would you?'

'No, of course not.'

'Well, then. And she of all people knows how much your work means to you. God knows, she's had reason to be grateful for it.'

'Yes, I suppose so, but to be honest, the best thing Virginia can do is help me to forget what's happened, at least while I'm with her. You should try to do the same,' he said, turning the tables. 'I know how deeply this has affected you. Make the most of some time with Marta, away from everything.'

Josephine gave him a wry smile. 'I'm fully prepared to be a Hollywood widow from the moment I step off the train. Marta's working all hours of the day.' She hesitated, guilty of dishing out advice that she found very hard to follow herself. 'Anyway, I wouldn't want to dwell on this with her,' she admitted. 'Marta's lost two children of her own, and she faces that every time she opens her eyes in the morning, so it seems wrong of me to be wallowing in someone else's grief, no matter how shocking it was.'

'It's not just about a child, though, is it?' Archie said seriously, and he was right. The profound sense of loss that Josephine felt had as much to do with a shattering of trust and the realisation that a place she felt safe in was as susceptible to evil as anywhere else; with the state of the world in general, and all that they stood to lose if the war went badly. 'And anyway,' he added, 'you can't help how you feel.'

'No, but I *am* going to Hollywood, so I won't be out of place if I pretend otherwise.'

A polite announcement came over the tannoy, filling the corridor outside and cutting short their conversation. 'All ashore who are going ashore. Please make your way to the exits. The ship is ready to depart.'

'That's my cue.' He got up reluctantly and she walked with him to the lower deck, where a line of lovers and parents and friends was snaking back from the gangway, all saying final goodbyes. 'You'll look after yourself, won't you?' Archie said, giving her a hug.

'Of course I will. You, too.'

'And write to me. I want to know about the apartment, and the stars you meet, and what you say to Hitchcock when he asks what you thought of his film – especially that bit, actually.'

Josephine laughed, if only to hide the fact that she was close to tears. She had separated different parts of her life now for long enough to accept goodbyes as par for the course, but there was nothing routine about this particular farewell, and she realised that she had no idea what sort of country she would be returning to in a few weeks' time, or what might happen to Archie once the bombing started over London. 'I promise you won't miss a thing,' she said eventually, when she trusted herself to speak. 'Now go, or you really will be looking for a cabin.'

'Give my love to Marta.' He headed for the steps, but something of her fear and uncertainty must have been on his mind, too, because he turned suddenly and came back to kiss her. Then she watched him disappear down the steps to the quayside, without another backward glance.

There was a sense of occasion on board now, although it was hard to say if it was genuine, or if the illusion of leaving everything behind was simply too seductive to resist. Josephine made her way to the Sun Deck and found a place amongst the line of passengers standing by the rail, waving down at the pier a hundred feet below. The gangways had all been removed and the ship was moving slowly away from the shore – smooth and serene, without a hint of the fracturing that its departure might actually mean. In a gesture of sentimentality that was uncharacteristic for her, Josephine stayed on deck, looking towards the horizon until England – and Archie – were long out of sight.

Reluctant to be alone in her cabin, she decided to explore and see what the ship had to offer. She had always believed the idea of a city afloat to be a cliché, but realised very quickly that there was something in it: it would have been hard to identify a luxury or home comfort that hadn't been thought of. The official booklet issued to all passengers had boasted enough recreational space to fill Wembley Stadium, and on her first turn around the upper decks she found squash and tennis courts, swimming pools and a state-of-the-art gymnasium, as well as enough bars and restaurants to undermine any exercise that she might do while on board. There was plenty of general entertainment available – cinemas, libraries and a lecture room – but more specialist facilities were also provided: a photographic dark room and a sound-proof studio, complete with Bechstein piano, and even a sizeable kennel block and exercise yard for dogs. Further down, on the Promenade Deck, an arcade filled with the world's most famous shops extended the width of the ship, selling clothes, flowers, cigars, jewellery and other souvenirs. Boredom certainly wouldn't be an issue during the crossing: there was far more here than anyone could realistically hope to get through in four days at sea, and plenty to distract her from her own thoughts and worries.

It was still early in the afternoon, so she went back to the Observation Lounge at the front of the ship, hoping to get her sea legs while the conditions were calm and sympathetic to a novice. The semi-circular room included a cocktail bar, and – like every other space that she had seen so far – it managed to balance comfort and sophistication. The bar itself was friendly and intimate, with red leather stools and a mural to celebrate the old king's jubilee week – a detailed dancing-party scene, whose flamboyant high spirits seemed very much in keeping with the generous array of bottles displayed below it. The star that gave the room its name, though, was at the other end, where a series of five-foot-high windows offered spectacular views ahead and to the sides. Not surprisingly, the lounge was already popular, but there was one seat left on a raised platform at the very front, and Josephine sat down, staring into nothingness over the bow of the ship. With the September sun so warm through the glass, and the light glistening on the water, the sensation was both magical and unsettling.

'Miss Tey – how lovely to bump into you already.' The familiar voice carried a faint Midlands accent, and Josephine turned to greet a pretty, red-haired woman in a smart trouser suit. 'I saw your name on the passenger list. Marta said that you were coming to visit sometime soon, and it's nice that we should end up on the same crossing.'

Josephine hesitated, wishing that she had thought to fore-warn herself with a quick glance at the same piece of paper. Her first meeting with Alma Reville, Alfred Hitchcock's wife, had been three years ago now, when the film director had bought the rights to one of her books. *Young and Innocent*, the movie that followed, was apparently Hitchcock's favour-ite amongst his British work; Josephine wished that she could say the same, but – judging by the changes he had made to it – *A Shilling for Candles* had obviously not been one of his favourite novels. She had kept up with the couple ever since through Marta's work for them, but found them far more agreeable as an anecdote than in person. 'It's very good to see you again,' she said, pulling herself together in an effort to be polite.

Alma raised an eyebrow, and her glasses couldn't obscure the twinkle in those bright hazel eyes. 'Have you forgiven us, then?'

The good humour reminded Josephine that – although she had disliked Hitchcock and still resented what he had done to her novel – she had shared a mutual respect with his wife from their very first meeting, and the director couldn't be all bad if he had secured the love and respect of such a talented woman, down to earth and creative in her own right. Alma was shrewd in her judgements and held strong opinions that she was never shy of expressing, and the Hitchcocks were partners in work as well as in marriage. She had begun her own career in film before her more famous husband, and was still fundamental to his success; it was to Hitchcock's credit that he readily admitted how much she had taught him. 'Let's just say I've learnt from past mistakes,' Josephine replied in kind, 'and it's done nothing to damage my royalty cheques.'

'I'm glad to hear it.' Alma glanced behind to her companions, who were obviously two more generations of the same family: a girl of around ten or eleven, who must be the Hitchcocks' daughter; and a small, fine-boned woman in her sixties, an older version of Alma. 'This is my mother, Lucy,' Alma said, beckoning them over. 'Mother, this is Josephine Tey, who wrote the original book that *Young and Innocent* was based on.'

Resisting the temptation to add the word 'loosely', Josephine held out her hand. 'Very pleased to meet you, Mrs Reville,' she said, noticing that the older woman's face had lit up at the mention of the film.

'Oh, I just love that story,' she said enthusiastically. 'I think it's the best thing they've done, don't you? So touching and romantic. You must have been thrilled when you saw it.'

Through no fault of her own, Mrs Reville had hit on one of the things that Josephine objected to most strongly about the adaptation – although even she had to admit that had she come to the cinema fresh to the story, without any vested interest in it, she would have loved the film just as much as everybody else seemed to. 'I really couldn't believe it,' she said truthfully. 'The transformation was quite remarkable.'

Alma smiled, appreciating the irony. 'And I don't think you've met Patricia?' she continued. 'She was away at school when we were all at Portmeirion.' Probably just as well, Josephine thought: it hadn't been a happy holiday, tainted by the sort of violence that Patricia's father specialised in all the time on screen but seemed ironically ill-equipped to cope with in real life.

'Do you travel a lot like this, Miss Tey?' Lucy Reville asked.

'No, I can't say I do. This is my first time on board.'

'Mine, too. Alma and Alfred have been back and forth . . .'

'I wouldn't say that, Mother! Two or three times, perhaps.'

'. . . and even Patricia's an old hand. She's been showing me round the ship. Isn't it exciting?'

'Yes, it is.'

The girl took her grandmother over to the other side of the room to look at the mural and Josephine watched them, not in the least surprised to see that the Hitchcocks had raised their child to be confident and curious. 'I'm surprised to see you here with filming underway,' she said.

'My work on *Rebecca* is done, really, so I've taken a few days out to collect my mother and bring her out to stay with us while all this is going on. I'm just relieved that she's been willing to make the move.' Alma sighed. 'Hitch hasn't been so lucky. His mother is refusing to budge – she says she made it through one war without a scratch and she's not about to let this one beat her.'

'I admire her spirit, but I can see that it must be a worry for you both, being so far away.'

'Yes, it is. At least she's agreed to move out to Shamley Green, so she won't be in the thick of the bombing, but who knows?' The phrase hung in the air, a simple expression of the uncertainty that everyone was feeling. 'Would you care to join me for dinner later?' The invitation came out of the blue and Josephine wavered before answering. She had expected a few days of peace and anonymity before being thrown into the Hollywood circus, and she was keen to hang on to them. 'I'd be grateful for the company,' Alma admitted. 'Pat and my mother eat early, and if I'm honest, the thought of going into that restaurant and eating alone fills me with dread. Too much time to think at the moment isn't good for me.' She smiled. 'It's short notice, though, so if you have other plans . . .'

'Actually, that would be lovely,' Josephine said, surprised to find that she meant it. 'I haven't made any plans, and too much time to think isn't good for any of us.'

'Wonderful. Does seven thirty suit you?'

'Perfectly.'

'Then I'll alter my reservation and leave you to find your sea legs. See you later.'

She walked off to join her family and Josephine went back to her cabin to unpack. There was a parcel from Marta in her case that she had been instructed to open on board, and in it she found everything she might need for her first trip to Hollywood, including sunglasses for the pool; a Los Angeles guide book, already marked up with restaurants, shops and galleries that they must visit together; and two tickets for the premiere of Bette Davis's new film at the Warner Bros Theater – a fictionalised account of Queen Elizabeth's relationship with the Earl of Essex, played by Errol Flynn, which Marta knew she would love. As exciting as that sounded, it was Marta's letter that really touched Josephine, full of the plans and preparations she had made for the time they would spend together. As she contemplated the freedom that the next few weeks offered, away from home and all the responsibilities that came with it, the sense of uncertainty that had been darkening her mood was suddenly exhilarating.

She found the copy of *Rebecca* that she had brought with her and read for a while until it was time to change for dinner, then headed to the next deck down. The *Queen Mary*'s main restaurant was known as the Grand Salon, and everything about it seemed designed to live up to the name. Josephine paused at the entrance, which was a vast work of art in its own right, a painting called *Merry England* in which idealised aspects of country life over the centuries were depicted in a tapestry style. A pair of elaborate bronze doors, massive in construction, had been incorporated into the painting, appropriately themed around Castor and Pollux, guardians of all sailors.

The entrance should have prepared Josephine for the magnificence of the dining room, but still it took her breath away. The Grand Salon was the biggest room on board, extending right across the ship, with high ceilings and a central dome. Like most of the *Queen Mary*, the room was characterised by rich polished woods in various autumnal shades, offset here by cream paintwork, tinted with pink at the higher levels, and chairs upholstered in a dark red leather. The restaurant was beautifully lit, and wherever the opulence threatened to become oppressive, a carefully judged plant or vase of flowers added a natural freshness to the space, lifting the mood of the room.

She announced herself at the desk and a waiter showed her to her table, giving her the chance to take in the true scope of the salon, which she found thrilling and intimidating at the same time. Alma had arrived already and was seated at a table for two by one of the large cylindrical columns that divided the room. She waved when she saw Josephine, cor-rectly reading the expression on her face. 'Quite something, isn't it? You can see why I'm glad of your company. I don't mind the razzamatazz when I'm with Hitch – he plays up to it, as you know – but it's daunting when you're on your own.'

'I'm pleased I'm not the only one who feels that way.'

'I suspect most of us do, if we're honest.'

They chatted about the ship while they waited for the waiter to take their order, and – as she had before – Josephine found Alma easy, entertaining company, which was just as well: dinner extended over seven courses, and promised to last most of the evening. 'It's straight to the swimming pool for me in the morning,' Josephine said, glancing at the dessert that had just been delivered to the next table. 'A lot of dam-age can be done in three or four days.'

'Yes it can, and the food is excellent.'

'It must be if *you* think so. Marta tells me that you're a very good cook.'

'Oh, I'm just an amateur, but I do enjoy it.' The wine

arrived and Alma raised her glass. 'To an uneventful crossing. Marta will be so pleased to see you, although I don't think she'll believe you're really coming until she actually sets eyes on you.'

Josephine had no idea how much Alma knew or had surmised about her relationship with Marta, but the two were good friends as well as business associates, so the comment didn't surprise her. 'It never seemed like the right time before,' she admitted, 'but then I suppose you realise how many years you could waste waiting for the perfect moment. There aren't many silver linings to another war, but it does focus you.'

'It certainly does, and it's funny you should say that, but it feels like we've been doing exactly that these past few years – waiting for the right time to try America. I'm not quite sure why it took Hitch so long to visit a country that's always fascinated him. He could reel off all the train timetables and theatres in New York as a boy, you know – it was as if he knew it would be important to him one day.'

'And what about you? How are you finding it?'

'I love it,' Alma said, without hesitation. 'I loved it from the moment I set foot in it – the weather, the orange blossom, the freedom. Especially the freedom. There's no stuffiness like there is in England. I feel we belong there. Even during the brief trip back to collect my mother, it's *this* direction that feels like coming home.'

'I'm pleased for you. The last time we met, you were worried about making the move.'

'And now I'm worried that we won't stay. There really is no pleasing me.' She smiled, and paused while another waiter brought the soup and topped up their glasses. Seated here, in the most stable part of the boat, Josephine found it disconcertingly easy to forget that they were actually at sea. 'Mind you, we should feel at home,' Alma continued. 'There was a military-style operation to ease us into things when we first arrived – the best restaurants, ex-pat parties every weekend, lectures and interviews for Hitch.' She caught the look of horror on Josephine's face. 'Yes, I know what you're thinking and I agree with you, but we've had the chance to find our own rhythm over the summer. There's a church that suits us in Beverly Hills, and Pat has a wonderful school on Sunset Boulevard. Hitch drives her there every morning. He makes a big thing about Hollywood meaning nothing to him as a place, and yet he shoots yard after yard of home film just riding around in a convertible like an excited kid.' Josephine listened, picturing the scene and liking the Hitchcocks all the more for their ordinariness as a family. 'We've brought our dogs out here with us, and our maid, and we've just found a wonderful German cook called Erna who can do absolutely anything with pastry. Most importantly, Pat adores it, too. The whole thing has been such an adventure for her. I don't think we've ever been so happy.'

'It sounds like you're settled for the long term.'

'I hope so. We're going to move out to Bel Air in the autumn. The Wilshire apartments are fine for a while – all mod cons, as you'll see, and very handy for the studios – but what we actually need is a proper house with a decent kitchen. The devil with a swimming pool, as Hitch would say.'

It sounded idyllic, but there had been no mention so far of her own career. When they first met, Josephine had been struck by Alma's drive and determination, by the sheer joy that she took from the creative partnership that she and Hitch had established. In her own right, Alma Reville had done every job in cinema except starring and directing, starting out as a tea girl at the London Film Company, and excelling even at that; it seemed unlikely to Josephine that she would be content with her roles as wife and mother, no matter how happy they made her. 'What about professionally?' she asked. 'I know you were worried that America wouldn't allow you to work with Hitch in the way that you could in England.'

'That's true, but we're finding ways around it. Hitch has a fair bit of clout already, and he's just negotiated his second movie here with Walter Wanger. He made sure they built me into the deal at a decent weekly rate, independent of Selznick International, so I have a separate contract. Joan, too – you know she came with us?' Josephine nodded. Joan Harrison was the Hitchcocks' right-hand woman, as good as a member of the family, and the three of them formed a tight-knit team; it was a role that Marta herself could perhaps have had if she'd agreed to move permanently to America. 'We've been working on a new script, ready for when Hitch is done with *Rebecca*, just like we used to at Cromwell Road, so it's not as different as I feared it might be – and the view is better.'

The lamb was cooked to perfection and far too good not to finish; by now Josephine was relieved that the remaining courses consisted only of salad, fruit and ices. 'How is Hitch getting on with Selznick?' she asked, curious to have Alma's take on a question to which she already knew the answer: there had been trouble brewing between director and producer, even before Marta left England.

'Well, they went to *The Wizard of Oz* together, but I don't think they'll ever be friends.' She rolled her eyes. 'They fell out over the script, as you may have heard. David wanted every scene from the book to end up in the film, and Hitch wants . . . well, you know from personal experience what Hitch wants from a novel.'

'An author who doesn't interfere?'

Alma laughed. 'Something like that. No, Hitch learnt his lesson with *Secret Agent*. A great novel can cast a shadow over a filmmaker. He's more interested in taking second-rate works and giving them his own vision.' If Alma was aware of how offensive that remark was in the present company, she showed no sign of it, and Josephine hid a smile. Privately, she could only wish that her own novels had been as 'second-rate' as Daphne du Maurier's; *Rebecca* had sold nigh on a million copies since its publication the previous year, and it didn't seem to need Alfred Hitchcock *or* David Selznick to make it successful. She was tempted to say something out of professional solidarity, but Alma hadn't finished. 'They both take movies seriously, though – the form, the language, the storytelling. They're obsessed by it, and that's what will make this work. They might come at it in different ways – David works until he drops and Hitch comes home to a proper meal every evening – but they both live for the film, and that's the saving grace.' She raised an eyebrow. 'That, and the fear of failure. Neither of them has the sort of ego that could brook that.'

'It's a gamble, though, and I admire your courage,' Josephine said. The Hollywood studio system was dominated by producers rather than directors, and by stars under contract who reigned at the box office. 'He's got to prove himself all over again. If he'd stayed in England, he'd be hailed as its greatest director for years to come.'

'But he can make better films in America.' There it was

again, the obsession that seemed to sacrifice all in its wake. Alma paused, as if reading Josephine's thoughts. 'And he wanted to get Pat and me out,' she said quietly. 'He's worked in Germany enough to know it quite well, and he's been sure about this war for some time. He wanted his family to be safe, and I love him for that, no matter what other people will say about it back in England. They'll call him a coward, and that will hurt him.' She seemed about to say something else, then changed her mind, apparently keen to lighten the mood. 'Mind you, the making of this film is a war in its own right.'

'Yes, Marta said things weren't exactly harmonious.'

'That's putting it mildly. Did she tell you about the screen tests?'

'A little. The last time I spoke to her, you still hadn't cast the female lead.'

The role of the second Mrs de Winter, playing opposite Laurence Olivier, was rumoured to be one of the most hotly contested in Hollywood. 'It was eleventh hour, certainly,' Alma admitted. 'Hitch was livid to have to sit through all those terrible tests with actresses he knew would be completely wrong, although we all agreed that Audrey Reynolds would have been *perfect* for the part of Rebecca.'

Josephine smiled, appreciating a backhanded compliment: the character of Max de Winter's dead first wife never actually appeared. 'I gather Vivien Leigh was quite keen to play opposite Larry,' she said wryly.

'Absolutely desperate – insisted on testing twice. David took a risk on her for Scarlett O'Hara and it's paid off, but she's completely wrong for this – far too strong and charismatic.'

'That must have called for some careful diplomacy.'

'It did, but David's hoping to find something that they *can* work together on.'

'Even so, I bet Larry will make things uncomfortable for a while. He's much better when he's getting his own way.'

'Aren't we all! You know him, then?'

'Not very well, but our paths have crossed. He was in a play of mine – Bothwell in *Queen of Scots*.'

'Yes, of course. I'd quite forgotten he was in that. How did you find him?'

'Charming, if a little sure of his own opinions, and that was five years ago now. He's had *Wuthering Heights* and an Oscar nomination since then, so I wouldn't be surprised if all that brooding on Penistone Crag had turned his head.'

'He *does* seem very well suited to moody scenes, both on and off camera. Personally, I rather got the impression that he was relieved to have some time apart from Vivien, but of course he can't say that.'

'So who *has* got the part?' Josephine asked, curious to know who had triumphed.

'Joan Fontaine.' Alma made an expression of distaste.

'You don't approve?'

'Not at all. She's far too coy and simpering for me. I can't stand the woman's voice – it's so irritating. I would have preferred Anne Baxter – she did a very touching screen test. She's only sixteen, but she had a lovely, natural quality, and I think audiences would have adored her. Or Margaret Sullavan – she's such an intelligent actress in whatever she does.'

'Didn't she play Mrs de Winter on the wireless?'

'With Orson Welles, yes, but David is smitten with Joan, and so Joan we shall have. He thinks he can pull off the same coup with a wild card that he has for *Gone With the Wind*.

Personally, I have my doubts.' The only time that Josephine had seen Joan Fontaine's acting was in a film with Fred Astaire, where she had been charmingly inept as his dancing partner; it was hardly a comparable role, but Fontaine had somehow managed the trick of being passive on the surface without ever coming across as a victim, and Josephine could see why Selznick might cast her as the shy, awkward second wife. 'Still, at least it will give Hitch a chance to prove that he can build a performance.' Alma sighed, unconsciously laying bare the ruthlessness of the film world. If Fontaine failed, it would be her own fault and she would be pilloried for her lack of talent; if she was a success, it would be down to Hitchcock's direction of her. Suddenly Josephine was glad to be a writer and out of harm's way, even if it did mean relinquishing control over her work.

'And Mrs Danvers?' she asked. Manderley's housekeeper – obsessively protective of de Winter's first wife and determined to intimidate his second – was one of the most memorable things about the novel, and her portrayal was likely to make or break the film. Josephine had been casting her mind over the actresses she knew, wondering who could pull it off, but so far she had failed to come up with anyone; when Alma responded, she saw it instantly.

'Judith Anderson. If you saw *Macbeth* at the Old Vic, you'll know her, too – she and Larry were playing opposite each other.'

'Yes, I remember. She was wonderful.' Perhaps it was the role she had seen her in, but Anderson gave the impression of being strong, formidable and ruthless, and would be perfectly cast as Fontaine's tormentor. Josephine listened as Alma reeled off a list of the other actors who were already hired, struck by how many of them were either British or had worked extensively in England; this might be Hitchcock's first American film, but at least he would feel at home with the cast, and she wondered if that had been a deliberate strategy to give him the edge in any power struggles with producer and crew. 'Perhaps it's as well that the war has closed our theatres,' she said. 'It sounds like everyone's over there.'

'It is a bit like that. There's a clique of Brits in Hollywood and they're a force to be reckoned with.'

It was late by the time they finished their coffee, but Josephine was surprised by how quickly the meal had passed and by how much she had enjoyed Alma's company; not only that, but she felt much more equipped to face the world of gossip and celebrity that she would soon be plunged into. 'Shall we have a nightcap?' she suggested. 'Not that I'll need much help in sleeping tonight.'

'Lovely idea, but let's have it in the lounge. In my experience, the next three days fly by and you get to New York realising that you haven't seen half the rooms you wanted to.'

Throughout dinner, Josephine had been seated with her back to one of the restaurant's most dramatic features, and she paused to look at it on the way out. The wall at the far end of the room was covered by an enormous decorative map of the North Atlantic, bold and stylised in red, gold and black. The ship's summer and winter routes were clearly marked, and an electrically operated crystal model tracked their actual progress from one coast to the other. 'Stunning, isn't it?' Alma said. 'Hitch loves boat travel, and he's like a boy when he sees this.'

'Well, Mrs Hitchcock! I'll be damned.' The volume alone would have drawn attention, even if the name and voice

37

hadn't been so famous, and Josephine glanced back to see Bob Hope making his way over to them, accompanied by a woman who she presumed was his wife. 'It's good to see you,' the actor said to Alma after the introductions had been made. 'Dolores and I only made it by the skin of our teeth. We've been in Paris, but we cut things short and headed for London as soon as we heard. We were lucky to get on board. Is Hitch with you?'

'No, not this time. I only went over to bring my mother back.'

'Good call. Seems to me that this little lady will be staying in New York for a while.'

'You think this will be the last crossing?'

'I'd put money on it. Look how many of us they've packed in – more than two thousand, I hear. Some of them are sleeping in the passageways.'

Josephine listened, astonished that they could be discussing the situation so calmly, then realised with a shock that she was the only one of this small party who needed to come back. A stab of panic hit her, and she tried to distract herself by concentrating on what Hope was saying about his new film, a comedy horror involving a murderer dressed as a cat, but the bizarre-sounding plot seemed somehow less surreal than the situation she now found herself in. Over Hope's shoulder, she watched as one of the diners got up from her table and approached them, standing at the edge of the group as if waiting to be noticed. At first, Josephine assumed that the woman was a fan, taking her chance to speak to the star, then noticed that she was staring intently at Alma. 'Mrs *Alfred* Hitchcock?' she asked, suddenly cutting into the conversation without any thought of decorum.

Alma looked surprised. 'That's right.' She stopped short of demanding who wanted to know, but her expression asked the question for her.

'We haven't met but you know my father. *Knew* my father, I should say. I'm Lee Hessel.' The words had a remarkable effect on Alma. The polite smile faded quickly from her face, and if frightened was an exaggeration, unsettled fitted the bill perfectly. 'He died, but I can see that you know that already.'

'Yes, and we were sorry to hear it. Very sorry.'

'And that's it?'

Out of the corner of her eye, Josephine noticed a waiter standing by, alert to the possibility of trouble and ready to intervene if asked, but Alma didn't seem inclined to shirk the conversation. 'Hitch, in particular, took the news very badly. He and your father had been friends for a long time.'

'*Friends?*' The word came out in a sob, and Josephine could see that Lee Hessel was struggling to contain her anger. 'It's your husband's fault that he's dead.'

Alma stared at her, making no effort to respond, and it was left to Bob Hope to intervene. 'Now, Miss Hessel, you've obviously had a little too much to drink,' he said, nodding towards the glass in her hand, 'so why don't you call it a night and go and find your cabin? Things will look clearer in the morning.'

'Don't patronise me,' the woman said, and not without some justification, Josephine thought. 'It's just a game for you all, isn't it? Get what you want, then move on to the next per-formance. But these are people's *lives* you're playing with. He wasn't even sixty, for God's sake.' She moved to throw her drink at Alma, but the waiter stepped forward to grab her arm and took the brunt of the wine. Undaunted, he led Lee

Hessel from the room and this time she didn't argue, other than a final parting shot at Alma. 'You *will* pay for this. Both of you.'

A murmur of conversation began again at the nearby tables, and Alma tried to shrug off the incident with a smile. 'I think I'll go straight to bed,' she said apologetically to Josephine. 'I'm suddenly very tired. Do you mind if we postpone our nightcap?'

'No, of course not.'

'Thank you. Now, if you'll all excuse me, I'll say goodnight.'

She left before anyone could ask for an explanation of what had happened, and Josephine said goodnight to the Hopes and headed back to her own cabin, choosing a route that would give her some air before trying to sleep. Even at this hour, there were plenty of people who apparently had had the same idea, and some seemed to be settling down for the night in the comfortable chairs that lined the glazed part of the deck; further down, beyond the wooden gate that separated one class of traveller from another, the passageway was even more crowded, giving substance to the rumour of a packed final crossing. Too anxious now to think of going to bed, Josephine stood by the rail for a long time and stared out into the darkness, wondering what the future might hold.

2

He was thrown by how similar it all was. Not the house, obviously, which had stood solid and unchanging for centuries, but the atmosphere, so redolent of when he was first here, in that fleeting, bewildering summer that had altered the course of his life. Milton Hall hadn't wasted any time in giving itself up for service again, and he watched from a window in the gallery as truck after truck pulled up outside, bringing soldiers and military equipment to fill the once grand rooms. It was a sobering sight so early in the war, and he felt the same old arguments bearing down on him. The khaki uniforms, the orders, the smell of fear along the corridors – they were still painfully familiar, so much so that he half expected to see the little girl again, just as she was all those years ago, with her blue dress and her questioning stare, looking up at him across the table. He had often thought of her during the intervening years, guilty for what he had asked of her. Strange that she should have been the one to bring him back here. Inevitable, perhaps, that he should see an element of fate in the way that things had turned out.

'Hey, Bart – are you daydreaming again?'

James Bartholomew smiled at the cameraman, acknowledging the truth of the charge. 'I can't help it if I'm more efficient than you, Frank,' he said good-naturedly. 'I've done everything I need to.'

In truth, he had very little business being here at all. The sets for *Rebecca* were well underway, and the miniatures of Manderley that he had sweated lovingly over for weeks bore very little resemblance to this particular English country house. But Selznick was keen to prove to an author he admired that his film would be as faithful to her book as he could make it, and so, when a second unit was dispatched to scout the house that had inspired those fictional rooms, James's familiarity with Milton allowed him to hitch a ride, using his knowledge of the building to suggest interior shots and details that would give authenticity to the special effects. He loved his work, no matter what the film, but *Rebecca* was especially important to him. No one would ever know it, but twenty-two years ago a young Daphne du Maurier had been his innocent go-between. He doubted that she would remember the event or had even given him a second thought, but still he wanted to do her justice, payment for a debt that she didn't know he owed. And he had wanted to see the place again, more badly than he cared to admit.

'How much longer will you be, Vic?' he asked, watching the unit's director stub a cigarette out in the nearest plant pot.

'An hour. Two at the most. If we miss that plane, Hitch will have our guts for garters.'

The peculiarly English phrase sounded strange in a Californian accent. 'Then I'm going for a walk,' James said. 'There's something I need to do.' It was a spur-of-the-moment decision, but as soon as he had spoken the words, he realised that it was his sole reason for coming here.

'He's got some woman tucked away, Vic,' Frank said, turning to his boss with a sly grin. 'Ten dollars says he's picking up where he left off, one more fuck for old times' sake.'

'Don't judge us all by your own standards.' James grinned to take the edge off his words, knowing from past experience that it was better not to rise to the bait. Frank Wheeler had a temper on him, and tensions in a small unit like this only made the work miserable.

'Least you could do is share some around, buddy,' Wheeler insisted, reluctant to let it go. 'We've got a long flight ahead of us. I could do with some exercise.' The cameraman paused and stared more seriously at James, who struggled to hold his gaze. 'What is it, Bart? What's so important? You've been miles away from the moment we got here. Who are you running off to see?'

For all his talk, Wheeler could be dangerously perceptive at times, and James was relieved not to have to answer him. 'Cut it out, both of you,' Victor said impatiently. 'We're tight enough for time as it is, without any more bullshit from you two. Don't hold us up, Bart. If you're not down there waiting when we're ready to go, you can make your own way back – that's if you still have a job to go back to.'

'I'll be there, don't worry.'

Irritated, James walked off, feeling Frank Wheeler's eyes on him until he had left the room. He stopped on the small landing where the two sides of the staircase met and looked down into the grand entrance hall, his mind instinctively visualising the way that the room would influence what was seen on screen. He had often heard Hitch say that *Rebecca* was the story of a house, and certainly they had spent as much time looking for the perfect location as they had for the perfect Mrs de Winter. Before he left England, the director had auditioned the various historic mansion houses near his country home in Surrey, sending notes, sketches and photographs back to the studio. When nothing proved satisfactory, they scoured the countryside around Hollywood, eventually extending the search as far as Canada, but their efforts were in vain and Manderley remained as elusive as it was in the dream sequence that would open the movie. All along, knowing that the house would eventually have to be filmed in ruins, the art department had argued against location shooting, and it seemed even less practical with a war hovering on the horizon. In the end, Hitch and Selznick gave in: they would build the house from scratch.

So far, their courage was paying off. It had been exhilarating to see the various interiors taking shape, like walking through the pages of the story – the boat house where Rebecca died, the coroner's court, the doctor's office – but nothing brought the script to life quite like the sets of Manderley itself, with those ornate rooms and towering staircases, the high doors and Gothic mouldings. Hitchcock's preparation was legendary, like many things about him, and not without good reason: his sketches were exhaustive, outlining every single camera movement and indicating where a real, three-dimensional set finished and a painted matte began. The backdrops added another layer to the illusion, with upper walls and ceilings, vast chandeliers and striking architectural details that would have been impossible – or far too expensive – to build, and the scaled models that James had created would allow Hitch to play God with the house, showing Manderley by day or by night, in rain or in sunshine, alive with laughter or charred and abandoned.

Excited by the challenges still to come, he continued down the stairs, feeling lucky that the magic of his work should thrill him now as much as it had when he walked onto his very first film set. To this day, he blessed the skills that his father – a furniture maker with a passion for miniatures – had nurtured in him as a boy. Unlike his dad, though, who would spend weeks perfecting one small detail on the leg of a chair, driving his mother to distraction as her housekeeping dwindled and the bills piled up, James thrived on the pressures of film work, loving the risk and the sense of moving on. Working on *Gone With the Wind*, they had literally burned down the back lot of the studios to film the flames of Atlanta. He had stood on set with the *King Kong* gates still visible through the towering flames, feeling the heat on his face and wondering if he would ever get the smell of kerosene out of his clothes, doubting that this Hollywood spectacle could ever be bettered. And yet here they all were, building something new, something that would – if they did it well enough – earn its own place in movie history. Manderley, too, would be consumed by fire, and his painstaking work along with it. There was a time in his life when the thought would have given him cause for regret, but that was long ago, before he had learnt what was truly irreplaceable. It scarcely mattered now what else was lost, as long as it served its purpose.

The grandfather clock in the hall struck the hour, reminding him of his curfew. He hurried out through the north door and across the lawns, where he had once watched the du Mauriers taking tea, envying them their carefree summer days. Autumn had come quietly to the woods that surrounded the house, he noticed. The trees were just starting to thin, the change only evident in the amount of light now coming through the canopy and the carpet of leaves on the ground, but the air still had that soft, gentle heat, unique to a fading English summer, and he realised suddenly how much he missed it. He joined the driveway, having cut off the sweep around the stable block, and the sound of his boots on the gravel took him back to his first time here, as a medical orderly during the last war, the flood of memories so vivid and insistent that he had to stop for a moment to catch his breath. It was his first posting, and the parting with his parents had been difficult and hurried, a sense of betrayal unspoken on either side: they hadn't wanted him to have any part in the war, not even caring for the sick if it meant patching them up and sending them back to fight. Like their parents before them, they were lifelong Quakers and this was the first time that he had ever been aware of any conflict in their faith, torn between their hatred of the war and their determination to let him follow his own conscience. It was a rift that would never heal: his parents had been killed by a German bomber on a rare day out in Folkestone, blown to pieces with a hundred other shoppers in Tontine Street. That awkward departure from the house, furtive and irritable, so different from the way they had always been as a family, was the last time that James had ever seen them.

He walked on with random thoughts of his parents playing in his head, still guilty after all these years for the manner in which he had left home. The sunset was on fire that night, he recalled, the sky ominously red as he boarded the Peterborough train and found a seat in the rear coach. They had crawled along in the darkness, as if the train were somehow colluding in his reluctance to arrive – so many tiny stations with unfamiliar names, and at each one he had had to fight the urge to get off and lose himself in the blackness of this unfamiliar fenland world. Every lighted window had filled him with a terrible longing for the homeliness that he was leaving behind. He felt something like it now in the pit of his stomach, brought on by being back at Milton, a yearning for something that had been so briefly and so unexpectedly his.

The walk to the cottage was shorter than he remembered it, and the sight of it up ahead surprised him, tearing him abruptly from his memories. He paused a distance away and looked it over – a modest estate house, one of several dotted across the parkland, but still a considerable prize for a retired servant to see out her days in, a reward for years of loyalty to a family that she had valued above her own, or so it had always seemed to him. The resentment flared again, disarming him with its intensity and making him doubt the wisdom of being here at all, but he hadn't travelled all this way only to lose his courage at the last moment. Before he could change his mind, he opened the garden gate and walked up to the door, knocking with a sense of purpose that was deceptive, even to his own ears. What was he hoping to achieve? he wondered. Were there things he needed to say, or to hear?

In either case, it looked as if he would be disappointed. There was no answer, even when he knocked again, and he was beginning to give up hope when he heard movement from inside, then the sound of a woman's voice muttering to herself in frustration as she fumbled with keys and bolts. He was shocked when she finally managed to open the door. The last time he had seen Marion Plummer, she stood proud and erect, matching him for height even in the flat, practical shoes that must have walked for miles each day along the corridors and stairs of Milton Hall. The woman in front of him was stooped with arthritis and used a pair of walking sticks, to which she clung pathetically, obviously frightened of falling. James found himself staring down at her, something that brought him no pleasure, even though the blend of humiliation and resentment in her face suggested that she thought it might. Her hair was grey now – the austere, lifeless sort of grey that hardened the softest of expressions – but she wore it in the same style as she had when he first knew her, swept up and fastened tight to her head, and something in that determination not to change only emphasised the toll that the years had taken. She was wearing a floral print dress with a pale pink cardigan, and although there was nothing odd in that for a woman of her age, it jarred on him, because he had only ever seen her in black. The crucifix that she had always worn was still around her neck, but it was less obvious now, nestled in its background of roses and forget-me-nots – diminished, somehow, and no longer the weapon that it once was. As if sensing that the clothes robbed her of her authority, she compensated by glaring at him with piercing dark eyes that were as sharp and as suspicious as they had always been, at least where he was concerned. In case she didn't recognise him, he gave his name, reluctant to let an elderly woman stand frightened of a stranger at her own front door, no matter how much he hated her.

'I know who you are. I'm not senile, if that's what they've told you.'

Her voice was weak and slightly rasping, and – although defiant – the words seemed to cost her a great deal of effort. 'No one has told me anything, Mrs Plummer,' James said, curious to know who 'they' were. 'I'm here because I need to speak to you. There are things I want to ask you about what happened to Matthew. Things I don't understand.'

She gave a scornful laugh. 'There were things *I* didn't understand the last time you were here, but I don't remember either of you being very sympathetic.'

'You never wanted to understand them.'

'I knew all I needed to know – and much, much more than I wanted to.'

James bit his lip, reminding himself that they had asked too much of her. He could never have expected her to understand how much he had loved her son, let alone condone it. As close as he had been to his own mother, she would have struggled to accept it had she lived to be told. 'Please, Mrs Plummer,' he tried again. 'I haven't got long. I'm catching a plane back to America and that's the last you'll ever see of me, I promise.'

'Of course it is. You'll be a coward in this war, too, no doubt. Have you really no shame?'

It had been naïve of him to think that grief could help them overcome their differences, or that a mutual animosity might have faded over the years. In truth, he longed to give vent to his own anger, but he needed to take this final chance to get to the truth. 'Please,' he asked again, trying to keep the impatience out of his voice. 'Just give me ten minutes of your time. Three questions, and I'll leave you in peace.'

Her mouth twisted into a smile, as if the last word were making fun of her, but she turned and walked slowly back into the house, leaving the door open for him to follow. The short hallway led straight through to a kitchen, and the sitting room was on the left; a door to the right – presumably her bedroom – was closed. To James's surprise, he heard the slamming of the back door and someone turning on a tap in the kitchen, and he wondered why he had assumed that Marion Plummer would live alone; it scarcely mattered to him that she didn't, but it was another reminder of how time had picked away at her independence.

The sitting room was sparsely furnished, with retirement offering no reason to change the frugal habits of a lifetime in service. There were two chairs by the fire, one with extra cushions to give it some height, and Marion Plummer lowered herself into it with difficulty, waving him away tetchily when he stepped forward to help her. The chair was angled towards the window and gave a fine view across the lake to the Hall, with shards of sunlight glittering on the water, the only moving thing in a scene of utter peace and tranquillity. The outlook was mirrored in a watercolour – skilfully painted – that hung over the mantelpiece, where a gold clock stood as the room's only extravagance, and James wondered if both had been gifts from the family to mark their housekeeper's retirement, or some other milestone over the years. For him, the most striking thing about the room was its absences: there were no trivialities to pass the time – no books or magazines, no wireless set, no bag of knitting or needlework basket, although her hands were gnarled and riddled with arthritis, which would have made sewing difficult. He wondered what she did all day, and imagined her staring out at the Hall as one long hour passed into another, lost in thoughts of who she used to be. In the corner, a small console table held a row of photographs and James scoured the collection of unfamiliar faces, but, as far as he could see, Matthew wasn't in any of the pictures.

The fire had been stoked up recently and the room was uncomfortably warm. He sat down on the other chair and she shrank back into hers, reluctant to breathe the same air. The silence between them bristled, another presence in the small space, and he cast his mind round for a way to open the conversation that wouldn't sound too aggressive or too trifling, wishing he had thought more carefully about why he was here.

In the end, someone else broke the silence for him, a woman wearing a black dress identical to the one that Marion Plummer had once sported with such pride. James looked at her, thrown by the uniform because the last time he had seen her she was dressed as a nurse – but otherwise twenty years had changed her very little. She faltered when she saw his face, her hesitation mirroring his own feelings of confusion and recognition. 'I'm sorry, I didn't know anyone was here. We weren't expecting you, James. I didn't think for a moment . . .'

She let the sentence fade away, and the words 'that you would dare to come here' were left unspoken, as if they brought too much of the past with them to be admitted. 'Hello, Evelyn,' he said. 'How are you?'

'I'm well, but I'm afraid I'm late for work. I thought you might like some tea before I go, Mother?'

'If I want tea, I'll make it myself. I'm not as helpless as you think I am.' It was an ungracious response, but Evelyn seemed used to it. He remembered suddenly how Matthew had complained that it was impossible to do anything nice for his mother, even on her birthday or the rare occasions that she felt unwell. He could hear him saying it now, '*You can never wait on a servant,*' and the voice sounded so vividly in his head that Matthew might easily have been in the room with them. The illusion took him by surprise, and he was glad to have time to compose himself while Marion Plummer was distracted by her daughter.

'I've left your meals in the kitchen,' Evelyn said. 'I'm on shift until ten tonight, but Mrs Wells is popping in to see you soon and she'll get you anything you need.'

Her mother dismissed her with an impatient wave of the hand, adding for his benefit while she was still in earshot: 'She's next to useless. I might as well do everything myself.' James saw the weariness in Evelyn's eyes as she left the room. He heard her go upstairs and come down again a few seconds later, then she left the house by the front door and walked quickly across the park.

'Does Evelyn work at the Hall now?' he asked.

'Thinks she can take my place. I swear she only does it to taunt me. They're all the same.'

There it was again, the paranoia that bitterness and resentment couldn't entirely explain, and James began to suspect that her opening comment to him had its roots in truth; perhaps she did fear for her mind. 'I've come to ask you about Matthew's death,' he said. She stared at him blankly, obstinately, and his eyes strayed once again to the table of photographs. What sort of woman had no pictures of her dead son, the son she claimed to have loved? 'Don't you want to remember him?' It sounded exactly like the accusation it was, and he tried to rein in his hostility, knowing it wouldn't get him what he wanted. 'Your son loved you. You can't just wipe him out and pretend he never existed – you're a Christian woman. He'd be so hurt if he knew how little you—'

'My son is there, on the left, very much alive,' she interrupted, stemming the flow of words.

Taken aback, and unable to avoid a brief, terrible glimmer of hope, James looked again at the photographs, wanting the face in the silver frame to be an older version of the boy he had loved, convincing himself that it could all have been a terrible mistake. A man in army uniform stared back at him, vaguely familiar but not the person he was hoping for. He realised that he was allowing himself to be sidetracked, and time was against him. 'No one ever told me what happened,' he said, annoyed to hear the emotion in his own voice. 'Matthew's suicide makes no sense.'

'You think you had a right to know? A right to anything where he was concerned?' Her scorn hung in the air as she paused to take a breath. 'He came here to be nursed. They made a special case for him to be brought here because he was a soldier from this house, wounded in the service of his country. You were supposed to be caring for him, and you abused that in the most despicable way.' She hadn't once used Matthew's name, James noticed, and he wondered if she had spoken it at all since his death. 'He was a fine boy, a *decent* boy until he met you. Why on earth would anyone talk to you about his death?'

'But he was getting stronger every day, and finally starting to believe that his life wasn't over because of what had happened to him. He was even getting some of his sight back.'

'Don't lecture me about my own son. How do *you* know what state he was in? You didn't see him before his death.'

'Only because you made that impossible, moving him out of the ward to a room I wasn't allowed anywhere near, separating us like naughty school boys. He must have thought I'd abandoned him.' She smiled, but there was no warmth in it; only triumph. 'He did, didn't he?' James said, horrified. 'He died thinking I didn't care.' He slammed his hand down on the side of the chair and stood up, barely able to contain his anger. 'Who told you about us?' She flinched at the final word, as if he had hit her, and he longed to make it worse by telling her things that she didn't know, things that were

53

intimate and private, but it would have been a betrayal of everything that he and Matthew had shared and he refused to desecrate something so precious by using it in anger. 'That day, when you found us together, who sent you there? Somebody must have told you where to go. You had no other reason to be there.' It was irrelevant now, but it seemed irrationally important that he should know who had started this whole destructive chain of events. It had been their place, the Gothic folly, a striking but rarely used building to the east of the Hall, surrounded by beautiful woodland. Matthew had played there as a child, and it was where they went when he began to convalesce, instinctively wanting to be alone after so many weeks on a ward where nothing was private. 'You never went anywhere near that place,' James reiterated, sitting down again and leaning forward to force eye contact. 'That was another reason for choosing it.'

She said nothing, and he hadn't expected her to. A woman who was professionally obliged to manage the secrets of a household was hardly likely to give up her own so easily. 'Will you at least tell me where you buried him?' he asked. 'Please, Mrs Plummer – I'll beg if I have to.' He remembered how secret and hurried everything had been in the aftermath of Matthew's death, with shame a far more powerful impetus than grief. He wasn't aware of the body leaving the house and he had been kept at arm's length from the funeral, denied the chance to pay his last respects, or to say the things that he needed to say. As a consequence, he realised now, he had never fully accepted that Matthew was dead. 'We're both mourning him,' he said quietly. 'No matter what our differences are, we have that in common at least. Tell me where he is.'

She shook her head. 'I couldn't protect him from you in life, but I'll damn well do it now he's dead.' Her hand went automatically to the crucifix to give strength to her words. 'Was that two questions or three? I'm afraid I've lost count.'

James saw the hatred in her face and knew that Matthew's resting place, the thing that mattered most, was for ever lost to him. 'There's one more,' he said, determined this time to get an answer. 'How did he get hold of the gun?' He had the satisfaction of her surprise, and pressed home his advantage. 'I'll never understand why Matthew blew his brains out, and I can see that you're not ready to help me. But I *will* find out how the man I loved left this earth, if it's the last thing I do. Who gave him that gun?'

In anyone else, such agitation would have distressed James. Marion Plummer plucked at her cardigan, her eyes tightly shut, and he could see her lips trembling – in grief or in anger, it was impossible to tell. Eventually she spoke, seemingly caught up in a world of her own. '"If it chance your eye offend you, Pluck it out, lad, and be sound."'

'What?' James looked at her, bewildered. The words were familiar to him from Housman's *A Shropshire Lad*, a book that Matthew had loved and made him read. He had returned to it many times since, although the poems were hardly a comfort in the wake of his lover's death, but he had no idea why Mrs Plummer should be quoting it now. Had she really lost her mind, he wondered, or was this just an elaborate ruse to close down the conversation? 'Answer my question,' he demanded, 'and then you'll be rid of me once and for all.'

She ignored him and continued to quote the verse, her voice growing steadily louder as the lines came effortlessly back to her. '"And if your hand or foot offend you, Cut it off, lad, and be whole."'

James stood up in disgust, abandoning any hope of getting what he had come here for. Only when he had reached the door, with the final words of the poem ringing in his ears, did he realise that she was answering his question after all. '"But play the man, stand up and end you, When your sickness is your *soul*."'

She spat the word out and he turned to look at her in disbelief. 'You gave him the gun, didn't you?' He waited, desperately needing her to deny something so abhorrent, willing to live with all his uncertainties if only she would tell him that he was wrong, but she didn't. 'Is that what happened? You told him to end it and put the means to do it in his hand? God, you disgust me.'

'How dare you talk to me about disgust, after what you turned my son into. He refused to give you up, you know. You should have heard how he spoke to me that day, the filth that came out of his mouth. I wanted him to do the right thing.'

'The right thing?' Even in his blind fury, James found it impossible to believe that Matthew would have left him like that. He stared at Marion Plummer and imagined her back then, as calm and composed as she was now, dripping poison into her son's ear, telling Matthew how quick his death would be and how painless, how easily he could end his suffering and how much better it would be for everyone if he were gone. '*What have you left to live for?*' He heard her whisper it so clearly that he wondered why her lips weren't moving. '*One moment of courage and it will all be over.*'

'Did you kill him?' he demanded. 'Did you cure Matthew of

56

his "sickness" by helping him pull the trigger? Is that what really happened?'

'It was better that way.'

James's rage was spent in seconds, but that was long enough – long enough to pick up the cushion from his chair and hold it tight over Marion Plummer's face, to obliterate the expression of triumph that tormented him so. Briefly, he felt her resist and saw her hand reaching desperately for her stick but clutching only at air; he heard a muffled groan and then the repeated thud of her heel against the wooden floor, beating out the pathetic rhythm of her own final moments. And then there was nothing. Just silence, except for the soft, insidious ticking of the clock that had signified her life's work, and now mocked her with its lack of regard for her death. James stared in horror at the cushion in his hands, scarcely believing that something so ordinary, so innocent, could have killed a woman, but Mrs Plummer was lifeless in her chair, her eyes closed and her head rolled forward, to all intents and purposes as if she were asleep. Frantic now, he knelt by her chair and shook her by the shoulders, pleading with her to open her eyes, angered by her vulnerability; if she had only struggled more, he might have come to his senses sooner and stopped himself in time. Now, there was no going back.

He stood up, disgusted with himself and trying to calm the panic that threatened to overwhelm him. Evelyn had seen him at the house, so there was no point in pretending he hadn't been here, and she could come back at any minute and catch him red-handed. He could tell the truth, and hope that someone would understand why he had reacted so violently, but Marion Plummer was a saint in the eyes of the house, and he had already left its walls once in disgrace; no one would believe him now if he said he was innocent. And anyway, was he? Innocent of the sins she had thrown at him, yes – nothing would ever convince him that his love for Matthew had been anything but noble. But this? Suffocating a helpless, elderly woman? He had lived for forty years by the principles that his parents had instilled in him, never hurting another living thing, refusing to take up arms even when the world spat at him in the street and called him a coward. And in thirty seconds, perhaps not even that, he had destroyed the integrity of a lifetime, betraying himself and the people he loved.

His eye caught something glinting on the floor – the crucifix, lying under her chair, next to its broken chain. Instinctively, he picked it up and put it in his pocket, knowing it was the only detail that hinted at anything but a natural death. After the shocking violence of the act, he marvelled at how peaceful she seemed and the very injustice of that helped him to make his decision. Even though he regretted what he had done with every fibre of his being, he grudged his victim that merciful oblivion when Matthew's death had been so violent, so driven by misery and self-loathing. Quickly and quietly, James left the house.

He made it as far as the woods before the reality of what he had done truly caught up with him, ambushing him like a physical blow. The sickness was sudden and violent, and he retched again, wishing he could expel his guilt so easily, but it was with him for life now, whatever happened in the short term, and he knew with an almost reassuring certainty that it would destroy him. He waited for the nausea to pass, then cut through the thicket and struck out across the parkland towards the Hall. The house had so many windows, and it seemed impossible that someone wouldn't notice him and know from his walk, from his panic, what he had done, but still he pressed on. To his left, he could see the folly peeping out of the trees, and he wished fervently that he had gone there today instead of to her, but that was impossible now. Everything about it was tainted by what he had just done.

There was no sign of Frank or Victor in the entrance hall, but he heard someone calling his name and looked up, horrified, to see Evelyn in one of the rooms that led off it, where the staff were packing things away and covering the furniture in dust sheets. He rubbed his hand across his eyes, hoping she wouldn't see that he had been crying, and caught the whiff of lavender on his sleeve – sweet and musty, like the room he had just left, a nauseating reminder of the old woman's clothes. He was tempted to pretend he hadn't heard, but she was on her way over to him now, and there was no avoiding her. 'James, are you all right?' He didn't answer, and she looked at him in concern. 'Don't let Mother get to you. It was always what she wanted.'

The past tense was used innocently enough, but it hammered home to him what he had done. 'I'm all right,' he insisted. 'It's not her fault. I shouldn't have gone.'

'I suppose you were the last person she expected to see in her sitting room. She was waiting for the vicar's wife.'

She smiled, shy and a little awkward, and her resemblance to Matthew was so painful that he couldn't meet her eye. She was wearing a wedding ring, he noticed, and he said more gruffly than he intended: 'I'm amazed you recognised me after all this time.'

'Oh, I recognised you.' He was surprised to see her blush as she led him back out to the driveway, where they could talk more privately. 'I knew you were here at the Hall, actually. I've been plucking up the courage to speak to you for days.'

'What about?'

'Matthew, of course. What else?' She took a deep breath and he wanted to tell her to stop; he didn't deserve her kindness or her confidence. 'There were things I should have said years ago. It's not right that you had to go away like that. You loved him. You had every right to know.'

'Know what?'

She paused, obviously frustrated with herself. 'I knew this would happen. Look – it's all in here.' She took an envelope out of her pocket and gave it to him. 'When I heard you were here, I wrote you a letter just in case I lost my nerve and couldn't say it to your face. And I was right – I can't, because I know you'll hate me for it and that's the last thing I want. I wasn't even sure I'd have the courage to give it to you, but when I saw you at the house just now, I knew you hadn't forgotten him, so I went back to get it. You need to move on, James. You need to forget Matthew and live your life, and I hope this will help, no matter what you think of me. Perhaps when you've read it we can talk.'

He looked down at the letter, torn between his need to leave before someone discovered what he had done and the temptation to hear what Evelyn had to say about her brother. 'There won't be time,' he said reluctantly. 'We're about to go, and I won't be coming back.'

'Bart! Hey, Bart! Where the hell have you been?' Frank looked furious as he came out of the north porch entrance, but his tone softened when he saw Evelyn. 'Vic's been looking everywhere for you. There's been a change of plan.'

'What do you mean?'

'We've got to stay a little longer. Some army guy has kicked off about us being here and wants to interrogate us all before we can leave. He seems to think we're some kind of threat to the war effort.'

'But we can't stay any longer,' James insisted, listening to the panic in his own voice. From what Evelyn had said, it was only a matter of time before the vicar's wife turned up and found Marion Plummer, and he needed to be well on his way out of the country before that happened. 'What about the plane?'

Frank ignored him and offered his hand instead to Evelyn. 'Frank Wheeler, Miss.'

'Evelyn Young.'

'Delighted to meet an old friend of Bart's.' He winked mischievously. 'You two *are* old friends, are you?'

'Cut the crap, Frank. Let's get this sorted so we can leave. Goodbye, Evelyn,' he said, keeping his voice as free of emotion as he could. 'It's been nice seeing you again.'

'I'll be at the folly at three,' she said, refusing to let him go without one last exchange. 'If you're still here then and you want to talk, please come.'

Frank grinned. 'Sounds like an offer you can't refuse, Bart – not when the lady asked so nicely.'

'All right, I'll do my best,' James said, with no intention of doing anything of the sort. 'But now we have to go.'

3

Josephine awoke the next morning to a very different ship. Overnight, the *Queen Mary* had been placed on full war alert, and the daily newspaper – slipped discreetly under her cabin door at eight o'clock – outlined what this meant for her passengers, all couched in a reassurance which was, by its very necessity, counter-productive. The liner would now be departing from its usual course, following a zig-zag path across the Atlantic and reaching New York a little later as a result, and, as she walked back along the Promenade Deck from breakfast, where a distinctly subdued atmosphere had prevailed at most tables, she saw that the portholes were being slowly but surely blacked out with paint; later, the deck lamps that had been so warm and welcoming the night before would be extinguished and they would sail in total darkness, now part of the oblivion that the lights had held at bay. Suddenly, for all the ship's strength and immensity, Josephine felt more vulnerable than she would have thought possible.

Determined not to be cowed by something she couldn't control, she settled down in the drawing room to write to Marta. The odds were even on whether she or the letter would arrive in California first – they both had a long train journey ahead of them when they reached the shore – but it comforted her to write it, and to show faith in the idea that they both *would* arrive. She gave a full account of the incident between Alma and the stranger at dinner, hoping that Marta might be able to explain it, but played down the delay and the growing sense of anxiety on board. Was this the shape of things to come? she wondered. Censoring their own letters, even before someone did it for them? Scrutinising every innocent phrase for its true, more sinister meaning? From the very early days, when they were still so shy and uncertain in each other's company, their letters had been brave and fiercely honest; now, it seemed that was to be the first, important, casualty of war, and it saddened her, no matter how well intentioned the deception.

By the time she dropped the letter off at the mail room there was still at least an hour to go before the next meal, and so – as the primary reason for being on board seemed to be eating and drinking – she decided to pass the time by doing something more active. She collected a swimsuit from her cabin and made her way to the pool, which lay beyond an obstacle course of other enticements, some more tempting than others: there were massage and steam rooms, Turkish and curative baths, and a whole menu of treatments that she had never heard of, let alone considered, but the area was hotter and more claustrophobic than any other part of the ship, and she couldn't help but feel that there were men in the boiler rooms downstairs who were having a similar experience without paying ten shillings for it. By now, she knew not to expect a strictly functional pool, devoid of flourishes, but still she was impressed by the splendour of the space: tiles the colour of straw were broken up with striking bands of emerald green and pillar-box red, and the pool itself was impressive in size, more than thirty feet long and overlooked by a balcony. At one end, inset into a broad double staircase, there was a glass panel etched with swans against a red and green background, but other than that it was left to the functional features of the room to provide the decoration – brightly painted poolside furniture, decorative water fountains, and carefully placed lighting bowls which illuminated a beautiful mother-of-pearl ceiling. The water was serene and inviting, and – like everywhere else on the ship – it was refreshingly hard to believe that the area didn't have its foundations in solid earth.

She changed quickly, pleased to see that only a handful of other passengers had beaten her to it, and took the steps that led down to the shallow end. A woman was coming up the other way, but Josephine didn't recognise her until she removed her bathing cap, and by then it was too late to turn back. She smiled awkwardly at Alma's adversary from the night before and moved to pass her, but the woman seemed as keen to start a conversation as Josephine was to avoid one. 'I'm sorry about last night,' she said, and Josephine noticed how young her face was without make-up; she couldn't be much more than twenty, but her boldness and determination to be heard in the dining room had made her seem older.

'Please don't worry. We all say things we regret, and it's forgotten as far as I'm—'

'No, no – I don't mean I'm sorry for *that*,' she interrupted. 'I stand by everything I said, and I wasn't drunk, in spite of what you all thought. As a matter of fact, I don't think I've ever felt more sober in my life. No, I just meant that I'm sorry to have roped you in and embarrassed you. I probably owe you an explanation.'

'Not at all, Miss Hessel. I was very sorry to hear about your father's death, but whatever his connection was with the Hitchcocks, it's really none of my business.'

She stepped away, but Lee Hessel caught her arm and there was something in her eyes that both intrigued and unsettled Josephine, a streak of vulnerability, masked by aggression. 'Please, I saw your face when they were trying to get rid of me. You didn't judge me like the others. You were interested in what I had to say – although I suppose I should be careful not to confuse curiosity with sympathy.'

The comment was such an accurate reflection of Josephine's own thoughts that she felt herself blush. 'I have sympathy for anyone who's grieving,' she said. 'I was only a little bit older than you when I lost my mother, and I was angry with the whole world. There are days when I still am, and that was sixteen years ago now, so I do understand – but lashing out only works in the short term. It doesn't help you find peace with yourself.'

Her kindness obviously disarmed the other woman. 'How are you involved with the Hitchcocks?' she asked, fighting tears by making the question sound more like an accusation.

'I'm not, really,' Josephine replied, deciding to keep any personal connection out of the conversation. 'A friend of mine works for them, that's all.'

'Then tell him to be careful. My father worked for them, too, but that made no difference. They don't care who they destroy. Tell him that from me.'

'I'll tell *her*, but I think she'd say that she can look after herself.'

Lee Hessel gave a wry smile, as if Josephine had somehow disappointed her. 'I've obviously misjudged you,' she said. 'Forgive me. I'm keeping you from your swim.'

She turned to go, and this time it was Josephine's turn to hold her back. 'Destroy is a very strong word,' she said.

'What happened to your father? And why do you blame the Hitchcocks?'

The other woman shivered. 'I need to dry off and feel the sun on my face,' she said. 'If you're really interested, come and find me on the Promenade Deck.'

She turned without another word and headed to the changing cubicles, leaving Josephine troubled and bewildered by the exchange. Her instinct was to go after Lee Hessel and finish the conversation there and then, but she knew in her heart that she would be wiser to leave things alone, so forced herself into the pool instead, hoping that some punishing exercise would get the curiosity out of her system. Twenty lengths later, it was sharper than ever.

A long row of deckchairs had been laid out with military precision on the Promenade Deck, complete with cushions, rugs and reading material. The deck was warm and inviting, particularly on the port side, where the thick glass that enclosed the whole level had trapped the warmth of the sun. Josephine set out on the circuit, hoping that Alma and her family had decided to spend their morning elsewhere; as much as she told herself she was a free agent, she didn't want to be caught fraternising with the enemy. At first, she thought that chance had solved her dilemma for her; there was no sign of Lee Hessel, and she was about to give up and go back to her cabin when she saw the woman she was looking for on a lounger, tucked away from the general thoroughfare. There was a vacant deckchair next to her, reserved by a wide-brimmed sun hat and bag, which were instantly removed when Josephine appeared. 'May I?' she asked.

'Please do. I thought you'd decided against it.'

'I hadn't really decided anything.' Josephine sat down, relieved that the seats were amongst the least conspicuous in the row, unlikely to be noticed by anyone taking a casual stroll. 'Are you sailing out or going home?' she asked. Lee Hessel's accent could not have been more English, but a significant section of the British film industry was calling America home now, as Alma had said, and there was no reason why the Hessel family couldn't be part of that. She tried to recall the name, but couldn't place it.

'Both. Neither.' She must have realised how frustrating her answer was, because she smiled and made an effort to explain. 'My father was English and my mother American, but they divorced when I was a little girl and I was part of the settlement, split scrupulously down the middle so that I never really knew where home was after that. I always preferred to be with my father, but now he's gone I've got no real ties in England and no reason whatsoever to go back there. I went over for his funeral, that's all.'

'I'm sorry. That must have been hard on your own.'

'I'm used to it.' She shook off the kindness, as if it were a threat to her. 'What about you? I'm sorry – I don't even know your name. And please, call me Lee. Hessel is my mother's name, and I hate it. She made me take it after the divorce. One more way to break my father's heart.'

Josephine introduced herself. 'So what was your father's name?'

'William Melrose. He was an actor. You probably won't have heard of him,' she added, reading the question in Josephine's eyes. 'It was bit parts, mostly, very low down the titles. That was another bone of contention between my parents. He was never ambitious enough for my mother's liking. He just saw it as a job that he enjoyed, a means to an end. He worked hard and loved his family, but I think my mother was almost embarrassed by that.'

'Is she an actress, too?'

'No. She's a Hollywood agent and an utter bitch – as hard as granite.' She must be, Josephine thought; even if the marriage was long dead, it was a hard-hearted woman who didn't put her own feelings to one side to support her daughter at the funeral of a father she had obviously adored – unless that was the problem, of course: parental jealousy. 'She's had to be tough to survive in that world, I suppose,' Lee continued, and Josephine was struck by the contrast between this calm, analytical assessment and the out-of-control anger she had witnessed the night before; it was an unsettling combination to be found in the same person. 'If she were someone else's mother, I'd probably respect her for it, but you want love, don't you?'

'Of course you do. It sounds like your father did his best to make that up to you, though.'

She softened, and for the first time the wariness dropped from her face. 'Yes, he did, without ever letting me know that was what he was doing. He was so much fun, you know – interested in everything and such good company. I remember my friends complaining whenever they had to spend time with their parents, but he didn't have a dull or boring bone in his body. I miss him.'

It was a deceptively simple statement, but Josephine knew exactly what she meant. When her mother had died, people had tried to comfort her by reminding her of the good relationship that the two of them had had, of the love she had enjoyed for twenty-six years, and while she knew how lucky she was, none of that had softened the pain. As selfish as it was, it had taken her a long time to stop resenting anyone who still had their mother to talk to. 'How did he die?' she asked gently.

'He had pneumonia. I thought he was getting better, but there were complications that no one expected.'

Josephine was surprised, although she tried not to show it. She had been expecting to hear about an accident, or even a suicide that was in some way connected to William Melrose's work, but she failed to see how the Hitchcocks could possibly be held responsible for an illness like pneumonia. 'That sounds like natural causes,' she ventured tentatively. 'Why are you so angry with Alfred Hitchcock?'

'Because he should have been more careful.' The words tumbled out, and would have sounded like the protestations of a petulant child had the subject not been so serious. She made an effort to compose herself, and Josephine waited patiently for the explanation. 'You know Hitchcock's *Jamaica Inn*?' Lee asked.

'I saw it when it came out.' She had gone out of loyalty to Marta, who had worked on the script, but not even love could persuade her to overlook the unforgivable changes to du Maurier's novel or the excesses of Charles Laughton's acting. As far as she was concerned, the film had been memorable for all the wrong reasons, although it wasn't the moment to speak those thoughts aloud.

'Then you'll have seen my dad. It was his last film – he played one of the wreckers in Joss Merlyn's gang. You'll probably remember those storm scenes, even if you don't remember him?' Josephine nodded. 'That's what makes it all the more senseless, really – Hitchcock could have put anyone out there in that costume. He didn't need to make my father do it.'

'I'm sorry, I don't understand.'

'The filming was brutal. Hours in the water with wind machines, day after day. Everyone went home with chills and shivers. Dad had a weak chest, anyway – he'd had bronchitis as a child, and he was susceptible to anything like that – so he felt it worse than the rest of them. He shouldn't even have gone back to the studio, but he was so bloody diligent – he wouldn't give up on a job he was being paid to do.'

'Did Hitch know he was ill?'

'Of course he did. Some of the others asked him to put a double in, and a couple of the crew even offered to stand in for him, but Hitchcock wouldn't have any of it. He just ploughed on with his precious film, no matter who got hurt in the process.'

Had it really been like that? Josephine wondered. Or had the actor been determined to play his part, shrugging off any concerns out of pride or sheer wilfulness, telling his director that he was fitter than he really was? Both scenarios seemed feasible, and she suspected that the truth lay somewhere in the middle, but Melrose's daughter was far too driven by grief and resentment to see beyond her own version of events. '*Were* they friends?' she asked, casting her mind back to the night before. Alma had sounded sincere when she talked about her husband's sorrow at the actor's death, and – in Josephine's experience – she didn't often say things she didn't mean.

'Yes, they'd known each other for years, since the Gainsborough days. Like I said, my dad had a great sense of humour and he was always up for anything, and Hitchcock liked that about him. He's a practical joker himself, but my father was one of the few people who could match him.' Josephine had witnessed one or two of Hitchcock's stunts herself at close quarters, and his humour relied far too heavily on cruelty and humiliation for her taste, but she kept quiet, reluctant to say anything that might imply a judgement on Melrose. 'He literally worked my dad to death,' Lee said disbelievingly, as if still trying to make sense of it herself. 'And do you know what really haunts me? Hitchcock didn't give a damn about *Jamaica Inn*. He just wanted it done so that he could get out of the country, and I can't bear the thought of my father being sacrificed for something that mattered so little.'

That much was true, or so Josephine had gathered from Marta: *Jamaica Inn* had fulfilled Hitchcock's contract in England, leaving him free to move. 'Had you thought of discussing this with them properly?' she asked. 'Or with Alma, at least. She's a reasonable woman, and I think if you approached her without making a scene and without a drink in your hand, she'd probably listen.'

'So she can explain it all away, and tell me that it's a tragic coincidence? That there's been nearly a year between the filming and my father's death, so it couldn't possibly be anything to do with them?'

'No, none of that. So that *you* can say what you need to say. It might bring you some peace.'

'Who says I *want* peace? What good is that to my father?' She had raised her voice, and their conversation was beginning to draw attention from further down the row. Josephine wished that she had listened to reason rather than curiosity, and wracked her brains for the easiest way out of the confrontation, but Lee seemed determined to make the most of her audience now that she had one. 'The Hitchcocks think I'm making all this fuss because I want to sue them,' she said, more quietly now but still taking Josephine by surprise; it had never occurred to her that last night's encounter wasn't the first time that the subject had been raised. 'You probably think that, too, but it's not about money, really it isn't.'

'So what is it about?'

'I want them to suffer,' Lee said, without a second's hesitation, and the words were spoken with sufficient detachment and strength of purpose for Josephine to believe that she might actually be able to make that happen; that she might, in fact, already have a plan. 'I want them to understand the meaning of loss, just like I do.'

'And is that what your father would want? Would that make him proud of you?' It was a cheap blow, but an effective one. Josephine stood up, taking advantage of the sudden silence. 'Please don't torture yourself like this,' she said kindly, 'and no – before you say it, I'm not taking their side. Far from it. I understand why you're angry, but there are other ways to honour your father's memory, ways that might be more in keeping with his life than his death.' She smiled. 'That name you hate, for example – you don't have to keep it. Lee Melrose has a very nice ring to it.'

She walked away before the woman could say anything to keep her there, and headed back to her cabin to change for lunch. The ship felt suddenly much smaller, rife with potential conflict wherever she turned, regardless of the war, and she was pleased to get through the afternoon without seeing Lee again or bumping into the Hitchcocks. Rather than face the main dining room, she decided to book for dinner in the Verandah Grill, only to find when she got there that Alma had had exactly the same idea, and was seated at a table in the middle of the room with her mother and daughter. It was a much smaller restaurant, and Josephine had no choice but to go over and say hello, although she was relieved to see that they were already on their dessert course and she wasn't invited to join them. 'I'm sorry about last night,' Alma said, when they had exchanged pleasantries about the day. She turned her head slightly so that her mother wouldn't be able to hear above the music. 'I know she's grieving, but the girl's behaviour was inexcusable.'

It was the second time in just a few hours that Josephine had had an apology that really wasn't necessary, and she made the same response. 'Please don't worry on my account. It wasn't of your making, and I've forgotten all about it.'

'It's significant that she's making a fuss now, I suppose.' Shortly after her father's death was probably the natural time to do it, Josephine thought, but she didn't interrupt. 'It's been a very high-profile move to America and it makes Hitch an easy target. I suppose she wants to capitalise on his success and make some money out of us.' It was so close to the script that Lee Hessel had written for Alma that Josephine had to work hard to keep her expression neutral. 'There's no truth in what she says,' Alma added, looking at her intently. 'Hitch isn't heartless in the way that she suggested. He doesn't exploit people, and if he'd known that there was any risk to William's health, he'd have taken steps to protect him. In any case, it was nearly a year ago now. There can't possibly be a connection.'

'I'm sure any resentment will die down naturally in time,' Josephine said, wondering who Alma was trying to convince. 'As you say, grief does strange things to people. With a bit of luck, you'll be able to avoid her for the rest of the voyage.'

'Perhaps, but Hollywood is a very small place.' She pushed

her plate away, leaving the pancakes untouched. 'Anyway, we mustn't keep you from your dinner, and I'm expecting a call from Hitch. Pat loves to say goodnight to her daddy, and he'll be in a much better mood for filming tomorrow if he's had a snatch of family time. Sometimes I think it's the only thing that keeps us both sane.'

She took her daughter's hand and Josephine watched them go, troubled by something in the back of her mind. If Lee Hessel really wanted to make the Hitchcocks suffer, she need look no further than any disruption to the tight family unit that was so precious to them. She shivered, as if the thought could somehow be father to the deed, and wondered if she should warn Alma tomorrow of what had been said; she didn't want to worry her unnecessarily, but if she kept her silence and something happened to Patricia, she would never forgive herself.

Her table was by the window, with a spectacular view of the sunset, and – after the awkwardness of the day – she took comfort from the solitude. The restaurant managed to be both exclusive and informal, designed with a nightclub atmosphere in mind, and there were cocktails and dancing on offer as well as good food. She had already fallen in love with the art on board the ship, a rich collection of paintings by the likes of Vanessa Bell, Cedric Morris, and Bertram Nicholls, whose landscape of the Sussex countryside she would happily have given houseroom to. Here, the decor was theatrical – large, flamboyant canvases by Doris Zinkeisen, a designer whom Josephine knew – and she suddenly felt very much at home.

She sipped her martini and looked out across the sea, shading her eyes against a sinking red sun that seemed reluctant to surrender its hold on the day. Approaching the halfway mark of the voyage, she still found the nothingness awe-inspiring, the vastness of the Atlantic that stretched out on all sides and made it possible to believe that there was nobody but this small band of travellers left in the world. Except today there was *something*, a vague dark smudge on the horizon that grew more defined as the sun lost its strength. Gradually, the grey silhouette of a vessel took shape, and Josephine was conscious of a lull in the conversation as everyone stared out to sea. They had passed several ships already en route, but this one wasn't moving; rather, it seemed to be waiting. As they drifted towards it, the music stopped, too, and an ominous silence fell across the room.

Some of the passengers seated in the middle of the room got up from their tables for a better view at the windows. One lady with a pair of binoculars offered them to Josephine by way of an apology for standing so close at her shoulder; she trained them on the horizon, but couldn't make out any markings on the ship. When someone finally found the courage to speak aloud what they had all been thinking, it was almost a relief. 'That's a German battleship, isn't it?' a man said gravely. 'I heard they were close but I didn't believe it.' One rumour quickly gave rise to others, and Josephine was shocked to learn that a British liner had already been torpedoed off the coast of Scotland with the loss of more than a hundred lives. Never in a million years had she dreamt that her family would be in danger so quickly; like most people, she had assumed that the immediate threat would be to London and the south-east of England, and she thought instantly of her middle sister, Jane, who was married to a naval officer; she must be worried out of her mind. They had

had a difficult relationship, particularly in recent years, but Josephine's heart went out to her now, and she cursed the distance that lay between them.

For the first time since she had been on board, she was conscious of a dramatic change in the ship's course. Clearly they were in serious danger, and it was the waiting staff who gave the game away most definitively: their discipline was shaken and she saw them looking nervously at each other, no longer able to maintain the illusion that their passengers were the only thing that mattered. A shout went up on the other side of the restaurant, and the diners moved as one to the opposite windows. Josephine went with them, and saw instantly that another, seemingly identical ship was positioned up ahead, only a fraction further away than the first. 'They've got us surrounded,' someone said. 'Bastards.'

The expletive was the only suggestion of panic in the room, and Josephine found the collective calm in the face of a crisis both heartening and remarkable. The head waiter – suddenly as white as his dress shirt – took control of the situation, and someone was dispatched discreetly to find out what was happening. The wait for news seemed endless, and the thoughts that passed through her mind were random and unsettling. She was no stranger to fear, but this was quite different from anything she had ever experienced, and she realised for the first time how many complicated emotions that simple, four-letter word covered. She had felt it first at her mother's bedside, nursing her through the final days of her cancer and terrified of what her loss would mean; she had been – and still was – frightened of her love for Marta, of what people would think and how it would shame her family if anyone but her closest friends found out; she had been a helpless bystander as Archie was shot, and she had faced a gun herself. And then, of course, there was the last war, when she had feared for someone she loved – with good reason, as it turned out. How far away the fighting had seemed back then, she thought; how sheltered they had been at home, like children playing a game they didn't really understand and weren't allowed to watch. This fear was something new, though – raw and visceral in the pit of her stomach, a selfish contemplation of her own death which she had lived surprisingly long without ever having to face. She looked around, and wondered how many other people were thinking about that cold, dark water, horrified because they felt so unprepared, because they still had so much left to say, and do.

'It's all right, they're ours.' The waiter stood in the middle of the restaurant, trying to catch his breath. 'The captain says not to panic. It's the Royal bloody Navy.'

It wasn't clear whether the final declaration was a direct quote or an embellishment of his own, but no one seemed to care. A cheer went up around the room, and the waiter was clapped on the back as if he were personally responsible for whatever stroke of good luck had summoned the ships in the first place. Several bottles of champagne materialised from nowhere, and the room was suddenly full of laughter and the sound of popping corks. It was a strange atmosphere, as febrile in its way as the trepidation had been just moments before, and it reminded Josephine of the months immediately after the war, when every pleasure had been that much more intense, that much more precious, because it was no longer taken for granted. Strangers moved from table to table, talking the night away long after dinner was over, and no one – herself included – seemed to want to go to bed. At the stroke of midnight, the tables were removed altogether, and a band took centre stage. The dancing lasted well into the morning.

4

Marta didn't need to spend much time in Culver City to understand exactly why Hitchcock had moved there, and why he had put his trust – and his career – in the hands of Selznick International Pictures. Selznick was an unconventional producer, and he and Hitch had been involved in a kind of professional courtship for months before the deal was signed, testing each other's limits and commitment, offsetting their obvious differences against their potential value to one another before deciding, on both sides, that the risk was worth it. It hadn't been the easiest of working relationships so far, and Marta doubted that it ever would be, but the studio's byword was quality, and Hitch would put up with most things for the integrity of the film.

When she had first walked onto the lot, the sets for *Rebecca* had taken her breath away, and there was no question in her mind now that it would prove to be the finest thing he had directed so far. The apparently limitless ingenuity of the art and special effects departments had fashioned a world which would never have been possible if they'd made the film in England – a fantasy manor house, steeped in atmosphere, with muscular walls and a patchwork of styles that gave every impression of a building evolved over centuries rather than a sleight of hand created in weeks. The interiors were hostile, confusing and claustrophobic, straight out of a Gothic novel, and they reflected quite brilliantly the mental state of the heroine. Marta could tell from the script, and from the handful of scenes already shot, that Manderley's isolation would be a powerful element of the story. If they'd shot on location, the temptation would have been to show the landscape around the house – the country lanes and neighbouring villages, the nearest market town – and the sense of mystery would instantly have been lost. But created like this, artificially and free of context, the house left the heroine with no one to turn to, and nowhere to go.

The set in use today was Manderley's dining room, decorated with expensive-looking antique furniture and paintings, all copied meticulously from English auction catalogues by a crew that seemed willing and able to turn its hand to anything. There was a roaring fire in the stone hearth, but not even that could soften the room's fundamental austerity, the only other comfort coming from a thick-pile cream rug that was big enough to hold the table and chairs. The doors and fireplace had classical mouldings, jarring convincingly with the otherwise Gothic atmosphere of the house, and family portraits looked down at them from the walls – although whose family the faces belonged to was anybody's guess. Hitchcock loved flowers, and it had been one of Marta's first responsibilities for him to make sure that bouquets were delivered to his home and his office twice a week; here, they were used as a weapon, with two enormous arrangements casting angry shadows onto the wall on either side of the double doors. Directly opposite, lending a symmetry to the room, stood two large urns, and Marta wondered if she was reading too much into the set to see Rebecca alive and dead in those particular details. In any case, the sense of menace was palpable, and the only authenticity missing from the room was the distinctive, slightly musty smell of an old country house.

Joan Fontaine sat fawn-like at one end of the long dining-room table, dwarfed by the vastness of the room, which conspired with the tension on set to give her the look of an awkward, frightened child. They were re-shooting a scene from the previous day, using new dialogue that Selznick had written himself, and nobody's temper had been improved by the delay. Fontaine flinched at every cross word, whether it was in the script or not, and Marta noticed how tired she looked. The twelve-hour days were beginning to take their toll, with long filming sessions on top of fittings and camera tests, and her apparent inability to cope was now a regular topic of conversation amongst the more experienced cast members, none of it particularly kind or understanding. There had already been far too many retakes this morning, and she watched as one of the crew stoked up the fire and put new candles in the elaborate silverware that dominated the dining table, making it even more difficult for the newly married de Winters to talk to each other. It was the fourth or fifth time that the candles had been changed today; if Hitchcock wasn't satisfied soon, half the budget would quite literally go up in smoke.

It was Olivier, this time, who fluffed his line. He swore and slammed his hand down on the table, making the cutlery jump and rattle like his co-star's nerves, and Marta had an uncomfortable flashback to her own childhood, when an overbearing father and a dutiful mother had made her frightened to let a word pass her lips at mealtimes in case it was the wrong one. Fontaine seemed to sink further into her seat, as if the ghost of Rebecca herself had just joined them for dinner.

'Cut!' Some directors paced and others gesticulated, but Hitchcock rarely moved from his chair once he had walked the scene through, exuding all the authority he needed from the calm courage of his own convictions. 'Let's try that again,' he said, smiling patiently at his leading lady, 'but we'll take a short break first.' He glanced at the secretary who had just come downstairs with a message for him. 'A little bird tells me that our producer is on his way to see us.'

Marta saw the frown on the woman's face, and realised that the announcement of Selznick's daily visit to the set had been meant as an incentive to keep working, not an instruction to do the opposite. Fontaine looked relieved at the prospect of a break, but Olivier glowered. 'Do we really have to prolong this?' he asked. 'For fuck's sake, Hitch, just get the girl to speak the damned lines.'

The director chuckled, apparently enjoying himself. It was always like this, Marta recalled: at the beginning of a new film, whatever the problems, Hitchcock glowed. 'I say, Larry old boy, do be careful,' he admonished, wagging his finger. 'Joan is a new bride, remember. Spare her blushes.' He could easily have been talking about her character, but Fontaine had married in real life just before filming started, cutting short her honeymoon when she heard she had got the part, and now – still only twenty-one – she had the unenviable task of adjusting to life as a newly-wed at home as well as at the studio.

Olivier looked at her, finally showing some interest. 'Oh? Who's the chap you married?'

Marta waited, hoping she might remind him that it was none of his business, but of course she didn't. 'Brian Aherne,' she said. 'We met on—'

'Aherne?' Olivier scoffed. 'Couldn't you do any better than that?'

He threw the remark over his shoulder as he strode from the set, a put-down that Mrs Danvers might have been proud of. Olivier's self-assurance was intimidating at the best of times, and it didn't help that he was still smarting with resentment because someone so inexperienced had beaten his lover to the part that every actress in Hollywood wanted. He would no doubt have behaved as badly with anyone, but that was no comfort to Joan Fontaine. Marta looked at her crestfallen expression and realised instantly that the words had had a devastating effect: Hollywood was a small, fickle place, where reputations were built and dashed in an instant, and it was as if she could see the pride draining from the actress's face along with its colour. After such a public humiliation, Fontaine would probably never look at her husband in quite the same way again. If Marta had been a betting woman, she'd have put money on the marriage failing within five years.

'What am I doing wrong?' Fontaine asked, looking to her director, and Marta had to remind herself that the cameras had stopped rolling and this wasn't Mrs de Winter asking for advice on how to fit into Manderley. From the moment she had arrived on set, the actress had been desperate to make her casting work, and Hitch had spent a lot of time with her already, guiding and shaping her performance, patiently explaining what he wanted from her in the same way that he had with Nova Pilbeam during the making of *Young and Innocent*. Fontaine's sense of exclusion hadn't been helped by her last-minute casting, which left her less familiar with the script than most other people on the payroll, and Marta wondered why they were shooting these crucial moments so early in the schedule rather than allowing her to familiarise herself with her character while the others pressed on with scenes that didn't include her. The obvious answer was that it suited Hitchcock to have Fontaine as awkward and vulnerable as the second Mrs de Winter, but their Pygmalion-style relationship only made her more isolated from the rest of the cast, who sat in each other's dressing rooms, swapping theatre stories that she could take no part in, even if she had been invited. It was far too much like being the new girl at school, Marta thought, wanting to belong but knowing that every attempt to fit in only emphasised your shortcomings.

Now, the actress stared earnestly at Hitchcock, repeating her question and waiting for him to offer some word of advice that would miraculously bring her into the fold. To Marta's disappointment, although not to her surprise, he did precisely the opposite, deftly establishing himself as her only friend on set. 'Try not to worry about Larry, my dear – or any of them for that matter. They might not like you, they might want you out, but we'll prove them all wrong, I can promise you that.' It was a ruthless strategy of divide and conquer, but it was already having the desired effect. Ironically, Fontaine's lack of confidence was adding to her performance, something that her director no doubt realised and would go on exploiting until the actress wondered where she ended and the nervous, paranoid Mrs de Winter began; if there was one thing that Alfred Hitchcock understood instinctively, it was insecurity. 'Now, go and take ten minutes to compose yourself and we'll get this finished,' he suggested kindly. 'Just remember what we rehearsed and you can't go wrong.'

The actress nodded and headed back to her dressing room. Marta stood to go after her, keen to offer some support that had less of an agenda behind it, but Hitch put a hand on her arm. 'Stay where you are – there are some things we need to talk through. Miss Schiller will look after Joan.' He smiled sweetly at the script editor, who sat just a few feet away. It hadn't taken him long to realise that Lydia Schiller was Selznick's eyes and ears on set, reporting back to the producer each day and raising the alarm if the director reneged on the smallest creative detail of what had been agreed. Hitchcock hated having an informant in his crew: loyalty was his most fundamental demand, and anyone who didn't offer it willingly was destined for a difficult time. Schiller scowled, obviously not appreciating being treated as a nursemaid, and Marta waited for her to argue, but she thought better of it and reluctantly followed Fontaine.

Her boss arrived almost immediately, and Marta felt Hitch bristle a little as Selznick walked onto the set, stopping occasionally to have a word with his crew. Their differences extended to their physical appearance: Selznick was tall and heavyset, with small, round glasses and an earnest expression that made him look studious; today, as always, his clothes were expensive but crumpled, a dark, three-piece suit that looked as if it had been slept in, and probably had. 'Why aren't the cameras rolling?' he asked without any sort of preamble, looking accusingly at his director.

'We had a slight problem with the cast. Nothing serious, but they're taking a break.'

'Really? Yesterday when I was here you had a slight problem with the cameras. I thought today I might actually see some work being done.'

Hitch shrugged and held out his hands, as if to stress that there was nothing he could do. 'Third time lucky tomorrow, perhaps?'

Marta hid a smile and settled down to watch. The regular sparring between the two men in charge of this film had proved as entertaining as some of the rushes. It had come as a terrible shock to Hitchcock to learn that a producer in America had a creative role as well as a financial one, and she would never forget how affronted he had been on the first day of shooting when a script girl informed him that Selznick expected to see how a scene had been set up before it was filmed. Since then, every trick under the sun had been employed to make sure that the cameras were mysteriously inactive whenever a visit was due, and although the studio head knew he was being hoodwinked, there had been very little so far that he could do about it. He was quickly coming to find that Hitchcock was unlike any director that he had hired – or fired – in the past, and if Selznick had won most of the battles over the script, Hitch was well ahead on points in the filming. 'You're using the new dialogue for this?' he said, gesturing back towards the dining table. Hitchcock nodded. 'Good. And I hope you've got the servants right this time. I thought you English were supposed to know about stuff like that. Christ, I've seen better-trained butlers in a Brooklyn apartment.' He drew up a chair and sat down heavily. 'I set aside some time to watch the rushes last night, only to find that there wasn't much to see. Is that all the footage there is?'

'I've filmed what I needed to film,' Hitchcock said, 'nothing more, nothing less.' The retort was a little defensive, perhaps because he knew it was a half-truth, open to conjecture. So far, he had only filmed the camera angles he judged necessary –

none of the normal middle shots or close-ups that would have given Selznick a chance to edit the film in different ways. It was a highly effective method of keeping control – risky, because it offered no safety net, but Hitch had more than enough confidence in his own singular vision to take that chance, and he knew that Selznick was far too busy with the editing of *Gone With the Wind* to put up much of a fight. 'You'll have everything you need,' he reiterated, obviously ready to argue his case in more detail, but Selznick waved the comment aside.

'I'll never get on with this goddamn jigsaw cutting of yours,' he said, 'but we do have to talk about the tempo. The whole thing needs more pace, Hitch. Why is Olivier so slow all the time? He's supposed to be thinking about a ball, not trying to run for president. And you're letting him throw away his lines. I know that's the modern style, but an American audience will never understand him and it will cost him points in the long run. It's all wrong, goddamn it.'

In the few interactions that she had witnessed between producer and director, Marta was always struck by how blunt Selznick was in his approach, and how diplomatic Hitch could be, employing a carefully calculated tact to get his own way on everything that mattered to him. 'I'll speak to Larry about it,' he agreed, ready to make this concession if it allowed him to stand his ground on something else. 'We'll speed things along.'

'Good. I'd much rather err on the side of too fast a tempo than the other way round. Except for Danvers, remember – she speaks more slowly than the others.'

'I hadn't forgotten.'

'I hear you've been allowing the actors to stand around while the camera crew lines up?' Hitchcock scowled at the script editor's empty chair, in little doubt as to where that information had come from. 'Then you keep the crew waiting while the actors rehearse. Where's the efficiency in that? Surely you can do both at the same time?'

'I can't rehearse while the crew is setting the lights. The noise disturbs the actors.'

'Then do it on the sidelines, for God's sake. We're behind schedule already, and it's only the first week.'

Hitchcock had been naïve about how closely his work would be monitored in Hollywood. There was a daily studio log that noted the beginning and end of a working day, as well as the number of script pages and film minutes completed; with that and a running commentary from those most loyal to him on set, Selznick could keep a much tighter rein on everything than anyone Hitchcock had worked with before. 'It's early days, as you say,' he insisted, his tone more conciliatory now. 'As soon as everyone is more settled, things will pick up.'

'I'm glad to hear it. Apart from anything else, there's the war to think about. We'll be in a fine pickle if they all sign up before the film's finished.'

'Not as much of a pickle as Poland, I suspect.'

'That's not what I meant and you know it. Now, the proposal scene – I was really disappointed with that. We need a close-up of the girl's reaction to it. She should blurt out her response like she actually *cares*. Put some emotion into it. Make her sound like she actually *wants* to marry him.'

'You asked me to handle her with restraint.'

'Yes, but not all the time. Don't underplay her when it matters or there'll be no variety in the picture. Come on, Hitch – a bit more Yiddish arts theatre and a bit less English repertory.'

'If you say so.'

'I do say so. There's no need to stray from the novel in that scene – it's perfect. Look at it again, will you? I want it word for word.' An instruction to go back to the source material was guaranteed to incite Hitchcock, and Marta didn't have to look at him to know that his expression would be thunderous. 'Did you get my memo?' Selznick asked.

'Which one?' The retort was instant, with a faint trace of sarcasm – the producer was infamous for his memos, some of them running into several pages – but it was carefully judged and Hitchcock got away with it.

'The most recent one, from this morning – the one about the budget. You're going to have to cut back on the wardrobe. It's not a damned period piece, so see what you can do.' Hitchcock nodded to Marta and she made a note, hoping that Selznick had finished and would go back upstairs to his office, but he had one more bee in his bonnet. 'I've been thinking about the final scene . . .'

Hitch's face suggested that he should play poker more often. 'Yes?' he said, looking innocently at Selznick as if nothing could be more welcome to him than advice on how to finish a film that he had barely started.

'We should have smoke from the fire curling up into a big letter "R" above the wreckage.'

Selznick drew it in the air with his hand, his enthusiasm for the concept giving the gesture a theatricality that was uncharacteristic. Marta looked curiously at Hitchcock, knowing that he would think the idea vulgar and silly, and wondering how he would convey that without actually saying so. 'Won't it rather imply that Rebecca's presence still lingers?' he suggested diplomatically.

'Not necessarily.'

'It's ambiguous, though. I thought we wanted to say just the opposite in those closing shots.'

It was hard to tell if Selznick knew already that he was beaten. 'But you'll think about it?' he asked insistently.

'Of course.'

'And where are we with the censor?'

'Miss Fox is on top of it.' Hitchcock looked conspiratorially at Marta. 'In fact, we were just discussing it when you arrived.'

It was the first that Marta had heard of it, but she nodded to back him up. 'That's right, and we're getting there. There are several routes that we could take – it's just a question of choosing the best one.'

'Good. Make sure you run it by me before you do anything.'

'Don't we always?' He kept his expression convincingly frozen until Selznick had left the set, then turned to Marta. 'These choices we have . . .'

'Fabricated, obviously.'

'Yes, I feared as much. You were very good, though, and it's a great improvement – you wouldn't tell so much as a fib when you first came to us.'

'And since then I've learnt from the master.'

'I'll take that as a compliment.' Hitchcock sighed heavily. 'I suppose we'd better talk about it, though, and preferably before David's spy has finished mopping up poor Joan.' He reached for his copy of the script, heavily annotated and filled with drawings for the camera shots he had planned; by the time filming was complete, Hitchcock's personal screenplay resembled a travelling artist's sketch pad. 'Where are we with the Hays Office?' he asked, using the informal name by which the censor's office was known.

'The revised script has just come back, and we've got two main issues to deal with. First of all, there's the relationship between Rebecca and Mrs Danvers – or, as they would put it, "the quite inescapable inferences of sex perversion". I really don't see a way of dealing with that, except to remove them completely from the script.'

'That's not the end of the world, I don't suppose. It's a shame, but we can show it in other ways.' Marta didn't doubt that. Hitchcock was a genius with suggestion and atmosphere, easily capable of outwitting the censors; by the time he had finished directing the key scenes between Judith Anderson and Joan Fontaine, the audience would assume without a second thought that the housekeeper's attachment to her first mistress was anything but platonic, although not even the most experienced censor would be able to identify the part to cut. 'I'd be sorry to lose the line about the nuns, though.'

Marta smiled. 'I'll see what I can do.'

'Thank you. The other issue is Max's guilt, I suppose?'

'Yes. If we follow the book . . .'

'As David wants us to do.'

'. . . we violate the Production Code and they'll never approve the film. Max can't be seen to get away with murder, and in the book he shoots Rebecca in the heart without a shred of remorse.'

'If it's the lack of remorse that's the problem, we could soften that – give him some regrets, show that it's been playing on his mind. That might go down well with the audience – a handsome, tortured man, imprisoned by his own conscience but ultimately redeemed by the love of an innocent woman.'

'I already tried that.'

'And what did they say?'

'He's still a murderer, and he can't go unpunished.'

'I will never understand why murder is considered such a lowbrow speciality in Hollywood. Crime doesn't have to be second-class literature, any more than tragedy is.'

'I agree with you, but – like it or not – there will be sections of the audience who support Hays. And not just the audience – we've already lost one actor over it.' Ronald Colman had been first choice for the role of Max de Winter but he had eventually turned the part down, reluctant to play a killer. 'We can't be seen to condone Rebecca's murder.'

'She was dying anyway.'

'Aren't we all? I'm not sure they'll view that as an excuse.'

Hitchcock smiled. 'There's the whole issue of provocation, though. It's made very clear in the book and in the script that Rebecca taunted Max because she wanted him to kill her and suffer for it. Can't we get some leeway out of that? If someone acts in the heat of the moment, responding to something too abhorrent to bear, is that really murder?'

'It depends on the jury, I suppose.'

'Well, the audience is *our* jury, and I know whose side they'll be on. After all, the book's been serialised in the *Ladies' Home Journal* without any obvious harm to the women of America. I haven't heard of a sudden increase in the homicide rate, have you?' Marta shook her head, although the question was rhetorical. 'We're all capable of it, though, don't you think?' Hitch continued, more serious now. 'We'd all kill for something.'

'Yes, we would.' Marta didn't have to use her imagination to answer him. There had been a period in her life when – from grief and injustice and anger – she had been ready to kill, and when she had despaired enough to put a gun in someone's hand in the hope that they would pull the trigger and put her out of her misery. The complex emotions of du Maurier's novel were real to her, intensely so, and she had played both Max and Rebecca in her time; perhaps that was why this film was so different from the others she had worked on. 'What about you?' she asked, although she thought she knew what he would say. 'What would drive you to it?'

'I'd kill anyone who threatened my family,' he replied without hesitation. 'The slightest possibility of any harm to Alma or Patricia, and I wouldn't give it a second thought – or regret it afterwards.'

'And I don't think anyone would blame you for that,' Marta said. 'The trouble is, Max's motive was essentially jealousy, and it will be very hard to dress that up as something more noble for the censors.'

Hitchcock sighed. 'So what are our options?'

'They're limited, obviously. We could make it an accident. Perhaps Max hits Rebecca and she falls, then he panics when he realises what he's done and has to get rid of the body, pretty much as he does in the book.'

'A woman having an accident doesn't hold quite the same tension, somehow.'

'But if we focused on that moment, on what it feels like for him . . .'

Hitchcock looked doubtful. 'That would be very hard to do without some sort of flashback, and it means bringing Rebecca in. We'd destroy the mystery completely.'

'So we do it through his testimony, when he's confessing to the girl. Thousands of people will see the film having read the book, remember, and they'll have his guilt at the back of their minds. It will make his narration of events unreliable, and that gives the whole thing an edge.'

'It's too clever, and we can't rely on prior knowledge. The film has to stand on its own or it will have failed.' He shook his head, obviously frustrated that the solution to their problem remained elusive. 'Do the best you can with it, then I'll go and talk to them. You never know, I might be able to win Joseph over.' Despite being so often at odds with him, Hitch had a good relationship with Joseph Breen at the Hays Office, and it was a dance of cunning that both parties seemed to enjoy. Sometimes, Marta suspected that the censors were as impressed by Hitchcock's success in smuggling things past them as they were alarmed by it. 'When are Victor and the crew due back from England?' he asked.

'Friday.'

'Good. I want you to go out to the coast with them at the weekend and scout for the Cornwall and Monte Carlo shots. Joanie will be back by then, and I can't spare her here.' Marta smiled wryly to herself, glad that she was one of the few people who could deal with being dispensable to Alfred Hitchcock; she liked and admired Joan Harrison, who rarely left Hitchcock's side during filming, and she had no interest in competing for that role on a permanent basis. 'Anyway, we want those scenes to be as authentic as possible, and you know Cornwall.'

She'd been there twice, but she wasn't going to argue. Getting away from the claustrophobic studio for a few days would be heaven; she enjoyed the freedom of working with a second unit, and got on well with the crew. Best of all, Josephine would be able to come with her; she wouldn't be welcome on set very often, and wouldn't want to be in the way, but out on the Californian coast they would have some time to themselves, away from the worries of home.

'It sounds as if everyone is getting out just in time,' Hitchcock said, unwittingly following her train of thought. He watched absent-mindedly as the candles were changed yet again and the cutlery realigned. 'I'll be pleased when Alma and Patricia are back. Alma seemed troubled when I spoke to her. She had something on her mind.'

'But she didn't say what?'

'No, that's how I know it's serious. She was very keen to pass me on to Pat.'

'Perhaps she was tired, or just a bit preoccupied,' Marta suggested, wondering if Josephine had bumped into Alma on board yet. 'It's easy to forget that there's a war on when you're here – too easy – but she's had to go back and face it, if only briefly. It's not surprising that she might be troubled.'

'Yes, I suppose so.'

He looked doubtful, and his concern was infectious. The Hitchcocks were a close couple, and if Alma was keeping something from her husband, it was almost certainly because she didn't want him to worry. Suddenly, Marta was anxious for Josephine and whatever might be happening out at sea: it had been foolish of her to assume that the ship would be safe the moment it left English waters. 'Will you be speaking to Alma again?' she asked, trying to keep her voice casual.

'If I can. The connection is a bit hit and miss.'

'Would you ask her if she's seen Josephine? And give her my love.' Marta had already decided to try a call herself, but it didn't hurt to have two chances of getting a message through.

'Yes, of course.' Hitchcock looked at his watch. 'We'd better have everybody back and get on with this blasted scene. I don't know why David had to interfere with the dialogue – it's just not working.'

'One more thing while we're waiting – the final scene . . .'

'Oh yes.' Hitchcock raised his eyes to the heavens. 'A smoking "R" in the sky – what a bloody ridiculous idea. I don't know why I bother if that sort of cheap gimmick is what he's after. We'd be a laughing stock.' He stopped and stared at her. 'You surely didn't *like* the idea . . .'

'No, of course not, but it might be effective to have the flames *consuming* a letter "R" as the final shot. Rebecca's signature, perhaps. We could see the fire destroying that poetry book she gave to Max – the letter "R" could be the last thing to burn. That would leave the audience with the right message.'

'Marta, my dear, you're a genius. That's a wonderful idea.'

'It is, but it's not mine, I'm afraid. Thank the author – page sixty-four.' She threw him her dog-eared copy of *Rebecca*. 'Sometimes it *is* useful to have the original to hand.'

He chuckled, and doffed an imaginary cap. 'Touché.'

'Tell Selznick it's faithful to du Maurier and he'll love it.'

Hitchcock winked. 'I'll tell him it's cheaper, too.'

Fontaine and Olivier returned to the set, ready to continue the scene. Once the camera crew had set up, Hitchcock prepared his actors, and Marta was interested by his approach. With Olivier, as with most of the experienced stars he directed, his guidance was negligible; with Fontaine, he was specific about everything, finding her character in the tiniest nuance of expression, and showing her rather than telling her what he wanted her to do. The director was a brilliant mimic, and the effect as he spoke some of her lines was uncanny.

Once he was satisfied that she was sufficiently rehearsed, he sat back in his chair. 'Right, twirl 'em,' he called.

They worked on the scene for another ninety minutes, and still Hitchcock wasn't happy. Fontaine was more self-conscious than ever, and it had obviously come as a shock to her that so much of an actress's time was spent doing exactly the same thing over and over again in exactly the same way, repeating for the close-up what she did in the long shot. It didn't help that Olivier was a master at it, even spilling his food in exactly the same spot in every take. 'It's David's fucking dialogue that's the problem,' Hitchcock exclaimed, drawing a gasp of disapproval from Lydia Schiller, although it was hard to tell which had disturbed her more, the obscenity or the slur against her boss. The director screwed up the extra page that had been added the day before and threw it over his shoulder. 'Right, let's try this another way.'

Marta watched as he went over to talk at length with his cameraman, and then with his actors, curious to know what he had in mind. When the scene began again, the camera was tightly focused on the lace napkin, embroidered with Rebecca's initials, that lay in the second Mrs de Winter's place setting. As Fontaine picked it up and unfolded it, the camera pulled slowly and steadily back until it was positioned behind and above Olivier, effectively abandoning the woman at the other end of the table, and making her seem more isolated and adrift than ever. In just a few minutes, Hitchcock had achieved the desired effect without any need for dialogue whatsoever. Marta shook her head in admiration, wondering how many more times Hitch would prove to David Selznick that he was worth every cent.

5

He didn't want his final thoughts to be filled with hate, but whenever he closed his eyes, all James could see was the broken crucifix lying on the floor and Marion Plummer's limp, useless body, succumbing so easily to him in those last few moments that he could almost have believed that she wanted him to do it, and that her brazen confession had been a deliberate ploy to make him put her out of her misery. She had known enough of his character, surely, to guess how he would suffer for it.

Now it was her ultimate revenge, or so it seemed, to stand between James and her son, even in death. His memory searched for Matthew's face but could summon only hers, twisted and triumphant with hate, her black, hollow eyes suddenly alive with the knowledge that – as frail and diminished as she was – she still held the power. On the flight from Southampton, when he had eventually fallen into a troubled, fitful sleep, Marion Plummer had visited him in his dreams, and he had awoken to Victor shaking him by the shoulders, telling him that he was disturbing the whole goddamn plane. God knows what he had said in those unguarded moments, but if he had spoken aloud the thoughts and fears that had dogged him since he left Milton, it was a miracle that he was still a free man. Relieved to have made it this far, he put his hand in his pocket and there, alongside a handkerchief and a train ticket to Pasadena that he would never use, his fingers brushed the crucifix.

He had managed to give Frank and Vic the slip as soon as they got to Chicago, excusing himself for some time on his own before the train journey back to the West Coast. Dearborn Station was busy in the early morning, with downtown commuters flooding into the distinctive building, oblivious to the way in which the September sun drew every ounce of colour from its pink granite walls, softening the sharp angles and steeply pitched rooftops, and making the clock tower shine more majestically than ever above the skyline. People missed so much, he thought, just by going about their daily lives; at least that was one regret he didn't need to have.

There was a crush in the entrance hall as travellers gathered around a cluster of ticket counters and waiting rooms. The restaurants were serving breakfast, but the smell of bacon turned James's stomach and he pushed his way through the crowd, his mind automatically taking him back to the day that he had first caught the train for Milton, the day that – in a roundabout way – had brought him to this point of no return. The platform reminded him of a Bruegel painting back then – boisterous and crowded, with all the oddities of life laid bare. By that stage in the war, only a handful of people were still in civilian clothes and he remembered brushing self-consciously at his suit, struggling to see over the shoulders of the men in front and stifled by the thick, coarse wool of their uniforms. The relentless masculinity of it all had overwhelmed him, and he had had to fight his way to the edge of the crowd, thanking God that he was excused from the army, no matter how cowardly and despicable that made him. Catching his breath under one of the arches, he had looked through to the next platform and seen for the first time the reality of war – rows of stretchers unloaded from a train, stacked two deep like travelling bunk beds, and waiting to be transported to a hospital. He would never forget how the idea that he was expected to care for these men had terrified him, and he realised now that it wasn't the station that had brought the memory flooding back to him, but the pit of fear in his stomach, physical now as it was then, and almost overwhelming.

He paused when he got to the trains, wondering where to go. As if in answer to his question, a voice came over the tannoy system, warning passengers that the next arrival at platform two was a through train which wouldn't be stopping. James made his way there as quickly as he could, and was relieved to find himself in a much quieter part of the station, with no train scheduled to board there for another half an hour. One or two early birds were waiting on benches, passing the time with a book or a newspaper, but no one paid much attention to him as he glanced up and down the platform, choosing the best place to die.

He pulled the handkerchief from his pocket to wipe the sweat from his forehead and walked a little closer to the edge. In the distance, he could see the through train approaching, blissfully ignorant of what he was planning, and for a second or two, James doubted himself, thinking about the man who was driving it, and who – through no fault of his own – would carry this burden for the rest of his life. It was almost enough to make him change his mind; almost, but not quite.

The train drew nearer, barely slowing as it came into the curve of the station, and James took another step forward, assessing how long it would be before it reached him, wanting to be sure. He felt sick with fear, and he wondered if the sense of calm that he had expected to feel would hit him during these last few seconds, or if it was another illusion that he had invented. To steady himself, he tried to imagine Matthew calling his name, but the voice that he had loved so much eluded him and he couldn't bring it to mind – or rather, he couldn't be sure any more that what he remembered was real. Somehow, in the shrill, piercing noise of the train's whistle, the voice became Mrs Plummer's again, goading him with words that she must have spoken to her own son. *'There's not much for you to live for. Why don't you try it? It's easy, isn't it, a quick, kind way?'* The taunting went on, insistent and repetitive, and suddenly James was glad to give in to it.

He was standing right at the edge of the platform now. The driver must have seen him, because the whistle cut knife-like through the air this time, louder and more urgent than before, but it was far too late for the train to stop. James closed his eyes and felt himself moving, but the fear and the roar of the engine disorientated him, and it seemed as if he were being dragged backwards rather than into its path. He felt a hand on his arm and reached out to take it, hoping in his confusion that Matthew had come for him, but he didn't really believe in that sort of salvation, and, when he was brave enough to look, he found that his guardian angel was a dark-haired woman of around his own age. Her lips were moving but he couldn't make out what she was saying against the noise of the passing train – a long goods vehicle that seemed to take an age to move through. The pause gave James a chance to compose himself, and the breeze in the train's wake seemed to bring him to his senses. He took a few steps back, trying to hide the unsteadiness in his legs.

The woman waited for the noise to die down, then held the crucifix out to him. 'This fell out of your pocket with your handkerchief,' she said, and he was surprised to hear that she was British. 'It looks precious, and it's not the sort of thing you want to lose.' He took the piece of jewellery and stared down at it in his hand, conscious of the irony that it should be this that saved his life. 'Are you all right?' she asked.

James forced himself to meet her eye, and realised instantly that she knew exactly what he had been about to do, but was too kind or too tactful to challenge him about it. His humiliation made him less gracious than he should have been, and he answered her gruffly. 'Yes, I'm fine. Thank you for this. Now, if you'll excuse me, I've got to go.'

The platform was beginning to fill up with passengers for the California train and he saw Victor further down the line, standing by their kit and waving to him to come and help. Hoping that his colleague hadn't seen anything of the incident, James stuffed the crucifix hurriedly back in his pocket, wondering if an unwanted talisman would turn out to be Mrs Plummer's final act of spite, keeping him safe against his wishes and blocking at every turn his efforts to find peace.

6

Penrose waited in a long queue at the lights, his patience frayed by a headache that defied both aspirin and fresh air. To his left, Hyde Park was still green and leafy, and it was hard to believe that the year had no more use for summer, but even those small, comforting illusions were soon snatched away by another reminder of the changes that September had ushered in. Further down the road, opposite Knightsbridge Barracks, he could see the outline of the steam shovels that now occupied the turf in many of London's parks – huge, crane-like machines digging mouthfuls of earth out of the ground and loading it onto the backs of trailers, ready to be funnelled into the sandbags that were already an accepted incongruity in every corner of the city. As the traffic began to inch slowly forward again, he could hear the sound of chains dragging across the ground in time with the machines' relentless rhythms, and it seemed a fitting soundtrack to the myriad new restraints that suddenly governed people's lives – restraints which, it seemed, were determined to claim even the blades of grass that might have brightened the darkest of winters.

The streets were busy, even at this early hour, and many of the cars that passed on the other side now had small notices fixed to their windscreens, marking them out as volunteers on official war work; most were driven by middle-aged women, he noticed, all determined to do their bit, and he couldn't help but admire their generosity when they were surely still smarting from the way they had been treated after the last war, dropped from most of the roles they had taken on as soon as the men came back to resume normal service. London had become such an earnest city, he thought, looking at the tight-lipped expressions on their faces; the war was not yet two weeks old and yet the restrictions on theatre and cinema and sport – all the things that brought people together and boosted morale – were worse than most people could have dreamt of. Occasionally, there was a snatch of patriotism in the streets – songs he found dated and nostalgic, although most people seemed to think them as good for 1939 as they had been for 1914 – but the general mood veered between gloom and a sort of invincible cheeriness that had nothing remotely natural about it.

Newspaper sellers lined Embankment as he approached Scotland Yard, one of the trades that seemed to have benefited from a fresh lease of life in these early days of war. London was buzzing with rumours, some more credible than others, and reports that the government was preparing for a three-year war had shocked many people. Penrose would have rejoiced had he believed it could be so short, but he did his best not to think about the future; the only way of getting through it was to take each day as it came, and there was no point in trying to speculate on what might lie ahead. Still, he couldn't help but wonder if Josephine would ultimately decide to stay in America, if Marta might persuade her that their safety and their life together mattered more than anything else. After all, Josephine could work wherever she was and there would be new opportunities for a talented writer on the other side of the Atlantic; she loved her father and enjoyed his companionship, but there were two younger sisters who could do more if she ever put her foot down and insisted that they take their share of those domestic responsibilities. In his heart, he knew that Josephine's sense of duty would never allow her to stay away, in bad times at least; she might consider her options after the war, but for now she would grit her teeth along with the rest of them and do what she could. So why had he had such a strong gut reaction to her departure the other day? Such a superstitious feeling of finality that had made him turn back for a last goodbye. He knew it was stupid, but it had preyed on his mind ever since and forced him to consider his own responsibilities to those he loved. How little it would take, he thought, to collect Virginia and the children and catch the next boat out of England.

There were more men at work on ladders with bags of London's earth as he drove through the gates of Scotland Yard. The defences were rising like a tide against the red brick, making the building's already sturdy walls sturdier still, and Penrose wondered – cynically – if there would be any green and pleasant land left to defend by the time that Hitler dispatched his planes. He got out of his car, short-tempered and in no mood to face the paperwork that awaited him in his office, but found a stay of execution on his desk – a note, or rather a summons, requesting his presence upstairs as soon as he arrived. Bracing himself for yet more procedural directives, he headed to the third floor and knocked on the head of CID's open door.

'Come in, Penrose. Take a seat.' Penrose did as he was asked and waited while the Superintendent knocked his pipe out and refilled it. 'How are you?' he asked, without looking up from his task.

The question was out of character. Alexander Bell was, like his more famous namesake, a proud, no-nonsense Scot, and even if his job had allowed time for social niceties, his personality would have shied away from them. He had the sharpest of minds and was responsible for overhauling many of Scotland Yard's methods of detection, particularly those concerned with criminal psychology, and Penrose had learnt a lot from him in recent years – but kid gloves were certainly not his style. Nevertheless, when it came to cases involving the murder of a child, like the most recent that Penrose had worked on, there was a certain etiquette to which even the brusquest of officers paid heed. The anger and helplessness that followed in the wake of such unspeakable violence turned the usual camaraderie and banter of the force into something deeper and more personal; its ripples spread throughout the building, from the top brass to the canteen staff, and no one remained untouched by it. Any officer of any rank who worked on those harrowing investigations felt the respect and sympathy of his colleagues, and was grateful for it.

'Fine, thank you, sir,' Penrose said. 'Just a bit frustrated over the Clifford murder.' The death of a rent collector in a Hoxton tenement building was proving stubbornly difficult to solve thanks to the collective silence of anyone who might have seen or heard something, and he thought it wise to pre-empt Bell's question before he asked for progress. 'We're no further on than we were when it first happened, and it's not for want of trying. We've knocked on every door and—'

'Aye, well, never mind that now.' Bell waved away his protestations along with a swirl of pipe smoke. 'I want you off the Clifford enquiry. You've wasted enough time on it already and Fallowfield can see it through. He's perfectly capable of taking over, and something else has come up. Something potentially sensitive.'

'Oh?' Penrose looked curiously at his boss, scarcely daring to hope that the 'sensitive' nature of whatever Bell wanted to discuss with him consisted of something more interesting than government red tape.

'You know Milton Hall? It's near Peterborough, up in your neck of the woods.'

It never ceased to bemuse Penrose that two years in Cambridge and an unfinished degree interrupted by the last war meant that anything in East Anglia would be for ever in 'his neck of the woods' as far as anyone who didn't know the area was concerned. He could have explained how different Cambridge and Peterborough were, how long ago it all was or how an insular university life rarely involved exploring the wider county, but Bell wouldn't have appreciated the waste of time, and anyway, Penrose was intrigued. 'I've heard of it, sir, but that's all. I've never been there.'

'Well, you're going there now. Suspicious death – one of the household staff. They found her overnight.'

He slid a piece of paper across the desk. Penrose skimmed the details but failed to see anything that might be interpreted as sensitive. 'Why isn't the local force handling it?' he asked, wondering what he didn't yet know. 'Does the family of the house feel entitled to special treatment? Are they involved in some way?'

Bell shook his head. 'No, nothing like that. It's got nothing to do with them, and they're not even resident there at the moment. The whole place has been handed over to the army for the duration and the family has moved out, at least for the time being. The house was requisitioned as a hospital in the last war, and they stayed put back then, apparently, so I suppose they know how uncomfortable it can get. Heart bleeds, doesn't it?'

Penrose smiled, although he had a certain amount of sympathy for anyone forced to leave a home they had loved for years, no matter how big or small it was; there was every chance that his own family would have to relinquish the house they owned in Cornwall, and he knew how painful that would be, even though they would do it willingly. 'They certainly haven't wasted any time,' he said non-committally, 'the family *or* the army. But I still don't understand why we're involved.'

'Partly because you've been requested personally,' Bell said, apparently enjoying the look of surprise on Penrose's face. 'The chap in charge there now is a friend of yours. Selwyn Scott? He's a colonel in the army, but I gather you were at university together?' He glanced up again from his notes, adding wryly: 'You might want to *pretend* you remember, even if you don't. It's never very flattering to be so easily forgotten, and he's obviously kept track of you over the years.'

'I can't think why,' Penrose admitted. 'Yes, I vaguely remember him. We were medics at Downing together, but I honestly can't recall a single conversation that I might have had with him. We were certainly never friends.'

'Well, all that's irrelevant, really. I'd have sent you anyway, even if he hadn't mentioned you. The murder of a woman in a government institution before the Germans have even got into a plane isn't a very auspicious start to the war. You'll have the full co-operation of the local force. There'll be a lot of press speculation, and they weren't keen to juggle that one.'

'Because they suspect that the culprit is in the forces?' Penrose queried.

Bell shrugged. 'It's got to be a possibility, hasn't it? But if you can offer an alternative explanation – something more personal, perhaps – I'm sure the Home Office will be eternally grateful to you, particularly if you can do it quickly. Speed is of the essence on this one, Penrose – I don't need to tell you that.'

'Of course not, sir. I'll get there as soon as I can. Is there anything else?'

'No, nothing else. You know as much as I do.' He looked at his watch. 'I'll get someone to meet you at the local station and take you straight to the Hall. And keep in touch, won't you? If there's anything you need when you've had a chance to assess the situation, just let me know.'

7

By the time the train reached Las Vegas, Josephine was heartily sick of luxury. On any other occasion, a journey by rail through the heart of Middle America would have thrilled her, offering an opportunity to see so much of a country that she had visited just once before, and then only fleetingly; coming immediately after four days at sea and a flight from New York to Chicago, she couldn't wait for it to be over. It was ungracious of her, but she longed for some time alone, with no one to wait on her – and not even the finest surroundings that the Santa Fe Railway had to offer could compete with the pleasures of standing still for more than ten minutes at a time, or pouring her own tea.

The *Super Chief* was the company's flagship, a miracle in red, yellow and silver that ran twice a week between Chicago and Los Angeles, eating up more than two thousand miles in under forty hours. Affectionately known as the 'Train of the Stars', it regularly transported celebrities to the West Coast. Fats Waller was rumoured to be on board this trip, and a woman in the dining car swore blind that she had glimpsed Carole Lombard, but the only people Josephine had recognised so far were those she had met on board the *Queen Mary* – Bob Hope and his wife, the Hitchcock family, and Lee Hessel, who seemed to have hooked up with a couple of American friends – both good-looking men, confident enough to be in the film industry. To Josephine's relief, Miss Hessel was far too preoccupied with her new travelling companions to want to continue, or even acknowledge, their earlier conversation.

She had dined with the Hitchcocks the night before, finding them to be every bit as weary with the journey as she was. Only Patricia remained as enthralled by the *Super Chief* as she had been by the *Queen Mary*, telling them excitedly about the time that her father had organised a special treat for her on the set of *The Lady Vanishes*. Hitch had cleared the stage one lunchtime, ready for what he called 'an important visitor'. A group of the studio's musicians were brought in to play specially selected tunes, while he and his daughter ate lunch together on board the film's train, complete with all her favourite foods and orange juice served in champagne glasses. It was a lovely story, so different from most of the details about the director that made it into the newspapers, and Josephine found herself warming to the family. She particularly liked Alma's mother, Lucy, who had no time for fools and a way with common sense that made Josephine long to be a fly on the wall when Mrs Reville came into contact with some of Hollywood's more ridiculous excesses. It was obvious now where Alma got her level-headedness from.

Except for Kansas City, where several new passengers had joined the train, there was no boarding or disembarking at any of the stops en route, and when the *Super Chief* did pull into a station, it was simply to change crews or service the engine. On an English train, that might have felt uncomfortably like being on board a moving prison, but rail travel in America couldn't have been more different. High-speed diesel trains like this didn't have the romance of traditional locomotives, but they made up for it with modern air-conditioned carriages, spacious private sleeping compartments and a crew of young, enthusiastic attendants who somehow managed to give the impression that the finest traditions of the railway were in their blood. Last night, Josephine had retired early to bed, exhausted by the transfer from boat to plane to train, but, in spite of the comfortable berth and the smoothest travel she had ever known, sleep refused to come. Eventually, she had pulled her window down and let the cool night air refresh her spirits. Unnerved by the incident at Dearborn Station, she couldn't stop thinking about the man who had been about to end his life, both horrified by what she might have witnessed and at the same time feeling faintly guilty about her instinctive need to stop him. She had always believed fervently in privacy of thought and deed, in a person's right to direct his own life if he was privileged enough to have a choice. Whatever had driven this man to the edge of the platform, that decision had taken courage, and Josephine wasn't arrogant enough to assume that she knew better. And she certainly hadn't saved him – she knew that, too: if he was serious, he would find another way.

She sat by the window for a long time, watching the lights gradually dwindle in the other carriages whenever the train followed the curve of a bend, then staring out into darkness, imagining the landscapes that passed unnoticed beneath the cover of night. Every now and again, she saw the man's face in her mind's eye, and was curious about the expressions that had passed across it as he stared at the crucifix she held out to him. It was an old-fashioned piece of jewellery – something his mother might have worn, perhaps – but he had looked at it first with such bewilderment that she had wondered briefly if she was mistaken in thinking it belonged to him at all; and then the expression had turned to hatred, pure and simple.

Hatred, tempered briefly by despair. His story intrigued her, but she could do nothing more than speculate about it now. The last thought she was conscious of before finally drifting off to sleep was an acute, if irrational, sadness that she didn't even know his name.

When daylight woke her, she greeted the unfamiliar landscape with renewed enthusiasm, knowing that by nightfall she would be with Marta, sleeping in the closest thing to her own bed that America could offer. Breakfast was announced by a violent ringing of bells along the train's corridor, and Josephine dressed half-heartedly, bracing herself for yet another meal. The gourmet food served on board rivalled the *Queen Mary*, and she hoped that Marta wouldn't have decided to celebrate her arrival with an elaborate meal in a fancy restaurant; right now, she could think of nothing she would love more than cheese on toast in bed.

They were well into the Arizona leg of the journey now, and she stared out across desert country as the morning passed, ticking off station names on a map she had bought in Chicago. The train slackened speed as they approached Kingman, arriving with a long, plaintive hiss of brakes. Staff moved down the carriages, announcing a half-hour break to replenish catering supplies, during which passengers were welcome to get out and stretch their legs; if the rush for the doors was anything to go by, Josephine's relief was shared by her fellow travellers. She went out into the corridor at precisely the same time as Clark Gable emerged from the compartment next door, and there was an awkward pause as she stared at him. The actor smiled, waiting – with a slightly apprehensive expression, she thought – to see if she was going to engage him in conversation, but she simply nodded and walked past, wondering how she was ever going to hold a conversation in Hollywood if she was tongue-tied every time she saw a famous face.

The sun shone on the gleaming train as she strolled up and down the platform, enjoying the novelty of moving under her own steam for a while. Alma was standing in a small group of passengers next to the station building and she beckoned Josephine over. 'There's someone here I want you to meet,' she said, when Josephine was close enough to hear her over the bustle of the station.

'Can it top Clark Gable?'

Alma smiled. 'You've rumbled him, then. He and Carole are both on board but they've been trying to keep a low profile. No, this is James Bartholomew. He worked with us on *Young and Innocent*.' She touched the arm of the man standing next to her, and James Bartholomew broke off from the conversation he was already engaged in to turn and greet her. 'Bart, I'd like you to meet Josephine Tey. She wrote the original novel.'

It was hard to say who was more surprised, Josephine or the man she had prevented from jumping in front of a speeding goods train. He looked so uncomfortable that she forced herself to recover quickly and rescue him for the second time. 'It's lovely to meet you,' she said and held out her hand, hoping he would realise that she had no intention of mentioning their earlier encounter. 'What did you do on the film?'

Talking about something as safe as his work seemed to relax him, as Josephine had hoped it would. 'I was in the special effects department,' he said, 'although I don't think I really appreciated what that could mean until I worked with Hitch.' He glanced at Alma, the words spoken with no motive other than genuine admiration. 'He pulled off some amazing moments in that film. The shots with the train, for example. You know they were all done with models?' Josephine nodded, recalling the scene as one of the few Hitchcock additions to her story that she hadn't resented, despite the fact that it played to the romantic bias of the adaptation. The moment occurred towards the end of the film, when the leading characters – on the run from the police – stopped their car under cover of night by a moonlit railway yard, and the director had created a truly enchanting setting, rich in mood and atmosphere. 'It was quite a complicated scene to achieve,' Bartholomew continued, and Josephine warmed to his enthusiasm. 'There were so many parts to it – the sideways tracking movement as the train goes under the bridge, the lights from the headlamps playing over the houses, that downward tilt of the camera as you get to the couple in the car.' He shook his head, smiling at the recollection. 'It took us ages to get it right.'

'Well, it was worth it. It's probably my favourite scene in the whole film.'

'Really?' He seemed genuinely pleased, and Josephine didn't spoil the compliment by adding that there was very little else about the adaptation that she could bear to watch. 'All most people ever talk about is the crane shot at the end where the camera finds the killer.'

'But he wasn't *my* killer, so you'll forgive me for not being able to watch that part with a great deal of pleasure.' She looked sideways at Alma, but the director's wife had drifted away into another conversation, leaving Josephine free to be as honest as she liked. 'With the script the way it was, I was grateful for some visual magic,' she admitted, 'and I would never have known that scene was done with models if I hadn't been told.'

'Wait until you see *Rebecca*.' He smiled, and the lines around his eyes became more noticeable, the only indication that he was no longer a young man. 'You're Marta's friend, aren't you?'

'Yes. How did you know?'

'She always sticks up for the author on set, even when no one is listening. Actually, she talks about you all the time.'

Josephine felt herself blush. 'You know each other well?' she asked, trying to remember if Marta had ever mentioned him.

'As well as you ever know anyone in this business. We're both left over from the quaint old English way of doing things,' he added, slipping into a very convincing Californian drawl, 'so we stick together. And we see things in the same way, I suppose.' A bell sounded, shrill and persistent, and the railway staff began to shepherd people back onto the train. 'Looks like our time's up. Can I buy you a cup of coffee when we're back on board? It's the least I can do, and I probably owe you an explanation.'

'You don't owe me anything, Mr Bartholomew. Really you don't.'

'Even so, just a coffee to pass the time – as long as you don't mind slumming it in the second-class part of the train? And please – call me James.'

Josephine was too intrigued to refuse. 'All right, that would be lovely,' she said, 'and slumming it would be quite a relief. If I'm honest, I've been longing to do that from half-way across the Atlantic.'

The bell rang again, signalling that they were about to

depart, and James opened the Pullman door for her, then led the way along the corridor. Second-class compartments were smaller and designed to be shared, more like berths on English trains, and the dining car was much less ostentatious than its first-class equivalent, but still spacious and pleasantly furnished. The huge locomotive set the train in motion, slowly at first through the railway yards, then out of town and onto the main line again, and James left Josephine to choose a table while he went to the counter for their drinks, returning a few minutes later with a pot of coffee and two cups. He sat down opposite her, and there was an awkward pause while both of them searched for the right thing to say. The manner of his invitation seemed to rule out the incidental conversation that had seemed so natural on the platform, but Josephine couldn't find an easy way to ask for the explanation he had promised her. 'Have you written any more books since *Young and Innocent*?' he asked eventually, and she was glad to have something ordinary and obvious to respond to – so glad that she forgave him for inadvertently re-titling her novel.

'A biography,' she said, 'but no more thrillers.'

'That's a shame. I enjoyed it. Marta gave me a copy,' he explained, noticing her surprise. 'I thought there'd be a sequel, especially with that one having been so successful, but maybe Hitch put you off?'

Josephine laughed. 'He might have put me off signing my work away without getting involved in the script, but I can't blame him for my own laziness. I'm not sure why I haven't followed it up, really. I started a novel a couple of years back, but it didn't work out. Things happened, and the book was too close to home, so I put us both out of our misery. Since then, I suppose, the right idea just hasn't—'

'Please don't tell Marta what you saw,' James said, interrupting her and avoiding her eye. 'I don't want anyone on set to know what I was planning to do.' So that was why he had asked her to join him, Josephine thought: not to explain, but to ask for her silence. 'It's a tough world and it's all about image,' he continued, 'even behind the camera. Weakness doesn't get you anywhere. There's always someone ready to take your place.'

'I don't think that what you were about to do was weak,' Josephine insisted. 'On the contrary. I can't imagine ever having that sort of courage.' She paused to give her words weight, and the silence forced James to look at her. 'Would you have gone through with it if I hadn't been there?' she asked.

He shrugged. 'Honestly, I don't know. Probably. It felt like the only option. The only thing that made sense.' His obvious love for his work had told a different story in Josephine's eyes, but she didn't want to insult him by claiming to know his own feelings better than he did. 'So will you keep it to yourself?' he urged again, a touch of desperation in his voice. 'I've got no right to ask for anything else from you, but I can't bear the thought of this getting out. People judge, don't they, whatever the circumstances, and not everyone will react like you.'

If he only knew, Josephine thought: Marta, at least, would understand better than most the emotions that had driven him to the edge of that platform. 'All right,' she agreed reluctantly, 'but I suppose there's no point in my asking you in exchange not to try it again?'

'I can't promise that.'

'No, I didn't think for a minute that you would.' She poured coffee for them both, wary of being intrusive but too interested not to hold him to his offer of some sort of explanation. 'So what *were* the circumstances?' she asked. 'Why were you so desperate?'

He stared out of the window, squinting against the midday sun, and Josephine couldn't tell if it was his emotions or merely the dazzling strength of the light that had brought tears to his eyes. 'I've let someone down,' he said eventually, 'someone I loved. I won't bore you with how or why, but I've betrayed everything I ever believed in. I should never have gone back there.'

'Back to England?' He nodded. 'What were you doing there?'

'Officially or unofficially?'

'Either. Let's start with officially.'

'I was there with the second unit. Mr Selznick sent us over to photograph the house that Manderley was based on – the interiors, anyway. The more he likes a book, the more faithful he tries to be to it – and he loves *Rebecca*.'

'Lucky Daphne,' Josephine said, a little more tartly than she meant to.

James smiled. 'If it's any consolation, Hitch is getting his way with plenty. We've got lots of visuals to show him, but he'll only use what works with the scheme he's already got in his mind. The models I've built for him – the ones he'll use for the exterior shots – are nothing like Milton. I'll show them to you if you're ever on set.'

'Thank you, I'd love that. So where is this house? I don't think I've heard of it.'

'Milton Hall? It's in Cambridgeshire, not far from

Peterborough. The du Mauriers were friends with the family, so they visited for the summer. Miss du Maurier was just a little girl then – a very curious little girl, as I recall, although perhaps I remember it that way because of what she's done since. She and her sisters had the run of the place with the two young boys of the family, and I don't know to this day who the ringleaders were. They were always getting up to something, and I don't blame them. It must have been a wonderful playground to have at that age – no wonder she's never forgotten it.'

'You were there too? When was this?' Josephine asked, fascinated by James's unexpected connection with the author of the story he was working on.

'During the war. The Hall was a hospital back then.'

'And you were wounded?'

'No, I was there as a medical orderly. My parents brought me up as a Quaker, and we didn't believe in the fighting.'

He spoke the words with a weary defiance, and Josephine wondered how often he had had to correct people's assumptions about that part of his life, based – as hers were – on his age and the more common experiences of war. 'I'm sorry for jumping to conclusions,' she said, acknowledging her mistake, 'and at the risk of sounding repetitive, that must have taken some courage.'

'I thought it would be difficult,' he admitted, 'caring for men who were prepared to do what I wasn't, and who were going through the most terrible suffering because of it, but it wasn't like that at all. I thought they'd despise me, but they didn't. When they talked about their life over there, there was never any bitterness in it, and that always astonished me. No bitterness, in spite of the pain – just sadness, and even that was hard to define, as if they'd learnt something about human nature that they'd never seen before. I only ever met one soldier who was angry all the time, and I don't think the war had much to do with that.' He smiled and Josephine waited for him to go on, moved by his sincerity and recognising much of what he said from her own experience of nursing as a VAD when she was young. 'I lived alongside those men at Milton,' he continued, 'and there was a friendship and a kindness there that I'd never known before outside of my family, a real bond. Somehow, that was strong enough to overcome all the differences in our attitudes to the war itself, and I'll never forget how appreciative they were of any small thing that we did for them. Very ineptly, sometimes – I'd never had that sort of responsibility in my life.'

'It's amazing how quickly you get used to it, though, isn't it? Even the most horrific injuries.'

'You nursed during the war?'

Josephine nodded. 'Yes, straight out of training college. It was a baptism of fire and we had to harden up very quickly, but the men were always patient and stoical, as you say. Most of them, anyway. Hiding how shocked we were and just getting on with it seemed the least we could do.'

'You must have been very young, though.'

Spoken with less sympathy and understanding, the observation might have sounded like a cheap attempt at flattery, but James just seemed pleased to have some common ground. 'No younger than they were,' Josephine said, 'or you, probably. And unlike you, I didn't have that difficult choice to make. Women were lucky in that respect. I've never had to interrogate my conscience about going to fight, and I can only imagine how that must have complicated things for you.

As it was, the emotions we felt for those soldiers back then were the most intense that most of us had ever known at the time. That was enough to cope with.'

James looked down, suddenly awkward, then responded to her earlier comment as if there had been nothing in between. 'It *was* shocking sometimes. The operations were the worst. Occasionally we'd have surgeons up from London to do special procedures that the resident doctors couldn't handle. A lot of them never even looked at the men when they were doing their rounds. They'd examine them as if they were specimens, without any feelings at all.'

'You must have got to know some of them very well,' Josephine said. James's fleeting awkwardness had not been lost on her, and she wondered if the emotions stirred up by his return to Milton Hall were general or related to somebody in particular. 'That must have been a great comfort to them, to have people they could talk to.'

'Yes, I hope so, but I remember often thinking that it was a privilege for us to do it.' He paused, and it was hard to gauge if he was going to tell her more or change the subject altogether. 'You're right, though – under those circumstances, you get to a level of trust with someone that would usually take years to find. There's no skirting round the important stuff, no stiff upper lip. One of the first men I got to know – he was badly wounded by a shell and he'd lost his sight, but he wanted to write a letter to the parents of a boy he'd served with who had died. They'd joined up together, and he felt responsible because they'd always looked out for each other up to then. Anyway, he asked me to write it all down for him, so I sat by his bed every afternoon for a week while he tried to find the words. It was incredibly painful for him to recall those days, and yet what he wrote was so tender and moving. I'm sure it was a tremendous comfort to the boy's parents, in spite of what they had to face, but it half killed him to do it.'

'There must be lots of memories,' Josephine said quietly. 'No wonder it was upsetting for you to go back there.' The bait was too casually laid and he didn't take it; instead, the silence was filled by a piercing whistle as the train thundered through another station, barely slowing down. Perhaps the noise took James back to those life or death moments on the platform in Chicago, because he suddenly seemed eager to find safer, less personal ground. 'I hope Miss du Maurier will be pleased with the film,' he said, a forced brightness in his voice.

'Does she know you're working on it?'

The idea seemed to amuse him. 'No. I only ever spoke to her once. I doubt she'd remember me.'

They had skirted around the unofficial reason for his return to England, and Josephine was keen to try once more before they drifted back into general talk about the film. 'The person you let down,' she said, deciding that directness was best, 'was it someone at Milton Hall? Is that why you really went back there? To make up for what you did or didn't do?'

'It's too late for that. Twenty-two years too late.' His voice was even, but Josephine struggled to remember a time when she had seen a face transformed so suddenly by grief. 'Jesus, can it really be that long?' he said quietly to himself. 'Sometimes, even now, the finality of it hits me so hard that it's as if I've just found out they're gone.'

'I'm sorry.'

'Don't be. I don't deserve anyone's pity.' He rubbed his hand across his eyes, but the sorrow there couldn't be so easily erased. 'They wouldn't recognise me now, anyway. I'm a different person. It's probably just as well they're not here to see what I've become.'

Josephine wondered who 'they' were, or if the pronoun was simply a convenient way of avoiding the use of 'he'. From what she had already heard, any close friend of James's at Milton was far more likely to have been a soldier than a nurse; she was an old hand herself now at keeping things vague when referring to the person she loved, and she recognised it instinctively in other people. 'Are you talking about your parents?' she asked, choosing to eliminate the safer possibility first.

'My parents?'

'Yes. The crucifix you dropped – it looked like an heirloom and I wondered if it was your mother's?'

'Good God, no,' he said, surprising her with the vehemence of his response. 'My mother would never have worn a thing like that. She carried her faith in her heart, and she didn't need to be branded by it.'

It was an interesting response, which somehow managed to convey as much about the owner of the jewellery as it had about James's mother, and Josephine saw the same extreme emotions flicker across his face that she had witnessed the day before – loathing, followed by despair. 'It seems a strange thing to carry around with you if you hate it so much,' she said.

He glanced at her as if she had caught him out in something and she thought she had overstepped the mark, but he simply nodded. 'You're right,' he said, standing up and reaching into his trouser pocket for the heavily jewelled cross and its chain. 'It's ridiculous to keep it.'

Before Josephine could say anything, he slid open the window and threw the crucifix out into the vast, alien landscape. 'That wasn't what I meant,' she protested. 'I hope you won't come to regret that, just because of something I said.'

'Don't worry. I'm much more likely to thank you for it. I feel better already.' He sat down again, conscious that his behaviour was drawing attention. 'If only everything were so easily eliminated.'

'What do you mean?'

James made her wait for an answer while he lit a cigarette, and Josephine began to wish that she had never sat down with him. The more he talked, the more convinced she was that he would one day carry out his promise to take his own life; and the more he talked, the more she found she cared. 'Some things stay with you, don't they,' he said, 'no matter how hard you try to escape them. And not every man on the run is lucky enough to have an Erica to save him from himself.'

The cryptic remark was a reference to her book and Hitchcock's film, and Josephine was about to ask him what he was running from when she was distracted by one of Lee Hessel's companions coming down the train towards them. To her surprise, he stopped when he noticed James and lingered by their table. 'I've been looking for you everywhere,' he said, glancing curiously at Josephine.

'Well now you've found me.' From his tone, there was obviously no love lost between James and the new arrival. 'What do you want?'

'An introduction would be nice. It's hard to stay on top of the women I find you talking to.'

James ignored the innuendo, except to raise his eyes apologetically at Josephine. 'Miss Tey, this is Frank Wheeler. Second unit cameraman and all-round pain in the ass.'

Wheeler grinned. 'Pleasure to meet you, Miss.' He picked up the jacket that James had cast aside and sat down in the empty seat. 'So how do you two know each other?'

Josephine saw the look of panic flash across James's face, still not entirely trusting her to keep his secret. 'We met on a film in England,' she lied. '*Young and Innocent*. I wrote the book, and I'm a friend of the Hitchcocks.'

The slight exaggeration of the truth seemed to do the trick. Her mention of his boss wiped some of the cockiness from Frank Wheeler's face, and just for once Josephine was grateful for the connection. 'So what do you want, Frank?' James repeated impatiently. 'We're busy here.'

Wheeler held up his hands, as if he wouldn't dream of interrupting. 'Okay, okay – I'll leave you to it. I just wanted to let you know that Vic and I and a few old friends are hitting the town when the train gets in if you fancy joining us?'

'No thanks. I've got stuff to do, and we've got an early start in the morning. You haven't forgotten you're working this weekend?'

'No, old man, I haven't forgotten. All the more reason to have some fun tonight.' He winked at Josephine, and she felt his leg move closer to hers under the table. 'How about you, Miss Tey? You're new in town, so if you want someone to show you round . . .'

He left the offer dangling, a faint grin on his lips as she blushed and moved further away. 'Thank you, but I already have plans.'

'So what about you, Bart? Jeez, you could do with a little lightening up, and it's just a few beers. Come with us.' James stared him down without bothering to refuse again. 'All right, please yourself. I'll see you at the studio in the morning.'

He stood up, tossing James's jacket back onto the seat, and Josephine watched him walk off down the corridor, wondering if Lee was one of the 'old friends' he'd mentioned. 'Sorry about that,' James said. 'He's an idiot.'

'No need to apologise. You can't always choose who you work with.'

'More's the pity.'

'Did you do anything on *Jamaica Inn*?' Josephine asked, suddenly realising that James might well have known Lee Hessel's father.

'Not much. Have you seen it?' She nodded. 'Then you'll know there wasn't a lot of visual magic involved, unless you count getting Charles Laughton onto a horse. Why do you ask?'

'Oh, just something that came up when I was talking to Alma on the way over. One of the actors has just died – William Melrose?'

'Yes, I heard about it. It's a shame – he was a nice man. We all liked him.'

'Have you ever met his daughter?'

James shrugged and shook his head. 'Not that I recall. To be honest, I didn't even know he had a daughter – but then I didn't know him very well, so that's probably not surprising.'

He was obviously curious about the course of their conversation, and Josephine explained. 'I was only wondering because I saw his daughter with your friend Frank earlier . . .'

'He's no friend of mine.'

'No, I know, but I thought I'd mention it because I have a feeling that she means to cause trouble for Hitch and Alma.'

'What sort of trouble?'

His cigarette had gone out in the ashtray and he reached in his jacket to find a lighter, pulling it out with a packet of Camels and a piece of paper, folded in half. He looked at the note as if he had never seen it before, and Josephine watched the colour drain from his face. 'Is everything all right?' she asked. James didn't answer and she tried to look at the message, but it was impossible to read without her glasses and she cursed her eyes for letting her down. All she could be sure of was its brevity, just a few words at most.

Without warning or explanation, James screwed the paper tightly into a ball and set light to it in the ashtray. 'I'm sorry,' he said. 'You were saying something about trouble for Hitch?'

Josephine began to explain, but she could tell that he wasn't really listening. The note had distracted him from anything she might have to say, and she was glad when he eventually brought the conversation to a close and excused himself. Wondering what it had said and who had sent it, she went back along the train to her own compartment and packed ready for their arrival in Pasadena. In the dining car, Patricia Hitchcock was enthralling her grandmother with yet another story, and Josephine was suddenly overtaken by a wave of nostalgia for the joy of being a child, when everything seemed possible and nothing was complicated. She smiled to herself, but the smile faded when she noticed Lee Hessel sitting a few tables back, watching the family intently.

The station at Pasadena had been introduced especially to allow celebrities to leave the train anonymously, without the razzamatazz – or press intrusion – of Los Angeles. For Josephine, the end of the journey couldn't come quickly enough, and she looked eagerly out at the long, lighted platform as it slid past them, gradually slowing until it was possible to make out individual faces amongst the people who had come to meet the train. Marta had positioned herself halfway up, and had obviously been there for some time because she was at the front of the crowd. She waved frantically as the train drew to a halt, and Josephine waited impatiently for the porter to put out the steps at her carriage door, tempted to do without them if it meant that she could be with Marta sooner. They hugged, and Josephine held her lover close; it was barely more than a week since they had last been together, but it felt like months, and only now did Josephine realise the toll that the ups and downs of the journey had taken on her. In particular, the conversation with James Bartholomew had unsettled her in a way that she found hard to quantify, and she knew that she would break her promise to him sooner or later and tell Marta all about it, but for now she was more than happy to put his worries to one side.

'Are you all right?' Marta asked, sensing – as she always did – that Josephine was troubled.

'Yes. Just exhausted and so pleased to see you. The more I think about it, the more surreal this journey has been.'

'Well, I want to hear all about it. I hope I've done the right thing, but I didn't think you'd want to go out after all that travelling. I thought we could have dinner at the apartment and an early night.'

'That sounds perfect.'

'Are you sure you're not disappointed? You weren't hoping for a swanky restaurant? Because I haven't booked and we won't get anywhere decent at such short notice.'

'I promise you, a swanky restaurant is absolutely the last thing I was hoping for. Right now I don't care if I never eat out again.'

'Good. Then let's find your luggage and get out of this chaos. I'm dying to have you to myself.'

8

Penrose was glad to leave the train at Wansford and avoid the hustle of Peterborough's bigger station; as it was, the platform on the other side of the tracks was busy, crowded with soldiers heading up to London and families who had come to say goodbye. The afternoon sun – as unseasonably generous here as it had been in the city – shone on a handsome station house, built in the Jacobean style from the limestone that was local to the area, and there was a serenity to the scene that – however illusory – Penrose found comforting. At home and at work now, his life veered between frantic planning and anxious waiting in a way that was becoming increasingly difficult to navigate. As the days passed, and the worst still failed to materialise, he found himself resembling a child on bonfire night, putting his fingers in his ears as his father set a match to the biggest rocket, only to find when he removed them that nothing had actually gone off.

He walked through the ticket office, carefully circumventing a large pile of mail bags that stood waiting to be collected, and headed outside. After what Bell had said about the sensitive nature of the case, he half expected the transport that had been arranged for him to be military, but the car parked at the main entrance was a standard police Wolseley, and a uniformed sergeant sat behind the wheel. He got out when he saw Penrose approaching, a man in his mid to late fifties, whose retirement had probably just moved a little further away as the war sapped the youth from the force. Already, Penrose was surprised and a little ashamed at how much he resented being in the older bracket, one of those left to fill in behind as the younger men went off to fight. There must be a good ten years between him and this man, and perhaps it was his imagination, but when the driver introduced himself as Sergeant Tunnicliffe and made a few generalities to break the ice, his attitude implied a camaraderie of age and outlook that instantly set Penrose's teeth on edge.

They set off, heading east on the main road through Wansford and out into the fens towards Milton. 'Looks like things are moving up a gear, sir,' Tunnicliffe said, nodding towards the local garage on the outskirts of the village, where a long queue was forming at the pumps, threatening to block the access roads in both directions. Petrol rationing was due to start that weekend, with a limit set at two hundred miles a month, and everyone seemed to be of a like mind to shore themselves up against the shortages to come. 'I expect you've noticed a few changes where you are.'

'I hardly recognise the place,' Penrose admitted, casting his mind's eye all too easily across the restaurant doorways buttressed with sandbags, the familiar red pillar boxes scarred with squares of yellow paint that changed colour at the first sign of gas. 'It seems we don't really need the bombs to destroy a way of life. Hitler could save himself a lot of trouble.'

'Fine chance of that.'

'Where are you stationed?' Penrose asked, keen to avoid another depressing conversation on the state of the world, and – more importantly – to get as much local knowledge as he could before they arrived at Milton.

'Peterborough, sir. I've been there since I joined the force, except for my training.'

'So do you know much about the Hall?'

'Not through the job, no, but the wife's mother used to be in service there, so I've heard a few stories. This was long before the last war, mind you. Different generation of the family from them that's there now.'

'And I suppose she'd retired by the time the house was last requisitioned?'

'Oh yes, sir. She was happy there, by all accounts, and I've not heard anything but good about the family. She always said they were decent to work for, and they do their bit for the local community as far as I know. You often see their name in the paper – charities and special events, that sort of thing.'

He slowed to take a left-hand turn, following a signpost to Marholm. 'Is Marholm the nearest village?' Penrose asked.

'We call it Marram round here, sir,' Tunnicliffe said, correcting his pronunciation, 'and yes – the estate land goes right up to the village and beyond. All the farms round here belong to the Hall. We'll be at the gates in a few minutes, and Marholm's a bit further down this road.'

Freshly ploughed fields stretched out to the left as far as the eye could see; on the right, as they reached the outer limits of the Milton estate, a protective ring of woodland appeared, thwarting the flat, featureless landscape that would otherwise have allowed them to see for miles in all directions. Suddenly, Tunnicliffe uttered an exclamation of annoyance, and Penrose, who had been peering in vain through the trees for his first sighting of the Hall, turned back to the road to find it blocked up ahead by a flock of sheep, herded at a leisurely pace from one field to another. 'Sorry, sir,' the sergeant said, as if he were personally responsible for the rhythms of the farming week. 'This might take a while.'

There was a gate further on leading into the estate, and Penrose took his opportunity to get a sense of the place before he had to engage with anyone. 'Not to worry,' he said, opening the car door. 'I'll just take a look through there while we're waiting. Give me a shout when the road's clear.'

He walked quickly along the verge, glad to be in the open air after the stuffiness of the car. The boundary of the estate was marked by a beautiful stone wall, uneven and irregular, scarred in deep green and yellow with the moss and lichen of years; when he put his hand on it, it was as if he could feel the warmth of a hundred summers. The gate was padlocked but easy enough to climb over, and he found himself at the tail end of a small copse – fifty yards or so of fir trees and bracken that opened out onto beautifully kept parkland, criss-crossed by wide, grassy avenues and dotted at regular intervals by majestic oaks. A long, hot summer had left its mark: the ditch running along the edge of the copse was bone dry and twigs cracked under his feet as he walked out to the parkland, parched in places and littered with fleece and pigeon feathers. There were horse jumps arranged on the gentle slopes, signalling one of the family's sporting interests, but the atmosphere was languid and still, disrupted by nothing more energetic than the occasional stirring of a sheep beneath the trees, the restless darting of a dragonfly.

He could see a lodge house over to his left now, next to the gates that Tunnicliffe had mentioned, and he wondered if anyone was watching him. A bramble snagged at the shoulder of his raincoat, as if trying to deter him from going any further, but he walked defiantly on, following the edge of the woodland towards more open ground. Still the Hall eluded him and he found that irrationally frustrating – a symbol, somehow, of the secrecy and concealment that surrounded any murder enquiry, likely to be made worse here by the timing and the different agendas that were already at work behind the scenes. Impatient to get started, he turned back to the road and was pleased to hear the periodic sound of moving traffic again; sure enough, Tunnicliffe appeared at the gate to beckon him back and Penrose raised his hand in acknowledgement.

At the gates, they waited while a convoy of army trucks turned in ahead of them, far more traffic than would usually have graced this quiet country lane. Penrose announced his business at the lodge, and they were directed via the shortest route to the Hall's north entrance and told to park by the stable block, where someone would meet them. When Penrose finally got his first clear view of the house, he could have been forgiven for forgetting why he was there: the Elizabethan mansion sat low in its rural setting, framed by wisps of soft white cloud against a watery blue sky, a picture of serenity in which violence seemed to have no place. The house was built of ashlar, and he was struck immediately by its elegant restraint – eight bays flanking a modest porch, with a predominance of windows so typical of its age. 'Quite something, isn't it?' Tunnicliffe said, correctly reading Penrose's admiration. 'My wife loves the weepies. She goes with her sister once a week – well, she did, before they closed the cinemas – and I used to laugh at all that sentimental stuff. I know how she feels now, though, when I look at something like that. With everything that's hanging over us, it's easy to get nostalgic for the things they haven't spoilt yet.'

It was true, Penrose thought. His appreciation of the house and surrounding lands was all the more poignant for its contrast with the city that he had just left. As instructed, they drove past the main entrance and headed for the adjoining stable block – an inadequate phrase for one of the most elegant buildings of its type that Penrose had ever seen. The stables were arranged around three sides of a courtyard, crowned by a clock turret and cupola, with a striking stained-glass window in the pediment above the door, and although he was no great expert when it came to horses, Penrose couldn't help but wonder at the quality of the animals that such a home must warrant. Their car bumped over the cobbles and Tunnicliffe pulled up by a small, octagonal building in the middle of the yard, used as a harness room. Even before the engine had died, an army officer was on his way out to meet them, and Penrose tried to assess if he would have recognised the man without the information that Bell had passed on to him; he knew without doubt that he wouldn't.

'Penrose, good to see you again after all this time,' Scott said, slapping him genially on the shoulder as if it were a college reunion rather than a woman's death that had brought them back together. 'Thank you for coming. It's a bit of a trek out here, I know, but we've got an awkward situation on our hands and I knew you'd be the man to understand.'

The assumption was not only a slight on Penrose's professional detachment, but an offence to most of the things that he believed in. 'I understand that a woman needs justice,' he said, before he could stop himself, 'and I'll do whatever I can to help her get it, no matter how awkward that might prove.' He stopped short of adding the words 'that's my job', but a polite smile couldn't entirely mask the barbed nature of the words. Scott seemed oblivious to anything other than his own agenda, though, and his air of camaraderie was so inappropriate to the situation that Penrose half expected him to produce a box of cigars and a large whisky. A flicker of recognition from his college days stirred in his memory, recognition of an arrogant twenty-year-old with an unquestioning sense of entitlement whom he had gone out of his way to avoid. Beside him, he sensed Tunnicliffe's seething resentment which a respect for rank could barely contain.

'I've got an office here,' Scott continued. 'We can talk in there.'

The stable clock struck four, an unnecessary reminder to Penrose that he needed to make the most of what was left of the afternoon. 'I'd prefer to go straight to the scene,' he said. 'I've kept everyone waiting as it is. Perhaps you could ask someone to take us there?'

'Yes, of course, but I thought you might appreciate some context first.' Scott drummed his fingers on the Wolseley's roof, his impatience belying any idea that the offer had been made for Penrose's benefit. 'She's been there for days, after all. Surely another half an hour won't hurt.'

'We can talk later,' Penrose insisted. 'When I've seen the pathologist, I'll have a better idea of what we're dealing with.' He had always believed that a sense of urgency was the very least of the courtesies he could offer to the dead, but there was no point in explaining that to Scott, so he fell back on a more practical justification. 'Time's getting on and I want to make the most of the light.'

'Oh, very well, but I'll take you there myself and we can talk on the way. We'll cut through the house. It's only a five-minute walk from there.'

Tunnicliffe was effectively dismissed, and Penrose wondered if that had been Scott's intention all along. He found it interesting that no senior police officer had come to meet him and brief him on the case; perhaps the detective concerned was still busy at the scene, or perhaps the army's efforts to take charge had met with less resistance at a local level – either way, Penrose was keener than ever to get started. 'Thank you, Sergeant,' he said, turning back to his driver. 'There's no need to wait. I'll telephone the station when I'm ready to leave, or get a lift from someone here.'

Tunnicliffe nodded and Penrose set off after his guide, who was already halfway across the stable yard. They entered the house through the servants' quarters, a baffling maze of stone-flagged corridors and half-open doors to kitchens, cellars and boot rooms. 'You seem quite at home here,' Penrose observed, as Scott led them unerringly up to the ground floor. 'When did you move in?'

'At the beginning of the week, but I know the house from last time. I was convalescent here for three months. They patched me up and sent me back when I thought I was finished, so I've got a lot of affection for the old place. I owe them my career – and it's been a good life.' He glanced back over his shoulder, looking curiously at Penrose. 'You weren't tempted to stick with the army, then, when it was all over?'

'All over? The last few weeks have made a nonsense of that idea, surely.'

'You know what I mean. Why the police? It's a long way from medicine, and you were always the brightest among us. You could have had any position you wanted in any hospital in the country.'

Scott struck him as the sort of man who would view lack of ambition as a weakness, and Penrose didn't feel inclined to share anything personal with him, to explain that his job placed a value on life that helped to dispel the senseless waste that he had witnessed: death's randomness on the battlefield had made him crave justice and order, or at least the illusion of it. 'It's a decision I've never regretted,' he said instead, as they emerged into the jumbled world of the ground floor, where khaki uniforms were mixing with the black and white of the household staff, one rigid hierarchy set suddenly against another. 'Not for a moment.'

Scott shrugged. 'Well, each to his own, I suppose.' He let the subject drop and they walked in silence through the main entrance hall towards the south front, past rooms where careful preparations were being made for the house's transformation. It was an unsettling collision of past and present; history being preserved so that a new history could be written. Penrose watched as ornaments and silverware were carefully packed away and faces from the family's past removed from the walls in their elaborate gold frames, imagining the bewilderment and relief of the men who were brought here to heal. He thought back to his own time in a Cambridge war hospital, when those quiet college cloisters had seemed a world away from the dirt and noise of the trenches, remembering the comfort he had taken from their beauty and permanence. That sense of history had sustained him through some of the darkest days of his life, and he hoped it would be the same for the men who came to Milton. 'It must be such an upheaval to add the running of a hospital to the work of the house and estate,' he said. 'I don't suppose they dreamt for a moment that it would ever happen again.'

'Who said anything about a hospital?' The question wrong-footed Penrose, and he realised in hindsight that Bell hadn't specified what the army would be doing with the house; the assumption of a hospital was his, based on what had happened during the last war. 'No, this time we're using it as a training base,' Scott continued. 'General training for now, but – looking to the future, as things become clearer – special operations. It's a good site and it gives us everything we need.'

Penrose glanced back at the south front as they left the house behind and walked out across formal gardens towards another belt of woodland. This part of the Hall had obviously been added later; it was softer than its Elizabethan counterpart and the circular lawns, paved paths and flower beds gave it a domestic gentility that the more austere north side lacked. Even so, Scott's words seemed to make a mockery of the romanticised, unspoilt England that Tunnicliffe had seen when he looked out at the vista in front of him, and Penrose could only imagine what changes the house might see before the family was allowed to return. 'What can you tell me about the victim?' he asked, seizing the initiative before any other agenda could raise its head. 'She was the housekeeper, I gather?'

'That's right.'

'Who found her?'

'One of the gamekeepers. Listen, you can talk to your lot about all that when we get there, but first and foremost I need you to understand how important it is that our operation here isn't tarnished in any way.'

At last there was an acknowledgement that they were potentially on different sides, and Penrose appreciated the honesty if not the sentiment. He decided to put an end to the games once and for all. 'A woman has been killed immediately after the army moves in and takes over the running of the house. It's hard to see how timing like that might not reflect badly on your operation once it gets out, and if you're asking me to cover something up to protect—'

'For God's sake, Penrose, of course I'm not asking you to do anything of the sort and I resent the suggestion. What I *am* asking is that you don't jump to conclusions, that you investigate *all* the possibilities. We weren't the only outsiders at Milton when she was killed, you know. There was a film crew here when we arrived, which would never have been allowed if we'd known about it, but it was agreed with the family and there was very little we could do. You need to check them out – one of them was here during the last war, I gather, so it's entirely credible that he knew her. Then there's the rest of the staff, of course. Perhaps someone had a grudge against her. That's got to be a possibility, hasn't it?'

'Did you?' Penrose asked, ignoring the question.

'Did I what?'

'Did you know her? You said you were here for three months during the last war, so it's entirely credible that you did.'

Scott looked uncomfortable, and Penrose was a little ashamed to find that quite so satisfying. 'I knew *of* her,' he admitted. 'Nothing more than that. She was close to a friend of mine – a friend of mine back then, I mean. He was treated here, too.'

'And what happened to him?' Penrose persisted, more out of devilment than a belief in its relevance to the investigation. There was a pause, and Scott refused to meet his eye. 'Well?'

'They got married.'

Penrose stared at him in disbelief. 'A friend of yours . . .'

'A *former* friend.'

'A friend of yours is married to the victim and you didn't think to mention it? Is he still in the army, by any chance?'

'Only in an administrative capacity. He was invalided out.'

'But he's here?'

'Yes, of course.'

'Then I can see why you'd want me to check up on the film crew.'

They were nearly at the edge of the woodland now, which lined one of the many small roads leading to and from the Hall, and Penrose's attention was taken by a distinctive building nestled in the trees, Gothic in style and decorated with stone finials and crenellations, halfway between a chapel and a folly. A once beautiful rose window sat above the arched entrance, but several of the glass panes were broken and, as they drew closer, he could see that the building was all but derelict. Two police cars were parked outside, with a mortuary van at a discreet distance down the road, and a uniformed constable stood guard in the doorway.

'She's in the woods at the back,' Scott said. 'I'll leave you to it, but I'd be grateful if you'd come and see me in my office as soon as you're done here. We need to decide what to make public.'

And more importantly, what not to, Penrose thought, but he said nothing. Leaving Scott to retrace his footsteps across the park, he made his way round to the back of the chapel, glancing through the windows as he went and noticing how ivy and the elements had reclaimed the small building, transforming it into a fairy-tale ruin. Two plain-clothes police officers stood redundantly by a group of young beech trees while a third man knelt a few yards away at the bottom of a thick bank of ferns, examining the ground intently. The pathologist's hunched figure was delightfully familiar, and Penrose was relieved to find an unexpected ally in the investigation. He introduced himself to the two local men, then cautiously approached the scene. Bernard Spilsbury raised his hand without turning round. 'Evening, Archie. Glad you could join us at last.'

'I'd have been here sooner but for the hospitality of the armed forces.'

The pathologist gave a cynical chuckle and struggled to his feet. 'Yes, it is a bit like that, isn't it? I was diverted from an afternoon at Newmarket when the local chap was suddenly and mysteriously unavailable. The Home Office was uncharacteristically grateful, although I suppose I should be thanking them – they've probably saved me a lot of money on the three fifteen.'

Spilsbury walked back up the slope, pausing briefly to rub the circulation back into his legs. He was in his early sixties now, but busier than ever and astonishingly fit for his age, and Penrose didn't doubt that he would face the added pressures of wartime with the resilience of a much younger man, not to mention the wisdom of one who had seen it all before. For the thousandth time, he blessed his colleague's obvious aversion to retirement: professionally, and as a friend, he would miss him. 'Can I take a look?' he asked.

'Of course. I've got most of what I need. I probably don't have to warn you that it's not a pretty sight. She's been there for at least four days, and the scavengers don't need a second invitation.'

They had worked together for many years now, long enough to be familiar with each other's methods, and Spilsbury hung back as Penrose approached the body, knowing that time alone at a scene was important to him, the only opportunity he would have to observe the victim where he or she had died, to get a sense of identity and circumstance before the artifice of science took over. He walked cautiously down the gentle slope, avoiding the area where the thick covering of ferns had been flattened, presumably as the body was dragged or rolled further into the woods. Even so, when he was in full view of the pitiful form in the undergrowth, he was surprised that more effort hadn't been made to conceal it.

Evelyn Young lay on her back, vulnerable and exposed in this deceptively gentle countryside. Predators from ants to foxes had done their worst to desecrate her body, ruthless at a time of year when the nights turned colder and a long winter lay ahead. The damage was severe, and they were lucky to have found her when they did; much longer, and the corpse might well have been destroyed completely. Penrose checked his own thoughts, conscious of how inappropriate the concept of luck seemed in relation to the horror that lay before him. He could see teeth marks on her face and neck where large amounts of flesh had been removed, and insects had been quick to target the wounds and soft tissues, making up for in voracity what they lacked in size and strength. The injuries around her eyes were particularly sickening: livid red wound margins crawled across her cheek and Penrose closed his eyes, trying in vain to halt the image of rats tearing into her skin. In his distress, the stark silence of the wood was anything but peaceful, as if even nature – no stranger to the presence of death – recognised the aberration and acknowledged that it had gone too far. When the call of a bird finally came, it wasn't the melodic song of an English woodland but the harsh, raw cry of a magpie.

There was very little left of her face, and no way of imagining the woman she once had been. The small clues that even a post-mortem examination offered to what those features might have looked like when they laughed or cried or loved were lost to him, and he would have to rely on photographs for a sense of the life he was now charged with investigating. She was dressed in black, the simple uniform of service, and his eyes strayed to the wedding ring on her left hand, to the lesions on her knuckles which he would have liked to believe were from manual work – but he knew that they were not, and he prayed to God that those who had loved her would be spared any attempt at a formal identification, and that dental records would suffice. Amid such violation, the wound that had actually killed her – a single gunshot to the forehead, obscured by the predation and barely visible to the naked eye – seemed absurdly merciful.

Penrose often felt anger or injustice when first viewing a body, but rarely had he experienced such utter desolation at a crime scene. It wasn't the injuries, although those were horrific enough; it was the sense of abandonment. There was something wretched about the way in which her body had been so casually discarded, a degree of contempt that affected him more deeply than he would have cared to admit. His nerves were already on edge from his conversation with Scott, but now he resented more sharply than ever the various agendas that threatened to obscure a woman's death, and it strengthened his resolve to get justice for Evelyn Young, no matter how unpopular that made him in the process. Impatient to make a start, he turned and strode back up the slope, taking his emotions out on Spilsbury by barking a question rather than asking it. 'Anything on the weapon?'

'The weapon? You didn't see it?'

'What?' Penrose felt rather than heard one of the local policemen snigger. 'You mean it's still with the body?'

Spilsbury nodded and led the way back to the scene. 'I left it where it was until you'd looked at it,' he said, a note of surprise in his voice that Penrose couldn't help but take as a criticism; it was unlike him to make such a careless mistake. The pathologist pointed to the gun, which lay tucked in the bracken by Evelyn Young's body. It was a pistol, army issue.

'No wonder Scott was so jumpy,' Penrose said. 'Is there any chance that she could have done it herself?'

'Almost certainly not. I can't say for certain until we get her back to the lab and I've had the chance to take a proper look, but I'd say she was shot from a distance of four feet or so. Obviously we don't have any soot or powdering to help us out – the animals have seen to that – but there's still a single large hole, and if you look closely at it' – he beckoned Penrose closer and held his magnifying glass close over the wound – 'you can see a slight scalloping around the edges. There, and there – do you see? Typical of what we call a rat hole, although I hesitate to use a phrase like that under the circumstances.' He stood up and gestured again towards the gun. 'There are some prints on there, so we'll double-check they're not hers first, of course, just in case the wound is misleading, but I'm fairly confident. You'll know as soon as I do.'

'Thank you.' Penrose stared down at the body again, still

smarting from his own lack of attention. 'So why leave the murder weapon behind?' he said, thinking out loud. 'And why go to so little effort to hide the body?'

Spilsbury shrugged. 'That's your department, Archie. It could simply have been panic, of course, but it strikes me that we're dealing with someone who stopped worrying as soon as the deed was done. Someone who was either foolishly confident of not being caught or too focused on the end game to care.' He grinned. 'Perhaps your job will be easier than you thought. Now, give me ten more minutes, then we can get the poor woman away from here.'

Still deep in thought, Penrose left Spilsbury to finish his work and walked over to glean what he could from the local detective inspector. 'She was found overnight, I gather?' he said.

'That's right, sir, by the gamekeeper – or by his dog, I should say. They've been having a bit of trouble with poachers, apparently. He went straight to the house and let them know there, and the butler phoned it in.' Rather than resenting the presence of someone from another force, DI Hughes seemed keen to share what information he had and discharge all responsibility, and Penrose couldn't blame him. 'Middleditch, that's the gamekeeper – he's got a cottage on the estate, and I told him you might want to speak to him. He's a bit shaken up, as you'd expect.'

'Thank you,' Penrose said, although he doubted that Middleditch would have anything more to add – or appreciate being made to relive the experience. 'It seems that Mrs Young has been here for several days – did no one report her missing?'

Hughes shook his head. 'Odd, isn't it? I spoke to a couple of people in the household about it before that army bloke intervened. She left them in the lurch at work and her husband said she'd been called away to look after her aunt, but the butler thought that was strange because she was usually so reliable and hardly ever took time off – certainly never without asking. What makes it even more peculiar is that she had another emergency in the family here that she should have been dealing with.'

'What sort of emergency?'

'Her mother had a stroke the same day she went missing. Marion Plummer – she used to be the housekeeper here, and her daughter took over from her when she retired. Someone found her at home, unconscious, and it sounds like they only just got to her in time. Naturally they wanted to get in touch with Mrs Young and the husband said he'd tell her, but still she didn't come back. The other staff couldn't understand it, more so as the days passed, but it wasn't their place to question it. If the family had been here, things might have been different, but . . .'

He let the thought tail off. 'Have you spoken to her husband yet?' Penrose asked.

'No, sir.' Hughes must have seen a look of annoyance flash across Penrose's face because he was quick to explain. 'It's not for want of trying, sir, but it wasn't encouraged, if you know what I mean.'

'No, I don't suppose it was, and I know exactly what you mean.'

'Perhaps you'll have more luck.'

'Damned right, I will,' Penrose said. 'We'll go and see Mr Young now – you can come with me. Where is he?'

'At home. There's a lodge house a bit further down this lane, where it meets the main road.'

'Good. Tell your DC to stay here and oversee the removal of Mrs Young's body, will you?'

'Yes, sir.'

Spilsbury had obviously finished his work and was busy packing away the large bag that was his constant companion, containing everything from his instruments, overall and rubber gloves to the specimen jars and private supply of formalin that he insisted on carrying. Penrose smiled to himself as the constable attempted to help him and was vigorously waved away: from the moment the pathologist began his examination, no one but he was allowed to touch that bag, not even to carry it to the car; it was discipline like this that made his evidence so reliable in court. With a quick promise to deliver his findings the following day, Spilsbury departed as unobtrusively as he had arrived, alone and preoccupied as he walked back through the trees to the open parkland, where a late-afternoon gloom now conspired with the woodland canopy to cast shadows across the whole estate.

'Right,' Penrose said, signalling to Hughes as the mortuary van moved slowly forward, ready for the grim task ahead. 'Show me where this house is and we can start getting some answers.'

9

The sun had sunk lower in the sky by the time they reached the Youngs' cottage, and a characteristic fenland chill took advantage of its absence. Penrose looked up at the house as he walked to the front door, built from the same York stone that featured in most of the Hall's smaller properties and traditional in style. It was beautifully kept, as he would have expected from the tenants of a respected country estate, but it was the garden that suggested love rather than simple obligation. A profusion of pink and white climbing roses framed the windows downstairs, throwing their scent onto the path, and the flower beds that had been cut from a neatly mown lawn were a joy to behold – an abundance of dahlias and chrysanthemums in fiery reds and yellows, offset by the gentle mauve of a Michaelmas daisy. Through an archway at the side he could see that the back garden was devoted to more practical efforts, with vegetable plots and a greenhouse. An old wooden bench, its paint chipped and blistered from a long, hot summer, was placed carefully to catch the last of the evening sun; Penrose tried to imagine Evelyn Young sitting there at the end of a busy working day, lifting her face to its warmth, but the pictures that filled his head had nothing of peace or contentment about them and he shook them away.

He knocked at the door, and the rapping was echoed immediately by a distant gunshot, the perfectly innocent sound of a gamekeeper at work or the partridge season underway, but – to Penrose's ears – it was a bleak reminder of what had brought them there. There was no response at first and Hughes set off to find a rear entrance, but Penrose called him back when he heard the sound of footsteps in the hall. The door was opened by a woman with ash-blonde hair swept up into a bun. She was tall and elegantly dressed in a fawn-and-green-checked woollen suit, and she could have been anywhere between forty and sixty; only the fine lines on her neck and around her eyes inclined Penrose towards the latter end of the estimate.

He produced his warrant card. 'I'm Detective Chief Inspector Archie Penrose from the Metropolitan Police,' he said, 'and this is Detective Inspector Hughes from the Cambridgeshire Constabulary.'

The woman nodded. 'Of course. You're here about Evelyn's death. We've been expecting you. It's a terrible time.'

'And you are . . . ?'

'Oh, I'm sorry – I should have said. Georgia Wells. I'm a friend of the family – well, of Marion, really. I was the one who found her on Monday, and I've been looking after her. A few of us are taking shifts to enable her to stay here. If she *is* going to recover, she's much more likely to do it in her own home.'

She spoke softly but with authority and no trace of an accent, and Penrose found himself wondering if she had once been a nurse, so perfectly matched was her voice to the calm of a convalescent bedside. 'Us?' he queried.

'Yes. Myself and a handful of women from the church. My husband is the vicar of St Mary's in Marholm, and Marion was an active member of the congregation in her younger days, so we're doing what we can to help. And it's fortunate that we're here now. Donald is devastated by the news, as you can imagine. He needs all the support he can get.'

'It's Mr Young we'd like to speak to. Is he here?'

'Yes, of course. Come in.'

She ushered them into the hallway and moved to close the door on the right, but not before Penrose caught a glimpse of the sick room beyond. A slight, elderly woman lay as still as death beneath the crisp white sheet, with a crucifix on the wall above her head and a jug of water on the bedside table, next to a crystal rose bowl of fresh flowers. 'How is Mrs Plummer?' he asked.

Georgia Wells seemed surprised by his concern, as if she hadn't expected kindness from a policeman on a murder enquiry. 'Very frail, I'm afraid. She suffers from arthritis, so her body was already under a great strain, and this has taken its toll. She's conscious, though, and we're starting to see some small signs of movement, which is encouraging, but it's going to be a very long road. The best we can do is keep her as comfortable as possible and pray for a miracle.' She sighed and dropped her voice even lower, so that Penrose had to strain to hear her. 'It's hard to see a blessing in all this, but at least she's not aware of what's happened to Evelyn.'

'Were they close?'

She paused. 'Yes, I suppose so.'

'You sound hesitant. Is there a caveat?'

'Not really – well, not in the way that I suspect you mean.' She looked at him shrewdly, a faint smile on her lips. 'In recent years, as Marion became less independent, she resented her daughter for having to care for her. Donald was a saint in her eyes, the son-in-law who could do no wrong, but Evelyn had the sharp end of her tongue whenever Marion's bitterness got the better of her. Then there was the Hall, of course. Marion ran that place like a military operation, even before it became one, and I often think it was the worst thing that Evelyn could have done, to try to fill her mother's shoes – for her own peace of mind, and for their relationship. Times change, don't they, and things are done differently, but Marion has a tendency to confuse modernisation with revolution. She was always the first to catch a whiff of betrayal where none was intended. Anyway, I must get back to her, so let me take you through to the kitchen. Donald's in there.'

She headed towards the room at the far end of the corridor but was beaten to it. The door opened from the inside, and a man – Donald Young, presumably – stood leaning on a cane, glaring at them suspiciously. 'What's going on?' he demanded. 'What are you all talking about?'

'It's the police, Donald,' Mrs Wells said gently. 'I was just telling them about Marion.'

'Why are you wasting time on that? You should be out there trying to catch the man who did this to Evelyn.'

It was an interesting assumption, Penrose noted, or perhaps Donald Young was simply the sort who thought of violence as a male preserve. 'We're here to talk to you about your wife, sir,' he said calmly, 'and I hope that whatever you can tell us will help us to do just that. May we come in and sit down?'

Young nodded, and stood aside to let them pass. Georgia Wells squeezed his arm sympathetically and returned to his mother-in-law's room, and Penrose and Hughes walked through to the kitchen. It was light and spacious, stretching the width of the house at the back, and it functioned as a living room as well, with armchairs at one end by a cluttered dresser and a dining table next to the stove. Young was obviously not much of a housekeeper, and – in his wife's absence – the line between comfortable and chaotic seemed to have blurred. Several days' worth of washing up was piled high in the sink and drainer, and the floor was covered with muddy footprints and leaves trailed in from the garden. Over in the corner, next to the back door, a handsome male tabby cat stared plaintively at two empty bowls.

'I'm very sorry for your loss,' Penrose said, as Young cleared some bills and an empty whisky bottle away from the dining table, making space for them to sit down.

He shrugged, an awkward, embarrassed gesture that suggested he was uncomfortable with sympathy. 'Do you want some tea?' he asked, putting his hand to the pot on the table. 'This is cold now, but I can make some fresh.'

'No, thank you. We don't want to put you to any trouble, but it's important that we find out as much as we can about your wife.'

'Yes, you said.' Young sat down heavily at the table, his face artificially lit by a nearby lamp, and Penrose saw for the first time how terrible he looked. He was a striking man, youthful for his age, but his eyes were red and swollen from crying and his hair needed washing, joining with a shadow of stubble to give him an unkempt appearance. His skin was pallid except for two crimson streaks on his cheekbones, livid and surreal, like crudely applied stage make-up. Even from the other side of the table, the whisky on his breath was overpowering. He looked at the notebook that Hughes had taken out of his pocket and rested on the table. 'What do you want to know?'

'How long had you been married?' Penrose asked, avoiding anything confrontational until Young was more relaxed.

'Just over twenty years. We were wed as soon as the war was over. I couldn't wait, if I'm honest. Evelyn was so beautiful – I couldn't believe my luck when she said she'd have me.'

His voice cracked over the last few words and Penrose waited for him to compose himself. 'And you met here, while you were convalescing?'

'That's right. I was wounded, and she was a nurse back then. They managed to save my leg, but it left me permanently lame, and Evelyn was the only thing that kept me going. I knew I didn't have a future in the army or in any other worthwhile job, for that matter. I was going to spend the rest of my life stuck behind a desk, but Evelyn made that bearable. It gave us something in common, I suppose – losing a job we loved. It was always going to be the army for me, and Evelyn never wanted to give up nursing but she knew that taking a place up at the house would make her mother happy.' Although by all accounts it hadn't, Penrose thought, remembering the resentment that Mrs Wells had spoken of. 'She did it because of Matthew, you see. She wanted her mother to have some sort of consolation for what had happened, something to be proud of.'

'Matthew?'

'Evelyn's little brother. He lost his sight out there – the same attack that killed Georgia's son. They were friends, Matthew and Robert, and they joined up together, but Robert didn't make it back. That's why Georgia's always been so good to Mother – to Marion, I mean. They helped each other through it.'

Penrose noted the term of endearment with interest. 'So Matthew died as well?'

Young nodded. 'They brought him back here to be nursed with his family, but there was no saving him. He blew his own brains out one day up at the Hall. Marion never forgave herself for leaving him on his own, and she could hardly bear the shame that he brought on her and the house, even though the family was good about it.' He shook his head, remembering. 'It was a terrible time and no one seemed to understand why Matthew had done it – but I did. If I hadn't had Evelyn, I honestly think I'd have gone the same way, poor devil.'

As tragic as this was, Penrose couldn't see how it might be connected to Evelyn Young's murder, and he needed to move things on. 'When was the last time you saw your wife?' he asked.

'When I left for work on Monday morning. It was a big day for me because the first of the lads were arriving and I was keen to get over there and make a start. I know it's only office work and it might not be for long, but it felt like I was part of it again after all these years, and it meant a lot to me that Scottie had put a word in and got me the job. He was my best man, you know – we've always had each other's backs.'

Penrose wondered how Young would feel if he knew that 'Scottie' had described him as a 'former friend'. He doubted that he would ever understand this yearning that some men had to return to the camaraderie of war, no matter what the cost, but he kept his silence; if it proved relevant, there would be plenty of time to look into Young's role in the new set-up at Milton. 'So your wife was still here when you left?' he prompted gently.

'Yes. I was hoping we could walk across together, but she was on a late shift that day.' He took a packet of cigarettes out of his jacket and patted the other pockets for some matches until Hughes obliged with his own lighter. 'I was in a hurry to be out of here,' he said, struggling again to hold his emotions in check, 'and I didn't even kiss her goodbye. It's stupid, I know, but I can't stop wishing that I'd gone back and done it, seen her just one more time, but all I could think about was the job. I let her down.'

Penrose watched him carefully, looking for any signs of dissemblance, but if Young was faking his grief, it was one of the most accomplished performances that he had seen. 'What time was she due back?'

'Ten o'clock, or thereabouts.'

'Why didn't you report her missing, Mr Young?' he asked. 'Surely when she didn't come home that night you knew something might be wrong? You must have been worried about her?' The man in front of him remained stubbornly silent, and Penrose caught Hughes's disbelieving eye. 'Had she stayed out all night before?'

Young shook his head. 'No, of course not.'

'Then why didn't you report it? What were you trying to hide?'

A look of genuine horror crossed Young's face. 'You think I did this? Is that what you're accusing me of?'

'I'm not accusing you of anything, but I don't understand why you wouldn't do everything in your power to find your wife? Even if you didn't report her disappearance to the police, surely you would ask after her at the house or check with her friends and colleagues? But you didn't. In fact, you lied to everyone and said she was with her aunt when you knew perfectly well that she wasn't. And all this at a time when your mother-in-law was gravely ill and needed your wife at her bedside. Why, Mr Young, if you claim to love her?'

156

It was the final suggestion that broke Young's resolve, as Penrose had suspected it would. 'Because I thought she was with someone else,' he shouted, slamming his hand down hard on the table in an effort to bring an end to the questioning. 'I thought she was leaving me for another man and I couldn't bear it, all right? Are you satisfied now?'

He stood up and walked over to a cupboard to fetch another bottle of whisky, but his hands were shaking too badly to open it, and in the end Penrose poured the drink for him. 'Why did you think that?' he asked.

'Because I saw her with him. I went to find Evelyn to tell her how well things were going and to thank her for putting up with me—'

'For putting up with you?' Penrose interrupted.

'Yes. I'm not the easiest man to live with, I'll admit that. I hate the things I can't do any more, and I get frustrated when I think about the life I could have had, and sometimes I take that out on Evelyn. Not physically,' he added quickly, correctly anticipating Penrose's train of thought. 'I'd never hurt her like that, I swear. But I have dark days, and they must be just as hard to live with sometimes.'

'So you were lying just now about the last time you saw your wife?'

Young nodded. 'Yes, I'm sorry. I saw her again later on, with him – about midday, it must have been. They were standing outside the porch together, talking. I watched them for a few minutes, and then I couldn't bear it any longer.'

'Did they see you?'

'No, I don't think so.'

'Do you know this man?' Penrose asked, thinking how easy it would be to invent a mysterious stranger and send them all off on a wild goose chase. After the convincing lie that had already escaped him, he felt much more wary of Young's sincerity.

'Yes. He was an orderly here during the war – a bloody conchie, at that.'

'Do you remember his name?'

'Of course I do. I remember *everything* about James Bartholomew. Teaching us to build matchstick bloody models while our boys were being shot to pieces – what sort of man is that? What did she see in him?'

More than a uniform, obviously, Penrose thought. 'Did you see any physical contact between them?' he asked carefully, and Young shook his head. 'So why did you assume—'

'Because she was in love with him, all right? All those years ago – she never said anything, but I knew it. She worshipped the ground he walked on, thought he was a bloody saint because of the way he cared for Matthew and the other men, me included.' He ground the stub of his cigarette hard into the ashtray and reached immediately for the packet again. 'And he was good at that,' he admitted grudgingly. 'If he hadn't been such a fucking coward, I'd probably have liked him. All the others did. Marion was the only person who could see through him.'

'What happened to James Bartholomew?'

'I don't know. He left Milton before the war was over. I never knew why, and I didn't ask. I was just glad to see the back of him.'

'And you hadn't seen him since?'

'Not until Monday.'

Penrose looked at Young's left hand as it gripped the walking cane, turning his knuckles white with the strain. 'It must have been a shock for you,' he observed. 'You must have been very angry to see them together like that.'

'Of course I was bloody angry! I wanted to punish her, God forgive me, and when I found out what had happened to Marion, I thought it would serve Evelyn right. She loved her mother, and I thought it would teach her a lesson if she missed the chance to say goodbye. She was forever feeling guilty about something.'

It was an uncomfortable comment, and Young seemed to take pleasure from it. 'Do you know why Mr Bartholomew was here?' Penrose asked. 'If he was a conscientious objector, he obviously didn't arrive with the army.'

'No – leopards don't change their spots, do they? There was a film crew here, and he was part of that. They'd been photographing the house for a few days, apparently. I had no idea he was with them until I saw him, but it explained a lot. Evelyn had been behaving oddly for a couple of days – she was quiet and withdrawn, and I got on her nerves even more than usual. She must have known he was there, and God knows what they'd been getting up to behind my back. The crew left on Monday, so that's why I thought she'd gone with him when she didn't come home. I thought he'd sweet-talked her into going back to America with him, and starting a new life together.'

'Do you *know* it was an American crew?'

'Yes. Scottie told me. Like I said, Bartholomew was a fucking coward, so it's just like him to be as far away from the war as he can get.' He smiled, but there was no humour in it. 'Hollywood, eh? When you put it like that, why *wouldn't* she have gone with him? He could offer her more than I ever could.'

'But you were wrong about that,' Penrose pointed out. 'She hadn't gone anywhere, had she?'

'No, and I suppose this is *my* punishment for doubting her.' He looked pleadingly at Penrose, tears once again in his eyes. 'You will get him for this, won't you? He can't get away with it.'

'We'll certainly track him down, yes, and see what he has to say.'

'What he has to say?' Young stared at him in indignant disbelief. 'Isn't it obvious what happened? Evelyn refused him and he got angry. She didn't go back to work after she met him. Surely you're not going to let him wriggle out of it?'

'As I said, we'll track him down and speak to him,' Penrose repeated, 'but I'm not making any assumptions. You've been very helpful, Mr Young, and we appreciate it, especially at such a distressing time. I just have one or two more questions and then we'll leave you in peace. Other than going to see your wife, were you at work all day on Monday?'

'Yes, I was. The boys will confirm that. They'll tell you I was there all day, and most of the evening.'

Penrose didn't doubt it. 'So what time did you leave?' he asked.

'Just after ten. I knew about Marion by then – Mrs Wells had telephoned from the hospital to tell me what had happened and to ask if I knew where Evelyn was because she wasn't at work. That was when it hit me, I suppose – she really had gone, and I just said the first thing that came into my head.'

'But you didn't go to look for your wife or ask somebody at the house where she was?'

'I couldn't, could I? Not when I'd just told a lie. I was angry and ashamed and worried about Marion, and I wasn't thinking straight. I stayed on longer at the office than I needed to. If I'm honest, I didn't want to go home to an empty house.'

At the risk of being taken for a fool, Penrose was inclined to believe him, and he would have to wait for a more precise time of death from Spilsbury before he could validate the alibi that Young was offering. 'Do you own a gun?' he asked, changing the subject.

The question wrong-footed Young and he took a moment to answer it. 'Yes,' he said cautiously. 'I've got an old army pistol, but I don't use it. I haven't fired a gun since I left the regiment. Why would I? I just haven't got around to getting rid of it. You never know . . .'

He stopped himself, obviously realising how incriminating the rest of the sentence might sound, so Penrose finished it for him. '. . . when it might come in handy? Quite. May I see it?'

Looking worried now, Young struggled to his feet and left the room, returning empty-handed a few minutes later. 'It's not where I thought it was,' he admitted. 'You'll have to give me longer to look for it. I can't remember when I last saw it, but it must have been years ago.'

It was Penrose's turn to hesitate, certain that one of Young's army chums would happily oblige him with a revolver to get him out of a fix. 'Perhaps you'd let Inspector Hughes here help you look?' he suggested, wanting to be sure in his own mind that there was no gun on the premises, even if he had trouble proving it later. 'I do have to stress that it's in your best interests if we can eliminate the gun you own from our enquiries.'

'Do what you like,' Young said, suddenly defeated. 'Search the whole bloody house if you want to. I've got nothing to hide.'

Penrose nodded to Hughes, who seemed relieved to have something practical to do. He left the table, and Penrose heard his footsteps on the stairs. 'Do you have a photograph of your wife?' he asked, seeing none when he glanced around the room.

'I got rid of them all the other night. I couldn't bear to look at her when I thought she'd gone off with him. Thank God I forgot about this one. It's all I've got left.' He took a photograph out of his wallet and slid it across the table, and Penrose tried to reconcile the woman who laughed up at him with the dreadful images still fresh in his mind. She was, as her husband had said, strikingly attractive, with long, wavy blonde hair and an open, good-humoured face, unencumbered as far as Penrose could see by make-up or any other artifice.

Young watched him as he studied the photograph. 'Can I see her?' he asked, almost as a challenge, and Penrose wondered if whoever had broken the news to him had had the sense to spare him the details of the state of his wife's body; it was the question he always dreaded most in circumstances such as this.

'I wouldn't advise it,' he said gently, 'but I assure you that she'll be treated with the utmost respect while she's in our care, and I'll let you know personally as soon as her body can be released for burial.'

'Thank you.' Penrose stood to leave, and Young looked nervously up at him. 'Is that it?'

'For now. I'll need you to make a formal statement, so someone will be in touch with you to arrange a convenient time, and we'll take some prints for the purposes of elimination. And I'll want to speak to you again myself when we have the results from your wife's post-mortem, and when

I've had a chance to follow up on everything you've told me today. Is there anything else you'd like to add?'

'Only that I loved her. You do believe me, don't you?'

'Goodbye, Mr Young,' Penrose said, resisting the temptation to add that absolution wasn't his to give, even if he had been inclined to do so. In any case, the sort of love that had been evident in the interview left an unpleasant taste in his mouth, and would certainly not have been an argument on the side of Young's innocence. 'Inspector Hughes will let you know about your missing weapon, and I'll see myself out.'

Hughes was obviously doing a thorough job upstairs: Penrose could hear furniture being moved as he went out into the hallway. The door to Mrs Plummer's bedroom was slightly ajar and he saw Georgia Wells at her bedside, keeping up a stream of conversation in the hope that a familiar voice would at least be of some comfort. She looked up when she sensed him watching her, then raised a hand to hold his attention and slipped quietly from the room. 'I was hoping to catch you on your way out,' she said, pulling the door to behind her. 'There's something I'd like to speak to you about. How is Donald?'

Unsure if the two things were one and the same, Penrose answered tactfully. 'He's been very helpful, but he's naturally distressed and still struggling to come to terms with what's happened. He's given us his blessing to look around,' he added, in response to another loud thud from upstairs, 'but as soon as that's done we'll leave you all in peace, at least for tonight.'

He waited to see if she had anything else to add. 'Forgive me if this is silly,' she began tentatively, 'but it's been bothering me for days and I've got to get it off my chest, if only for you to dismiss it.'

'Is it to do with Mrs Young's death?'

'No, at least I don't think so, which is why I'm reluctant to bother you with it when you have so much else to do. It's just that Marion's crucifix is missing, and I find that very odd. I honestly don't think I've ever seen her without it in the thirty years I've known her.'

'Her crucifix? You mean a piece of jewellery?'

'That depends on your point of view, I suppose.' The smile came again, ironic rather than admonishing. 'My husband might disagree with you. Marion certainly would. Her husband gave it to her when they were married, and he died very young, so it has a sentimental value for her as well as a religious one. She wasn't wearing it when I found her on Monday, and I've looked in all the obvious places while I've been here, but it's gone. I really don't see how that happened, unless . . .'

'Unless someone took it?' She nodded. 'Could she have lost it before Monday?'

'She was wearing it on Sunday when Donald brought her to church.'

With someone else, Penrose might have asked if she was sure, but he already had a healthy respect for Georgia Wells's observations. 'Where was Mrs Plummer when you found her?'

'In her sitting room. I noticed straight away that the crucifix was missing, but it was an emergency and not the right time to worry about it.'

'So it couldn't have gone astray in the hospital, either.'

'No, absolutely not. She didn't have it with her when she went in, and I remember thinking at the time that it seemed rather a bad omen.'

'Did you notice if anything else was missing from the house?'

She shook her head. 'Not as far as I could see. You think it's strange, too, don't you? I'm so glad. My husband accused me of getting things out of proportion.'

Penrose smiled. 'There certainly doesn't seem to be an obvious explanation. I'm glad you mentioned it. Perhaps you'd let me know if it turns up?'

'Yes, of course.'

'Can I ask you, Mrs Wells – what was Evelyn Young like?'

She looked back at him in surprise. 'I would have thought Donald was the best person to answer that. I'm not sure what I can add.'

This time, it was Penrose's turn to allow himself a sardonic smile. 'A less partial view, perhaps. A husband, particularly a grieving husband, isn't always the most rational witness, and with very good reason. And you said you've known the family for many years.'

'Yes, I have.' She thought for a long time before answering. 'The word that keeps coming to mind when I think of Evelyn is disappointed.'

'Disappointed? What do you mean by that?'

'I'm not sure I know, exactly. But most of us fall into one of two camps, Chief Inspector. We're either happy with our lot, or at least content with it, or we're bitterly unhappy and looking for someone to blame. That's my experience, anyway, going right back to my own parents, and forty years of living amongst my husband's parishioners certainly hasn't changed my mind. But Evelyn was neither of those things. She certainly wasn't happy, but neither did she seem bitter. As I say, she was disappointed.'

'By what?'

She shrugged. 'By life, by herself, by her marriage – that, I couldn't tell you. I'm sorry not to be of more help, but – as I said – it's Marion I know best.'

Penrose was tempted to ask which camp Mrs Wells placed herself in, but Hughes came down the stairs before he could decide whether or not the question was impertinent. 'Well?' he demanded impatiently, looking at the inspector.

'Nothing yet, sir. Do you want me to do down here now?'

'Yes, please.'

'Will you need to come in here?' Mrs Wells asked anxiously. 'I understand if you do, but I'd rather Marion weren't disturbed unless it's absolutely necessary.'

'It's not,' Penrose said, directing Hughes to the other door. 'We'll just do the sitting room and the kitchen.' In his heart, he was already certain that they had found Donald Young's pistol in the woods, next to his wife's body. Its sudden absence from the house was too much of a coincidence otherwise, and his instincts told him that Young had been lying when he claimed not to have seen it for years. What they didn't tell him – at least not yet – was whether he was also lying when he said that he hadn't fired it.

10

Josephine woke early to the sound of Marta making breakfast in the kitchen. She got out of bed and pulled the curtains, keen to savour her first glimpse of the area in daylight, and was greeted by a glorious vista of sunshine, space and greenery, inside and out. The apartments that Selznick International had leased for Hitchcock and his associates were in the Wilshire Palms on Wilshire Boulevard in Westwood, just beyond the Beverly Hills boundary – a new, low-rise building with stunning views of the mountains and ocean. Chosen for its ten-minute drive to the studios, the apartment had plenty of other features to recommend it. It was beautifully appointed, with pastel carpets and drapes, and modern, simple furniture that was nonetheless attractive to look at. The softly coloured walls absorbed and intensified the light, while a series of geometric mirrors – the only harsh lines in the apartment – threw it back into the room, giving everything a radiance that felt fresh and hopeful.

All the windows were wide open, and the gentle breeze coming through was already warm for this hour of the morning; once the day got into its stride, it was set to be a scorcher. In typically extravagant style, Marta had filled everywhere with flowers, ready for Josephine's arrival, and the scent of gardenias – green and earthy, with a subtle sweetness – greeted her as she walked through to the living room. 'Good morning.' Marta put a tray down on the coffee table and gave her a kiss. 'Sorry about the early start. I was going to bring this through to you in bed. You were dead to the world when the alarm went off.'

'I can't remember when I last slept so well. Somehow I wasn't expecting Hollywood to be peaceful.'

'I'm sure the journey must have helped. That and goose down – please don't ask me how much those pillows cost.'

'Whatever it was, they were worth it.' Josephine looked round, taking in the general air of space and luxury that Marta's natural untidiness hadn't been in residence long enough to obliterate. 'Actually, I should be honoured that you come home at all. This is exquisite.'

'I'm glad you like it, although there's one thing that it can't compete with.' Marta drew her close and kissed her again. 'But now that thing is here, I might never see England again.' There was a time when such a comment would have filled Josephine's heart with dread, no matter how playfully it was made, but she just laughed, marvelling at how far they had come. That her love for Marta should be the anchor in life now rather than the thing that threatened to throw the world off its axis was a source of joy and amazement to her. 'We'll eat in here now you're up,' Marta said, 'and if you think this is the height of sophistication, you should see Hitch and Alma's place. They're in a three-bedroom penthouse on the top floor. They've even got a bar.'

'This is fine by me. I don't need a bar.'

'No, I don't think they do, either. It's all white walls and monochromatic furnishings, and they don't feel at home there, Alma especially.'

'So she said. She told me they were looking to move somewhere with a proper kitchen.' Josephine raised an eyebrow.

'Carole Lombard's house, I gather, when she moves into Clark Gable's ranch. How the other half lives. Can I do anything to help? I've been waited on for days.'

'No, it's all in hand and there's nothing that needs much effort. Just sit down and make yourself at home.' She set out fresh rolls, cheese, fruit and orange juice, and went back to the kitchen for the coffee. 'We've got an hour or so before we have to leave, so let's enjoy the peace while we can. A weekend with the second unit is bound to test my patience, even if it is in beautiful surroundings.'

'Are you sure it's all right for me to tag along while you're working? I don't want to get in the way, and I won't be the slightest bit offended if it's easier for me to stay here. Didn't you say there was a pool?'

'And a tennis court, yes, but you won't be in the way. It's only a scouting trip, and two days should be plenty of time to get through what we need to do. I'll make sure they're efficient so that you and I can spend some time together. Unless you'd rather stay here? A long car journey might be the last thing you're ready for after all that travelling, and we are in the middle of a heat wave, so if you'd prefer a couple of days by the pool, that's fine by me. I'll be back tomorrow night if everything goes smoothly.'

'No, I'd much prefer to come. I want to spend all the time I can with you while I'm here, and a weekend at the coast sounds wonderful. Where are we going?'

'Point Lobos State Park. It's up near Monterey, about a six-hour drive from here. You'll love it – rugged cliffs and stunning views, and it's a nature reserve, so the wildlife is wonderful. We went there in the summer for a recce, and I remember wishing then that I could show it to you.'

'So how are they using it in the film?'

'It'll be Cornwall and Monte Carlo.'

'Very versatile.'

'Yes, and it works uncannily well for both. There's a shot at the beginning where Max is standing at the edge of a cliff and Fontaine's character thinks he's about to jump, so we're doing that there, and another Monte Carlo scene a bit later on with Fontaine and Olivier on the hotel veranda – well, it won't be them, it'll be their doubles, so no close-ups. Then some more general shots for the opening credits.'

'Who else is going?' Josephine asked, hoping that James Bartholomew might be spared the discomfort of watching a man contemplating suicide.

'Victor, Frank and Bart. Don't worry, though,' she added, misreading Josephine's expression, 'we'll take my car so I don't have to play referee with the boys for the whole journey. And that way we can stay as long as we like. I haven't told you before just in case it was cancelled at the last minute, but I've got Monday off so we can have the whole day to ourselves. We can stay up in Monterey or come back here and I'll show you round, whichever you prefer – no need to decide until Sunday night.'

'It sounds like the perfect weekend, especially your day off. That's a lovely surprise – I thought you'd be working round the clock.'

'I suppose I will be once things really get going, so it's good that you're here at the beginning.'

'And I'm relieved that we're going to the coast on our own. I met Frank briefly yesterday on the train – there's no love lost between him and James, is there?'

Marta smiled. 'It's just banter. Bart's lovely, and far too

easy-going to rise to any of Frank's nonsense.' James had struck Josephine as many things, but easy-going wasn't one of them; she thought back to his short-temperedness on the train, particularly after he had read the note in his pocket, and wondered again what had happened in England to make him behave so differently from the man that Marta obviously knew. 'He's talented, too – you should see the miniatures he's created for *Rebecca*.'

'He promised to show them to me if there was time.'

'Then he must like you. He's normally far too modest to show off his work.'

'Well, we were talking about *Young and Innocent*. He obviously enjoyed working on that very much.' She was tempted to tell Marta what had really brought them together, but she still felt bound by the promise she had made and it wasn't the right time; perhaps later, when she had had the chance to talk to James again and judge his mood. 'He met Daphne du Maurier when she was a little girl,' she said instead. 'Did you know that?'

'No, I had no idea. Where?'

'At Milton Hall, where they've just been filming. Apparently the du Mauriers were friendly with the family.'

'How interesting. I knew Bart was at the Hall – that's why they sent him over there – but he's never talked about it. I wonder what Daphne was like as a child? I still can't get used to the fact that she's so young, you know. I keep thinking of her as our age, and then I realise that she's written this extraordinary, complex book that's sold over a million copies and she's still barely more than thirty. Makes you sick, doesn't it?' She drained her coffee and stood up. 'We'd better get dressed.'

In spite of her excitement about the weekend, Josephine thought longingly of the cool, white sheets she had just left, but a shower and the prospect of a visit to Selznick International soon revived her spirits. 'Who should I be keeping an eye out for?' she asked on the way down to the car, remembering what Marta had said about the Palms being home to a steady stream of Hollywood newcomers and stars from broken marriages.

'Billy Wilder's just moved in upstairs, and Franchot Tone's been nursing his wounds here for a few weeks now.'

'Really? How exciting.' Josephine had a soft spot for the *Mutiny on the Bounty* star, who had recently gone through a high-profile divorce from Joan Crawford. 'You must tell me which apartment. I'll take him a casserole. And what about that – who lives there?'

She pointed to the building next door, a French-style castle with turrets and leaded-glass windows; only the vines – young and just beginning to climb the walls – betrayed the fact that the building was much newer than its appearance suggested. 'That's Chateau Colline,' Marta said. 'Oil men. Playboys. Bette Davis in the early days.'

They drove out onto Wilshire Boulevard, a long, wide corridor that linked Santa Monica in the west to downtown Los Angeles, cutting through the heart of Beverly Hills, and Josephine took her opportunity to get a feel for the neighbourhood. As Marta had promised, the Westwood district was blessed with a fine selection of shops, restaurants and cinemas that she looked forward to getting to know, but what struck her most was how very familiar it all seemed. 'It feels so English,' she said, looking at the street lamps and Tudor-style houses, the well-kept lawns and road signs sporting the names of British towns; the area had an old-world charm about it that – were it not for the palm trees and the scale of everything – could almost convince her that she had never left the suburbs. 'Alma was telling me about the ex-pats. I can see why they feel so at home here.'

'Pretty much all of this district was designed by Anglo-philes,' Marta explained, stopping at the lights by the Los Angeles Country Club. 'I read up on it before you arrived so that I could give you the full tourist experience. They brought in a man from Kew Gardens, apparently, and he planted a different species of tree for every street. I've lost count of how many there are, but I love it.' It *was* beautiful, Josephine thought, looking at the different varieties – magnolia, elm, eucalyptus, palm and sycamore, to name just the ones that she recognised. In this part of town, the trees were comple-mented by curved streets and triangular parks that seemed a world away from the uniform, grid-like patterns that she had been expecting.

Marta pointed out a few more landmarks as they approached Culver City, but Josephine didn't need to be told when they were in sight of their destination. Selznick International Pictures had its headquarters in a magnificent white colonnaded mansion on Washington Boulevard, southern plantation style and familiar as the iconic opening shot of all of the producer's films. The imposing studio facade had originally been built as the set for a silent film, then subse-quently converted to an administration building by Cecil B. DeMille. Having seen it so often on the cinema screen, there was something faintly illusory for Josephine in approach-ing the grand pathways, wide green lawns and ornamental hedges that separated the mansion from the road, and she felt more than ever like Dorothy en route to the Emerald City. 'Are all the studios in this area?' she asked.

'Quite a few.' Marta gestured over her shoulder. 'MGM's about a mile in that direction, and Fox is back towards Wilshire. Then there's Hal Roach just up the road – Laurel and Hardy territory.' She drove round to a parking lot at the rear and Josephine saw instantly that the main building, though impressive, was just the tip of the iceberg: the site as a whole was vast and sprawling, home to a motley collection of outlying bungalows and structures that resembled warehouses or aircraft hangars, rising high above the studio's more elegant public face. 'This must go on for miles,' she said, trying to take it all in.

'It's about forty acres in total.'

'How do you remember where everything is?'

'I don't have to. The only things that concern me are the soundstages and Hitch's bungalow. As long as I can get from one to the other I'm fine, and there's always someone around to ask if I get lost.'

'Hitch has a bungalow as well as a penthouse?'

'Oh yes. They don't work at home – he's got a suite to write in with Alma and Joan and me. It's very cosy – nice kitchen and bathroom, a bit like the old days in London when we all used to work at Cromwell Road.' She laughed when she saw the expression on Josephine's face. 'He's very important here, you know. Selznick's invested a lot of money in him already and he'll expect a good return on that, so they need to keep each other happy. A bungalow is nothing if it gets results.'

'It really is a different world, isn't it? Perhaps I should have stuck at that scriptwriting business.' A few years ago, at the height of her success in the West End, Universal had commissioned Josephine to work on the scenario of a romantic novel that they were filming, but she had hated the experience, finding little to inspire her in working from someone else's characters and ideas. 'I'm looking forward to seeing you at work, though,' she said, genuinely interested to understand more about Marta's role in this huge and complex operation.

'Well, I hope I don't disappoint you. By the time we get to this stage, it's mostly waiting about and shouting at people.' She took the parking space nearest the main building and got out. 'We'll go and sign in first, and then I want to take you over for a quick look at the set. They're working on one of the scenes in Rebecca's bedroom today, and it's stunning. There's just time to do that before we have to hook up with the boys.' Josephine followed as Marta signed them both in at reception and led the way along a succession of corridors with diligently polished floors and a bewildering number of doors to either side. 'It's mostly administration in this building,' Marta explained. 'Selznick has his offices up on the first floor, but out here is where the real magic happens.'

It seemed scarcely possible that two such different worlds could exist on either side of a simple door. The back lot stood in sharp contrast to the attractive gentility of the main building, with its painted shutters and old-world white stonework. It was far more industrial – grey and dusty and noisy – and anyone might have been forgiven for doubting that such elaborate fantasy worlds could be conjured up in these drab and characterless surroundings. As Marta had said, there were people working everywhere, and Josephine's immediate impression was of a small, self-contained town; she wondered if any other industry brought together so many different skills and crafts. 'Is it always this busy?' she asked, stepping to one side to allow a lorry to pass.

'I can only speak for the last couple of months, but it's always been like this whenever I've been here. They've got three pictures in various stages of production at the moment, though – *Intermezzo* and *Gone With the Wind*, as well as *Rebecca* – and that's not very common, so I suppose it'll quieten down.'

Through a process of elimination that wasn't entirely obvious to Josephine, Marta quickly found the soundstage she was looking for, where preparations for the day's work on *Rebecca* were already well underway. Sound crew members seemed to have been at their posts for some time and were busy connecting power lines, suspending microphones and testing equipment, while others – script in hand – checked small details on the set itself. To Josephine's novice eye, the activity seemed chaotic and baffling, but there was an atmosphere of calm over the whole room, and she had no doubt that everyone involved was in complete control of his or her particular task. She saw Hitchcock straight away, dressed in his familiar white shirt and dark suit, in earnest discussions with his cameraman over a selection of lamps and reflectors. His solid figure would have been difficult to overlook in any room, but it wasn't his weight that drew her attention; it was his vitality and his obvious enthusiasm for the task ahead, and she remembered from their last meeting how infectious that could be. 'Are you sure we're not in the way?' she whispered, self-conscious at being the only person in the room without a clear purpose.

'I'm positive. Hitch specifically asked me to bring you in to say hello before we left.'

'Did he really?'

Marta smiled at her surprise. 'I know you find it difficult to believe he has a human side, but yes, he did. While you and Alma were living it up on the *Queen Mary*, he and I were worried sick about you both having to cross the Atlantic with a war going on. It was actually quite nice to have someone to panic with.'

Josephine watched the director, completely at ease and joking with his crew as if he had never had a moment's panic in his life. 'You like him, don't you, over and above admiring his work?'

'Yes, I like him very much, and I think you would, too, if he'd never filmed one of your books. We'll go over when he's finished talking to George, but come and have a closer look at the set.'

The invitation only served to strengthen Josephine's sense of intrusion, not because she was still wary of being in the way, but because of the extraordinary atmosphere that Hitchcock and his set designers had created around Rebecca's bedroom. Even if she hadn't known from the novel that the dead woman's room had been preserved by her loyal housekeeper as a sanctuary that very few were allowed to enter, she would have sensed it from this meticulous recreation of twisted devotion. In spite of the room's sophisticated elegance – the ornate chandelier and four-poster bed, the heavy drapes and the ivory-handled hairbrushes on the dressing table – there was something tomb-like and forbidding about it, something in the vase of white gladioli and the heavily framed photograph that seemed more akin to a mausoleum than a bedroom. The simplest domestic details were redolent with menace, even the dog sitting obediently at the edge of the set, and Josephine couldn't help but think that only

Alfred Hitchcock could make a well-trained black spaniel look sinister.

'Ah, Miss Tey – how very nice to see you again.' The director was obviously in a good mood, and he greeted Josephine as if she were a long-lost friend, the acrimony that had surrounded their last encounter obviously forgotten, on his side at least. 'Marta and I are very pleased to have you and the duchess back on firm ground. My wife tells me that it was a long and sometimes weary journey.'

'Yes, and not always a harmonious one,' Josephine said, curious to see if he would offer an opinion on Alma's confrontation with Lee Hessel, but he seemed oblivious to it.

'No, I can't imagine that believing yourselves to be surrounded by the German navy was a very comfortable sensation, no matter how quickly it passed,' he said, misunderstanding what she had meant. 'What do you think of our set?'

'It's stunning, although as bedrooms go I wouldn't choose it for a restful night's sleep – which I imagine is exactly the point.'

Hitchcock chuckled. 'Precisely. Now, you must both come to dinner with us while you're here. How does Chasen's on Thursday suit you? It's the finest restaurant in town – Marta will tell you how good it is. They serve the best steak you'll ever eat and a cocktail that I've devised myself.'

'It sounds lovely,' Josephine said, with more conviction than she felt. 'We'd be delighted.'

'Good, I'll tell Alma. It will just be the family, so don't expect a big party – more than eight people at a time is an insult to my friends.'

'We'll look forward to it.'

'And talking of insults, I think I'm about to take my fair share. You must let me introduce you to our esteemed producer.' Hitchcock fixed a smile, looking over her shoulder, and Josephine turned round to see a tall, owlish man with glasses who had just walked onto the set, looking – with some justification – as if he owned it and everyone on it. 'David, come and meet Josephine Tey,' the director said, and Josephine wondered if she was being used as a convenient deflection from whatever altercation had been about to take place. 'She's the wonderful writer whose book inspired us to make *Young and Innocent*.'

To his credit, Selznick quickly lost his scowl and replaced it with a smile that seemed genuine. 'What a very intriguing and exciting picture that was, Miss Tey,' he said, taking her hand. 'Hitch has a lot to thank you for. It was *Young and Innocent* that convinced me he was the greatest master of this type of melodrama.' Josephine was sceptical of both the melodrama in her work and Hitchcock's mastery of it, but she took the compliment in the gracious spirit that it was given. 'In fact, I thought Nova Pilbeam would have been perfect for Mrs de Winter,' Selznick continued. 'She's gauche and she's awkward, but with proper guidance she could become a real star. Hitch didn't agree with me, though.'

Josephine listened with interest, reminded of how fickle the film industry was. According to Marta, when Hitchcock had been making *Young and Innocent*, Nova Pilbeam – the British actress who had played the female lead – could do no wrong and he had championed her cause at every opportunity. 'She was right for the book but not for the film,' the director argued, obviously feeling the need to defend his decision.

'Yes, well, Miss Tey and I probably aren't quite as clear about that distinction as you are. Now, Hitch, we need to talk about last night's rushes.' Josephine turned away, reluctant to intrude on their private business, but it was impossible not to hear what Selznick was saying. 'Were you listening at all when we discussed Joan's make-up? Christ, those eyelashes – she looks like Dietrich at her very worst. I said *light* make-up – she shouldn't look as if she's wearing *any*. She's supposed to be a naïve kid. What can I do to get you men to throw away your kits and your tweezers. You're destroying these stars one by one – and tell Miss Anderson to stop plucking her eyebrows.'

Josephine looked round for Marta, but she was deeply engrossed in a conversation with another woman about the script, so she found a chair out of the way and watched the comings and goings on set. Hitchcock seemed to have taken his dressing-down with remarkable good humour, either because he was used to it or because he had every intention of ignoring any instructions he didn't like, and Selznick turned his attentions to his star. No one else seemed to have noticed that Fontaine had arrived on the set. She stood at the edge of the proceedings as if she didn't really belong there, nervous and uncertain, and wearing an old-fashioned white dress – presumably her ill-fated choice of costume for the Manderley ball. Josephine couldn't hear what they were saying, but she could tell from their body language how deferential the producer was and how grateful Fontaine seemed. It was kind of him in the short term, but she remembered what Alma had said on the boat coming over; Selznick certainly did appear to be smitten with her, and Josephine couldn't imagine that going down well with the rest of the cast. From time to time, she had been involved in a theatre production where a star was the teacher's pet of the director, and it had never ended well.

'You made it down here, then. I'm pleased – we didn't get the chance to say goodbye properly yesterday.' James stood beside her, looking much more relaxed than he had on the train, and Josephine was genuinely pleased to see him. After the despair of the day before, she had half expected him simply not to turn up for work. The relief must have shown on her face, because he smiled and added: 'No need to look so worried. There's only one man standing on the edge of a cliff today, and it won't be me.'

'I don't know whether to be reassured or concerned by the fact that you can joke about it.'

Marta saved him from having to reply. 'I'm sorry, but something's come up and I can't leave just yet. Joan Harrison's running late, so I've got to stay here until she arrives, just in case anybody questions an if or a but in the script. You can get going if you like, Bart, and Josephine and I will follow on as soon as we're ready.'

'We're a cameraman short at the moment,' James said. 'Frank hasn't shown up yet. He's probably nursing a hangover somewhere, and Vic's fuming about it, so take your time.' He turned to Josephine. 'I promised to show you the tricks department – do you want to take a look now?'

'I'd love to,' she said, pleased to have an excuse not to hang around in the studio once the work began in earnest.

'Okay. Follow me.' He led the way out of the soundstage and over to the one next door. 'I didn't know you were coming to Point Lobos.'

'Neither did I until last night. Marta says it's fabulous.'

'Yes, I'm looking forward to going back there. We've

finished the construction work on set now, other than any changes that come up as the filming progresses, so it's nice to get out and see more of California. It's full-on here when the sets are taking shape, and it's easy to forget what's real and what isn't – although sometimes that's not a bad thing.'

'You said you've learnt a lot from Hitchcock.'

'Yes, I have, and from Mr Selznick, too. He's always been way ahead of the field when it comes to special effects. Most producers only use them as a last resort, when there's something that they can't achieve in any other way or when things get too expensive, but he actually looks for opportunities to create them in the script – optical effects, matte shots, any small detail that might improve the production design of the film.'

'I imagine *Gone With the Wind* tested you.'

'It certainly did. We used over a hundred trick shots in total, but I bet you don't spot more than half a dozen of them when it gets to the screen.'

'That sounds like a challenge. When does it come out? I can't wait to see it.'

'Just before Christmas, and neither can I. I'll let you into one secret, though – we never built the exterior of Twelve Oaks at all, only the doorway. It's all matted in, even the trees.'

'So what about Manderley? How have you managed that?'

'With several versions, all different sizes. Let me show you.' He gestured for her to go ahead with the air of a showman pleased to have an attentive audience. 'This is the first one.'

Whatever Josephine had been expecting, it wasn't this vast recreation of a country-house facade, complete with adjacent landscaping and a sky backdrop, almost as big as the cavernous soundstage that held it. She stared at it in amazement, scarcely knowing whether to be more impressed by its ambitious scale or by the minute attention to detail. 'Why on earth do you call it a miniature?'

James laughed. 'It makes a nonsense of the term, really, doesn't it? But technically speaking, a miniature is anything carefully scaled that works as a substitute for the real thing – a car or a train, like in *Young and Innocent*, or even a whole scene. We build them as big as we can get away with, because bigger models are easier to light and photograph, and they're more believable on the screen.' He glanced proudly up at the chimneys and crenellated rooftops, all so utterly convincing. 'They're not usually *this* big, though, I'll give you that. Manderley might well be the largest scale miniature ever built – for now.'

'So how do you use it?' Josephine asked, looking at the constricted space between the model and the back wall of the soundstage, which surely wouldn't allow a camera much room for manoeuvre.

'For close views of the house. There's a scene from outside, for example, where you can see a light moving from room to room, so we'll do that here.' He grabbed a torch from a shelf to demonstrate and dimmed the lights, then went through Manderley's front door, and Josephine saw the light passing through the ground-floor windows, exactly as he had described. 'It looks amateurish now,' he said, rejoining her, 'but once the lighting and the camera angles are right, it'll be so atmospheric. Everyone will assume they're looking at a real house that's been standing for three hundred years, and think how much it would have cost us in time and money to film on location. Miniatures are quite expensive as visual effects go because they have to be so detailed, but they pay their way ten-fold.'

'It's the detail I find so extraordinary,' Josephine said. 'Even close up, like this, it feels authentic. There must be so much work involved.'

'There is, especially when you consider how little screen time the outside of the house actually has. You'll notice when you see the film, Manderley is hardly visible, and even when it is it's usually obscured by rain or clouds or flames. It all adds to the air of mystery, though. If we'd filmed out in the countryside and given the house a precise location, it wouldn't feel anywhere near as isolated. This way, Hitch really hammers it home that she's got no one to turn to.'

James beckoned her onto Manderley's 'lawn', and Josephine hesitated. 'Are you sure?'

'Don't worry, you can't hurt anything – and anyway, no one's at home.'

From a distance, the trees in front of the terrace looked as lifelike as everything else, but, on closer inspection, Josephine saw that they consisted of poles of varying lengths, ingeniously cloaked in burlap and plaster, with real leaves fastened to them. James grinned. 'We lacquer the leaves to keep them looking fresh. And you see the entrance over there?' She nodded. 'Well, we've built that and a few other sections to full scale, but they all match the details here exactly, so again, you'd never know one door frame from the other – or stonework from papier mâché.'

'You said there were several models – how do the others compare in size with this one?'

'The one on the next stage down is half the size, and that allows us to take full shots of the building. You can see there's no room to do that here. There's one long panning shot as they approach Manderley for the first time after the honeymoon, and it really gives you the feeling of arriving at a big house when you don't feel like you should be there.' He was talking about Mrs de Winter, but the words sounded heartfelt and Josephine guessed that his mind had also gone back to his first glimpse of Milton Hall as a young man. 'I'll show it to you in a minute, and you'll understand exactly what I mean. That one's surrounded by a forest, with a winding road leading through the woods. It's the opening scene of the film.'

'Like the dream she has of Manderley?'

'Exactly. Jack's filming that – Jack Cosgrove. He's our special effects supervisor, and he's a genius. He'll use some of the shots we get from Point Lobos, and cut them in with the camera travelling through the undergrowth on the model – high up, Hitch says, because a ghost doesn't have to walk on the ground.' The image was startling, and Josephine found she could picture the scene even before she saw the model or the landscape that Marta had described. 'Eventually the camera gets to Manderley to find that it's been gutted by fire. The other miniature will stand in as the ruin, but this is the one we'll actually burn down, so they all have their uses.'

'You're really going to burn this down? Doesn't that break your heart?'

'Only if we suddenly remember another scene we need it for. Destroying a model is about as final as it gets.'

'And there's only one take to get it right, I suppose.'

'Yes, although we use several different cameras and angles to make sure there's plenty of variety for the editing. It took a fair few cameramen to burn down Atlanta in *Gone With the Wind*.'

Josephine laughed, happy to listen to stories like this all day. She had been torn over coming to the set, and not just because she didn't belong there; she had loved film since she was a little girl, sharing her mother's delight in the early days of cinema, when everything had seemed so magical and so mysterious, and part of her didn't want that sense of wonder destroyed by too much knowledge of how films were actually made. But rather than spoil things for her, she found that James's insights only made the whole business more thrilling than ever. 'Is it your job to come up with the ideas?' she asked.

James smiled and shook his head. 'One day, maybe, but at the moment I just build what I'm told to build. I work out the scales and hope I've got it right, but there aren't any hard-and-fast rules in special effects. You learn as you go, and I was lucky because my father gave me a head start.'

'He worked in film, too?'

'No, but he was a carpenter. He was so clever, and I have him to thank for all of this, really. He showed me that anything was possible, that a well-crafted miniature can fool anyone – and he didn't even need cameras to pull off the trick. He just made me believe in whatever he was doing.'

'It's an extraordinary talent, to be able to envisage all this,' Josephine said.

'You get used to it, I suppose, until it's second nature. It's a hazard of the job, seeing things that aren't there.' He looked at her, suddenly more serious, and seemed to read her thoughts because he added: 'Yes, I know what I would have missed if I'd gone through with it, and I owe you . . .'

'If you're about to thank me, please don't. Just remember the promise I asked from you.'

'I haven't forgotten, but I won't make it until I know I can keep it.'

'That's a slight improvement on yesterday, I suppose,' Josephine said with a wry smile. 'We're getting there – and thank you for showing me all this.'

'Why don't you go and have a closer look, then I'll take you next door to see the other one.'

Josephine didn't need to be asked twice. She walked across the terrace and between two convincingly solid-looking stone pillars, finding herself disorientated by the peculiar scale, which was big enough to move around in but too small to be exactly lifelike. The model was a typical country house jumble of different architectural features, modified and added to over generations, with turrets, parapets, mullioned windows and Tudor-style gables, and the patchwork of sloping rooftops and towering chimneys made for a dramatic skyline. Over to the right was an archway and she walked through it, keen to know how it would feel to stand within Manderley's walls, even if they weren't made of stone. She paused for a moment, waiting for her eyes to get used to the darkness, and was struck by the smell of fresh wood and glue, which couldn't be further from the musty, stale damp that characterised most of the country houses that she had spent time in. Just as she was about to venture further in, she heard the door of the soundstage close and another voice in the room. 'What are you doing here all on your own, Bart?'

There was a pause before James answered. 'Just checking some stuff. Why? Are we ready to go?'

He sounded defensive as well as surprised, and Josephine noticed that he hadn't argued about being alone. She stayed where she was, guessing that she really wasn't supposed to be here after all and not wanting to get James into trouble. There was no way of seeing who the new arrival was, but James's response suggested a member of the crew and the drawl sounded like Frank Wheeler's.

'Did you get my note?'

'No. What note?'

'The note I sent you on the train yesterday.'

'I've had nothing from you, but you're here now. Whatever you've got to say to me, just say it.'

'Are you sure you didn't get it? You seemed pretty jumpy when we got to Pasadena. Anyone might think you had something to hide.'

The words carried a mocking tone, and Josephine was caught in an impossible situation – embarrassed to be party to a private conversation, yet shamefully curious to know what was going on. There was nothing she could do to extricate herself, though, so she began to move as quietly as she could towards the nearest window, afraid of missing something and keen to confirm the identity of the second speaker. After a lengthy silence, she heard James's voice again, low and taut with anger. 'I don't know what you're talking about.'

'I know what you did, Bart. I know what you *are*. You think I wasn't watching you like a hawk when we were on that trip? You think that people didn't talk about you? It's my *job* to notice things, and I noticed *you*. I saw you with that woman.'

'You have no idea what you saw.' For the first time, there was a note of uncertainty in the words which undermined their conviction, and Josephine sensed that James's bravado was waning. She was tempted to show herself and intervene, but knew that he wouldn't thank her for it – and anyway, the threatening turn that the conversation was taking frightened her. Conscious of the irony, she suddenly understood exactly how Mrs de Winter must have felt, trapped in the isolated house with someone who meant her nothing but harm. 'So what do you want from me?' James asked with a sigh.

'Nothing – at the moment. You're in my debt now, though – and don't you dare forget it.' Josephine saw James flinch as if he had been hit, but it must have been the vehemence of the words because the other man was still near the entrance, stubbornly out of her sight. 'I'll let you know when I need you, and if you've got any sense, you'll do what I ask.'

'If I've got any sense, I'll knock the hell out of you here and now.'

'You a fighter now, then? Really? That's not what I heard back in England. Just the opposite, in fact.' There was another pause and Josephine waited, fearing that James might be foolish enough to retaliate, but the defiance seemed to have been knocked out of him and he looked utterly defeated. 'You're a smart man, Bart. Don't let me down – and don't even think about mentioning our little conversation to anyone.'

Josephine waited a minute before emerging to make sure that James was alone. She found him sitting on the edge of the set, his head in his hands, and he jumped when she put a hand on his shoulder, as if he had forgotten that she was there. 'Are you all right?'

'No, not really.'

'Was that Frank?'

James didn't deny it. 'Did you hear everything he said?'

Josephine nodded. 'You can't let him blackmail you like that. So what if he saw you with me at the station? He can't prove what you were going to do, and even if he could, it's your business, no one else's. The only person you were going to harm was yourself – and you didn't do it. I'll talk to him if it helps, and deny that was even your intention.'

He stared at her as if she were mad. 'It's not that. Don't you understand? That's not what he was talking about.' The impatience in his voice implied that she was to blame for the lack of understanding, and she tried in vain to follow his train of thought. 'I don't know how he knows, but he knows. I've done something terrible, something I can't undo, and you can't help me. No one can.'

Josephine was stunned by the finality of the declaration, and by the sudden realisation that her liking for James had blinded her to the possible motivations behind his suicide attempt. Throughout their long conversation, she had assumed that the emotion driving his decision was grief; not for a moment had she considered that it might be guilt. 'So the woman Frank was talking about – that wasn't me at the station.' James shook his head. 'Who was it?'

'Someone I knew a long time ago.'

'And what did you do?'

She was almost relieved when he refused to answer; there were very few things that couldn't be undone, and in her heart she didn't want to believe him capable of any of them. 'I'd better take you back to the set,' he said, standing up and effectively drawing a line under their conversation. 'Marta might be ready to leave by now. She'll be wondering where we've got to.'

'But you can't just ignore this,' she insisted, afraid of what he would do. 'Whatever it is, I can't believe that you don't regret it, or that you did it without good reason, so . . .'

'Oh there was a reason. But I *do* regret it.'

'Then tell someone. Make sure it's your story that counts, and don't do something else you'll be sorry for just because of Frank. Take that power away from him by doing the right thing.'

He met her eye, and Josephine knew that no argument she could ever come up with would be a match for the sorrow she saw there, for such a complete absence of hope. 'Don't be kind to me,' James said. 'Please. I don't deserve it.'

11

Marta watched as Hitchcock walked Judith Anderson through the scene, assuming the Danvers role himself and showing the actress how to position herself for optimum camera effect, always leaving space in the frame for the ghost of Rebecca herself. As ever, the director was utterly engaged in what he was doing and Anderson clearly had great faith in him. She seemed to relish the chance to learn from her first major film role, not with the Svengali reverence that Fontaine occasionally fell into when Hitchcock was around, but as someone who wanted to push her craft to its limits. From the very first day, she had been one of the most confident people on set, secure in her role as if she understood the character of Mrs Danvers inside out – and they certainly had their self-assuredness in common. For a newcomer to Hollywood, Anderson had made the most extraordinary demands even to audition – a thousand dollars a week, plus transport, expenses and a written guarantee that Hitchcock himself would direct her screen test; it was a degree of imperiousness that had not only won her the part, but would also make her great in it.

Hitch was giving her his final notes, explaining how he envisaged the balance of the scene to play out. 'Go to the window, open it, look at her and look away,' he instructed, standing by the Gothic window that supposedly looked down onto the rocks, miming the actions as he spoke then. 'Then say, quite matter-of-factly, "You need a little air, madam." Don't overplay it. The camera will do the work for you.'

He went back to his chair, and Anderson and Fontaine took their opening positions. The scene was the moment when Mrs de Winter follows Danvers to Rebecca's bedroom after being humiliated at the Manderley ball; it brought to a climax the hostility that had been simmering between the two characters for the first part of the film, and it was one of many in which Fontaine was supposed to break down in tears. Four takes later, Hitchcock still hadn't got what he wanted. 'Let's try that again,' he said patiently.

'But I'm all out of tears,' the actress pleaded. 'Can't we try it some other way?'

Hitch hauled himself up and went over to the bed. 'What would it take to make you cry, Joan?' he asked, sticking out his lower lip like a disappointed child.

It occurred to Marta that telling his star the truth about her salary might help; Olivier was being paid more than four times her daily rate, and Anderson nearly double. Instead, Fontaine answered with something just as practical but much more direct. 'I don't know. Maybe if you slapped me?'

Marta was horrified, and exchanged a glance with Lydia Schiller. Surely even Hitchcock wouldn't resort to such an extreme measure to get what he wanted – but of course he did. The slap resounded through the dumbfounded set. Fontaine reeled, then staggered out in front of the camera looking fragile and hurt, exactly as the scene required her to look. Catching Marta's disapproving eye, Hitch smiled and gave a defensive shrug as he returned to his chair. 'Twirl 'em,' he ordered again.

From then on, the natural tension on set seemed to work with the scene. Hitchcock started with a wide camera angle, then moved forward into the room, involving the audience in the drama and allowing the passion of the characters to fill the screen. Throughout the filming so far, Marta had noticed how effectively he used the camera in the scenes between the two women, moving always with Anderson and towards Fontaine, giving the housekeeper the power while her prey remained static and unable to escape. Now, Fontaine lay sobbing on the bed while Anderson stood over her, a stern column of black with the look of Bela Lugosi, and Marta tried to think of another actress who could deliver such a quality of menace simply by folding her hands. She glanced back at the crew, wanting to share the excitement of the moment with someone, and noticed that Josephine was standing at the back of the soundstage with Bart; they must have slipped back in during the break in filming. Josephine was transfixed by the scene playing out in front of her, but it was Bart who drew Marta's attention. Staring intently at Mrs Danvers as she stood over the bed, he looked absolutely terrified, exactly as if he had seen a ghost.

Distracted now, Marta turned back to the set and quickly checked the script. Anderson had opened the casement and looked back at Fontaine on the bed, her eyes drawing her victim to the window before she had even uttered a word. Then she spoke, her voice seductive and encouraging, delivering the lines exactly as Hitchcock had instructed – quietly and gently, and all the more terrifying for that. Out of the corner of her eye, Marta saw Josephine say something to Bart and he nodded, but still he didn't take his eyes off the actress.

Crying harder than ever, Fontaine pressed herself against the stone framework of the window as Anderson urged her to leave Manderley. An electric fan placed out of shot made the drapes billow gently, bringing the chill air of the sea into the room like the breath of the dead Rebecca. Marta saw Bart move closer to the set, breaking all the rules of the studio, and she heard Hitchcock tutting quietly beside her, but the performances were too good to interrupt. 'He doesn't love you,' Anderson said, her voice now lower than ever. 'You've nothing to stay for. You've nothing to live for really, have you?' She stood stock still behind Fontaine, her face almost touching the actress's bare shoulder, the parody of a hesitant lover. 'Look down there. It's easy, isn't it? Why don't you? Go on, go on. Don't be afraid.'

'No!' The cry was full of such raw, inconsolable emotion that it took Marta a second to realise that it wasn't in the script. There was a noise to her right as Bart left the sound-stage, knocking over one of the lighting ladders as he went, and she stared in confusion at Josephine. Hitchcock slammed his script down on the floor, his fury giving him an unusual grace as he leapt from his chair and bellowed at his crew. 'Cut! Will someone please tell me what the fuck is going on?'

12

Penrose sat at a desk in the room he had been allocated at Milton Hall, waiting impatiently for some of the enquiries he had made to pay dividends. He would much rather have gone back to the familiar efficiency of Scotland Yard, where everything was designed to help rather than obstruct his investigations, but as his immediate tasks revolved around long-distance telephone calls and questions for those who lived and worked on the estate, it seemed sensible to stay where he was and not waste time travelling back and forth from London. The room was part of the stable block, and he probably should have been flattered that both the house staff and the army had seemed so keen to offer him hospitality, but he knew that he was potentially disruptive to both and it was little wonder that they wanted him where they could keep an eye on him. In the end, Scott's rank and persistence had won the battle, and Penrose found himself in a small room just a few yards down the corridor from the colonel's own office, conveniently in earshot as the bustle of the day dwindled.

Thankful of the time difference that gave him an eight-hour advantage over the working day in Los Angeles, Penrose looked at the sheet of paper that the butler had handed over, somehow managing to convey as he did so that – had it been down to him – no film crew would have been allowed within a five-mile radius of Milton Hall, especially if it came from Hollywood. There were three names on the list: Victor Petrie, Frank Wheeler and James Bartholomew, the man whom – according to Donald Young – his wife had loved enough to leave their marriage for. All three were employed by Selznick International Pictures, and Penrose could still scarcely believe that of all the films they could have been working on, it should be *Rebecca*, the one that had taken Josephine out of the country. It was irrational, but the sense of foreboding that had struck him so powerfully as she left renewed its grip, and he wondered if there was any way of getting in touch with Marta.

It was heading for ten o'clock, and the shadows beyond the window didn't help his mood. Strange, he thought, that this heavy, unfathomable darkness should be so much more unsettling when it fell over an alien landscape, when really it should make no difference. He stared at the telephone, willing it to ring, then jumped out of his skin when it obliged him. The response was quicker than he had dared to hope for and he grabbed the receiver eagerly, quickly dismissing the operator and developing a healthy respect for the Los Angeles Police Department's efficiency.

'Is that Detective Chief Inspector Penrose?'

The American voice placed the accent on the second syllable, something that Virginia had always done when they first met, and the small reminder of a more normal life lifted his spirits. 'Yes, it is. Thank you for—'

'This is David Selznick,' the caller said, completely wrong-footing him. 'I've got two officers from the LAPD here, asking to speak to my crew, and they say you sent them.'

'That's right, yes.'

'Then would you mind telling me what the hell is going on?'

Penrose took a breath, wisely ignoring the obvious retort. It didn't surprise him that someone in Selznick's position should assume that only his own time mattered, so he patiently repeated the information that the officers who had been dispatched to the studios would no doubt already have shared. 'We're investigating the murder of a woman at Milton Hall, Mr Selznick. She was killed on Monday, while your crew was working at the house, and it's important that we speak to everyone who was present here to eliminate them from our enquiries and to gather any valuable information that they might have. We would greatly appreciate your co-operation, and theirs.'

'You don't think they had anything to do with it, though?'

Fleetingly, Penrose wondered how many times he had heard that during his career. 'As I said, we'd greatly appreciate anything they can tell us, and it is a matter of some urgency. I'm particularly keen to speak to James Bartholomew, as we have a witness who claims that he was known to the victim. Her name is Evelyn Young, and I gather that they met during the war, when Bartholomew was last at Milton.'

Penrose had the satisfaction of a slight pause at the other end, as Selznick digested the fact that there was more than a coincidence of time and place to link his employees with the murder. 'How long will this all take?' he asked.

'That very much depends on what your men have to say.'

The ferocity of Selznick's response made it hard to believe that there was really five thousand miles between them. 'You want my entire fucking second unit out of action for God knows how long?' he exploded. 'We're supposed to be filming four script pages a day. That's not much to ask, for Christ's sake, but do you know how far behind he is already?' It was a rhetorical question, and Penrose had no chance to intervene before the producer continued his tirade. 'Three days, that's how far. We're more than a week into the schedule and he's only turned in eighteen minutes of usable film. The budget's going to be well over a million at this rate.'

Did Selznick really expect him to put justice on hold while Hitchcock got *Rebecca* back on track? Penrose wondered. Heartily wishing that he could have got to the men before they left the country, he tried again. 'I understand your frustration, sir, and I give you my word that your crew won't be detained any longer than is absolutely necessary – but it's vital that we're given the opportunity to question them, and if you won't co-operate, I'll have no choice but to ask the officers present to take all three back to the station for more formal questioning.' Selznick was silent, obviously weighing up his options, and Penrose could only imagine Hitchcock's anxiety when the LAPD arrived on his set; as he had discovered to his advantage during their last meeting, the director was terrified of the police. 'I probably don't have to tell you that those formalities will be more time-consuming in the long run,' he added, 'but we will of course try to keep any inconvenience to a minimum.'

'Inconvenience doesn't come anywhere near it. Location trips are expensive, and you've just shot mine to hell. We'll have to do it all over again if you haul them back now.'

'Haul them back? Why? Where are they?'

'Point Lobos State Reserve, up on the coast near Monterey. They left three or four hours ago and they're due back tomorrow night. Couldn't this wait until then, Chief Inspector? In any case, it might be difficult to get hold of them while they're out on location.'

Penrose's heart sank, but he found it very hard to believe that Selznick International Pictures would send a valuable crew anywhere without a means of contacting them in an emergency. 'Surely you know where they're staying tonight?' he said, a note of belligerence entering his voice at the thought that Selznick was playing him for a fool. 'Perhaps you could get a message to them and ask them to return at their earliest convenience, and I'd be grateful for your discretion. The sooner we can speak to them and eliminate them from our enquiries, the sooner we can leave you in peace to get on with your film.'

There was a pause at the other end and Penrose thought for a second that he had been cut off, but then he heard Selznick speaking to someone else in the room – muffled, as if he had his hand over the receiver. 'My secretary will do her best to get in touch with Miss Fox,' he said grudgingly when he came back on the line. 'She's co-ordinating things up there, and we'll ask her to get everyone back here as soon as she can. I can't promise you when that will be, but someone will let you know when they're here.'

'Miss Fox?'

'Yes. She's one of Hitchcock's people,' he clarified, misunderstanding the tone of confusion.

'And she's there with them?' Penrose made an effort to keep his anxiety out of the question. It had occurred to him that Marta would probably know the men he was after, but never for a moment had he dreamt that she'd be stranded in Monterey with them.

'Of course she's there. Like I said, she's co-ordinating everything.'

'And who else is on this trip?'

'Trip? You make it sound like a damned vacation. The three men you want to talk to are up there, with Miss Fox and a friend of hers. They're working at North Point on the Cypress Grove Trail.'

'And do you have a telephone number for Miss Fox? A private number, I mean.'

'Why would you want that? I told you, my secretary will deal with it.'

'It's just a precaution, sir, and I would appreciate it.'

There was more muttering in the background, but eventually the producer provided Penrose with the number he had asked for. 'I hope that helps,' he said, his tone a little more conciliatory, 'and please – keep this as quiet as you can, Chief Inspector. The censors won't even stomach a murderer on the screen, so the last sort of publicity I need is one on my own payroll.'

'Of course. Thank you, Mr Selznick.' Penrose hung up without saying goodbye, an economy that the producer might have approved of had it not been so rude. He made an effort to rationalise his thoughts. Of course Josephine would be with Marta; they had only just been reunited, and a trip to the Californian coast would be idyllic, even if Marta had to work while they were there. And there was really no good reason to suspect that any of these men were dangerous. Young's determination to pin his wife's murder on a man who had known her twenty years ago was driven entirely by jealousy, and there was no corroborating evidence: none of the household staff he had questioned remembered Evelyn Young even talking to the film men while they were at the Hall. No, it made much more sense to look closer to home for the culprit, particularly if the missing service revolver couldn't be found and the prints on the murder weapon turned out to be Young's. As soon as he had confirmation from Spilsbury, he would almost certainly be making an arrest – and it would have nothing to do with three innocent men on the other side of the Atlantic. An image of Evelyn Young's body forced itself into his mind once again, strong enough to drive all logic from his thoughts. He picked up the receiver to book his third long-distance call of the evening. Over-reacting he might be, but he was taking no chances with this one.

By the time Penrose had persuaded someone in the LAPD to talk to someone in Monterey, another hour had been lost. He put the phone down, exhausted, defeated and above all frustrated by having to rely on distant strangers to do something so important – and he had no real hope that anyone there would take him seriously enough to embark on a wild goose chase out to Point Lobos; if he were in their position, he would consider it a terrible over-reaction and a criminal waste of resources. It was nearly midnight, far too late to call Virginia without disturbing the children, and he really should go to bed and get some sleep, ready to start afresh in the morning, but he couldn't bring himself to leave the telephone. He was just calculating how long it would be before he could reasonably hope for news of any sort, when there was a knock at the door and Colonel Scott appeared carrying a bottle and two tumblers. 'Sounded like you might need one of these,' he said, putting the whisky down on the desk without waiting for an answer. 'Those film chaps giving you the runaround?'

'I wouldn't say that, but it's not easy at this distance,' Penrose said, sounding more defensive than he intended. 'Still, we're making progress.'

'Good. Then I'll forgive you this little slip.' Scott walked across to the window with an exaggerated gesture of dis-approval and pulled the blackout curtains across, replacing one square of nothingness with another and making Penrose feel like a naughty school boy. 'Just like old times,' he said, taking the vacant chair and pouring two large whiskies. He slid one across the desk and Penrose was grateful for it, even if he couldn't remember a time when they had ever shared a nightcap in their college days. 'I've been waiting for you to come and see me – how did you find Donald?' Scott asked.

It was that sort of practised nonchalance that got a man promoted, Penrose thought wryly. 'Angry,' he replied, know-ing that Scott had very little interest in Young's emotions; what he wanted was information, and Penrose had no inten-tion of giving it to him. 'Grieving one minute and bitter the next, just as you'd expect from someone in his position.'

'Of course.' Scott nodded thoughtfully. 'Look, there's some-thing you should know, Penrose. He came to see me after you left him and asked me to lend him a revolver. Apparently his has gone missing and you think it's the murder weapon, but he swore blind that he had nothing to do with Evelyn's death. He knows the gun looks bad, though, and he asked me to help him. Naturally, I refused.'

'Naturally.'

'And he begged me not to tell you that he'd asked.'

'He thinks a lot of you, doesn't he? He must do to trust you with something like that.'

The observation hung in the air between them, more a charge of disloyalty than of any wrongdoing, and its subtext wasn't lost on Scott. 'All right, it was a dilemma for me, I admit that. I was fond of Donald back then and we were friends, but it was a long time ago and my priority has to be our job here now. Full transparency, Penrose – you have my word on that. If Donald is guilty – and from what I hear, things don't look good for him – he must take what's coming. I can't help him.'

If Scott had added the words 'he's not one of us any more', his meaning could hardly have been clearer. He suddenly seemed very keen to point the finger at his old army friend, and it crossed Penrose's mind that he might be protecting something more personal than the reputation of his regiment. 'You were Mr Young's best man, weren't you?'

'Yes, I was. What's that got to do with anything?'

'Nothing, probably, but I'm keen to understand as much as I can about Evelyn Young and her family – and if you were best man at their wedding, you must have some insights. What was she like?'

'I told you – I really didn't know her, except as one of the nurses.'

'But were they happy together, from what you could see?'

'Donald was happy, certainly. I didn't see much of them together after the wedding, so I couldn't speak for Evelyn.'

Scott drained his glass, and Penrose wondered how much more to say. The last thing he wanted was to reveal too much of his own thinking, but he had very few witnesses to life at Milton during the last war, and – if that was as significant as he suspected – any perspective was valuable. At least two people from the Hall's past were here again, and Evelyn Young had died. In his heart, Penrose didn't believe that was a coincidence. 'You mentioned that one of the film crew had connections here. He was an orderly, and his name is James Bartholomew. Do you remember him?'

'Vaguely, yes.'

'You didn't mention that when you raised the subject.'

'Why should I? I hardly knew him. He wasn't my sort.'

'Because he was a conscientious objector?'

'No, because he was a fucking shirtlifter, if you must know. Can you believe it? A fucking queer around all those vulnerable men.' He must have seen the expression of surprise on Penrose's face because he was quick to justify the outburst. 'I'm sorry, but the very thought of it makes my skin crawl. God knows what he was getting up to.'

'Are you sure about that?' Penrose asked, careful to keep his voice neutral. 'Donald Young thinks that there was something between Bartholomew and his wife. He claims that Evelyn was in love with him.'

'She liked him, yes, but she was barking up the wrong tree there. It was Matthew he was interested in.'

'Her brother?' Scott nodded. 'How do you know that?'

'It was obvious – well, obvious to me, at least. Were you ever wounded, Penrose?'

'Yes, a couple of times.'

'Then you'll know that convalescence is excruciatingly dull. You have lots of time to watch people – it's about all you bloody can do. I saw how much time Bartholomew spent with Matthew Plummer, right under his family's nose. He was a good orderly, I'll give him that. He was attentive to all of us, but he was *very* attentive to Matthew. Unnaturally so. They were off on their own whenever they got the chance – fresh air and exercise, all in the name of recuperation.' He scoffed. 'I can only imagine what sort of exercise. Bloody disgusting it was. They used to go to that folly to be alone.'

'The folly where Mrs Young's body was found?'

'That's right. I'd see them walking off together across the lawns, with Bartholomew guiding him and holding his arm. Any excuse to touch him.'

Scott had done himself an injustice by using the word 'vague', Penrose thought; his recollections of James Bartholomew seemed surprisingly vivid. 'But his sister wasn't aware of this?' he asked.

'Not until I told her. She confronted Matthew, I know that much. She was horrified. No wonder she turned to Donald.'

'Why did you tell her?'

'What do you mean?'

'Just that – what good did you think it was going to do?' To Penrose, such a rash betrayal of something so private seemed an unnecessarily spiteful and destructive thing to do, with terrible consequences for all involved.

'I'm afraid I don't understand why you're even asking that, Penrose. The man was abusing his position, for God's sake. He needed to be stopped. Matthew was a gentle soul, and he was vulnerable. Bartholomew took advantage of that.'

Still, Penrose wondered why Scott had chosen to tell Evelyn Young – or Evelyn Plummer, as she was then – rather than take a more official route. Perhaps it was simply because he didn't think he would be believed or didn't want to tarnish his own record with any sort of involvement in the matter. Perhaps he wanted to do his friend Donald a favour by making it clear to Evelyn that she had no future with James Bartholomew. Or perhaps there was something far more selfish and personal at the root of it; if he had been asked to put a name to Selwyn Scott's motivations back then, or to the emotion that coloured his words now, Penrose would have called it jealousy. 'Is that why Matthew Plummer killed himself?' he asked quietly. 'Donald told me it was because of what had happened to him during the war, but was it really shame that drove him to it? Fear of being exposed as a homosexual? Despair at what his family might think?'

Scott shrugged. 'I have no idea why he did it, but if you're implying that it's somehow my fault . . .'

'I'm not implying anything.'

'Good. Bartholomew blamed himself for what happened, and so he should.'

The last observation was delivered with a degree of satisfaction that sickened Penrose. 'So you were still here when it happened?'

'Oh yes. I remember that day very clearly.'

'Tell me about it.'

Scott refilled his glass and handed the bottle over. 'We're straying a long way from the point, aren't we, Penrose?'

'Humour me. I've got a long night ahead while I wait for this call, and the more I know about James Bartholomew, the better.'

'Very well. As it happens, he was with me that afternoon. We were in the Long Gallery, which they used as a day room back then. Walter Glynne was on the gramophone, I remember that, and we were sitting at one of the tables by the French doors. It was the middle of summer – a beautiful day, but I was still in a wheelchair and I couldn't abide being pushed about, so I stayed inside. Bartholomew took pity on me, and he tried to interest me in one of those wretched matchstick models he was always making. Can you believe it? We were soldiers, for God's sake, not that he'd know anything about that, and they had us fucking around with matchsticks and jigsaw puzzles as if we were five years old.' Penrose smiled, recognising some of Scott's frustration with convalescent therapies, even if he didn't share his bitterness. 'There was a child there – a little girl. She must have come to stay with the family, because I saw her often after that with the children of the house, but that day she was on her own. Precocious little thing, she was. She was looking at the model, so Bartholomew beckoned her over. Any chance to show off, and he wasn't fussy who his audience was. He talked to her for a bit to gain her confidence, and then he took a small model of the Gothic folly out of his pocket. He'd found his go-between, you see, his chance to get to Matthew.'

'What do you mean? Why did he need a go-between?'

'Oh didn't I mention that? Matthew had been taken off the ward by then. Evelyn told her mother what had been going on, and she made sure of it. She was the housekeeper in those days, and she ruled that house with a rod of iron, even though she didn't have any official remit over the hospital side of things. They put him in one of the rooms in the west wing and wouldn't let Bartholomew anywhere near him. He hadn't seen Matthew for over a week, and you could tell it was driving him mad, so he used the child.'

'To do what?'

'He gave her the model and told her where to take it. The folly was their place, you see – I suppose he thought it would prove to Matthew that he hadn't forgotten him. He asked her to come and tell him when she'd delivered it.'

'And did she?'

'No. I watched him waiting and waiting, but she never came back, and it became obvious that something was going on. The atmosphere in the house changed completely, and we could see people running about in the corridors. Then a mortuary van pulled up outside – nothing unusual about that, of course, but this was different somehow. Everyone was white-faced and tight-lipped, and nobody would tell us what was going on.'

'Did you hear the shot?'

Scott shook his head. 'I don't think we'd have paid much attention. There was always shooting going on in the woods or vehicles backfiring outside, and there'd been a particularly heavy convoy of casualties that day, so the corridors downstairs weren't exactly peaceful. I couldn't get over how quiet the place was when I came back last week, you know – like a different world. No, it was well into the evening before word got out that Matthew had blown his own brains out. God knows how he got the gun.'

'Wasn't there an investigation?'

'To emphasise the embarrassment, you mean?' Scott raised a cynical eyebrow. 'I don't know what they did about it, but I rather got the impression that everyone was simply relieved that the tragedy was self-inflicted, with no one else involved.'

Had Bartholomew's well-intentioned gift been the catalyst for the suicide? Penrose wondered. Had it been a shameful reminder to Matthew, or had it taunted him with something that he could never have? Or perhaps the little girl had failed in her mission and was reluctant to admit it. In hindsight, he hoped that she had: God forbid that she should have been anywhere near the room when it happened. 'How did Bartholomew react?' he asked.

'It destroyed him. He smashed the model of the house to smithereens when he heard. I've never seen anyone so angry, but then he always had a temper on him. He was gone within a month of Matthew's death. They threw him out.'

It was hard to know if Scott was oblivious to how badly

the story reflected on him, or if he simply didn't care. Then again, Penrose thought wearily, perhaps it was his own reaction that was the aberration; most of the men he had served with would have reacted with disgust to the idea of an affair between two men. 'It's a wonder that Bartholomew could bear coming back here at all,' he said.

'It is, isn't it? Makes you think that he must have had a good reason. Revenge, perhaps? He must have been *very* angry with Evelyn for her part in Matthew's death.'

And so would you have been, Penrose thought, if you cared about Matthew Plummer more than you were willing to admit. Scott finished his drink and stood to leave. 'I've had enough of reminiscing for one day,' he said. 'See you in the morning, Penrose.'

The phone rang almost immediately, but it was army business and not for him. There was little point in making the night any longer, so he made his way to the main house via the route that Scott had taken earlier in the day. The servants had all retired for the night, leaving the entrance hall in darkness except for a feeble lamp by the stairs, and he was glad to have brought a torch as he made his way up the grand staircase, his footsteps echoing loudly on the stone. His accommodation was on the first floor of the west wing, a small room at the end of a long corridor, basic but comfortable; in all probability, a room very like the one in which a man had chosen to end his life. As he stood by the bed in the darkness, the hollow silence of the house was filled in his imagination by the bustle of a wartime hospital, by the cries of the wounded and the sound of running feet, by the violence of a gunshot. Exhausted though he was, it was a long time before he slept.

13

With so much to talk about, the drive to Monterey passed by in a flash. Josephine brought Marta up to date on her various conversations with Bart, finally sharing with her exactly what had happened on the station platform in Chicago. 'Jesus, I've worked with that man on and off for three years now,' Marta said, 'and I had no idea he was so troubled.'

'Well, I rather got the impression that he'd learnt to live with his demons, whatever they might be, but something must have happened this time at Milton to bring it all back. God knows what, though. He wouldn't say – only that he'd done something and it could never be undone.'

'And are you thinking what I'm thinking? Has he hurt someone?'

'Let's just say it did cross my mind that we shouldn't be going into the middle of nowhere with him.'

'I really can't believe we're having this conversation. Bart is one of the gentlest people I know. He's a Quaker, for God's sake – a conscientious objector. It goes against everything he believes in to harm a fly. I'm sure he wouldn't be violent.'

'So what else could it be?'

There was a long silence while they both thought about it, and it was Marta who conceded defeat first. 'Do you think we should tell someone what he told you?'

'But who? And what exactly would we say?' Josephine took off her sunglasses and wiped the sweat from the bridge of her nose. The car was sweltering, and the temperatures showed no sign of falling as the day wore on. 'I did wonder if we should try and find out if something *has* happened at Milton Hall,' she suggested. 'If there's been a crime, that's the most obvious place to look for the scene of it.'

'You can't just ring up a stately home and ask if everything's all right. If it is, they'll think you're mad, and if it isn't, you'll look suspicious.' Marta shook her head and thumped the steering wheel in exasperation. 'I really don't understand why he reacted so badly to that scene, do you? That might be the key to everything.'

It was something that they had both been speculating on since they left the studios, going round in circles with the limited possibilities. 'Perhaps it really was just the suicide angle and the prospect of her jumping out of that window,' Josephine said with a sigh, repeating something she had said at least twice before.

'It seemed so much more than that, though. Did you see the look on his face?'

'Yes, I did. He was haunted.' She thought for a moment, and a new idea occurred to her. 'Do you think he might have driven someone *else* to commit suicide? That certainly couldn't be undone, and it's marginally easier to believe than the thought of his actually killing someone.' It was the first time that either of them had spoken their most extreme suspicions out loud, and it made their conjectures seem more outlandish than ever. 'Or perhaps it was just a cumulative thing. The suicide reminder might have been the last straw after what I overheard on the soundstage.'

'That's another thing that doesn't really make sense. I can't see Frank having the brains for blackmail,' Marta said bluntly. 'If he saw something, he'd call it out on the spot and make a big thing of it. He wouldn't have the patience to bide his time or calculate how to make the most of it.'

'Well, he sounded pretty calculating to me – and don't forget the woman who's hanging round with him.'

'The one who confronted Alma?'

'Yes. She obviously means to cause trouble somehow, and perhaps they thought they'd involve Bart. He's closer to Hitch and Alma than any of them.' They were making good time and Josephine looked down at the map on her lap, ready to give Marta her next set of instructions. 'Do you know James well enough to talk to him?' she asked.

'Not really, and anyway, that would show you've betrayed his confidence.'

'I'm sure that horse has already bolted. He can't honestly think that we're going to be in the car for six hours and not talk about it, especially after what happened on set. He must know I've told you everything by now.'

'And I don't suppose for a moment that will make things more awkward than they are already.'

The comment was heavy with sarcasm, and Josephine looked at her in concern. 'You will be careful, won't you?' she said, more seriously this time. 'I hate the thought of you on your own with a blackmailer and a potential murderer. What's Victor like?'

'The strong, silent type. Always grumpy. Likes his own way.'

'That's not exactly reassuring. Can't you think of something for me to do so that I can keep an eye on you?'

'It's not a bad idea to stick together. Let's see how the mood is when we get there. They've had six hours cooped up in a truck, so they'll either have got it all out of their system or killed each other three miles west of Culver City. At this point, I'm not sure I really mind which.'

'Do you think you'll still get everything done by tomorrow night?' Josephine asked, thinking selfishly of their precious Monday together. 'You must have lost two or three hours this morning.'

'It should be fine as long as Vic's in a decisive mood, and we can claw back some time by getting an early start tomorrow. I'm not sure any of us wants to hang around longer than necessary. Five more weeks of filming is starting to sound like a very long time, and that's if Hitch finishes on schedule. There's not much chance of that if we have many more days like today.'

Point Lobos was situated a few miles south of Carmel, and it had just gone five o'clock when Marta left the main highway and turned in at the entrance. A tree-lined dirt road stretched out ahead of them, and she pulled over after a hundred yards or so and cut the engine to get a feel for the place. Families and walkers were enjoying their Saturday afternoon, and the cool shadows of the forest on either side offered a welcome refuge from the heat of the day, but not even the playful cries of children or the occasional barking of a dog could destroy the essential mystery of the place, the essential peace. It was already atmospheric, and as Josephine looked up at the trees growing over the road, their branches misshapen and entwined, she thought immediately of the dreamlike opening sequence that Bart had described. 'Ghosts don't walk on the ground,' she said, recalling the phrase he had used.

'Have you been reading the script?'

'It was James, quoting Hitchcock. I thought that was wonderful, and you can really believe it in a place like this. It's magical.'

'It is good, isn't it? Mind you, Bart will know how those ghosts feel if he's not careful. Any more stunts like this morning and *his* feet certainly won't be touching the ground.'

They drove on, heading north-west to the park's coastal boundary and stopping occasionally to appreciate the views. 'If we can get everything we need from North Point today, that will leave us tomorrow to concentrate on the forest sequence and Gibson Beach,' Marta said, thinking out loud. 'Some early-morning mist would be nice in those trees.'

'And what's at Gibson Beach?'

'An old set of wooden steps going down to the cove – it's perfect for the scene where Mrs de Winter loses the dog and finds the boathouse. And it's a great place to swim.'

North Point was at the very tip of the reserve, next to a vast grove of ancient Monterey cypress trees. 'This is beautiful,' Josephine said in delight. 'No wonder you wanted to come here. I bet they're inundated with film crews, aren't they?'

'Not any more. They used to allow full-scale location shooting, but all the sets and hordes of people trampling everywhere were destroying the park and eroding the cliffs. Then someone made a film called *Evangeline* here and nearly burned down a whole pine forest. The commissioners did some aerial surveys to show how much damage had been done over the years, and since then it's been strictly background footage only and a limited crew each time.'

'Good for them. It's quite heartening to know that Hollywood can't buy everything, although I suppose I shouldn't be saying that.'

'Oh don't worry – I agree with you. Those cypress groves are sacred, and I've had to jump through hoops to get us in. You should see the list of things I've had to promise we won't do. The good folk of Carmel will be up in arms if we contravene anything, but we're lucky to be here at all.'

To Josephine's relief, they seemed to have arrived before the rest of the crew and she was pleased to have some quiet time with Marta after the heat and effort of the journey, made all the more uncomfortable by their topic of conversation. They left the car in the shade and walked out across the cliff top, taking in the sweeping views across granite headlands and a glittering blue sea, all framed by the age-old cypress trees that Marta had mentioned. The trees – exposed to the elements on outcrops of rock – reminded Josephine of the windswept, sculpted firs at Loe Bar in Cornwall, near Archie's childhood home, twisted into wild, mysterious shapes by years of fierce sea winds. They had a striking visual quality that made them perfect for filming, and she could see why this particular stretch of the north Californian coastline had been chosen to stand in for Manderley's Cornish setting: it had that same quixotic quality – magical in this weather, with the sun sparkling on the azure-blue sea, but very different, no doubt, in rain or mist, when the atmosphere would be far more forbidding. In these steep, rugged cliffs and foaming waves, Hitchcock would find all the drama he could ever want.

'The greatest meeting of land and sea in the world, someone called it,' Marta said admiringly.

Josephine smiled. 'They've obviously never been to Portknockie on a summer's morning, but that could just be my childhood talking.'

They found a pocket of shade with a gentle ocean breeze,

and Josephine dozed, suddenly realising how tired she was, while Marta made some notes. She was woken by the slam of a door, and opened her eyes to find a pickup truck now parked next to Marta's Dodge. 'Brace yourself,' Marta said. 'I think I'm going to be terribly English about this morning and just not mention it unless somebody else does.'

Josephine watched as she went over to greet the three men, sympathising with James for what must have been a difficult ride. He seemed quiet and despondent, with none of the appetite for the trip that he had spoken of earlier, and in spite of her misgivings, she felt sorry for him. Marta introduced her to Victor, the unit director, and Josephine recognised him from the *Super Chief* as the second of Lee Hessel's travelling companions. He turned away after a cursory greeting, making it perfectly clear that he couldn't understand why she was there, and began issuing instructions to the other two. Josephine stared at him, suddenly struck by his voice.

'Don't let him make you feel uncomfortable,' Marta said. 'He's like that with everyone. It took me weeks to break the ice.'

'It's not that.'

'Then what's the matter?'

'I'm not sure, but his voice sounds familiar. I think it might have been *him* talking to James this morning.'

'Victor?' Josephine nodded and waited for Frank to say something, but the two men sounded so similar in accent and tone that she could hardly tell them apart. She looked to James to see if his body language gave anything away, but he seemed equally detached from them both. 'That would be more in character, I suppose,' Marta said thoughtfully. 'I mean, Vic's smart and he'll stand up to anybody, but I don't see what his motive would be. He's always respected Bart.'

'Perhaps I'm wrong. I just wish I had more than a voice to go on.'

'Well, I'll keep an eye on them both. Will you be all right here while we make a start?'

'Yes, of course.'

Josephine took a walk along the cliff while Marta got to work, keeping her in sight as much as possible but careful not to get in the way. The sun was much lower in the sky now, and she went back to the car to fetch a cardigan, noticing that James was on his own by the pickup, making some sketches. He seemed absorbed in his task – deliberately so, as if he didn't want to make eye contact, so she left him to it. The rest of the crew had moved inland, further into the cypress grove, and Frank was busy hacking through the vines and underbrush that impeded their access while Marta tried to stop him. 'Bart?' Victor yelled. 'Bring us the machete and some bolt cutters.'

He did as he was asked and Josephine followed him across to the trees, perfectly happy to be thought interfering if Marta needed her help. 'Frank, you really can't do that,' Marta objected. 'We're supposed to leave everything exactly as we found it. This area is protected.'

'What's your problem? It's just a bit of weed. I'm doing them a favour.'

He grinned, and Josephine could see that Marta was struggling to keep her temper. 'Let him get on with it,' Victor said. 'We need to get further in there to take a look. Did you take down the note about the platforms I asked for?'

'No I didn't, because you can't build platforms over there,' Marta objected. 'You'll crush those trees.' She pointed to some young cypress saplings that were not yet fully established. 'Do you have any idea how much trouble we'll be in if we damage anything?' She looked to James to back her up, but he was already on his way back to the truck, taking as little part in the day as he could. 'I marked on the map where we can and can't go, and the opening sequence has to be done near the entrance,' she insisted. 'Anyway, it's perfect for what we want.'

'It's not bad, but this is better. It's just what Jack needs. Now, let me have those cutters.'

Frank handed them to him and Victor strode over to a heavily chained gate, where a warning notice declared that the area was out of bounds for conservation purposes. 'Vic, you can't,' Marta shouted.

'Watch me.' He made light work of the chain and it fell uselessly to the floor. 'Come on.'

He pushed through the scrub and disappeared, and Frank followed him. Marta looked at Josephine. 'I hate it when they stick together like that and treat me like a glorified fucking secretary. I don't mind taking it from Hitch, but I won't have it from a second unit director and a cameraman. They'd never behave like that in the studio.'

'So what are you going to do?'

'Go after them and limit the damage – I've got no choice. If they ban us from shooting here, Hitch will be livid and Selznick will probably shut down the whole film. He's already having doubts about it.'

'All right, but be careful.'

'You, too.'

Josephine saw Marta's eyes move automatically to James. 'Don't worry. Whatever his troubles are, I honestly think the only person he's a threat to is himself. Go and sort the others out. I'll be fine.'

Marta nodded reluctantly and Josephine watched her disappear into the trees, kicking the telltale broken chain into the undergrowth as she passed. James had picked up his sketchbook again, but he sat on the cliff top with it, staring out to sea, and she walked over to join him. 'Do you mind if I sit down?' He shrugged, but didn't argue. 'What are you working on?' she asked, glancing at the half-finished drawings, but the question sounded as hollow and forced to her as it obviously did to James, and she knew that they were past such incidental small talk; if she was to have any chance of helping him, or getting any of the answers she so desperately wanted, she would need to be more direct. 'What happened on the set this morning?' she asked. 'Why did you react like that?'

'I threw away my job, that's what happened,' James said bitterly. 'The only thing I really cared about, and now it's gone. There's no way that Hitch will forgive me for that kind of behaviour. He can't bear a lack of discipline on set. I'm surprised he didn't fire me on the spot, but I might as well not bother going back.'

'Hitch isn't stupid. He must know how important you are to the film, and from what Marta tells me, that always comes first.' She smiled, hoping to reassure him. 'And anyway, if he tries to fire you, I don't doubt that Alma will show him the error of his ways. She obviously values your work tremendously, and he always listens to her.'

'That's true.'

'So what *did* upset you about that scene? Was it Mrs Danvers? You looked as if you'd seen a ghost.'

James stared at her as if she had uttered something far more insightful than a tired cliché. 'It was the first time I'd seen Miss Anderson on set and it came as such a shock,' he said. 'They hadn't started filming when we left for England, so all I had to go on was what's in the script, but it's never the same as when the scene is there in front of you.' And Hitchcock had brought the words to life with a peculiar intensity, Josephine thought; no wonder James was affected if there was the smallest grain of truth in it from his own experience. 'You're right,' he admitted. 'Danvers did remind me of someone I used to know.'

'Someone at Milton Hall?'

'Yes. Her name was Marion Plummer. She was the housekeeper there, but that's not the only similarity. She was full of hate, just like Danvers is. She bullied people.'

'She bullied you?'

'No, not me, but someone I loved – at least, I thought she did.'

He hesitated, but this time as somebody who wanted to go on but didn't know how, and Josephine did her best to make it easy for him. 'Tell me about him – the person you loved, I mean.' James's expression was a familiar mixture of wariness and relief, and she wanted to show him that she understood. 'I remember so clearly the first time I trusted someone enough to talk about Marta,' she said. 'I won't judge you – you must know that, surely?'

'Yes, I suppose I do, but it's not easy, is it? Not after a lifetime of being careful.'

'No. It's never easy.' Particularly with people like Frank and Victor to fool, Josephine thought, imagining the sort of charade that James must go through each day to protect his secret. 'What was his name?'

'Matthew.'

'And was he one of the soldiers you cared for or another orderly?' Her use of the past tense echoed James's, but she would have guessed at his loss from the grief in his eyes alone.

'One of the soldiers, but Milton was his home. The woman I was telling you about, Marion Plummer – she was his mother, so he'd grown up there.' Josephine was about to say that it must have been comforting for Matthew to have somewhere familiar to heal, but home wasn't a sanctuary for everyone, and facing people you knew when you were injured and frightened must have been hard, so she kept her silence and waited for James to speak. 'I'd only been at the Hall for a month or so when he arrived, and I'll never forget the first time I saw him. He'd lost his sight – permanently, as far as they knew – and he had to have an operation on a wound in his shoulder. They sent me to fetch him afterwards and bring him back to the ward – and we all hated going anywhere near that operating theatre, so I was dreading it.'

'That sounds familiar. The smell of chloroform still turns my stomach.'

'Mine, too. It was so strange to be back there last week and to see that room again. You'd never know now that it had been turned into an operating theatre – it's just another big room in a country manor house.'

'Not for you, perhaps.'

'No, not for me. It was all still there – the heat from the fire and the blood in the washstand, and someone shouting at me not to faint whenever I was helping out with an operation.'

'And did you faint? I know I did.'

'Only the first time – it was an amputation. But I got used to it. You do, don't you, and I can never decide if that was a mercy or a pity. The men barely seemed human when they were on that table, the flesh didn't even look like flesh. It seemed so barbaric after what they'd already suffered.'

He fell quiet for a moment and Josephine waited for him to go on, but he seemed lost in his thoughts and she knew that she would have to prompt him. 'So you went to fetch Matthew?'

'That's right. Me and another orderly helped to get him off the operating table and back to the ward, and then the matron told me to sit by his bed and wait for him to regain consciousness. He was like a caged animal when he did, shouting and struggling, railing against being there and wanting to die. I hadn't seen a man break like that before. Everyone else I cared for was so stoical, so damned grateful – but not Matthew. It was almost a relief, really, even if I didn't have the faintest idea how to handle it. At least it felt honest.'

'So what did you do?'

'The only thing I could. I held him and talked to him, while everyone around us was eating their Sunday roast.' He laughed and shook his head, disbelieving of the memory. 'It was all so surreal, but eventually he slept. After that, I started spending time with him each day – more than I should have done, but they let me do it when they saw that it was helping. His sister was a nurse there, and obviously I knew his mother, and they appreciated what I was doing for Matthew – at first, that is, until they understood how close we were getting.'

Josephine listened to James's story, his tone gentle and full of emotion, and found it easy to imagine how such a voice might bring someone back from a darkness that seemed all-consuming. 'Did he feel the same way about you?' she asked.

The smile lit his face, but disappeared as quickly as it had come. 'I thought he did, although it took a while. He resented me for a long time, I could tell that, even though he wanted my company. A part of him would have hated anyone he was so reliant on – he was that sort of man. Then one evening all that changed. It was a Saturday night, and some of the fitter men had been in to Peterborough and brought some drink back. They were getting rowdy around the billiard table, swearing and showing off, and one of them lurched up to me with a cue in his hand and started threatening me – it was buggers like me who should be in the trenches, he said. I don't think he meant anything by that. He was having a go because I was a conchie and the term was just unfortunate, but Matthew was there and he stood up for me. No one had ever heard him speak out like that before – he was always so quiet in the day rooms – but he was fearless in what he said about my beliefs, and how it took courage *not* to fight. I had no idea until then that he respected them so much. The chap even wrote me a letter of apology the next day, after he'd sobered up.'

'You were equals after that, I suppose – he'd done something for you for a change.'

'Yes, and when he stopped resenting me – or rather, resenting what I did for him – things were different between us. It was as if we could get to know each other properly, without his injuries getting in the way – and he was growing stronger every day. Once he was up and about, I'd take him round the rooms and describe the paintings so that he could see them in his mind's eye or remember the ones he knew from his childhood. And it was a beautiful summer, so we spent a lot of time outside. It was the first time I'd lived in the countryside, so I saw the small changes of the seasons every day. I took more notice, I suppose, and I shared that excitement with Matthew. I wanted him to realise that his blindness needn't be the end of everything that was joyful or beautiful. And then, day by day, he began to get his sight back in one eye. It was like a miracle, and it gave him hope – well, it gave us both hope for the future.'

'They sound like very special days. It's good to know that something tender could come out of all that hate.'

'It seemed too good to be true,' James admitted, 'and of course it was.'

'Why?' Josephine asked quietly. 'What happened?'

'Someone found out about us. I don't know who or how because we were so careful, but we had a special place that we used to go – a folly out on the estate. It was special to Matthew from his childhood. He used to kid around there with his friends, pretending he was lord of the manor. One of them, in particular, was special to him – they'd run away together to join up and the friend was killed out there.'

'The one whose parents you helped him write to?'

He seemed surprised that she had remembered. 'Yes, that's right. Matthew was full of guilt about it when he first came back – he'd been the ringleader, you see, so he blamed himself. Neither of them was of conscription age, so they didn't have to go, but he'd wanted the adventure. He asked me to take him to the folly to remember Robert, and after that we started to go there to be on our own. His mother found us together one day, and that was the beginning of the end. They moved him off the ward that night, and I never saw him again.'

'Because you left Milton?'

'I suppose you could say we both did. Matthew had been

225

gone from the ward for just over a week when it happened. I did my best to see him, but he was in the west wing of the house where we weren't allowed to go, and his family closed ranks and made sure I was kept busy elsewhere. It was driving me mad, the thought of him all alone up there, thinking I'd forgotten him. You remember I told you I met Daphne du Maurier there?'

'When she was a little girl, yes.'

'It was on that terrible day. She came into the day room, looking for her sisters, and I was with one of the other soldiers, showing him how to make a model. She was obviously interested, so I called her over to look at it – nothing more than that. Then it occurred to me that she had the run of the house and she was obviously curious, so she might be able to do me a favour. I knew where Matthew was because I'd heard the nurses talking about it, so I gave her a model I'd made for him of the folly and asked her to take it to him. It was supposed to be a celebration of his sight returning. I'd made others for him before but this was special because of where it was. I thought it would prove to Matthew that I was thinking about him, that I still cared.'

'And did she do it?'

'I don't know. She went off with it but she didn't come back. Then later the chaplain called some of the staff together and told us that there'd been a terrible accident and Matthew had died.'

'An accident?'

'That's what they called it, but it didn't take long for the rumours to start. He shot himself – I don't know if they were trying to spare our feelings or the family's shame, but that's what had happened.'

226

He was fighting back tears now, and Josephine tried to imagine how he must have felt, dealing with a grief that he couldn't acknowledge, separated in death from the man he had loved. 'I suppose you blamed yourself for Matthew's isolation,' she said, knowing that in his position she would have done the same. 'I suppose you thought you should have tried harder.'

James nodded. 'And not just for that. I blamed myself for what I asked of that little girl, too. I shouldn't have involved her in something she was too young to understand. It's ridiculous, isn't it? Look how successful she is – it's not as if it's scarred her for life and I doubt she's even given it a second thought. She probably threw that model into the bushes and went back to her family. But it's bothered me all these years that I sent her running into something she should never have seen. What if she was there when he did it? What if she got into trouble for it? Perhaps it's just a distraction from things that are too terrible to face, but it haunts me, what I asked a child to do out of my own selfish desperation.'

'Is that why you care so much about this film?' Josephine asked, thinking of the love and work that had gone into the miniature he had shown her; she had thought at the time that it was simply talent and ambition on display, but it made sense now that the brilliance should have come from something much deeper.

'Yes, I suppose it is, although I've never really thought about it like that. But you're right – this film does matter to me more than anything. That's why I'm so angry with myself for what happened this morning. I can't bear the thought of not being around to finish the job.'

It was hard to know in what sense he spoke of not being

around. 'Did you stay at Milton after Matthew died?'

'Not for long. I was given a convenient transfer to ambulance duties in the Red Cross. At one time, that was exactly what I was hoping for, but not after Matthew. I didn't much care what happened to me after that, but I hated not being able to mourn him with everyone else or to ask questions about what had happened – and I know that his mother had a hand in getting me moved on. I never even found out where Matthew was buried. That's why I did everything I could to be sent back to Milton for the film – I went to get some answers.'

They had been avoiding the subject of what had happened during that visit, and Josephine realised suddenly that she didn't want to know. No matter how much she sympathised, whatever James had done was likely to set them on opposite sides. 'Is Matthew's mother still at the Hall?' she asked uneasily. 'Did you see her when you went back?'

'Yes, she's still there, in a cottage on the estate. I shouldn't have gone because I knew I'd lose my temper, but there was so much that I didn't understand about Matthew's death. I was an idiot for thinking that talking to her might bring me peace. Nothing that came out of that woman's mouth ever gave anyone comfort.'

'So what *did* she tell you?'

'That my love for her son disgusted her so much that she put a gun in his hand and goaded him into pulling the trigger.'

'She admitted that?' The shock of his response was all the more potent for the explanation it offered of why he had found the scene in Rebecca's bedroom so charged. 'James? Did she really say that's what she'd done?'

'She said it was better that way. She talked about the sickness of his soul.' The two things were very different, but

Josephine could tell from the uncertainty in his voice that she didn't need to point that out. 'I was so angry,' he admitted. 'She wasn't even sorry for what she'd said, but I'd give my life to go back and change that moment, I swear I would.'

He was crying now, his body wracked with regret, and she put a hand on his shoulder. 'Did you hurt her?'

She wanted him to say that he had lashed out in his grief or pushed her by mistake, but his answer left her cold. 'I took a cushion from the chair and I held it over her face until she was dead. God forgive me, I didn't mean to kill her, but that's what I did.' He stared at her, almost defiantly. 'I bet you're judging me now, aren't you? I don't blame you for it, but you can't be as hard on me as I am on myself.'

Josephine didn't answer immediately, knowing that her voice would prove him right even if her words didn't. 'Was it *her* crucifix?' she asked, remembering what James had implied about the person who owned the jewellery, and horrified to think that she might have encouraged him to throw away vital evidence. He nodded, and she wondered suddenly if he was being exceptionally clever, manipulating her emotions and deliberately framing his crime in a way that he knew would elicit her sympathy. For all she knew, he could have planned the killing and fabricated the mitigating circumstances, but could she really have been so wrong about him? 'You know I'll have to tell someone what you've told me, don't you?' she said cautiously. 'I can't just let it go because I feel sorry for you, and I can't take it for granted that you'll do the right thing. I have to speak out.'

'So you do feel sorry for me?'

'Rightly or wrongly, yes, I do. But that's not enough, and what I feel really doesn't matter.'

'It matters to me.' He rubbed his sleeve across his eyes and looked properly at her for the first time. 'I think that's why I'm talking to you like this – because I know you *will* tell someone. I don't trust myself to do the right thing any more, and I despise myself for running away, almost as much as for the violence itself. All my life people have called me a coward, and now I've proved them right.'

'You were frightened. It's understandable.'

'But it's not an excuse. And once I got back here and went to work, I started to think it might be all right. I wanted to get away with it so that I could continue to do what I love. It was all too seductive, but life isn't like the movies, is it? I don't deserve a happy ending. By telling you, we can both make sure that I don't get one.'

'There are things that will speak in your favour, though,' Josephine insisted. 'If you believe that she really did aid and abet Matthew's suicide . . .'

'It's not as simple as that.'

From where Josephine sat, none of this was simple, but she waited to see what else he was going to tell her. 'That *is* what I honestly believed when I did it, but since then . . .' He paused, apparently trying to get things straight in his own mind before sharing them with her. 'Matthew's sister, Evelyn – she was there briefly when I called to see her mother, but then she left for work at the Hall.' It was the first time he had mentioned that there was a witness, Josephine noticed – a witness, at least, to his presence at the house where the murder took place. 'I thought I'd get away without seeing her again, but she caught up with me later on and said that there were things she'd been wanting to tell me about Matthew. She'd written me a letter and had been plucking up the courage to give it to me.'

'What did it say?'

'I didn't read it immediately. I was in such a hurry to get out of there, and I could hardly bring myself to look at her after what I'd done, so I just took it and said goodbye. Then I got to thinking that it might give me the answers about Matthew's death that I'd been looking for. At least it might say something about how much he had loved me, and that would have made things more bearable, but it didn't say that at all. Just the opposite, in fact.'

'You shouldn't set too much store by that. If the family didn't understand or approve of your relationship, it's only natural that they'd try to deny it or write it out of history. You know in your heart what you felt for each other.'

'It wasn't like that, though. Evelyn was trying to be kind, that was obvious, but she said that I hadn't known what Matthew was really like, and if I'd met him before he went to war, I would have hated him.'

'Hate is a very strong word. Did she say why?'

'She said that he had a cruel streak, and that he wasn't the man I thought he was. She accused him of doing some terrible things to his other friends, especially to Robert, and she said she hadn't wanted the same thing to happen to me, so she'd had to put a stop to it.'

'What did she mean by that? Was it Evelyn who had Matthew moved out of the ward? You said she was a nurse.'

'Perhaps, or perhaps she meant something worse. Anyway, I didn't believe a word of it at first. I know Evelyn had a soft spot for me back then – Matthew always used to tease her about it – and I tried to tell myself that the letter was just written out of jealousy of our relationship.'

'But now . . . ?'

'Little things keep coming back to me. All the times that Matthew was angry or sulky if I gave too much attention to the other men. The subtle way he'd manipulate me into doing exactly what he wanted. The stories that he'd tell me about his time in the trenches – there was a ruthlessness to them, but I always thought that was just the nature of war.' He shrugged and held up his hands, a gesture of helplessness. 'Now I'm so confused and I really don't know what to believe. I only wish I'd talked to Evelyn about it when I had the chance.'

'You haven't lost the chance – not if you confess to what you did and let justice take its course.'

James hesitated, then replied a little scornfully. 'You think she'll talk to me once she knows what I did to her mother? No, I should have gone to meet her like she asked me to.'

'Why didn't you?'

'Partly because I was in such a panic, but mostly for Evelyn's sake.' He could see that she didn't understand, and tried harder to explain. 'That anger I felt when I killed her mother – it came from nowhere, and I didn't recognise it. It was like nothing I've ever felt, before or since, and it lasted seconds – but look at the damage it did. I couldn't risk hurting Evelyn like that, and if she *did* do anything to Matthew . . .'

He didn't need to finish the sentence, and Josephine knew that she was out of her depth. More than ever, she wished she had Archie there to talk things over with; suddenly, London felt a very long way away. 'Have you still got the letter?' she asked, hoping that there might be something to testify to what had happened all those years ago; it wouldn't exonerate James, but it might at least prove that other people had questions to answer.

'No, I got rid of it. I didn't need to read it again. I'll never forget what it said, more's the pity, and I didn't want it to be true. As it is, I can't live with what I've done, but I can't bear the idea that I killed Marion Plummer for something she didn't do, or for a man who wasn't worth it.'

'Then all the more reason to tell the truth and let someone investigate what really happened. It's not just your story, now, is it?'

'What do you mean?'

'That there's more at stake than what happens to you. It's about justice for other people now – for Matthew, if someone really did make him take his life, and for this other boy, Robert, if what Evelyn told you is true. You owe it to them, and to yourself, to get to the truth, but you'll never do that by merely ending it all – and I know that's what's in your mind.'

'No one will care about that. It's all too long ago.'

'You might be surprised,' Josephine said, with more conviction than she felt; she was all too aware that her friendship with Archie gave her a more positive view of the law's interest in truth than was always justified. 'How does that phrase go? Old sins cast long shadows – and not everyone wants to brush them under the carpet.' James didn't say anything, and in the silence Josephine thought back over their conversation. 'When Matthew's mother talked about the sickness of his soul, she might not have meant your love for him,' she said. 'If what Evelyn told you about his cruelty is true, she might have been referring to that. Matthew's death, everything that went on, it might have been private within the family and nothing to do with you.'

She had meant to comfort him, but her thoughts seemed to have the opposite effect. James got up without answering, and Josephine found it impossible to tell if she had made any difference at all. 'Will you promise me one thing?' she asked.

'If I can.'

'Don't let Victor use whatever he thinks he knows to make you do something else you'll regret. It *was* Victor I heard trying to blackmail you, wasn't it?' James nodded. 'How could he know any of this?'

'I've driven myself mad trying to work that out. Frank said that Victor went looking for me at the Hall, so perhaps he saw me leaving the cottage. Maybe he just noticed the state I was in and how desperate I was at the train station and took a lucky punt. I was stupid to react in the way I did. Everything he said was so vague now I've thought about it, but I behaved like a guilty man because I am one.'

'So he might not know exactly what you've done?'

'No – but he'll find out soon enough now. I think you were right, though. Whatever he wants from me, it's got something to do with Hitch. After what you told me on the train, I sounded Vic out on the way up here whenever Frank was out of earshot – I said a few derogatory things about Hitch and the way he works, made it seem as if I had a grudge against him that goes way back, and Vic was egging me on. At one point, he started to talk about . . .'

Josephine was suddenly distracted from whatever he had been about to say by a pencil-thin line of grey rising up into the sky above the cypress grove. 'Please tell me that's not smoke,' she said, beginning to panic. 'What on earth can they be doing? Where's Marta?'

She got hurriedly to her feet but James caught her arm. 'I'll go. You stay here, just in case there's trouble, and don't worry about Marta – I'll find her.'

He was true to his word. After about ten minutes, which seemed like ten days to Josephine, he and Marta reappeared through the trees, looking absolutely furious and trailing Victor and Frank behind them. All of them were dishevelled from the terrain, and Marta's arm was bleeding through a tear in her shirt. As they drew closer, Josephine could see livid patches of red on their skin where they had been grazed or stung in the undergrowth. Victor showed no emotion whatsoever, but Frank seemed his usual cocky self. 'Thank God you're all right,' she said, glancing back to the grove, where the last traces of the fire had smouldered to nothing.

'No thanks to these two.' Marta gestured impatiently behind her. 'One of them thought it was a good idea to throw a cigarette butt into the bushes.'

'What's your problem?' Frank objected. 'I put it out, didn't I?'

'Not before time. And let's call it a day, shall we? I've had enough. We can start again in the morning.'

'You look exhausted,' Josephine said, when the others had wandered back to the pickup, 'and we need to get you back to the motel to bathe those cuts. Some of them are deep.'

Marta looked down at her injuries as if it were the first time she'd noticed them. 'How about you? Was everything all right with Bart?'

'I'll tell you all about that later. Right now, I just want to forget about the lot of them and concentrate on you.'

14

By Sunday morning, Penrose had more than enough evidence to arrest Donald Young on suspicion of his wife's murder. Spilsbury had telephoned first thing with the salient points of the post-mortem and forensic reports. Interestingly, Young's prints and his wife's were on the murder weapon, but the distance and direction of fire ruled out suicide; it was possible that they had struggled over the gun, but the condition of Evelyn's body made it impossible to say with certainty if there were any minor injuries to support the theory. The time of death had been narrowed down to between three and six on Monday afternoon, and accounts of Young's presence at his desk during those hours had varied; two of his colleagues were happy to testify that he was there, but – after his attempt to coerce Scott into offering a substitute weapon – any prosecution counsel worth his salt would be able to make such an alibi look less than solid to a jury. That desperate request would probably prove to be one of the most damning pieces of evidence against him, Penrose thought. Together with the very plausible motive that Young had inadvertently presented during his questioning the day before, the nuts and bolts of the investigation were coming together smoothly and efficiently, just as Superintendent Bell – and the Home Office – had hoped for.

So why, he wondered, couldn't he share their enthusiasm for a swift result? Why did a little voice inside his head keep offering alternative arguments? Young's prints were obviously going to be on a gun that belonged to him, and someone else could have used it and worn gloves. His grief and bewilderment had seemed genuine. An alibi existed, even if it was tenuous. If it *had* been Young, he would have removed the gun from the scene. And last but not least, Young, with his very personal motive, was the solution least damaging to the wider politics of the war – or, for that matter, to the politics of Hollywood. No one would remember Donald Young once the initial scandal had blown over, and Penrose was forced to come to the uncomfortable conclusion that – in his heart – he didn't want Selwyn Scott to be let off the hook quite so easily.

There was still no word from Selznick International, but he had expected the producer to bide his time in recalling his crew. In any case, Spilsbury's reports made that situation much less urgent than it had seemed during the long, dark hours of the night before, and Penrose offered up a prayer of thanks for the clarity of the morning and the ease of communication that he had come to take for granted; if the prime suspect *had* turned out to be one of the men in America, his job would have been made so much harder. He decided to book a transatlantic call to Marta's number for later that day, hoping that she and Josephine would be back from Monterey by then; even if the case was coming to a conclusion, it would be good to speak to Josephine and make sure that she was all right. As he left the stable block and walked over to the north entrance, the thought of adding the expense of another long-distance call to the army's hospitality put a new spring in his step.

Two police cars were waiting by the porch as requested, and Penrose used the short drive to the Youngs' cottage to bring Inspector Hughes up to date on the overnight developments. Hughes stopped short of saying that he had known Young was guilty all along but his face suggested as much, and Penrose didn't doubt that the Cambridgeshire force would be questioning why it had needed Scotland Yard to secure such an obvious result. They passed the folly, where the brilliance of the sun on the honey-coloured stone made yesterday's horrors seem almost unimaginable, and drew to a halt by the Youngs' picket fence. The sound of the cars brought the movement of a curtain from one of the downstairs windows – the room that Marion Plummer was in – and Penrose wondered if it was Georgia Wells again or another of her husband's faithful parishioners. He rather hoped that it would be the vicar's wife: her reaction to the arrest might be interesting, and he was keen to see if she could tell him more about Matthew Plummer and his suicide.

Hughes knocked loudly at the door and this time it was answered quickly, and by Young himself. 'I'm sorry to disturb you again so soon, Mr Young,' Penrose said, 'but we'd like to ask you some more questions.'

'Can't it wait? I'm looking after Marion and there's no one else here.'

Penrose hadn't really considered what day it was, but of course the faithful would have a prior engagement on a Sunday morning. If he took Young into custody, that would be an added complication. 'I'm afraid it can't. May we come in?'

'Yes, I suppose so.'

His obvious tiredness couldn't blunt the fear in his eyes as he pulled one door to and showed them into the sitting room opposite. 'How is your mother-in-law?' Penrose asked, glancing at the watercolour above the fireplace, which was a particularly well-executed likeness of Milton Hall, full of light and soft colours, and a welcome contrast to the bleakness of the unlit grate.

'There's no change. I keep imagining signs of improvement, but it's probably just wishful thinking.'

'Have you managed to find your pistol?' Penrose asked, although he already knew the answer. The change of subject sounded brusque to the point of heartlessness, but he saw no point in stringing this out with a conversation that Young wanted even less than he did.

'No, but I haven't had the chance to look properly, what with Marion to take care of and everything else.'

The excuse was as half-hearted as it was improbable. 'Mr Young, I must inform you that your fingerprints were found on the weapon that killed your wife. Do you still deny that the gun is yours?'

'Yes, I do.'

'Then how do you explain it?'

'Oh, I don't know.' He sank down onto one of the two armchairs, his head in his hands. 'I don't know how this can be happening. It must be mine, mustn't it? But I didn't use it to kill Evelyn. I *swear* I didn't. You've got to believe me. I've never taken that gun out of this house.'

'We have a witness who says you asked him to lend you an identical weapon. Is that true?'

The expression on Young's face was painful to watch, a disbelieving smile followed by a sense of betrayal that seemed to hurt him more than Penrose's accusations. 'No,' he said. 'No, that can't be right. Scottie wouldn't have said anything.'

'Is it true, Mr Young?' Penrose repeated quietly, although his question had just been indirectly answered.

Young nodded. 'I'm sorry, but I didn't know what else to do. I knew what it looked like and I knew what you'd think, and it was the only way I could put myself in the clear.' He looked imploringly at them, turning first to Penrose and then to Hughes. 'Someone must have taken it – that *must* be it. There's no other explanation. What about Bartholomew? Have you asked him?'

'We're still trying to get hold of him.'

'Well, perhaps *he* took the gun.'

'Did he come here, to your knowledge?'

'I don't know, but he could have done, couldn't he? Evelyn might have met him and brought him back here. It's possible, isn't it?'

'Yes, it's possible, and we'll certainly ask him about it.'

'Even if you do, he'll lie his way out of it. God, I wish Marion could talk to you. She'd tell you what sort of man he was.'

He was growing angry now, and Penrose brought the scene to a close before it could disturb the woman in the room across the hallway. 'Donald Young, I'm arresting you on suspicion of the murder of Evelyn Young . . .'

'But I was at work, I swear it. You've got this all wrong.'

'You'll be taken to the station now for further questioning. Do you understand?'

'Yes, but what about Marion? I can't just leave her.'

'I'll arrange for someone from the Hall to come and sit with her until more permanent arrangements can be made.' He signalled to Hughes to dispatch one of the constables waiting outside, and turned back to Young. 'She won't be left alone, I assure you. Is Mrs Wells due to come here today?'

'Yes, but not until later this afternoon. She's busy on Sundays.'

'Then I'll talk to her myself and make sure that everything is taken care of.'

'Does she have to know about this? What will she think of me?'

Penrose was surprised that Georgia Wells's opinion preyed so heavily on Young's mind when he had plenty of other things to worry about, but perhaps he had meant his mother-in-law; in either case, the answer was unlikely to bring him comfort. He took Hughes to one side and instructed him to take the suspect back to the station and conduct the first interview as soon as Young had a solicitor. 'Don't you want to do it, sir?' Hughes asked in surprise.

'You know just as much as I do about this, Inspector, and by rights it should be your case. We'll talk later. Ask one of your constables to stay here with Mrs Plummer until some-one from the Hall gets here.'

'Yes, sir.'

Hughes went about his business and Penrose took the opportunity to have a quick look round the house. There were two bedrooms upstairs, and he noted that the Youngs had obviously slept separately. The bigger room – at the front of the cottage with a view of the Hall – had a meticu-lous sparseness about it, as if the man who occupied it were poised to move out at any moment; it hardly testified to twenty years of marriage, but it was a trait that Penrose rec-ognised from other ex-military men, and he was pleased not to share it himself. The only thing not tidied away in drawers or cupboards was a group of half a dozen photograph frames that sat on a chest by the window. He walked over to look at them and saw Young in his army days, before the injuries that had brought him to Milton Hall. There was a wedding picture, too, of the groom and his best man, and the likeness of Selwyn Scott as Penrose had known him brought back a flood of new memories, none of them positive. The bride was poignantly absent from the image, and he remembered what Young had said about destroying the photographs of his wife when he thought she had betrayed him; three of the frames were empty, two of them broken, and Penrose felt the hurt and anger in the cracked glass and splintered wood.

By contrast, Evelyn Young's room was warm and welcoming – touchingly so – and not just because it faced the morning sun. She had obviously loved colour: the same joyful exuberance that he had admired in the garden was present here in the bedclothes and the cushions and the rugs, in the floral pictures on the walls and in a vase of dying roses on the dressing table. There was a small bookcase in one corner, and Penrose saw that she favoured women writers – Stella Gibbons, Elizabeth Bowen, Dorothy Whipple – with a smattering of P. G. Wodehouse and Beverley Nichols. It was pure speculation, and the kind of observation that he only ever allowed himself in private, but he imagined that someone with a collection like this was probably good company herself. A copy of *Rebecca* sat on the bottom shelf, and he wondered if she had bought it because of the Hall's significance to the story, but *Jamaica Inn* was there, too, and *The Loving Spirit*, so she must have been a du Maurier fan.

He stood and looked round, taking in the peace and personality of the room, sensing that here he would be as close as he could get to the real Evelyn Young, free of her mother's demands and expectations and of the marriage that – in Georgia Wells's words – she had found disappointing. To him, the room suggested a quiet self-containment and a pleasure in ordinary things, and he hoped that she had had time to enjoy it. There were no photographs on display, but when he picked up the book on the bedside table – an old, well-thumbed gardening manual that she had marked up with jobs to do and shrubs to plant – he discovered one used as a bookmark. It pictured one of Milton's grand rooms when it had been used as a hospital, and Penrose spotted the dead woman quickly amongst the nurses tending to the sick. The ward was full, its beds pushed close together, and more men – the walking wounded – stood around the edge or perched awkwardly on chairs. Some of them had bandages over their eyes, others nursed broken limbs, but all wore that same shy half-smile, caught somewhere between pride and guilt, life and death. Orderlies in uniform dotted the room, and he wondered which one was James Bartholomew. With no real reason for doing so, he slipped the photograph into his jacket pocket.

Back downstairs, he gently pushed open the door to Marion Plummer's room. She seemed to be sleeping peacefully, and he took a few steps inside to look around, but stopped when she suddenly opened her eyes and stared at him with an expression of abject terror. She tried to speak, but the sound came out as an anguished moan and Penrose retreated quickly, raising his hands to show that he meant her no harm. Unsettled, he closed the door behind him and was relieved to see a woman dressed in a maid's uniform coming up the garden path, obviously sent over from the house. 'It *was* him, then, was it?' she said without any further introductions. 'Evelyn didn't deserve that. She made the best of that marriage.'

'I'm afraid I can't tell you anything at this stage,' Penrose said diplomatically, imagining the gossip that must be circulating in the servants' quarters, 'but thank you very much for coming at such short notice.'

'They should bring her over to the Hall now she's got no one,' the woman said. 'It's the least she deserves after all those years of service. Milton was her life. Only right that she should die there.'

'That may be the best solution,' Penrose agreed, not knowing which to admire more – the woman's obvious respect or her down-to-earth practicality in the face of tragedy. 'But in the meantime, if you could wait until someone is free to take over, I'd be very grateful.' He left the house, but turned back as an afterthought. 'How far is Marholm from here? I'm looking for the church – could I walk there?'

'Oh yes. It's only a mile or so from this end of the estate. Carry on down the track to the gates and turn right onto the road. There's a footpath across the fields, and that's the shortest route. You can't miss it once you get to the village.'

'Thank you.' It was a spur-of-the-moment decision, but Penrose was glad that he had made it. Some time alone to think, free of the house and its ghosts, was just what he needed. For the first time, the brightness of the day had a seasonal edge to it, and the morning could have been fashioned from a list of everything that was most beautiful about an English autumn. His heart lifted as soon as he left the boundaries of the estate, with its ever-present reminders of both this war and the last, and by the time the rooftops of Marholm appeared up ahead, he had almost convinced himself that peace and sense would prevail.

His first view of the village church gave credence to the lie. St Mary the Virgin was one of those timeless, rural churches that seemed bound together by a way of life as well as by bricks and mortar. It stood bathed in sunlight, except for a squat Norman tower that fell under the shadow of a group of ancient cedar trees, and was separated from the surrounding meadows by a ha-ha, with cows grazing in companionable proximity to the dead. The morning service had obviously just come to an end, but most of the congregation seemed to have lingered in the churchyard, talking in small groups or to the vicar, and a sober atmosphere prevailed; it was a close-knit community, and Penrose guessed that much of the service had consisted of tributes to Evelyn Young and prayers for the health of her mother.

He couldn't see Georgia Wells with any of the parishioners, so he headed to the porch to look for her inside. The churchyard was striking, and the path to the entrance was lined on one side with old, elaborately carved gravestones, and on the other with rows of chest tombs, their names obscured by the ivy that crawled around and inside, invading the privacy of the dead. The vicar watched him curiously as he went in, quick to notice a stranger amongst the faithful. Inside, the church was light and welcoming, with a particularly impressive chancel. Mrs Wells was busy collecting hymn books, but stopped as soon as she saw him. 'Mr Penrose, is everything all right? Oh God, is it Marion? Has something happened?'

Her face showed such concern that he was pleased to be able to put her mind at rest, at least on that score. 'No, it's not Mrs Plummer, but I'm afraid we've had to take Mr Young into custody.'

She seemed shocked. 'That was very sudden. So Marion's alone – that must be why you're here.'

'Yes, it is. I've arranged for someone from the Hall to sit in

245

for now, but I thought you'd want to know so that you can make arrangements.'

'Of course. That was very thoughtful of you. I'll rally the troops – several of them were asking this morning if there was anything else they could do. You feel so helpless at a time like this, don't you? And now there's more trouble, it seems.'

'From what I gather, the staff would be happy to look after Mrs Plummer at the Hall if it's too much for you.' The words sounded patronising, and Penrose was quick to make amends. 'If Mr Young's absence leaves too many hours to fill, I mean. It would have to be cleared with the family and with the army, of course, but I can't imagine there'd be a problem, not for a woman who's given such long service.'

'It's an idea, but I think Marion would much prefer to stay in her own home if at all possible. Most of us would, wouldn't we? If Milton were going to be a hospital again, that would be different, but there's nothing at the Hall that we can't manage between us with a little goodwill and organisation.'

'That's very kind of you.'

'Not at all. Marion *must* get better. She really must.' She said it as if her own life depended on it, a dogged determination in her voice, then saw Penrose's surprise and pulled herself together, adding by way of explanation: 'There's already been far too much tragedy in the family – and now this. I find it so hard to believe that Donald would do such a thing.'

She resumed her task with the hymn books and Penrose made himself busy on the other side of the aisle. 'It would be helpful for me to have a more precise understanding of where Mr Young was on Monday afternoon,' he said. 'What time did you call on Mrs Plummer?'

She glanced at him, obviously wondering why that was

relevant, but didn't argue. 'It was just before three o'clock. There was no answer when I knocked, so I went round the back and let myself in that way. Nothing unusual in that – Marion has arthritis, as I believe I mentioned to you before, and she sometimes struggles to get about. But then I found her in her sitting room. To be honest with you, I thought I was already too late. There was still a faint pulse, though – very faint, so I telephoned for an ambulance straight away.'

'And what about Evelyn Young? Did you try to get a message to her?'

'Yes, of course. I telephoned the Hall as soon as I knew the ambulance was on its way and spoke to one of the footmen. It was the break in Evelyn's shift, apparently, and she'd told them that she was going back to the cottage to check on her mother. She did that most days, even when Donald was at home. I was hugely relieved that she was only a few minutes away.'

'But she never arrived?'

'No. The ambulance came very quickly, thank God, and they didn't waste any time. They wanted to get Marion to the hospital as soon as possible, and I waited behind so that I could follow on with Evelyn in the car. When she still didn't arrive, I rang the Hall again but there was no sign of her there and I didn't know what to do. In the end, I went to the hospital on my own and asked the staff at the Hall to tell Evelyn when she came back to work.'

'How long were you at the cottage?'

'Only for a few minutes. Twenty at the most – I wanted Marion to have someone with her, just in case she came round and was frightened.'

'Did you try to contact Mr Young?'

'Not until later, I'm afraid. To be honest, I'd forgotten he was starting work at the Hall that day, so it didn't occur to me. All I thought about was Evelyn.'

'When exactly did you speak to him?'

She thought carefully. 'About a quarter past five, I suppose. I telephoned the Hall again from the hospital to check on Evelyn. She wasn't back at work, but of course they'd just assumed that she was with her mother. They suggested that I speak to Donald, which I did – that's when he said that Evelyn had been called away.' She sighed heavily and took the hymn books from Penrose. 'I suppose I should have been more sceptical about that, Chief Inspector, but I was so worried about Marion that I just accepted it. And what other explanation could there have been?'

'Did he know about his mother-in-law by then?'

'No. He was horrified that no one had thought to tell him. They were very close – Marion treated him like the son she'd lost.'

'Would you mind if I asked you a few more questions about the family? There aren't many people who've known them as long as you have.'

'No, I don't suppose there are. By all means, if it helps.'

'Matthew's suicide must have been a terrible shock for Mrs Plummer. Do you know why he did it?' Georgia Wells's face clouded over, and Penrose instantly regretted the insensitivity of the question, but it was too late to take it back. Distracted by his more recent conversation with Scott, he had forgotten that the Wellses' son had been lost in the battle that blinded his friend. 'I'm sorry,' he said. 'It must bring back painful memories for you, too.'

'Yes, it does.'

'Then please don't feel you have to answer.'

'Why did you ask about it, though? How is Matthew's suicide relevant to Evelyn's death?'

'I'm not sure it is, but a witness who was there at the time suggested that Matthew was having a homosexual relationship with one of the orderlies, and that he killed himself before it could be exposed. Do you know if there's any truth in that?'

Perhaps it was his imagination, but she seemed to choose her words carefully. 'Marion certainly never mentioned anything like that to me, and I didn't hear it from anybody else. Even if it *were* true, how is it relevant?'

'The same witness also said that it was Evelyn who betrayed her brother's secret. The orderly in question was at Milton recently, and I'd like to eliminate every other possibility from—'

She interrupted before he could finish. 'You're not certain it *was* Donald, are you? Is this orderly another suspect?' There was something like hope in her voice, and Penrose suddenly remembered her hand on Donald Young's arm the night before and the detached way in which she had spoken about Evelyn; fleetingly, he wondered if there was anything between Georgia Wells and the grieving widower. 'It would be such a relief if Marion didn't have to face that as well as everything else.'

'As I said, we need to eliminate all possibilities. I gather Matthew and your son were very good friends?'

He hadn't meant it as a euphemism, but Georgia Wells was quick to object. 'What are you suggesting, Chief Inspector? I can't prove or disprove what you say about Matthew, but I will not have you making accusations about my son when he's not here to defend himself.'

'I wasn't suggesting anything, Mrs Wells – only that Matthew and Robert were friends. They joined up together, apparently?'

'That's right. And to go back to your earlier question, I always thought *that* was why Matthew killed himself. They ran away to war, you see. Robert didn't even say goodbye to us – he just took a suitcase and left. Michael and I wouldn't have known for certain but for Matthew writing to Marion. Robert was under age, you see – he didn't have to go and he knew we'd try to stop him if we could – but he followed Matthew in all their schemes. Matthew was always the ringleader – he admitted that much afterwards – but he came back and Robert didn't. Missing in action.'

Her eye strayed automatically to the church's war memorial, a large bronze plaque on the west wall with a cross in high relief at the centre and a stylised rose in each corner. There were ten names on the memorial, and Penrose was interested to see that Robert Wells was not amongst them. She knew he had noticed it but didn't offer an explanation, and he didn't press her; lots of missing men's families avoided having their loved one's name added to the official memorials, confirming something that they didn't even want to admit to themselves. 'That must have tested your friendship with Mrs Plummer,' he said instead. 'Part of you must have blamed Matthew for Robert's death.'

'You'd think so, wouldn't you, but strangely enough I didn't blame him. Perhaps it was naïve, but I truly believed that he'd looked after Robert once they were out there. I found comfort in the idea that Robert had died with a friend by his side. And anyway, none of that was Marion's fault. It was the most terrible time of my life, and I honestly don't know how I'd have got through it without her. When Matthew died, it was the least I could do to return the favour.'

'What can you tell me about that day?'

'Nothing. I wasn't there.'

'I was.' The voice came from behind them, and Penrose turned to see the vicar standing in the doorway.

'Michael, this is Mr Penrose, the detective I was telling you about.'

'Pleased to meet you.' They shook hands, and Wells – polite, but guarded – asked: 'How can I help?'

'You were at Milton when Matthew Plummer died?'

'Yes, I worked as chaplain to the soldiers there. It was down to me to break it to his friends and colleagues. My God, that was an awful day.'

'Do you remember an orderly called James Bartholomew?'

The Reverend Wells nodded. 'I certainly do. He was inconsolable, far beyond any words of comfort that I could offer. The military had to step in, for his own safety as well as everyone else's.'

'Why? What happened?'

'Well, for a Quaker and a conscientious objector, violence seemed to come very easily to him. He was out of his mind with anger, and he started to smash up some of the furniture in the day room – a couple of the men were innocent bystanders. Just cuts and bruises, but it could have been much worse.'

'But he didn't hurt anyone deliberately?'

'No. It was mostly anger turned in on himself – but there were threats, too.'

'Threats against whom?'

'Evelyn, her mother, God. As blasphemous as it might sound, I remember thinking that of the three of them, Marion was probably best placed to withstand them – she was always such a formidable woman.'

'Do you remember the threats?'

'Very clearly – that they'd be sorry, that he would make them pay, no matter how long it took. I gather there had been some sort of unhealthy attachment between Bartholomew and Matthew, and the Plummers had put a stop to it, but that wasn't common knowledge at the time. I didn't think for a moment that he meant any of it, and the anger didn't last, but he was moved on soon after that to avoid any more trouble.'

'Did you see Mr Bartholomew when he was back at Milton last weekend?'

'No. I had no idea he was here.'

Georgia Wells was looking at her husband as if it were the first time that any of this had been mentioned, and Penrose decided to leave them to it. 'Thank you for your time,' he said, getting up to go. 'You've both been very helpful. Mrs Wells, can I leave it to you to liaise with the Hall about Mrs Plummer?'

'Yes, of course. I'll go over there as soon as I've finished here. Is there anything else we can do?'

'Not for the moment.' He walked to the door, then thought of one final question and turned back to the vicar. 'Is Matthew buried here?'

'That wouldn't have been very popular with most of the congregation, Chief Inspector, even if I'd thought it appropriate. In any case, Matthew was cremated.'

'His ashes, then?'

Reverend Wells smiled in acknowledgement of Penrose's persistence, but his wife seemed close to tears. 'Let's just say there's a young oak tree on the north side of the churchyard that Marion Plummer always spent a lot of time by. It seemed the least we could do after her son's kindness to ours.'

15

Selznick's cagey but firm directive that the second unit should return to Hollywood first thing on Sunday morning turned out to be a blessing in disguise. Marta had spent an uncomfortable night after her battle with the undergrowth at Point Lobos, and the cuts that had concerned Josephine were less of a problem than the painful, blistering rash that had subsequently appeared on her arms and face; by eight o'clock, when they were due to leave the motel, she was running a slight temperature and neither of them had slept for more than a few hours. In the end, James – who seemed to have escaped any ill-effects – offered to drive them back and Josephine willingly agreed, hardly caring if the offer was made out of kindness, a reluctance to spend more time cooped up in a truck with Frank and Victor, or a wish to limit what she could say to Marta about their conversation from the day before; all she wanted was to get them both back to that cool, peaceful apartment, where they could shut the door on everything else. As far as Josephine could see, the only silver lining to the whole weekend was that the crew's two troublemakers were suffering from the same allergic reaction as Marta, and their symptoms appeared to be marginally worse.

'I'm so sorry,' Marta said, collapsing on the sofa back at Wilshire. 'You've come all this way and it's a fucking disaster.'

'That's hardly your fault.'

'But poison ivy – what a ridiculous thing to do. I should never have followed them in there – thank God I didn't drag you in with me.' She stood up again and walked over to one of the mirrors. 'Just look at my face – how can you even bear to look at me?'

Josephine had to laugh, in spite of the circumstances. 'If that's all you're worried about, then don't be. I still love you, but you're doing what you're told and going straight to bed.'

'Not before I've been upstairs to tell Hitch what's happened.'

'That can wait until tomorrow.'

'It really can't. It's only fair that he has some warning about all this before he goes to the studio and finds out from Selznick.'

'Then let me go. I'll explain the basics and you can meet with him in the morning – *if* you're feeling better by then.'

'All right, thank you. I won't argue, but I need a cold shower before I go to bed. It's the only thing that might stop me scratching myself to death.'

'Don't forget to keep all the clothes you've been wearing separate so they can be washed – and the first sign of this getting any worse and I'm calling the doctor.'

While Marta was in the shower, Josephine changed into something less creased and more authoritative to face the Hitchcocks in. She put a jug of iced water and some calamine lotion by the bed and was on her way out of the apartment when the telephone rang. She picked up the receiver, scarcely daring to believe her luck when the operator told her that she had a long-distance call from England, then heard Archie's voice – distant and a little distorted, but even more welcome than usual. 'Are you both all right?' he asked.

'Yes and no. We think Marta's got poison ivy, but it's too long a story for a transatlantic call. We've been to the coast.'

'Yes, I know. It's my fault you were hauled back.' Josephine listened while he explained the reason for his call, astonished that the conversation she had wished for should be so unexpectedly offered. 'It's less urgent than it was,' Archie admitted. 'All the evidence is pointing to the woman's husband and we've made an arrest, but we'll still need to speak to Marta's crew – and I wanted to make sure that you were both safe.'

'You've arrested her husband?' Josephine was confused. Not once in any of their conversations had James mentioned Matthew's father. 'Why have you done that?'

Even at this distance, she could sense his surprise. 'Well, I can't go into detail but the forensic evidence on the weapon is fairly conclusive.'

It sounded strange to hear a cushion described as a murder weapon. 'Archie, you can't arrest her husband. I know who killed Marion Plummer and it wasn't him. You were right all along to think of the crew. James Bartholomew did it. It wasn't planned, but she goaded him and he—'

Whatever feeble excuse she was about to make, Archie's words cut through it. 'What are you talking about? Marion Plummer isn't dead.'

'What?'

'She's had a stroke and she's seriously ill, but she isn't dead.'

'I don't understand. You said you were investigating the murder of a woman at Milton Hall.'

'I am, but it's not Marion Plummer. It's Evelyn Young.'

'Her daughter?'

'That's right. She was shot on Monday afternoon. So why are you talking about Marion Plummer? How do you even know who she is?'

'James talked to me about her. He said he'd suffocated her.'

The noise Josephine heard at the other end was either a crackle on the line or Archie's patience running out, and she knew which she would put her money on. 'Listen, Josephine – I haven't got time on a call like this to ask *how* you know these things, but you must tell me *what* you know. All of it – don't leave anything out.'

She did as he asked, repeating the details of her three conversations with James as succinctly as possible. 'So all this time he's been thinking that he killed her.'

'It takes a lot longer than a few seconds to suffocate someone, if he's telling the truth about that. But stress can bring on a stroke, so he's still culpable.'

'But it's not murder?'

Just for a moment, Josephine allowed herself a glimmer of hope on James's behalf, but it was short-lived. 'Not yet, but it's touch and go. And attempted murder is still serious, you know – the difference is just a matter of argument in court.'

'Not for James it won't be. The difference will mean all the world to him.'

Archie didn't seem to be listening. 'I can't believe I've been so stupid,' he said. 'Everyone's been telling me to look to him and I've ignored them all. Young's right – he could have taken the gun from the cottage now that we know he was there.'

Josephine was horrified. 'You're surely not suggesting he did both?'

'Face the facts, Josephine – the two women who betrayed his love for Matthew are attacked in the time that he's back at Milton Hall. Are you telling me that's a coincidence?'

'No, but his presence might have been the catalyst for Evelyn's murder. James told me that she liked him – perhaps the husband was jealous.' She could tell from his silence that her stab in the dark had hit home. 'Anyway, James has no idea that Evelyn's dead. He was hoping to have another chance to talk to her.'

'He could have been bluffing. That's a very clever deflection.'

And thinking back, Josephine realised that it was she who had raised that possibility, not James. 'Well, if it was a lie, it was a brilliant performance,' she said, a little belligerently.

'Where is he now?' Archie asked.

'How would I know? We've only just got back and I've been far too worried about Marta.'

'So he tells you all this and you don't do anything about it?'

'What did you want me to do? Slip on the handcuffs that I always carry with me and take him straight to the LAPD? Christ, Archie.'

'Sorry. That was unreasonable.' She forgave him instantly, knowing that his exasperation was rooted in his concern for her, but decided not to antagonise him any further by mentioning the crucifix that was for ever lost in the Arizona desert. 'So Bartholomew thinks that either mother or daughter forced Matthew to take his own life?' Archie clarified.

'That's right.'

'Where's this letter that Evelyn wrote to him? Did he show it to you?'

'No. He said he'd destroyed it.'

'How convenient, especially as the person who wrote it can't confirm his story.'

'I don't think it's a story, Archie – he didn't want to read that letter, but now that he has, he's desperate to find out what really happened in that room.'

'Except the two women who might know aren't in a position to talk.'

'He did mention one person who might be able to help.'

'Go on.'

'Daphne du Maurier. James used her as his go-between.'

She expected to have to explain, but Archie surprised her. 'So *she* was the little girl! How extraordinary.'

'You knew?'

'Only part of the story. One of the soldiers who was here at the time remembered a child but he obviously didn't know the significance of who she was.'

'Could you talk to her? Find out if she remembers anything?'

'Josephine, I can see you believe he's innocent, but I can't waste time interrogating novelists about what they might or might not remember from twenty-odd years ago. I've got a perfectly good suspect who needs to be brought into custody and questioned about two crimes, at least one of which we know he committed. That has to be my priority.'

'Even when you're as curious about what happened as I am?'

She knew him far too well, and heard him laugh as he relented. 'As it happens, I'm back in London soon. There's a meeting tomorrow morning that I have to attend, so they've recalled me, at least for the time being. If I get a chance, I'll leave a message with Daphne du Maurier's publisher and ask if I can speak to her. *If* I get time.'

'Thank you. If you do manage to speak to her, tell her

how sorry James is for putting her in that position. He's haunted by the idea that she might have witnessed something terrible.'

If she thought that would convince Archie of James's essential compassion, she was wrong. 'But the first thing I'll be doing is calling the LAPD,' he said. 'I'll have to get them to bring him in for questioning.'

'He might beat you to it. I believe him when he says he'll confess.'

'It will be in his favour if he does.'

'What will happen to him?'

'That depends on what he's done.'

'But if you confirm that he didn't kill Evelyn?'

'Then he should be praying that Marion Plummer makes a good recovery. You're not going to see him again, are you?'

At the back of Josephine's mind was a determination to let James know that he wasn't a murderer, and she wondered if a lie counted at such a distance. 'No, of course not. And don't worry about me. Just do what you need to do, and let me know what happens when you can.'

Marta came out of the shower as she replaced the receiver, and Josephine was horrified by the angry-looking marks on her skin. 'Does that feel any better?'

'Marginally, but I don't expect it will last. Who was that?'

'Archie. Believe it or not, he was calling about Milton Hall.'

Marta listened as she explained, torn between surprise and relief. 'Did you tell him about Bart?'

'Yes.'

'Thank goodness. I might be able to sleep now. I hate the thought of your being confidante to a murderer.'

'He might not be a murderer. The woman isn't dead – yet.'

'What?'

'I'll explain when you've had some rest. Now I'm going to see Hitch, so wish me luck.'

As it happened, she didn't need it. Hitch was out with Patricia, and Josephine was relieved to be able to talk to Alma on her own. 'We didn't expect you back so soon,' she said, leading Josephine through to the kitchen, where she was in the middle of making a roast dinner. 'Is everything all right?'

'Not really. I'm afraid that's why I'm here.'

'Please don't tell me there's more trouble. I've had to send Hitch out for ice cream with Pat to cheer him up. He's been so down today. There are problems back at home.'

'What's the matter?'

'Some of his former colleagues have been knocking him in the press for deserting his country.' Alma pushed a copy of a New York newspaper across the table, open at a page that carried an article about British actors and directors who were currently languishing in Hollywood, away from the perils of war. Central to the piece was a scathingly drawn cartoon, advertising a film called *Gone With the Wind Up*, directed by Alfred Hitchcock. 'He's so upset – we both are, of course, but Hitch in particular.'

'I can't help thinking that jealousy must have a lot to do with this,' Josephine said.

'I couldn't agree with you more. Several of the people who've spoken out have had creative differences with Hitch and I might have expected it of them, but it's Michael Balcon's comments that have really hurt him.' She stabbed angrily at a section of the article. 'We honestly thought he was a friend.'

Josephine skimmed the offending paragraphs, which didn't mention Hitchcock by name but referred to a plump junior technician whom Balcon had promoted to become one of the country's foremost directors, and who was now in Hollywood while the British were left short-handed to harness their industry to the war effort; she could only imagine how the article's bold use of the word 'deserters' had stung. 'It's so unfair,' Alma continued. 'Hitch has already agreed to make films with the Ministry of Information in London. He'll do his bit and I'm proud of him, but just because he doesn't shout it from the rooftops like the rest of them, he's branded a shirker.'

'He'll fight back, surely?'

'I hope so, although part of me asks why he should have to – how he helps his country is his business. It does make me angry, though. Thank God we *are* here. If I have my way, that's exactly where we'll stay.' She opened a vast refrigerator and took out a jug of something pink and full of fruit, passing a glass across to Josephine and pouring one for herself. 'It's more alcoholic than it looks, but I know I need one, and forgive me for saying so but you look like you do, too.'

'Is it that obvious? I'm afraid I'm bringing more bad news, but Marta wanted you both to know as soon as possible. She'd be here herself but she's not well.'

'Nothing serious, I hope,' Alma said, looking genuinely concerned.

'I hope not, but it might be if she doesn't take care of herself. We think it's poison ivy, and she got it from Point Lobos. Frank and Victor have the same symptoms.'

Alma groaned. 'That's all we need. Do you know, I'm beginning to think this film is cursed. Please give Marta our love and tell her not to come to work until she's well enough.'

'I will, but that's not all. You might want to sit down for

this.' She outlined the last couple of days for Alma, filling in the details of why the unit had been recalled and seeing no reason to hold back anything about James.

When she had finished, the director's wife sat in silence, stunned by what she had heard. 'It's funny – I was going to say that I can't believe it of Bart, then I realised that's not true. It's always been obvious that he feels things very deeply, and although I never would have said that he was violent, it actually doesn't surprise me at all that he'd lash out for the reasons you've suggested.'

'You'll keep it confidential, won't you?' Josephine said. 'There's bound to be a time when all his secrets are out in the open, but I'd hate this to make trouble for him any sooner than it has to.'

'Hitch will be devastated. He thinks so much of Bart.'

'He'd be pleased to know that, I think. He's convinced that you were going to sack him for what happened yesterday.'

'Not at all. He'll always get the benefit of the doubt from Hitch – well, from both of us. Did Mr Penrose say what will happen to him?'

Josephine shook her head. 'We didn't get the chance to talk about that in much detail. I expect Archie will be in touch if there's anything he can share.' She hesitated, wanting to get back to Marta but keen, too, to talk to Alma about the other matter that was worrying her. 'Can I ask you something else in confidence?'

'Yes, of course.'

'How well does Hitch know Victor Petrie?'

Alma shrugged. 'Not very well at all, as far as I'm aware. He met him for the first time when they started on *Rebecca*, and he hasn't said anything to me about him. Why do you ask?'

'Because Victor is blackmailing James, and I thought you should know. At best, it will cause trouble on set; at worst, I think it might involve you and Hitch personally.'

'What makes you think that?'

'Victor knows Lee Hessel. I saw them together on the *Super Chief*, and she'd already talked to me on the crossing about her father. She still seems very bitter about what happened to him.'

'Yes, I gathered that from her performance in the restaurant. There really is no truth in what she says, though – it's important to me that you believe that.'

'I do believe it. That's why I wanted to warn you to be careful.' She drained her drink and got up to go. 'I must get back to Marta. I'm sorry to have laid so much trouble at your door.'

'Not at all. I appreciate your loyalty, and so will Hitch. A little intrigue from an adversary closer to home might actually take his mind off the things that he *can't* change at the moment – and forewarned is forearmed. Give Marta our love, won't you?'

'Yes, of course.'

The telephone rang as they were saying goodbye and Josephine left Alma to answer it, but stopped at the door when she heard the anxiety in the other woman's voice. 'Hitch? Where are you? I expected you back by now.' There was a long pause, and then Alma spoke again, more troubled than ever. 'Hitch, slow down – you're making no sense. What do you mean? She can't have just vanished. All right, all right – tell me exactly where you are and I'll come and find you.'

When she replaced the receiver and turned to Josephine, the colour had drained from her face and she seemed to have aged a year for every minute of the phone call. 'It's Patricia,' she said, making an obvious effort to keep the panic out of her voice. 'Hitch went off to the kiosk to get them another drink, and when he came back she was gone.'

16

'Nice work, Penrose.' Alexander Bell perched on one of the empty desks in the CID office and smiled broadly at his Chief Inspector, resembling a proud parent at the end of term. 'Quicker than I dared hope, and a damned sight cheaper than hauling someone back from America to face charges.'

'Thank you, sir, but I wanted to talk to you about that. I didn't realise you were still here.' Penrose saw the Super brace himself for whatever complication was about to present itself and chose his next words carefully, hoping to imply that his information had come from somewhere more official than a phone call to his closest friend. 'Something else has cropped up during the questioning, though – something we might want to take a look at.'

'Oh yes?'

'James Bartholomew, the orderly who was back at Milton with the film crew . . .'

'I know who he is, Penrose – I'm not likely to forget those telephone bills.'

'Well, there's a suspicion that he assaulted Marion Plummer, the victim's mother.'

'What sort of suspicion? Spit it out, man – it's not like you to beat around the bush.'

'He admitted as much to someone else on the film set.'

'Why would he do that?'

'I gather it's preying on his conscience. He's under the impression that Mrs Plummer is dead.'

'So he fled the scene, thinking he'd got away with murder?' Penrose nodded. 'And is this witness reliable? No grudges against Bartholomew that we should know about?'

The words were hopeful, and Penrose was sorry to have to dash them. 'Completely reliable. I've no doubt whatsoever that Bartholomew made the confession.' He gave a few more details of Bartholomew's time at Milton and the possible motives behind the assault. 'Obviously it's hearsay at the moment, but I think we should check it out.'

'Of course we should. Have you spoken to the hospital yet? Any signs of assault or a struggle when she was brought in?'

'I tried just now, but the doctor who treated Mrs Plummer isn't back on shift until tomorrow. I'll call again then, and I'll also speak to the woman who found her and got her to the hospital. It's too late to disturb her now.'

'And how is Mrs Plummer? Will she live?'

'It's touch and go.'

Bell stared warily across the desk at him. 'Are you muddying the waters, Penrose? I'd rather have the bad news all at once, so if you're going to tell me that you suspect Bartholomew for the Young killing as well, please do it now.'

'I'm keeping an open mind, sir. If there's any truth in the rumours surrounding Matthew Plummer's death, then Bartholomew had a clear motive for both attacks, and he certainly had the opportunity to kill Evelyn Young.' He thought back to Josephine's words and her conviction that Bartholomew was telling the truth; she didn't give her trust easily and he was inclined to have faith in her judgement, but there was too much at stake here to rely on instinct. 'And Donald Young is still adamant that he's innocent,' he added. 'I spoke to Inspector Hughes earlier, and they've got nothing new from him yet. The clock's ticking before we have to charge him or let him go.'

'All right. See what you can find out, and if you have to go back up there to question Young again, so be it. And get our American friends to bring Bartholomew in.'

'Already requested, sir. I'm hoping to hear from them soon.'

'Good, but don't wait up all night for it. I need you firing on all cylinders tomorrow, so go home and get some sleep. That's an order.'

It was an order that Penrose was happy to comply with. He left the Yard on foot, glad of some fresh air and – despite the new restrictions – finding the familiar freedom of London's streets a refreshing contrast to the claustrophobic atmosphere at Milton Hall. The beauty of the night sky came as a shock to him in the city, hidden as it usually was by the glare of the street lights, and he wondered how long the small, unexpected treasures of the blackout would compensate for its inconvenience. He reached into his pocket for his torch – allowed for the time being as long as the beam was pointed downwards and covered in tissue paper – and walked back to his flat in Maiden Lane, a narrow cobbled road running parallel with the Strand. The brief journey was punctuated by voices swearing aloud in the darkness as they missed their way or tripped over a carelessly parked bicycle, but the frustration was still good-natured, one of those shared endeavours of wartime that people were only now beginning to take seriously. The restaurants he knew so well were black and faceless, though, and the noise coming from inside seemed strangely disembodied and unreal, a relic of past pleasures to which they were no longer entitled. Usually, at this time of night, he'd be battling through the crowds spilling out of the Vaudeville Theatre, and he was surprised by how much the theatre's locked doors saddened him: such a small thing in the grander scheme, but such an important one, and he took more hope than he perhaps should have from the news that the restrictions on entertainment were soon to be lifted.

His flat was on the top floor of a four-storey building that he shared with his cousins, Lettice and Ronnie, and their housekeeper, Dora Snipe. He let himself in to the sound of a gramophone and found the door to the downstairs flat amiably ajar, as it invariably was whenever Lettice was at home. He put his head round the door to say hello, and found his cousin sitting in the middle of the living-room floor, framed by a backdrop that could easily be mistaken for the back-stage area in any West End theatre. The Motley sisters were two of the most sought-after stage and costume designers in London, and Penrose was more than used to tripping over a mannequin in the hall or doubling as a model for their latest male lead, but the scene in front of him took working at home to another level: every surface was covered in dresses of varying sizes and fabrics, and the rug in front of the fire seemed to have had Selfridges' entire shoe department tipped unceremoniously onto it. 'Archie! What a lovely surprise,' Lettice said through a mouthful of pins. She finished the hem she was working on and stood up to give him a hug. 'Mrs Snipe and I began to think you'd moved without telling us. Has Virginia kicked you out?'

Penrose smiled. 'No, not yet. She's away for a few days, taking Teddy back to school in Cambridge.'

'Then you can stay and have a drink with me. It's nice to see you, and I've got a long night ahead of me working on this lot. Whisky all right for you?'

'Perfect. Have you heard from Ronnie lately?' Lettice's sister had been in New York for the past month, working on a Broadway production that their company had been commissioned to design, and Penrose knew that Lettice was worried about her.

'Only once since everything kicked off here. She's perfectly all right and the play is going well, but God knows when she'll be back.' Lettice sighed as she passed him his drink. 'It's all starting to fall apart, isn't it?'

The comment was uncharacteristically despondent; Lettice was the most optimistic person he knew, irritatingly so at times for someone of his own, more cynical, disposition, and he knew how deeply the separation from Ronnie must be affecting her, personally and professionally: completely different in character and outlook, the sisters were not only perfectly matched creative partners but also the best of friends. 'They'll be back soon enough,' he said, unconsciously pairing Lettice's concern for Ronnie with his own for Josephine, 'and at least we know they're safe over there.'

'Yes, I suppose that's something,' she agreed, with an unconvincing brightness in her voice. 'Have you eaten? There's some cold roast pork left over from lunch. I could make you a sandwich.'

It was invariably the first or second question on Lettice's lips, and Penrose suddenly realised how hungry he was. 'I'd love a sandwich, but I'll make them. Will you join me?'

'I shouldn't, but I will – only because I'm worried, though.'

'Of course.' Penrose grinned, and went through to the tiny kitchen. 'Where's George?' he called.

'Still at the theatre.' Lettice's fiancé was an actor and manager, who had recently started directing. The couple lived and breathed theatre, and Penrose occasionally envied the way in which their shared careers made them so close; until Virginia, whose past gave her an intuitive understanding of his darkest days at work, his profession had kept him detached from most of the people he loved. 'The reopening has taken us all by surprise, as you can see. We never dared to hope they'd change their minds quite so soon.'

'Good news, though.'

'It certainly is, and God knows we need some.'

He brought their supper through, generous doorsteps of which Mrs Snipe would have been proud. 'Have you got a copy of *Rebecca*?' he asked, glancing at Lettice's bookshelf.

'Pining for Josephine already?'

'No, don't be silly. I need to know who published it.'

'We do have a copy, but I think George has taken it with him.'

'Just in case he gets bored with his play? That doesn't bode well.'

Lettice stared at him, exasperated. 'There was a time when you used to take an interest,' she said, a serious edge now to the familiar teasing. 'That *is* the play. He's directing *Rebecca* at the Queen's. They've just started rehearsals.'

Penrose looked at her with mixed emotions, scarcely able to believe his luck but realising, too, how detached his life had become from his cousins' over the last few months, and how much he missed them. 'I'm sorry,' he said, a little sheepishly.

'It's all right. You're forgiven. Why do you need Daphne's publisher?'

'To get in touch with her. It's to do with the case I'm working on.'

'Of course it is. And I don't suppose you can tell me anything about it?'

'Not yet, but you'll be the first to know when it's over. Do you think George could get a message to Daphne? I need to speak to her, and it's quite urgent.'

'He can do better than that. She's breathing down his neck at rehearsals at the moment, with a script change in every other speech. I'm sure he'd be grateful if you distracted her for a while. I'll talk to him about it in the morning.'

17

Marta was still sleeping soundly when Josephine went down-stairs to check on her, before returning to the Hitchcocks' penthouse, where she had agreed to wait in case Patricia came home before her parents had the chance to find her. There was an optimism in the phrase that Alma had used in making the request, and Josephine was happy to go along with it: the alternative was unthinkable, and she passed the time anxiously and unproductively in thoughts of how she might have averted disaster by speaking up sooner, should her worst fears prove to be justified.

The telephone rang and she grabbed the receiver before it had even finished its first peal. 'Hello?'

'Josephine, it's Alma. I'm calling from the beach. Is she back yet?'

The disappointment was overwhelming, and only when she felt it did Josephine realise how firmly she had believed that Hitch would have found his daughter by the time that Alma got to him, innocently distracted by a dog or a game or a new playmate, by all the things that children were drawn to on a trip to the beach. 'No, I'm sorry. There's been nothing. You haven't found anything?'

It was a ridiculous question, one of those obvious state-ments that people make in a crisis when they don't know what else to say, but Alma didn't give it the contempt it deserved. 'No, nothing at all. We've been up and down the beach and we've asked everyone nearby, but nobody can tell us anything.'

'Are the police there yet?'

'They've just arrived, and Hitch is beside himself. His daughter is missing and still he can barely bring himself to speak to them because of this ridiculous phobia he's got about policemen.' She stopped herself and took a breath, and Josephine sensed the strain that she was under: it was the closest that either of the Hitchcocks had ever come to criticising the other, at least in her presence. 'It was stupid of me, but I left in such a panic that I didn't think to bring a photograph and it's the first thing they asked for. Could you choose a couple from the ones we've got out and run them down here? I know it's a lot to ask, but . . .'

'Don't be silly. It's nothing. I'll do it right away. Tell me exactly where you are.' She made a note of the address and directions on how to get there, then brushed away Alma's thanks. 'If Pat should come back while you're gone . . .'

'Don't worry. I'll leave a note on the door just in case and tell the concierge to take her to Marta if she turns up downstairs.'

'But if Marta's ill, she won't want to be bothered.'

'Of course she will. I'll let her know what's happening on my way out. And it's Patricia who'll be bothered when she sees the poison ivy.' Alma gave something that was halfway between a laugh and a sob, and Josephine spoke more seriously. 'Try not to worry. We'll find her, I'm sure of it.'

'Thank you. We'll see you as soon as you can get here.'

She rang off and Josephine went quickly round the apartment, choosing two photographs that seemed to have been taken recently and finding it poignant in the present circumstances that a man who was famed the world over for his imagery should surround himself at home with ordinary photographs of his family, photographs that any father and husband might have taken. Downstairs, she collected the car keys and explained the situation to a bewildered Marta, relieved to find her looking so much better than when they had arrived home. 'Are you sure you don't want me to come with you?' Marta asked. 'I could drive you there at least – you've only been here for forty-eight hours and you'll soon have seen as much of California as I have. I've had more sleep, too – you must be exhausted.'

'Not really. I lost all thought of tiredness as soon as I heard Patricia was missing. Anyway, it's important that you rest, and the last thing you need is more sun. Stay here, just in case she comes home.'

Marta caught her hand. 'You're worried that's not going to happen, aren't you?'

Josephine nodded. 'I feel cold every time I think about her. I was convinced that woman meant her harm, and I should have said something to Alma sooner.'

'Don't you dare blame yourself for this. And anyway, we don't *know* that's what's happened.'

'I'd better go. They're waiting for these.' She picked up the photographs she had chosen, her attention caught again by the one on top – a picture of Patricia with her parents on board the *Queen Mary*, presumably taken during one of their earlier journeys to or from America. She seemed to have inherited their genes in equal measure, bearing a strong resemblance to both her father and her mother, but the most striking thing about the little girl was her smile and the sense of adventure that Josephine had seen for herself on the crossing from England; even if she had never met the family, she would have known from that one photograph that Patricia's happiness and self-confidence stemmed entirely from an unquestioning faith in her parents' love. 'I'll let you know if there's any news.'

'Just let me know that you're all right – and promise me you'll be careful.'

'I will.'

Josephine had been far more apprehensive of the drive than she had admitted to Marta, but Alma's directions – straight down Wilshire Boulevard until she reached the ocean – proved to be as simple to follow as she had promised they were, and Josephine made the journey in good time, arriving at the coast in less than half an hour. Santa Monica had the ease of a small town combined with the high spirits of a holiday resort, and in any other circumstances she would have relished her visit, but today she had no appetite for the long stretch of beach or the roller coasters and shooting galleries that were delighting couples and families in either direction. She saw Hitch's baby Austin as soon as she arrived at Ocean Park, out of place amongst the Cadillacs and Packards but mercifully easy to find, and she parked in the closest available space. Alma must have been watching out for her because she was beside the car before Josephine had the chance to get out and look for her. 'Thank you for coming so quickly,' she said, 'and these are perfect.' She looked down at the photographs, and Josephine saw her choke back a sob. She put a hand on Alma's shoulder, and waited for her to regain her composure. 'I'm sorry,' she said eventually. 'I was holding myself together, but seeing her like this – happy and safe with us . . .' She held up the pictures, as if to emphasise what was at stake. 'I don't know what we'll do if we've lost her. I really don't.'

'What can I do to help? Would you like me to take these to whoever's in charge?'

'No, I'll do it. It will help to keep me focused. Will you let Hitch know where I am? I've had to make him go and sit down. He was about to give himself a heart attack, rushing about in this heat. And he blames himself, of course.' She stared out to sea, unwilling to meet Josephine's eye. 'It's awful, I know, but I can't bring myself to reassure him that it's not his fault – not yet, not until I know she's all right. He's over there, by the kiosk.'

Josephine found the director sitting in the shade of an umbrella. He looked utterly defeated, his face red from the sun and his shirt soaked in sweat; as she got closer, she could see that he was breathing heavily, no match for the exertion of looking for his daughter or the state of panic in which he found himself. She remembered the last time she had met him, three years ago in Portmeirion when they were discussing the terms of his filming her novel; a series of murders had taken place there, all with their roots in his work, and it had surprised her then how ill-equipped he had seemed to cope with the fear that he was so good at creating in others. But not even that could compare to the desolation she saw in his face now; this was personal, and if it turned out badly, she knew it would destroy him. 'I've given the photographs to Alma,' she said, sitting down next to him. 'She's taking them to the police. That will help.'

'Thank you.' He tried to smile, but the lie was too much. 'My job is to see things,' he said instead, 'and I missed my daughter being abducted. Alma would never have missed it. Pat would have been safe with her.'

'You don't know she's been abducted,' Josephine insisted. 'From what I saw when we were travelling, she's adventurous and very independent. She might have gone off to explore.'

'Yes, she does that all the time. We chose somewhere safe to live to make sure that she could.'

'Well, then – perhaps she just went further than she meant to and got lost.'

'But she always tells us where she's going. Always. You're very kind,' he added, making it sound as if it were an affliction to be pitied, 'but Alma told me about Miss Hessel.'

'Did you mention her to the police?'

'Alma did, yes.' He sighed, and took a handkerchief out of his pocket to wipe the perspiration from his face. 'I didn't know her father was ill, you know. I would never have let him on set if I had. Contrary to what people will tell you, the film *isn't* everything. I care about the people I work with, and William was a good friend. We'd grown up together in the business. He was a competent actor, but a very fine man. I understand why his death was such a blow to his daughter.'

'Why is she so convinced it was your fault?'

'There were one or two rumours in the press just after he died, but it's hard to say if she started them or vice versa. And rumours aren't unusual – several people have a grudge against me. These bothered me, though, because I liked William so much. I even tried to speak to his doctor to find out one way or the other if I could have been responsible, but he wouldn't discuss it. We wrote to Miss Hessel to give our condolences, but she never replied – until that night on the *Queen Mary*, of course. Alma thinks she wants money.' He looked at her, interested in her silence. 'You don't agree?'

278

'I think it's more personal than that.' She remembered what Lee had said about making the Hitchcocks suffer, but didn't torment Hitch by repeating it. 'Grief is a terrible thing. You're not yourself, are you? Sometimes not for years.'

'I'm afraid I wouldn't know,' Hitch admitted. 'My father died when I was fourteen, but we weren't particularly close. Everyone I love is still here, so all I can do is imagine it – and I'm certainly imagining it now.' His expression darkened, but Josephine resisted the temptation to fall back on platitudes again. 'Ironic, isn't it? I once made a film about a couple whose child was kidnapped.'

'Yes, I saw it.'

'I was quite pleased with it at the time, but I realise now how inadequate it was. Perhaps I'll remake it one day, and get it right.' From what Josephine could recall, the film had captured quite brilliantly the fear of the child concerned; as if following her thoughts, Hitch added, out of the blue: 'I hope she's not frightened. When I was a child, I woke up one evening and found that my parents weren't in the house. I had no idea where they were or if they were ever coming back, and I've never forgotten it. I felt so abandoned. We made a vow, Alma and I, that we would always be there for Patricia until she was older, that she'd never call out for us and find us gone.'

Josephine was deeply moved by Hitchcock's sadness and longed to say something to help, but she sensed that more hollow reassurances wouldn't be welcome. 'I don't know if Alma told you, but Lee Hessel is friends with Victor Petrie,' she said, changing the subject to something more practical. 'Is he one of the people who might have a grudge against you?'

Hitch shrugged. 'David hired him. I barely know the man.'

Once again, Josephine wondered what James had been about to tell her at Point Lobos, before the fire interrupted them. Her conversation with Archie had unsettled her where James was concerned; without trying to, he had managed to make her feel naïve for having such faith in someone she barely knew, and – as much as she tried to tell herself that Archie would feel the same if he had met James – a little sliver of distrust had got under her skin and refused to be dislodged. By the sound of it, Victor could have no possible motive to take against Hitchcock, unless it was purely in support of Lee, and she wondered if James was manipulating her by inventing a resentment that simply didn't exist.

Hitch looked at his watch. 'She's been missing for three hours now.'

Her thoughts ran straight back to the child who had gone missing from her own Suffolk village, to that dreadful watching of the clock that brought more fear and less hope with every single movement of the second hand. She was torn over whether to stay or go back to the apartment, reluctant to leave Hitchcock and Alma to their worst nightmare, but conscious that Marta would be worried and still seduced by the faintest possibility that Patricia might return home safe and sound. She scoured the beach to her left, wondering if Alma was all right, and her attention was drawn to a couple walking along the shoreline from the direction of the amusements. It was the woman she recognised, rather than the little girl who was holding her hand. 'What's Patricia wearing today?' she asked, careful not to raise his hopes.

'A yellow sundress with a hat to match.'

'Thank God. Look.'

Hitchcock leapt from his chair, calling his daughter's name at the top of his voice. When she heard him, Patricia dropped the hand she had been holding and ran across the sand to meet him, laughing with delight and obviously unharmed. Lee Hessel made no attempt to stop her or, Josephine noticed with interest, to leave them to it. She glanced round, keen that Alma shouldn't have to suffer a moment longer, but she was already on her way over, drawn to the commotion of delight, and Josephine followed. Alma hugged her daughter tightly, then turned to the woman who had taken her. 'What the hell do you think you're playing at?'

Patricia looked at her mother in surprise, bewildered by her parents' tears of relief and clearly oblivious to the danger that everyone had imagined for her. 'It's all right, Mummy. We had fun while Daddy went to fetch you. Lee took me to the park like you asked.'

'Is that what she told you?'

Patricia nodded. Hitchcock put a protective arm around her shoulder and led her over to Josephine, then went back to stand by his wife. Lee stared defiantly at him. 'Do you understand now how it feels to lose something precious? The thing that you love most in all the world?'

'Yes, Miss Hessel, I do. The last three hours have been a living hell for both of us.' He glanced at Alma and she took his arm, her anger and any recriminations against her husband completely overcome by the knowledge that her daughter was safe. 'Thank you for giving us our life back. I only wish I could return the favour.'

The quiet sincerity of his words did more to defuse Lee Hessel's hatred than any amount of threats or allegations. Without another word, she turned and walked away, and

Josephine could see that she was crying. 'Do you want me to get the police?' she asked.

Hitchcock shook his head. 'Not for her, if that's what you mean. We must let them know that Patricia is safe, of course, but we'll tell them that she was lost and that someone brought her back to us – if Alma agrees?'

'Yes, I do. Pat is obviously fine.' She removed her daughter's sun hat and kissed the top of her head. 'We've got everything we need right here. There's no sense in making things worse.'

Josephine hesitated, wanting to raise the possibility that Lee might try the same thing again if she were allowed to get away with it, the next time with more serious consequences – but somehow she knew that she wouldn't. Now that she had made the Hitchcocks suffer, albeit briefly, her rage was spent, and Josephine felt sorry for her. She turned and walked up the beach, keen to give the family some privacy to enjoy their reunion and wondering if there was anything she could say to make Lee feel less desolate. She could still see her up ahead and she quickened her pace, then paused when she saw Lee stop and exchange a brief word with someone else before moving on again and disappearing into the crowd. To her astonishment, the person Lee had spoken to was James.

Josephine called his name, hoping that he wouldn't run when he saw her, but he turned and waited for her to catch up with him. 'What are you doing here?' she asked, a little breathless. 'Why were you talking to Lee Hessel? Did you have something to do with what she was up to?'

'What?' His disappointment in her was obvious, and he spoke angrily. 'Of course not. I didn't even know the woman existed until you told me about her. I was trying to help. I made her bring the girl back.'

'But how did you even know she had her if you weren't involved?'

'Victor told me. They were planning it together, but the opportunity to take her came sooner than they expected. Lee called Victor to come and meet them, but he's too ill, so he thought he could make me do it. I agreed because I wanted to talk her out of it – and I did, didn't I? Lee was never in it for the money like Victor was. She did it because she wanted to punish Hitch for taking what she loved, and God knows I understand how that feels. You do believe me, don't you?' Josephine had no idea how to answer him, but her silence did the work for her. 'Of course you don't, and why should you? Why would you believe that a murderer could ever do anything good?'

'You're not a murderer. Not yet, at least.'

'What do you mean?' He stared at her in disbelief. 'I told you what I did, so why would you say . . .'

'Marion Plummer isn't dead. She had a stroke, but you didn't kill her. There's a small chance she'll pull through.'

'I don't understand.' In his distress, the words sounded almost petulant. 'She was dead, I know she was.'

'You *thought* she was, and you panicked. Did you stop to check? Did you feel for a pulse?'

'No, I just wanted to get out of there.'

'There you are, then. She was alive when you left her, and someone found her in time. They saved her, and that might save *you* if you hand yourself in now and tell the truth about what happened.' Josephine longed to tell him about Evelyn Young, hoping that his surprise would be obvious and justify her belief in him, but she knew that she had already said too much; if she jeopardised Archie's questioning by revealing his

283

trump card, she could say goodbye to their friendship. 'You need to give yourself up, James,' she said. 'If you do it now, before they track you down, it will work in your favour.' She had assumed that her news would make him more willing to hand himself over and let justice take its course, but it seemed to be having the opposite effect. 'Now's your chance,' she urged. 'There are policemen right over there, and they'll be fair to you, I promise. I'll even come with you if it helps.' He hesitated, and she could see the fear in his eyes. 'I was wrong to trust you, wasn't I? You're not going to confess to anyone. You have no intention of doing the right thing – so I'll have to do it for you.'

She turned and left him before he could try to stop her, furious with him and with herself for proving Archie right, but by the time she had found a policeman and convinced him of her story, James Bartholomew was nowhere to be found.

18

Perhaps it was down to his family, perhaps simply to his own sense of history, but there was little that Penrose found more appealing than the magic of an empty theatre. He looked around the Queen's exquisite auditorium, admiring its beautifully judged elegance: the restful cream and gold decor; the three tiered boxes on either side of the stage; the baroque domed ceiling, adorned with eight seated muses. Sprague's design was magnificent, but even the most run-down of old theatres would have given him the same thrill: standing there with no one but the theatre's ghosts was like taking a breath from the outside world, caught between night and day, reality and fantasy.

As his eyes accustomed to the semi-darkness, he saw a woman sitting in one of the stalls with a notebook on her knee, framed by the corner of the proscenium, and it reminded him of the solitary figure in the Edward Hopper painting that he loved so much. She was watching him intently, and she stood to greet him when she saw that he had noticed her. 'Chief Inspector Penrose?'

'That's right.'

'A policeman who appreciates theatre architecture – even more intriguing.' She held out her hand. 'Daphne du Maurier.'

The writer was younger than he had expected, slender in a dark trouser suit, with a high forehead, appraising eyes and a wide, expressive mouth. 'It's good of you to see me at such short notice,' he said.

'Well, it's not every day that Scotland Yard comes calling – and George gave you a very good reference.'

Penrose smiled and waved to George, who was in the wings, talking to a woman who looked vaguely familiar. 'Who's in the cast?' he asked.

'Do you know the book?'

'I can't think of anyone who doesn't.'

'Celia Johnson is Mrs de Winter, Owen Nares is Max, and Margaret Rutherford is playing Danvers.'

It was Rutherford whom he had recognised backstage. 'That's an interesting choice.'

'Yes, it is. I wasn't sure at first, but George convinced me and he was absolutely right. She's actually trying to get under the skin of the woman and play her as she is in the book.' She tucked the script she was holding into her notebook, and Penrose noticed how heavily annotated it was, remembering what Lettice had said the night before. 'What did you want to talk to me about?'

'Milton Hall in 1917.' He smiled apologetically when he saw the surprise on her face. 'It's a long time ago, I know, and you were very young, so I'll quite understand if you don't remember much about it.'

'On the contrary. I remember it very vividly and I've been thinking about it a lot recently, with everything that's happened to *Rebecca*. There would be no Manderley without Milton.'

'So I gather. Do you know that a film crew was there last week?'

'Yes.'

'Well that's why I'm here. Someone in that unit was there in 1917, too, and he remembers meeting you. I'm hoping you might also remember him.'

'This sounds far more interesting than I dared to hope. Who is he?'

'His name is James Bartholomew.' She looked blank, and Penrose was disappointed. 'Perhaps you'll remember if I tell you more about it. Will we be in the way if we stay here?'

'Actually, do you mind if we walk while we talk? It always helps me think, and anyway, I could do with some fresh air.' She raised her voice deliberately, so that it carried to the stage. 'And no doubt the director will be pleased to see the back of me for a while. I've got more changes for him this afternoon.'

'Take as long as you need,' George called back, answering in the same wry spirit. 'It's nice to see you, Archie. Don't be such a stranger.'

Daphne led the way over to a set of steps by the side of the stage, then swore and retraced her footsteps, scrabbling under the seat for her gas mask. 'I don't think I'll ever get used to the damned thing,' she said, as they went out through the wings to the stage door. 'What a bloody mess we're in.'

They walked round onto Shaftesbury Avenue, where a gang of workmen sticking paper trellising onto the shop windows seemed to underline her sentiment. 'I feel like I've been rescued,' she admitted, 'and we've only just started working on the play.'

'It must be satisfying to adapt your own book.'

'Yes, but it's difficult in ways I never expected. I finished the script in June and I thought that was that, but then you bring it to the table and find out what's wrong with it. There was nowhere near enough dialogue for the stage, and now

I've written more, it feels as if I'm changing the story.' She sighed heavily. 'Still, it could be worse – I could be at home. My husband and I have just moved to Hythe and the house is in chaos. The children are driving me up the wall, so it's nice to be away from them for a bit.' His face must have given him away, because she added: 'Sorry – I didn't mean to shock you. That wasn't very maternal, I suppose, but each to her own. Do you have children at home?'

'A boy and a girl, ten and three. I'm afraid I'm smitten.'

'Of course you are. You're a policeman – you work long hours.'

Penrose laughed, surprised by how easy he found her to talk to. 'Actually, they're my partner's children. It's complicated, but I missed out on my elder daughter's childhood, so I suppose I'm making up for it.' He paused, then conceded her point. 'When I'm at home, that is.'

In Piccadilly, work had begun on protecting the city's landmarks, and they stopped to watch as men on ladders clothed Eros in a timber construction filled with sandbags, both of them wanting a final look at the statue before it disappeared indefinitely from view. 'So, dear old Milton,' Daphne said, resuming their walk in the direction of Green Park. 'How can I help? I'm sorry I didn't remember the name you gave me. Who is he?'

'He was an orderly at Milton during the war. I'm told that he asked you to deliver a gift for him.'

'You mean my magician?' Her face lit up at his explanation. 'That's what I've always thought of him as – he told me his name but I would never have remembered it. Of course I remember *him*, though. I've always wondered what happened to him.'

'He's a film technician now, working for Alfred Hitchcock.'

'On *Rebecca*?' Penrose nodded. 'How extraordinary.'

'His job is in special effects, particularly models and miniatures. I think it was something along those lines that he asked you to deliver for him?'

'That's right. A model of one of the buildings at Milton. To my shame, I still have it.'

Unwittingly, she had answered Penrose's next question. 'So you didn't actually do what he asked?' he clarified, thwarted to think that she wouldn't be able to help him if she hadn't gone to Matthew Plummer's room.

'No. I got as far as the door, but a woman came out and chased me away.'

'What was the woman like? Can you remember?'

'Oh yes. She was Mrs Danvers – at least in my mind. I have no idea who she was or what she was really like, but she terrified me then and I realised quite recently – when I was talking to Margaret Rutherford, in fact; she asked me where Danvers came from – that it was the unknown woman at Milton who had handed the character to me all those years ago.' They entered the park, and Daphne sat down on one of the benches to light a cigarette. 'I was about to say how wonderful it is that my magician should be working on *Rebecca*, then I remembered that I was talking to a policeman and you wouldn't be here unless something was wrong. Is he all right?'

'I'm afraid he's a suspect in a murder enquiry, and he's also facing charges of assault and attempted murder.'

'*What?* How terrible. What on earth happened?'

'A woman was shot while Hitchcock's film crew was at Milton Hall, and another woman – Marion Plummer, your

Mrs Danvers – was assaulted. She's fighting for her life. The murder victim was her daughter, Evelyn.'

'And you suspect him of both? I can scarcely believe it.'

'He's admitted the attempted murder, and it may be that he had a strong motive for the shooting as well.'

'But I still don't understand what you want from me. I haven't been anywhere near Milton for several years, and if you're asking me to testify to his character, I met him so briefly and I was a child who believed he could do magic—'

'No, it's nothing like that,' Penrose interrupted. 'Did you know who you were taking the model to? His name was Matthew Plummer, and he was Marion's son.'

Daphne thought back. 'I think he gave me a Christian name – he must have done – but I don't remember what it was. And he told me I'd be helping a wounded soldier. What girl doesn't want to do that?'

As succinctly and methodically as he could, Penrose outlined Bartholomew's relationship with the Plummers and the speculation that had surrounded Matthew's suicide. 'What happened in that room might have a bearing on why those two women were harmed. If you can give me any insight into that, I'd be very grateful.'

'So you're asking me to convict him? Forgive me, but I'm quite glad I can't think of anything that could possibly be relevant.'

There was little point in arguing with her reasoning, when she was right about what he wanted from her. 'Did you know at the time that someone had committed suicide?' he asked.

'No. I had no idea until you told me just now. My parents probably knew, but we were shielded from anything difficult or messy, anything that needed too much explaining. And other than that day, when we'd just arrived, we were strictly confined to the garden and the family's part of the house. The hospital was out of bounds, and after my encounter with that woman, I did as I was told.' She thought for a moment, staring off into the distance, and Penrose gave her time to reflect, without the bother of further questions. Eventually, his patience was rewarded. 'My God, surely it wasn't . . .'

'What have you remembered?'

'I think I heard the shot, but I never realised what it was. Could that be possible?'

'Where were you?'

'On the main staircase, running down to the grand hall. It wasn't a very loud noise – more like a pop or the crack of a whip than what I'd imagined a gun must sound like.'

'It depends on what sort of gun it was. A pistol can make a noise like that.'

'And of course I was too frightened to think about it. She was coming after me and shouting, and I just wanted to get back to my parents.'

'Marion Plummer was following you when you heard the shot?'

'If that's what it was, yes.'

'She couldn't have been in that room when the gun went off?'

'No, absolutely not.'

He didn't insult her by asking again to make sure. 'Can you remember what she was shouting?'

Again, she thought for a long time. 'I'm reluctant to say anything, because I know how important this must be and I honestly can't be sure if I *actually* remember or if I merely imagine I do. I know that she wasn't in the room when I heard that noise – I'd stake my life that she was on the stair-case – but I couldn't swear to what she was saying.'

'I'll bear that in mind if you'll tell me what you think you heard.'

'She was calling me a wicked girl, I'm fairly sure of that, and I probably deserved it. Then she said something like this: "It's evil, what you're doing. I won't have any part of it." I think that was it, or words to that effect.'

'And was all that aimed at you, or could she have been talking to someone else? Did you see anyone else nearby?'

'No, I didn't – but I wasn't hanging about to look.'

'And did you hear any sort of commotion behind you? Anyone crying for help, or any other signs of an emergency?'

'No, not that I can recall.' She looked at him apprehensively. 'I don't know whether to hope that's been helpful or not.'

'It has. Thank you. Could I ask you one more question?' He reached into his inside pocket and took out the photograph that he had found in Evelyn Young's bedroom, the one of the ward at Milton. 'I'm assuming that one of those orderlies is James Bartholomew,' he said. 'Do you recognise him? This might sound ridiculous, but I've never met him and I'm curious to know what he looks like – or what he looked like then.'

'It doesn't sound ridiculous at all.' She took the picture and pointed straight away to the orderly standing at the same bedside as Evelyn Young. 'That's him. I'd recognise that smile anywhere. His eyes were a very deep blue, I remember, and he had the most beautiful voice I'd ever heard.' Her delight faded as she returned the photograph. 'It's silly, isn't it? One chance meeting, all but forgotten until today, and yet now he's going to haunt me. I know he will.'

'I'm sorry to have brought that about, but I do appreciate your help.'

She was about to say something, then changed her mind and gestured to the photograph. 'Hang on a moment – give me that back.' He did as she asked, and thought that she was staring again at Bartholomew, but then she pointed to Evelyn Young. 'That's the nurse who passed me on the stairs. I would never have remembered if you hadn't shown me this, but it's her hair – it was so long, tied back in a plait like it is here, but down below her waist. I'd never seen anything like it. I honestly thought I was looking at Rapunzel – or some sort of angel, dressed in that uniform.'

'She passed you on the stairs as you were running away?' Penrose asked, wondering if he finally had the evidence that would prove that neither Evelyn nor her mother was in the room when Matthew pulled the trigger.

'No, she overtook me as I was going up. I thought she was going to tell me off and send me back down, but she barely seemed to notice me. Who is she?'

'Evelyn Young – or Evelyn Plummer, as she was then.'

'The woman who's been killed?'

Penrose nodded. 'That's right. Did you see where she went? Was she anywhere near that room?'

'I couldn't say that for sure, but she turned into the corridor. There were several doors there, though. She might have gone to any one of them.'

'Yes, of course.' Even with that caveat, Penrose had heard enough, at least to know what was possible. Bartholomew had been wrong in his initial conviction that Marion Plummer was present when her son killed himself, and with catastrophic results – how must he have felt when he began to suspect that? When it became clear that Evelyn might have been the one to betray her brother? If she really had killed Matthew for loving another man, or had at best forced him to put a gun to his own head, her actions were despicable and he sympathised with Bartholomew's anger; but the revenge, too, had been brutal in its execution. Somehow, that resonated with the contempt and sense of abandonment that he had witnessed in those woods – far more so than the jealousy of a possessive husband – and he knew that Bartholomew must be tracked down as a matter of urgency.

Daphne looked at her watch, reminding Penrose that he also needed to be getting back to his desk: the doctor from Peterborough hospital was due back on shift soon, and he hoped to start building his case. 'A friend of mine is working on the Hollywood *Rebecca*,' he said, as they made their way over to Shaftesbury Avenue.

'She's not called Kay Brown, is she?'

It was spoken with venom, and Penrose laughed. 'No, she's not. What's Kay Brown done to offend you?'

'Omitted to breathe a word about Alfred Hitchcock when she was negotiating the rights for Selznick. Fifty thousand dollars would never have been enough to go through that again. I made them take my name off *Jamaica Inn*, you know. I'll do it again if this one doesn't turn out any better.'

Penrose remembered Josephine wishing she'd done the same thing when she first saw the changes that Hitchcock had made to *A Shilling for Candles*. 'Do you know anything about the film?' he asked.

'No, I've tried to keep out of it. I didn't want to write the screenplay, but I keep getting messages from Miss Brown to reassure me that they're staying as faithful as possible to the novel – which of course worries me more than if she hadn't said anything at all. The last note I had from her was to request a page of the book proofs with my corrections that Selznick could frame for his wall.'

'If he's such a fan, that probably bodes well.'

'Perhaps. Margaret Mitchell obliged him, apparently, but I think I'll hold back until I've seen the end result, otherwise the author's note I'd be tempted to write won't be to his liking.' She stopped outside the stage door and spoke more seriously. 'Will you let me know what happens to Mr Bartholomew?' Penrose hesitated, and she understood immediately. 'What*ever* happens, I mean. I'd like to know, even if the news is difficult.'

'Yes, of course,' he said. 'Thank you for your help, and I hope the play goes well. I'm looking forward to seeing it.'

Back at Scotland Yard, he found that the doctor had beaten him to it and already responded to his message. He telephoned back immediately and was put straight through. 'Dr Berkley? Thank you for telephoning. I wanted to ask you about Marion Plummer – she was admitted to you last Monday after suffering a stroke.'

'Yes, I remember, but Mrs Plummer has been discharged. She's no longer under my care, so perhaps it's the district nurse you should be speaking to?'

Dr Berkley must be either very busy or very discreet to show so little curiosity about a call from the Metropolitan Police, Penrose thought. 'I realise that, but it's the circumstances of her admission that I'd like to speak to you about,' he explained. 'We have reason to believe that Mrs Plummer was the victim of an assault earlier that day. Did you see any signs of that when you treated her? Any bruising or scratches? Anything at all that suggested she might have struggled with someone?

You might not have appreciated its significance at the time, but now, in hindsight, could there have been something?'

There was a long silence at the other end, then the rustling of some papers, and Penrose guessed that the doctor was checking back through his notes. 'No, I certainly don't recall anything, and nothing's been recorded.' Penrose was disappointed but not surprised: suffocation was notoriously difficult to prove. 'You might be better off talking to the woman who called for the ambulance,' the doctor added. 'She came in later that evening to see how Mrs Plummer was and left her number in case there was any change overnight. Perhaps she noticed something amiss when she found her.'

'She came in during the evening?'

'That's what I said.'

'Do you mean Georgia Wells?'

'Hang on a minute. Yes, that's right – Mrs Wells. She gave her address as the rectory in Marholm, and I remember thinking that her husband would soon be of much more use to Mrs Plummer than we were. She was in a very bad way.'

'But I understood that Mrs Wells came in *with* Mrs Plummer – or shortly afterwards, at least. She told me that she followed the ambulance and stayed with her friend so that she wasn't on her own.'

'Then there must have been a terrible hold-up on the Peterborough road, because Mrs Plummer was very much on her own for several hours. There was some talk about a daughter that no one could find, but Mrs Wells definitely arrived in the evening – about six, I would say. I remember because I was about to leave for home and she only just caught me to ask for news.' Penrose listened, wondering if he could simply have misunderstood what Georgia Wells was telling him, but he was certain that he hadn't. 'Is that it?' Berkley asked impatiently. 'I've got patients to attend to if there's nothing else?'

'Yes, of course.' He had wanted to ask the doctor if he thought that Bartholomew's attack could have led directly to the stroke, but that could wait until he knew more details about exactly what had happened. 'Thank you, Dr Berkley. I won't hold you up any more.'

'How is she, by the way? If I'm honest, I'm surprised she's still with us.'

He said it as if Marion Plummer's resilience were an affront to his professional judgement. 'I gather from those looking after her that there are small signs of improvement,' Penrose replied.

'Hm. Wishful thinking, I'm afraid. We sent her home because it was the compassionate thing to do.'

Penrose said goodbye and replaced the receiver, then picked it up again immediately to phone the vicarage. There was no response there, so, with a growing sense of unease, he tried the Youngs' house. 'Hello, Marholm 341.'

'Mrs Wells?'

The familiar voice sounded surprised. 'Yes. Who is this?'

'DCI Penrose. I was hoping to catch you. How is Mrs Plummer?'

'Ah, Chief Inspector. There's been no change. She's comfortable, but that's as positive as I can be.'

'I see. Do you mind if I clarify one or two things with you?'

'What sort of things?'

She sounded wary, and he did what he could to distract her from his true purpose. 'It's Mr Young's alibi, I'm afraid. There are some discrepancies in his story, and I need to build some reliable timings around it. I'm sorry if that compromises your loyalty to him, but we do need to get to the truth.'

'Yes, of course. Fire away.'

Was it his imagination, or was there a note of relief in her voice? 'I believe you said you telephoned him from the hospital at a quarter past five to let him know about Mrs Plummer – is that correct?'

'About then, yes.'

'You're absolutely sure of the time?'

'Within five minutes or so on either side, yes. Does Donald disagree?'

There was no way that she could confer with him as long as he was in custody, so Penrose risked the lie. 'He claims it was earlier that afternoon, between half past three and four.'

'Why would he say that?'

'I suspect to try to prove that he was at his desk then. I knew that wasn't possible, because I remembered distinctly that you'd called from the hospital, and you can't have arrived there until, say, four at the earliest?' She didn't answer, and he would have given anything to know what was going through her mind. 'Is that right, Mrs Wells? Four o'clock at the hospital?'

'What? Oh yes, I'm sorry. I was just thinking about how bad things look for Donald.'

There was a genuine sorrow in her voice, and Penrose was bewildered. Why would she lie about where she was when she made that telephone call? The obvious answer was that she didn't want him to know where she had really been. 'Mrs Wells, is everything all right?' He heard the click of the receiver and tried to call her back, but this time there was no reply.

19

Georgia Wells sat by Marion's bedside, waiting for her to die and accepting – finally – that there was nothing more that she could do to prevent it: Marion's body – already a traitor to her in recent years – had proved a match for them both. She took a clean handkerchief and dipped the corner in a jug of water on the bedside table, then gently moistened Marion's parched lips. There was very little response, just a slight furrowing of the brow as if she found the care an irritation, a delay of the inevitable when she wanted to be gone – and it wouldn't be long now. The skin on her feet and legs was mottled with a telltale blue and her breathing was shallow and irregular. It would be a miracle if she lasted through the night.

The room was stubbornly quiet, offering nothing to distract Georgia from her own thoughts. She got up and walked over to the window, needing to stretch her legs but unable to bring herself to go anywhere in the house except this one sepulchral chamber. It wasn't right, somehow, to tread the stairs that Evelyn had used every day, to touch the cups that she had drunk from or glance in a mirror that had once reflected her face; silly, but she couldn't bring herself to do it. A draught was coming through the glass, and she shivered as the night pulled in around her, darkness settling early on a day that had never truly been light. The lake and the parkland faded quickly before her eyes, eventually disappearing beneath a moonless sky, and she could just make out one or two small oblongs of yellow in the distance as the lights came on at the Hall. Deep within the woods at the back of the cottage, the dry, staccato bark of a fox fractured the air, two or three cries at a time, allowing her to chart the animal's progress as it moved closer. There was something ominous about the sound, something threatening; feeling hunted, she drew the curtains quickly to shut it out.

She went back to the bed, noting the barely discernible rise and fall of the sheet, and took Marion's cold hand in hers, the hatred of the past few days replaced by a desperate, all-consuming grief which was as much for herself as for her friend. It was over for them both, she knew that now. Even if Penrose hadn't begun to put two and two together, she would have to speak out after Marion's death – and then it would begin, the rapid, relentless unravelling, bad enough for her but so much worse for Michael, who had done nothing wrong. And what had it all been for? Their son was still lost to them. Terrified and ashamed, Georgia bowed her head and wept.

When she raised her eyes to the pillow again, she saw that the muscles in Marion's face had relaxed. Astonishing, she thought, that something as momentous as a final breath could ever slip by unnoticed, but there was no question that Marion's struggles were over, in this world at least, and now it was up to those who waited for her in the next to make their peace. Georgia whispered her goodbyes and then – as a final act of reparation for the empty chair at the bedside, where Evelyn should have been sitting – she unclasped her own cross and chain and fixed it gently in place around the dead woman's neck.

A rapping at the front door made her jump out of her skin, and in her misery, for one fleeting moment, she actually believed that Evelyn had come to fetch her mother. Pulling herself together, she left the bedside and went to answer it, expecting to see her husband; she had told Michael not to come, but he was bound to worry when she didn't answer the phone, and in hindsight she would be glad to have him with her. She pulled back the bolts and opened the door, but her face fell when she saw that Michael was not alone. 'I met the Chief Inspector by the lodge,' he said, looking pointedly at her. 'He wants to ask you some questions. I told him it wasn't a good time, not with Marion so near the end, but apparently it can't wait.'

She stood aside to let them into the hallway. 'Marion's gone, I'm afraid.' There was a catch in her throat and she saw the suspicion in Penrose's eyes. 'I didn't hasten her departure, Chief Inspector, if that's what you're thinking. On the contrary, there were things I needed to ask her. I longed for that final conversation more than you could possibly know.'

'Georgia, darling – wait a moment—'

'I have to talk to him, Michael,' Georgia said, interrupting her husband quickly before he could incriminate himself with how much he knew. She turned to Penrose. 'Anyway, you know what I've done already, don't you? That's why you're here.'

'I know you lied to me on the telephone this afternoon. I'm here to find out why.'

Georgia nodded. 'I'd rather my husband weren't present,' she said. 'He'll have to know what I've done, I understand that, but I can't bear to see his face when he hears it. Can we speak alone?'

'I'm not leaving your side,' Michael insisted, and she stared pleadingly at him, begging him to save himself and leave this to her. 'Georgia, what can you be thinking? This affects us both. I won't let you do it alone.'

'Please, Michael. Go and sit with Marion. Say some prayers for us all. God knows, we need them.' He looked at Penrose, who nodded. 'Thank you, Chief Inspector,' Georgia said with relief. 'Let's go through to the sitting room. It feels disrespectful to do it here, and anyway, that's where this all started.' She glanced back through the open bedroom door, surprised by her own superstitious reluctance to admit to everything she had done in front of Marion. 'I'm sorry,' she whispered, scarcely knowing if she was talking to her husband or to her friend; she had wronged them both.

She lit a lamp in the sitting room, unable to avoid seeing Marion in her chair as she had been that day, slumped over and scarcely breathing, beyond all hope. The same knot of panic twisted inside her, but this time it was selfish. As pointless as it seemed to rail against these things, she couldn't help but wish that Marion hadn't fallen ill, that she hadn't been the one to find her, that they had gone to the hospital together. Those small twists of fate threatened to open the door to more dangerous regrets – letting Robert grow up too soon, leaving so many questions unasked simply because she feared the answers – and she forced them back, knowing that she had to get through this. She took Marion's chair, if only so she didn't have to look at it, and offered the other to Penrose.

'You weren't at the hospital when you phoned Donald Young, were you?' he said.

'No. I was at home, at the vicarage. I didn't get to the hospital until later, as I'm sure you know.'

She expected him to interrogate the lie, unpicking the details fact by incriminating fact, but instead he looked at her patiently – kindly, she would have said, under any other circumstances. 'Tell me what happened that afternoon, Mrs Wells.'

The simplicity of the request threw her for a moment and she gathered her thoughts. 'Most of what I told you is true,' she began, struggling to find firm ground. 'I came to Marion exactly as I said I did, and I phoned for an ambulance and spoke to someone at the Hall about Evelyn. They said she was on her way over to the cottage, so I kept looking out for her while I stayed with Marion, willing her to arrive in time to go with her mother to the hospital.' She closed her eyes, seeing her friend's pale face, remembering what it was like to watch her slipping away when they had been through so much together. Marion was the only person who truly understood how she felt about losing Robert. She had shared her grief with Michael, of course she had, but even he could never truly comprehend a mother's guilt at having failed to protect her son. 'It was dreadful, seeing her like that,' she admitted. 'I felt utterly helpless, and time was passing so slowly – at least, that's how it felt. I needed to do something practical to help, something positive – and God forgive me, I wanted to get out of that room, just for a moment. It was all too much. So I went next door to Marion's room and collected some things together, things that I thought she'd need in hospital – a clean nightdress and a change of clothes, her Bible. I looked there for her crucifix, too – I thought the chain might have broken while she was dressing or something, but there was no sign of it.' She saw a flicker pass across Penrose's face, but he didn't interrupt her. 'There was nothing to put it all in downstairs, so I checked that Marion was still with us, then popped upstairs to see if I could find an overnight bag or a little suitcase. It felt like the right thing to do,' she added, trying not to let her emotions get the better of her. 'An act of faith, if you like. Marion would recover, and she would need her things about her.'

'Yes, I understand.'

'One of the doors was open off the landing, so I tried that room first. It was obviously Evelyn's.' She stopped, recalling the sense of intrusion she had felt as she looked around and realised that the Youngs slept alone; she doubted that Evelyn would ever have wanted another woman to know that, but even at the time it hadn't surprised her. 'There was a suitcase on top of the wardrobe but it was far too big, so I opened the wardrobe door and looked inside to see if there was something more suitable.'

'And?' Penrose prompted when she had been silent for a while.

'And I found a small overnight case, perfect for the job. The strange thing was, it was something I recognised. Something I never thought I'd see again.'

'I'm sorry, but I don't understand.'

'How could you? I didn't either – not straight away. I told myself that I must be mistaken, that it couldn't possibly be Robert's. Then I opened it, and his things were still inside. His favourite pullover and the socks that Michael's sister had given him for Christmas. The book that he was reading when he left. Pyjamas that I'd ironed for him myself – all the things that I thought he'd taken to war. Just for a second, it was like having my boy back.' The last few words were barely audible, and she was grateful to Penrose for letting her cry without pressing her to continue. 'I didn't even try to work out what it meant at first,' she managed eventually, 'but then I found these. He would never have gone away without them.' She took the reading glasses out of her pocket, where she had kept them close, and laid them on the table, cracked where Robert had dropped them while she was hurrying him into the car one day. How many times had she reproached herself for not finding time to get them repaired before he left? For letting him down? 'Selfishly, I once hoped that his eyesight might save him from conscription,' she admitted. 'How could I have known that it wouldn't be an issue?'

'Are you saying that you don't think Robert went to war?' Penrose asked.

'I *know* he didn't,' she retorted angrily. 'Robert never went to the Front. He never even left this estate. All those years of wondering, and he was here all along. Matthew was the enemy, not some faceless German soldier.' She saw that she had confused him and pulled herself back, determined to tell her story logically; it was the only way she could get through it. 'The ambulance arrived while I was still upstairs,' she said. 'I went down to let them in, and while I was doing that I saw Evelyn across the park, but she wasn't coming to the cottage – she was heading to the woods, to the folly to be precise. I opened my mouth to call out to her, but something stopped me. I should have put Marion first, but I couldn't get the suitcase out of my mind. I needed to challenge Evelyn, to ask her what it all meant and why she had my son's things tucked away in her wardrobe – so I let Marion go on her own and I said I'd follow. Please believe me when I say that I'll never forgive myself for that. Things could have turned out so differently.'

'So you went over to the folly?'

'Not immediately, no. I needed to make sure that I hadn't imagined things in all the shock over Marion, if that doesn't sound silly, so I went back upstairs and looked more carefully at what I'd found in the wardrobe. The case was definitely Robert's, there was no doubt about that, and most of what was in it, but there were other things, too – photographs and a model, and right at the bottom, wrapped in a pillowcase, there was a gun.'

To her surprise, he ignored her last remark, almost as if he hadn't heard it. 'What sort of model?'

'The model?'

'Yes. What was it?'

'A house, made from wood.'

Penrose seemed satisfied with the answer. 'And the gun – army issue?' She nodded. 'The weapon that you used to kill Evelyn Young.'

It wasn't spoken as a question but she answered anyway, astonished by how calmly she could utter the three simple words that would damn her. 'Yes, that's right.'

'Please go on, Mrs Wells – and take your time.'

'I closed the case and took it over to the folly to confront Evelyn. She was standing inside the ruin with her back to me, but she turned round when she heard me approach and started to speak. I heard her say "you came", as if she were surprised, but her smile faded when she realised it was me. I didn't know who she was waiting for at the time, but Donald told me later what he suspected. He'd been drinking – well, you saw that for yourself when you came to question him that night – but he was right, as it happens. Evelyn was in love with this Bartholomew chap.' She glanced down, feeling his eyes on her and unable to meet them. 'Before you ask, I feel very ashamed of what I let you put Donald through. I should never have allowed it to go so far.'

'So you confronted Mrs Young,' Penrose said, moving her on a little brusquely, and only when he denied it to her did she realise how badly she had wanted some sort of understanding from him – but what she had done to Donald was unforgivable, she knew that.

'Yes, I confronted her, and she was horrified when she saw what I was carrying. She stumbled back and put her hand on the wall to steady herself. I thought she was going to faint, but then she recovered herself – to tell me a pack of lies, or so I thought, but I was wrong. I asked her what had happened to my son, and she told me. It seemed almost to be a relief to her.' The anger was still there, Georgia realised suddenly – the searing blast of injustice that she had discovered within herself as every word of Evelyn's confession seemed to lighten the woman's burden, while her own despair only deepened. She thought that guilt had replaced the fury of that day, but the fury came back to her now as she tried to put it into words for a stranger, and she was forced to acknowledge that it was and would always be part of her, for ever woven into her love for her son. Perhaps it shouldn't have, but the thought gave her strength.

'What did she tell you?'

'Well, the story was that Matthew and Robert had signed up together – you know that, I believe, and it was certainly the plan. Michael and I knew that Robert was desperate to be out there – lots of boys were – but we never dreamt that he'd go without telling us. He went off one morning but I didn't see him go because I was worrying about some wretched committee meeting that I was attending on Michael's behalf.

My son was leaving home for the last time and I was organising a fundraising buffet. I can't even remember what we were raising the money for.' It was almost inconceivable that she had missed that final goodbye: she could see him now, in her mind's eye, going down the drive with that little suitcase, as real as if she had been standing at the window in the dining room. 'I didn't find his note until after lunch,' she continued, 'and by then it was too late to stop him.'

'The note said that he'd gone to sign up?'

'He and Matthew, yes. He asked us not to be angry with him, and he promised to make us proud. We were so proud already – how could he not have known that?' She held her head in her hands, unable to go on for a moment. 'Anyway, we tried to tell ourselves that it was only what thousands of families were going through all over the country, and we waited for him to write to us to let us know that he was safe, but nothing came. Then Marion had a letter from Matthew to say that they'd arrived. They were getting on famously, apparently, and looking out for each other. She brought the letter round to show me, said that mine must have got lost in the post. I'll never understand how she could lie to me like that. I thought we were friends.'

'And you heard nothing more as time went on?'

'No. Matthew wrote to his mother once or twice, saying that Robert sent his love, but there was always some excuse why he couldn't write himself – he'd sprained his wrist or gone down with flu. All the news we had was second-hand.'

'But that day Evelyn told you what had really happened?'

'Yes, if she and Matthew are to be believed. Robert packed his case and went off to meet Matthew at the folly, just as they'd planned, but a hospital convoy was arriving at the gate as he got to the lodge, and he saw everything – the blood, the missing limbs, the reality of war. No newspaper reports could have prepared him for that, and he was horrified – horrified, and frightened out of his wits. When he got to the folly, he told Matthew he wasn't going. He'd changed his mind.'

'And Matthew didn't take it well?'

'No. He was always a bully at heart and we'd have preferred Robert to have other friends, but he worshipped the ground that Matthew walked on.' She stood up and walked over to the window, unable to meet Penrose's eye. 'I don't know if there was anything more to it than that,' she said. 'What I said to you yesterday was the truth – I don't believe that Robert was like that with Matthew, but I can't swear to it, and now that you've put the thought into my head, I can't stop thinking about it.'

'I'm sorry. It was never my intention to upset you.'

'We all do so much that we don't intend, don't we? Isn't that why you and I are here?'

'Did Matthew kill Robert?' Penrose asked gently.

'Yes. They fought, apparently, when Robert said he was staying behind. Matthew had his hands around Robert's throat, and he went too far. He swore he never meant to hurt him, but I don't believe that for a moment, and I don't think Evelyn did either – but that didn't stop her and her mother covering it all up. Evelyn swore to me that she'd tried to help Robert when Matthew went to her in a panic and told her what he'd done, but she got to him too late. He was already dead.'

'And Marion Plummer was involved, too?'

'Of course she was. It was a real family affair. Matthew went off to war and continued the lie from there, while his mother and his sister cleaned up at home.'

'But you've tended to Mrs Plummer so diligently. I saw you myself the other night – you've done everything you could to help her and your concern for her was genuine, I'm sure of it. How could you bring yourself to do that when she deceived you? Was it out of guilt because you killed her daughter?'

'Partly that, of course, but you credit me with too much compassion, Chief Inspector. I needed Marion to live – desperately. I needed her to tell me what they did with Robert's body, where my son is buried, otherwise all this has been for nothing.' The estate stretched out in front of her, surrounded by miles and miles of woodland, desolate and unfathomable. 'Evelyn wouldn't say, you see. I begged her to help me and I swore on my own life that I wouldn't give her away if only she would tell me where Robert was so that Michael and I could go to him – privately, if we had to, just to have somewhere to mourn him.'

'But she refused.'

'Yes – as long as her mother was alive. She said that Marion would never stand the shame of it, and she wanted to protect her. She promised to tell me when Marion was dead.' Georgia caught his expression. 'Ironic, isn't it? I told her what had just happened, that Marion was on her way to hospital and how dangerously ill she was, but she didn't believe me. She thought I was making it up to fool her. I was desperate, Mr Penrose. I took the gun and I held it to her head to try to make her tell me, but still she said no.'

And that was when she had pulled the trigger. She had felt nothing, even as she dragged Evelyn's body into the undergrowth and threw the gun down beside her – nothing except this dreadful, inescapable blankness which she had told herself was shock.

'What did you do afterwards?' Penrose asked, when she had described the shooting to his satisfaction.

'I took the case back to the cottage and telephoned the Hall again to ask where Evelyn was,' she admitted, knowing how calculating that must make her look, but determined to keep any cards she had left for her husband's benefit. 'Then I went home. I had to change and compose myself before Michael saw me, and luckily he was out.' If only that had been true, she thought, remembering her husband's face as he met her in the hallway, his grief when she told him what she knew and what she had done. 'Later on, I telephoned Donald, pretending to be at the hospital.' That had been Michael's suggestion and she had known at the time how flawed it was, but panic had set in by then and she didn't have a better idea. 'We went later – Michael drove me there, and we arrived just after six. You know the rest.'

If she had thought he would leave it there, she was wrong. 'Let's go back to Robert's disappearance,' he said. 'You told me he was missing in action, but you can't have had any official notification of that if he never enlisted.'

'Of course we didn't. Michael badgered the authorities but he couldn't get any answers that made sense to us – not at the time, anyway; they make perfect sense now. But the official records were chaotic by then, if you remember, and if I'm honest, I didn't want to know. Ignorance was hope – but then Matthew came home, wounded, and he told us that Robert was dead.'

'Dead or missing?'

'Dead. I'm sorry, but I lied to you yesterday. Robert was never missing, not even in Matthew's version of events.'

'Did you talk to Matthew about it when he came back here?'

'No. Evelyn and Marion kept me away from him, and I understand why now. But Matthew wrote us a letter – well, he dictated it to one of the orderlies, the one you say he was in love with, probably, although I doubt that Matthew Plummer ever knew the meaning of the word. Do you know what he said?' Penrose shook his head. 'Of all the despicable lies that he could have come up with, he chose to tell us that our son – the son he murdered – had been shot for cowardice.' She looked down at her hands, wondering why they hurt her, and saw the whiteness of her knuckles, the red marks where her fingernails had pressed into her palms, almost drawing blood. 'It was a twisted sort of truth, I suppose. Robert died, in Matthew's eyes, because he was a coward. What he told us just changed one or two of the important details.'

'I'm so very sorry,' Penrose said, visibly moved by what she had told him. 'I can't even begin to imagine how that must make you feel.'

'Thank you.'

'Have you still got the letter?'

'I asked Michael to destroy it so that no one else could see it, but I don't know if he did. You'll have to ask him. It's funny, but in spite of the shock and the bewilderment, that letter actually brought me comfort. Matthew was so caring in what he said about Robert, so outraged and full of a sense of injustice, so adamant that Robert was innocent. I believed every word of it, and it worked beautifully.'

'What do you mean?'

'It stopped us looking for answers. Marion knew me well enough to be certain of that, so perhaps it was even her idea. I begged Michael to stop making enquiries after that.'

'Because you didn't want confirmation that your son was a deserter?'

'No, it wasn't that. I would have stood up for him, no matter what. It was because I didn't want to believe in the fear and the loneliness that would have *driven* him to desert. No one wants to think of her child alone and frightened like that. So we stopped searching. Michael didn't want to, but I was ill and he was terrified for me. I had a breakdown shortly after we got the news. It took me years to recover, and I'd never have done it without his love.'

There was silence in the room except for the ticking of the clock above the fireplace, the one that Marion had been given on her retirement in recognition of her loyalty, and Georgia suddenly longed to pick it up and smash it to smithereens. 'Did Evelyn kill Matthew for what he'd done?' Penrose asked out of the blue. 'Or force him to take his own life, at least.'

She stared at him in astonishment. 'How could you possibly know that?'

'I don't, but I'm hoping you'll confirm it. I'm hoping that she told you what really happened.'

'Yes, she did. I think she hoped that it would make me feel differently towards her, that I could somehow be grateful to her for killing my son's murderer.'

'Did Mrs Plummer know what she was planning?'

'Marion was against it, apparently, but Evelyn might just have been saying that to protect her mother. We'll never know now – but your orderly played his part, too.'

'Bartholomew was involved in Matthew's death?'

'No, I didn't mean that, but Evelyn loved him, as I said. She was horrified when she found out that there was something between him and her brother, but not out of shame or jealousy. I think she knew that there was more malice in what Matthew had done to Robert than he ever admitted, and she didn't trust him not to do it again – this time to someone she loved. "Matthew had to be stopped." Those were the very words she used.'

'Do you think Donald helped her?' Penrose asked, almost as if he could read her mind. 'Did he get her the gun, perhaps, and might that be why she married him? To repay the debt and secure his silence?'

'I don't know that for certain, but the thought has occurred to me. Yes, I'm sure that's why she did it.'

'Thank you.' Penrose stood up and gestured to the door. 'You'll want to talk to your husband before we go.' He spoke with regret, as if he wished there could be some other way, but to her surprise Georgia felt only relief. 'What did you do with the suitcase?' he asked.

'It's in Marion's room, under the bed. I was going to ask her about it as soon as she was strong enough.' Instantly she saw him regret his kindness that night, when he had refused to search a dying woman's room. 'I never intended to punish her for the part she played in obscuring Robert's death,' she insisted, with a final glance across to the Hall and the convoy of army trucks parked outside, 'but there's a dreadful symmetry in all this, isn't there? We think we've learnt our lessons from the past, but we never really get beyond an eye for an eye.'

20

The atmosphere on set was tense and exciting, and Josephine was glad that Marta had recovered sufficiently to be part of it. The last three weeks had been beset with problems for the production, starting with the poison ivy incident and the revelations about James and Victor, followed by setbacks of varying seriousness: a three-day wildcat strike from the stage-hands' union; a fly on the set which had delayed filming for several hours; and now a serious bout of influenza which had laid Fontaine low and made her unavailable for work. In a fit of pique, spurred on by his producer's mounting anxieties over time and money, Hitchcock had completely revamped the schedule, bringing forward the few scenes that didn't require the presence of his female lead. To Josephine's delight, one of the most anticipated – the burning of Rebecca's bedroom, which would close the movie – was now scheduled for her last full day in Hollywood, and although she would have liked more time alone with Marta, she relished Hitch's invitation to take a ringside seat at the spectacle.

There were far more people on set than the last time she had been here. Alma was there with Patricia, and perhaps it was Josephine's imagination but she seemed to be keeping her daughter just that little bit closer than before. Memories of those terrifying three hours hadn't entirely gone away, and neither had Lee Hessel: coverage of the murder at Milton Hall had spilled over from the British press to the more creative American newspapers, and one piece in particular – a story about the 'lethal legacy' of Hitchcock's movies, citing *Jamaica Inn* and now *Rebecca* – had her influence all over it.

Today, Josephine watched the preparations for filming with mixed emotions, knowing that there was one person absent who deserved more than most to be here. As far as she knew, James still hadn't been found. Archie had told her all about the outcome at Milton Hall, and had telephoned briefly that morning to wish her a safe flight home the following day. There was still no word on James's whereabouts, not even the most tenuous of sightings, and she began to think that they would never know what had happened to him. Perhaps he had done what he was always destined to do, in spite of her best efforts to interfere and the Los Angeles Police Department's attempts to find him – and if that was the case, she knew she would regret until her dying day their final meeting. She had been too harsh on him, too lacking in the compassion that might possibly have made a difference; instinctively, she had liked and trusted him, and she was honest enough to acknowledge that – in his position – she might not have acted so very differently from him.

But at least he had been spared the sight that greeted her now, a sight that would have horrified him. Two Mrs Danvers were present on set, the actress who was playing her and the stunt double who would take Judith Anderson's place for the most dangerous parts of the take. They were wearing identical black dresses, their hair styled in the same way, and were of similar slender build, and Josephine had no doubt that no one would notice the difference by the time that Hitch and his editor had finished. Even with the trick laid out so clearly in front of her, Josephine couldn't look at Danvers now without thinking about the woman who had inspired her, and she wondered how the book's author would feel when she finally saw her character on the screen.

'All set, cock?' Hitch asked Anderson as she made her final preparations.

'Yes, but I was rather surprised when you sent the wardrobe people to my home to fit me for a new dress. Why do I need an asbestos lining? You assured me that this scene would be safe.'

'It's perfectly safe.'

Hitchcock beamed and Anderson glanced sceptically over to the firemen who were a new addition to the crew. 'Tell me honestly, Hitch – am I in any danger?'

'None whatsoever. It's just a precaution.'

'Very well, then. Let's get on with it. I'll be glad when this is finished, though.'

'He sounded confident,' Josephine observed, as Marta joined her.

'Let's just hope he's right. We haven't exactly been blessed with good luck so far, have we?' She handed Josephine an envelope. 'Someone left this for you at reception.'

'For me?' She took the letter, which had only her name on the front and had obviously been hand delivered. 'Why would anyone write to me here?'

'Maybe it's Selznick making you an offer you can't refuse.' Marta's smile faded as she watched Josephine open the envelope. 'What's the matter? Who's it from?'

'It's from James.' She read it out loud, so that Marta could hear:

'Dear Josephine,
So much has changed since we last met. For the briefest

of moments, what you told me on the beach gave me hope, and for that I thank you from the bottom of my heart – but Marion is dead, I know that, and I can't live with myself as a murderer. There was a terrible inevitability in what I set in motion that day, and now I must finish what I started.

Your kindness was one of the few things that has made these past few weeks bearable. That, and my love for Matthew – but I realise, of course, that even that was a hollow fantasy, an illusion every bit as manipulative as those that once brought me such joy – and you were right about that: once the trick is revealed, the magic is spoilt for ever.

I meant it when I said that your good opinion matters to me, and I want to do something worthwhile before I go. Not to make up for what I've done – that would be impossible – but to ease the pain of those whose lives have been destroyed. I've read enough in the newspapers to know that somewhere at Milton there's a young man who's still lost, and parents who will never be at rest until they find him. I've thought a lot about this, and about the times that Matthew and I spent together, and I believe they'll find Robert's body a hundred yards or so to the west of the folly, by the remains of a vast old oak tree which I pray are still there. Matthew used to insist on going to that tree whenever we went to the folly; he told me once that his favourite pet had been buried there.

For his parents' sake, I hope I'm right about the location, but I can't wait around to be sure, to have proof that the man I loved – the man I did this for – was so little deserving of any affection. And I'm truly sorry for the part I played in the letter of lies to his parents, even though I did it with the best of intentions.

Say goodbye to Marta for me, and cherish your love for each other. The world has far too little of it.

The film will be spectacular, by the way. Leave a seat free by your side when you see it, and know that – if the dead do indeed come back and watch the living – I'll be there with you.

Sincerely,

James.'

Josephine read the note again, this time to herself, struck by its immense sadness and by the poignancy of the quotation from *Rebecca*; it seemed to her recently that the living had been spending far too much time preoccupied with the dead. 'Do you know when this was left?' she asked.

'No, I've no idea. I picked it up about ten minutes ago with a pile of other mail.'

'I need to go and find out.' She hurried from the soundstage, cursing the circuitous route back to the main building and the actors in costume who obstructed her path. 'Excuse me,' she said breathlessly to the woman on duty, holding out the envelope, 'someone left this for me and I wondered if you could tell me when?' The woman raised an eyebrow, asking with a directness that needed no words if Josephine knew how many people passed through the studios each day. 'I'm sorry, that was silly. But it was left by a technician who used to work here – James Bartholomew – and I thought you might have remembered him if you saw him?'

The woman shook her head. 'I'm very sorry, Miss Tey, but I've only been here a week. I've never met Mr Bartholomew.'

She turned away to answer the telephone, and Josephine walked quickly back to the soundstage. 'Any luck?' Marta asked.

Josephine shook her head. 'I suppose I'll have to let the police know,' she said reluctantly, torn between a stubborn desire to let James find his own peace before anyone could stop him and the urgency of the information in the note.

'Already done,' Marta said. 'I know how hard that would have been for you. Lydia's gone across to phone from the office. I couldn't possibly let Hitch overhear when he's about to shoot one of the biggest scenes of his life.'

As if on cue, Selznick appeared on set, looking nervous. 'You're positive everything is ready?' he asked his director.

'As ready as it can ever be, wouldn't you say, Ray?'

Hitch turned to the man whom Josephine assumed was the film's production manager. 'We're ready. Hell, we burned down Atlanta – this is a piece of cake.'

It wasn't said in arrogance. The sequence had been planned for weeks – every move, every camera position, every safety consideration designed to give Hitch as much control as possible over each aspect of the scene and to maximise its impact: even with a director who could work wonders, the fire could only rage for so long. Josephine watched as Marta went between the different cameras, checking angles and lenses before conferring with Hitchcock one last time, and then everyone was told to move back behind the safety ropes. Silence fell across the lot, and almost immediately the main lights went out. After another brief pause, Hitch's voice cut through the soundstage: 'Start the fire.'

The production manager nodded to the men who were working the pumps, feeding the oil mixture through the pipes. The set had been wired in strategic places so that when a contact switch was pressed, sparks would ignite the gasoline; a minute went by and Josephine looked round, wondering if something was wrong, then everyone jumped as a loud whoosh ignited the oil-soaked wood and fabric. 'Action!' Hitchcock called.

Flames began to lick at the framework around Rebecca's bedroom window, as if they, too, were under the director's spell. Josephine caught sight of an arm clad in black, and then, as the double moved further into the room, she saw Mrs Danvers more clearly, turning first to the right and then to the left, her arm held up to her face, trapped by the fire that she had started. Oblivious to her distress, the blaze continued to consume the bedroom, engulfing the couch and the chairs and making short work of the drapes around the bed. Even at a distance, Josephine could feel the heat on her skin, and the dry hiss and crackle of the flames was an effective soundtrack to the destruction playing out in front of her. Meanwhile, at another window to the right of the set, Judith Anderson stood for a close-up shot, her face anguished and demented, the very picture of tortured evil.

At the back of the soundstage, a chink of light drew Josephine's attention as someone opened a door and slipped inside. To her amazement, she recognised James, but before she could say anything or take a step towards him, he walked over to the set and into the fire without a moment's hesitation, looking neither left nor right. The appearance was so fleeting that she could easily have imagined it, nothing more substantial than a shadow thrown onto the wall, but seconds later there was a piercing scream of utter terror from the set, and all hell seemed to break loose around Josephine as – one by one – the crew began to realise what was happening.

Anderson was rushed from the burning set, followed by her double, whose clothes were starting to smoulder. There were cinders on her face and in her hair, but her distress clearly stemmed far more from what she had witnessed than from any danger to herself. The fire crew moved forward and began to douse the flames, but before they could make any impact, there was a dreadful, ominous groaning from above and the beams started to cave in. The fireman who had ventured in to find James was dragged back by a colleague, and a woman's voice yelled hysterically at the crowd to stay back.

Josephine clung to Marta, her heart pounding, futile cries of anguish coming from her lips, but – like everyone else – she was powerless to put a stop to the horror unfolding in front of her. People were screaming now, as panic replaced shock, and she had a fleeting glimpse of Hitchcock's face, contorted with fear and disbelief. He didn't know who had died, she realised – probably only she knew that – and how much worse it would be for the director when he did. In spite of everything, he had cared for James Bartholomew.

The fire crew began to usher everyone from the set and out into the lot. Josephine threw a final glance over her shoulder, but fate was kind to her that night: there would be no image of horror for ever imprinted on her mind, no charred or burning body to obliterate. As she stared back into the flames, she could see nothing more tangible there than shadows and dancing silhouettes.

FEBRUARY 1940

I would have dearly loved to go inside, to walk along those corridors again and climb Milton's stairs, daring my ghosts still to be there, but the years have made a coward of the trespasser I once was, so I left the car by the side of the road and walked down through the woods. The bright February morning had something ominous about it, I thought, its early promise of spring not entirely to be trusted. The air was too still, the ground too soft, with no way of knowing what was to follow. Or perhaps that was just my mood, unsettled by what I had come here to do, and by why I felt the need to do it.

I realised as soon as I saw her that I had been fooling myself all along. The house was tainted for me now. As beautiful as she looked in the pale sunlight, with the last of a sharp frost holding strong on the front lawn, where we had once taken tea, she was no longer dear old Milton. She had fooled me for all those years, and I wasn't inclined to forgive her.

I turned and walked back up the slope, then took the short drive into the village. The church stood on its own, surrounded by fields, and the pungent smell of a bonfire – earthy and nostalgic, so perfectly in tune with the melancholy of the day – reached me as soon as I got out of the car. The gate across the ha-ha was cold and rusty to the touch, and the churchyard – though beautiful – was unsettling: as I wandered through the old tombs, brushing the moss aside to make sense of long-lost names, the skulls and the urns and the hourglass seemed to defy any promise of peace.

The new stone to the side of the church stood out amongst its ancient friends and made the grave I was looking for easy to find. There was no need here for a symbol of life's brevity: the boy's age – sixteen – said all that was necessary. I removed the dead roses, their heads bowed from the frost, and replaced them with the daffodils that I'd cut from my garden the day before, wondering if Robert – this boy I never knew – would mind that the flowers were left not only for him, but for the man who had done wrong and tried to put it right.

The model was still in my pocket. It had seemed right to return it to the place where it was made, and – like the house – its magic was tarnished, indelibly stamped with the grief it now stood for. Hoping that my magician would approve, I followed the smoke to the edge of the graveyard. A young oak tree – diseased, perhaps – had been felled on the north side of the church, and the wood was still burning. Before I could change my mind, I threw the model into the fire and watched as its own small flames flickered for a moment, shot with crimson as it disappeared into the embers. It was gone for ever, its sorrow with it. And I knew that he was watching as I turned and walked away.

Acknowledgements

After delays from strike action, illness and poison ivy, shooting on *Rebecca* finished in December 1939 and the film was premiered on 28 March 1940 to glowing reviews. The following year, it led the field at the 13th Academy Awards with no fewer than eleven nominations: Outstanding Production; Director; Actress (Joan Fontaine); Actor (Laurence Olivier); Supporting Actress (Judith Anderson); Adapted Screenplay (Robert E. Sherwood and Joan Harrison); Cinematography (George Barnes); Art Direction (Lyle Wheeler); Film Editing (Hal C. Kern); Original Score (Franz Waxman); and Special Effects (Jack Cosgrove and Arthur Johns). The film won two Oscars – Outstanding Production and Cinematography – and although Joan Fontaine lost out to Ginger Rogers, she would win the following year for her role in another Hitchcock film, *Suspicion*. The Oscar for Best Director went to John Ford and *The Grapes of Wrath*. Although Hitch would be nominated on a further four occasions, he never won.

David O. Selznick remained true to the original *Rebecca* to the very end of production. On 3 March 1941, he cabled Daphne du Maurier, sending thanks and best wishes from the entire studio for the 'splendid' novel that had made it possible for them to win the Academy Award.

The stage play of *Rebecca*, adapted by Daphne du Maurier from her own novel and directed by George Devine, opened at the Queen's Theatre on Shaftesbury Avenue in April 1940 and ran successfully for more than five months. Margaret Rutherford's performance as Mrs Danvers was highly praised. The production was brought to a premature end when the theatre was bombed on 24 September, remaining closed for the next twenty years.

The Hitchcocks remained happily settled in America for the rest of their lives. Hitch was deeply hurt by accusations of desertion during the war years and, despite the restrictions of his contract with Selznick, did accept the invitation from the Ministry of Information to shoot propaganda films. His final contribution to the war effort was a 1945 documentary on the concentration camps. My apologies must go to Joan Harrison, who has been unfairly sidelined by Marta for fictional purposes here but who was indispensable to the Hitchcocks during this period. Harrison's life and creative achievements are brilliantly documented by Christina Lane in her book, *Phantom Lady*, which also gave me a wonderful insight into Hollywood life at the time of the Hitchcocks' move to America.

In his conversations with François Truffaut, Hitch described his film of *Rebecca* as 'the story of a house', and so is *Shot With Crimson*: the house that we see on screen, and the house that – many years before – sowed the seeds of Manderley in an author's imagination. Daphne du Maurier visited Milton Hall for the first time as a little girl in 1917, when it was being used as a military hospital, and she returned many times. 'Dear old Milton' made a tremendous impression on her, and, in a letter to Oriel Malet, she explained that the Hall was really the *Rebecca* house, even more so than her beloved Cornish home, Menabilly; her son, Kits Browning, has subsequently said that Milton also provided her with her first glimpse of a housekeeper figure who would eventually inspire Mrs Danvers. Hitchcock and Selznick sent a second unit to scout the Hall in 1939, and during the Second World War Milton was occupied by the Czechoslovakian army and used by the British Special Operations Executive as a training base for Operation Jedburgh. I'm indebted to Reginald Payne's book, *The Watershed*, for its detailed account of life at Milton as a medical orderly during the First World War, but the characters who people Milton in this novel, and all that happens there, are entirely fictional and exist only in my imagination. St Mary the Virgin in Marholm is an exceedingly beautiful church, but Archie has never had reason to call on anyone living at the rectory.

Amongst the vast amount of research material available on Hitchcock, Selznick and the making of *Rebecca*, the following were particularly valuable: *Alfred Hitchcock* by Peter Ackroyd; *Memo From David O. Selznick* by Rudy Behlmer; *It's Only a Movie* by Charlotte Chandler; *No Bed of Roses* by Joan Fontaine; *David O. Selznick's Hollywood* by Ronald Haver; *Film Magic* by David Hutchison; *The Wrong House: the Architecture of Alfred Hitchcock* by Steven Jacobs; *Footsteps in the Fog: Alfred Hitchcock's San Francisco* by Jeff Kraft and Aaron Leventhal; *Hitchcock and Selznick* by Leonard J. Leff; *Alfred Hitchcock: a Life in Darkness and Light* by Patrick McGilligan; *Showman: the Life of David O. Selznick* by David Thomson; *Hitchcock* by François Truffaut; *Rebecca: the Making of a Hollywood Classic* by Jennifer Leigh Wells; *The Twelve Lives of Alfred Hitchcock* by Edward White; and *Rebecca* (BFI Film Classics series) by Patricia White. The Criterion Collection special edition DVD of *Rebecca* contains fascinating interviews and commentary on the making of the film, and the Daphne du Maurier website at dumaurier.org is an invaluable resource for anyone wanting to know more about the author and her work, as is Margaret Forster's wonderful biography. I would dearly have loved to travel on the *Queen Mary* as it was in Josephine's time, but, in the absence of that possibility, David Ellery's *RMS Queen Mary: the World's Favourite Liner* and C.W.R. Winter's *Queen Mary: Her Early Years Recalled* helped me to see all the glory of this magnificent ship in my mind's eye.

It's such a pleasure and a privilege to celebrate the life and work of Josephine Tey in these books, and my respect for her achievements and her unique contribution to crime fiction grows hand in hand with the series. As far as I'm aware, she never went to Hollywood, but she did have a brief and unsatisfactory flirtation with scriptwriting for Universal in the 1930s. Fortunately, it didn't put her off the magic of cinema, which she loved throughout her life.

Love and thanks to my editor, Walter Donohue, from whom I learn so much with every book, and to everyone at Faber for working so hard on the series; to my friend and agent, Veronique Baxter, and to Sara Langham and all at David Higham Associates; to W. F. Howes and Sandra Duncan for giving the books such a rich and vivid audio life; to Nathan Burton for his stunning cover designs; to Marni and Arthur Graff for love and insights from across the pond; to Denise Collins for always being on hand to guide Josephine's life in Scotland; and to Jenny Uglow, who unwittingly opened up one crucial aspect of *Shot With Crimson* for me with a characteristically generous remark.

There's a page in my notebook for this novel which is headed 'Mandy's brilliant idea' (of which she has many). My thanks and love not just for the idea but for living once again with the Hitchcocks, for never complaining when we had to watch *Rebecca* 'just one more time', for the day in the Cambridgeshire countryside that refocused the whole book, and for bringing joy to the days that I write and the days that I don't.